OTHER BOOKS BY LIZA CODY

Anna Lee series
Dupe
Bad Company
Stalker
Headcase
Under Contract
Backhand

Bucket Nut Trilogy
Bucket Nut
Monkey Wrench
Musclebound

Lady Bag Double
Lady Bag
Crocodiles and Good Intentions

Other Crime Novels
Rift
Gimme More
Ballad of a Dead Nobody
Miss Terry
Gift or Theft

Short Stories
Lucky Dip and other stories

As Editor
1st Culprit (with Michael Z Lewin)
2nd Culprit (with Michael Z Lewin)
3rd Culprit (with Michael Z Lewin & Peter Lovesey)

MY PEOPLE

and other crime stories

LIZA CODY

Columbus, Ohio

MY PEOPLE and other crime stories

Published by Gatekeeper Press
2167 Stringtown Rd, Suite 109
Columbus, OH 43123-2989
www.GatekeeperPress.com

Cover Design © Sam Camden-Smith and Olivia Rhodes

Turning It Round, (2003) BBC Radio & Ellery Queen Mystery Magazine
Art, Marriage and Death, (2004) Ellery Queen Mystery Magazine
The Old Story, (2005) Ellery Queen Mystery Magazine
Kali In Kensington Gardens, (2006) Crippen & Landru
Mr Bo, (2009) Crippen & Landru
Whole Life, (2009) Ellery Queen Mystery Magazine
I Am Not Fluffy, (2012) Ellery Queen Mystery Magazine
A Hand, (2012) Ellery Queen Mystery Magazine
Day Or Night, (2013) Severn House
Ghost Station, (2016) Sphere
Health And Safety, (2017) Ellery Queen Mystery Magazine
Life And Death In T-Shirts, (2017) Ellery Queen Mystery Magazine
My People, (2020) Ellery Queen Mystery Magazine
When I'm Feeling Lucky, (2020) Hyakawa Mystery Magazine
Hard Hearts, (2021)

The cover design and editorial work for this book are entirely the product of the author. Gatekeeper Press did not participate in and is not responsible for any aspect of these elements.

ISBN (paperback): 9781662913112
eISBN: 9781662913129

CONTENTS

A FOREWORD OF WARNING

I'm writing this in the summer of 2021 when lockdown restrictions, such as they were, are being lifted in England.

Nearly all the stories included here were written before Covid forced us to change our lives. And I wonder how culture will be altered longterm. Will it be like the difference between pre- and post- World War II novels? Pre-War was, for instance, a world of toffs and servants. Post-War was far more utilitarian, and attitudes which had been taken for granted then strike us as horribly sexist, racist, and anti-Semitic. This left space for ordinary women, like me, to put women of all sorts at the centre of their work.

I don't yet know what a post-Covid world will look like. I'll have to wait and see how cultural norms will have changed.

One change I'm already facing is a cultural revolution accelerated by the reliance we all placed on social media while we were isolated. I had seen it coming, but from a distance. I watched while people – professors, writers, journalists, media stars, sports men and women, etc. – lost their jobs, their reputations and their livelihoods: not just for real crimes but sometimes for voicing an unpopular opinion, or for something as simple as a joke or a careless word.

'This can't apply to me,' I thought – confident that I'd always been on the side of the underdog and those who fight bigotry. But I was also scared, and thus wilfully blind to an assault on discussion, free thought and free speech. In retrospect it was there to be seen – a swelling atmosphere of criticism for anyone who disagreed with whatever was deemed acceptable by opinion-makers. At the time it seemed paranoid and fanciful to compare this trend to Mao's Cultural Revolution or Soviet Russia – where nothing but state-approved work would be published and writers could be imprisoned, re-educated or executed.

My blindness might have been caused by the fact that nowadays it is not the state that is responsible. It is ordinary people gathering on social media who are putting on the pressure. An unprecedented level of 'hate-speak', abuse, and on-line bullying is making people afraid to voice their opinions in case what they say is turned against them.

While I was looking the other way publishers, media outlets, schools, and universities were beginning to hire 'sensitivity experts' to warn them of what the likely result would be of causing discomfort or offence to this or that group. Everyone, including those I rely on for my living, seems to be terrified of the punishment suffered by causing offence to anyone at all.

This is a toxic environment for those of us who think about ideas, characters, consequences and following a story where it wants to go rather than where a sensitivity expert says it *ought* to go.

What saddens me most is that a lot of this bullying has begun in support of just causes – those I've supported all my life. But the fight against bigotry seems itself to have engendered bigotry.

If you want to live in a healthy society you do not want your creative people to be looking over their shoulders, terrified of the consequences of making a mistake: frightened that the next knock on the door may be for them.

So here are my stories, warts and all – about My People, warts and all. And I want to thank the people who were brave enough and free enough to publish them – warts and all.

Liza Cody, 2021

To Michael Z Lewin, Peter Lovesey and all the other wonderful short story writers who have been pathfinders for me.

MY PEOPLE

and other crime stories

I AM NOT FLUFFY

One night I decided to fight back.

I don't want to be a victim, I said to myself, so why am I always walking in other folks' piss? This was literally true at the time: I was going down a steep flight of steps between Paragon Hill and Sharp Harbour. There's a pub at the top and a nightclub at the bottom and it's where all the drunks choose to empty their tiny bladders as they stagger between one venue and the other. Sadly it's on my way home from the nightshift.

I hopped and danced from one small dry patch to another.

These are my good shoes, I thought. Why should I contaminate the soles of my good shoes with drunken piss? Why should the soles of my shoes contaminate my carpet with drunken piss? Because evil never stops in one place. It corrupts whatever it touches. Once it has touched your sole or soul, you carry it with you wherever you go.

*

Mark paid me and when we were done I got out of the car. I call them all Mark, for the sake of confidentiality. This one offered to drive me home, but obviously I didn't want him to know where I lived.

He was a big guy who comforted himself with steak and potatoes. His third son weighed eleven and a half pounds when he was born, and after that his wife refused to have sex with him anymore. He thinks his wife's mean. He thinks she's made of latex.

'He's a good bloke,' Pearl said. 'He could of just got his self a girlfriend and left her and the kids with nothing – like my bastard Bobby did.'

'Don't worry, be happy,' Bob Marley sang out of the chip shop speakers. 'Ev'ry little thing gonna be alright.'

*

I worked as a hostess and greeter at a bar-restaurant for six nights a week for five years while Harvey qualified to be a tax lawyer. And for two nights a week Harvey was going round to Alicia's flat to bounce on her bones. 'You were never there,' he complained. 'What was I supposed to do all by myself every night?'

'You said you were revising,' I shouted. 'I was supporting us and giving you time and space to study.'

Alicia used to be a friend of mine. She didn't want him to move in with her until he was qualified and could support *her*. So that's why I didn't find out till five years later.

Now he's earning gazillions so she wants to get married.

The divorce papers came in the post months ago. He wants me to sign them and send them to the court. No contest divorce, I think they call it. Easy peasey. The papers are sitting on my glass coffee table. I can't seem to find a pen.

*

Mark is getting married next week. He's only nineteen and he told me that his mates said they didn't want him to 'die a virgin.' So they all pitched in to corrupt him. He's sweet and simple. He couldn't understand what they meant by it, but he got interested anyway. He didn't seem to see it as corruption – more as further education. I cried, and he didn't understand that either.

*

2

Alicia will demand the theatrical white wedding me and Harvey couldn't afford when we went through our short, shabby, civil ceremony six years ago. She bought a MaxiMart chocolate cake for our wedding lunch. I was so grateful to her. She wore a scarlet silk dress for the occasion and looked way more sexy than the bride. I should have learned something from that. But I was in love so I learned, saw, heard, nothing. Love deletes obvious deductions from your brain and should be avoided.

The divorce papers, the proof of corruption, were sitting on my table, corrupting my home. So one night I decided to fight back.

I began passively by taking the papers and a box of matches outside and setting fire to them in the gutter. If asked, I would claim I'd never received them.

But later that night I decided that if *he* wanted a no contest divorce, *I* would give him a contest. After all, what had behaving lovingly, helpfully and supportively ever done for me?

I might just as well have presented my arse to him with a sign stuck to it saying, 'Kick me here'.

But contests require lawyers and cost cash. He had lots. I had little.

The very next night, my manager, Oliver D, asked me to do him a favour. He said, 'See that fat tart in the pink strappy number, chatting up those public school tossers at the bar? Get rid of her.'

'Why?' I said. 'She isn't doing anything wrong.'

'She's a whore,' he said.

'How do you know?'

'Just do it.'

'But that's *your* job.'

'*Do it!*' he said, and scuttled upstairs where the woman in the pink strappy number wouldn't see him and maybe say, 'Hello, how are you?'

That's how I met Pearl. She isn't fat; she just has an exuberant bosom. Also she has a much bigger heart than the manager of a bar-restaurant. And she was earning ten times more in a night than I was in a week. If she wanted a lawyer she could just pick up the phone.

*

I was feeling very tangled up on Tuesday. Mark said, 'See you next week. Wear that little red skirt and the black boots.'

'Black and red,' I said, 'the devil's colours.'

'Now you're talking,' he said and drove away. They never listen and that night I really needed to say something.

I keep a fold-away shower proof coat with a hood in my bag. I put it on and made for the steps between Paragon Hill and Sharp Harbour. It wasn't a weekend so there were hardly any drunks out and the steps were fairly dry. No one was looking. I took a huge chunk of snow white chalk out of my pocket and wrote on the ground, 'Only men with tiny willies have to wee in public places. Signed – Fluffy.'

I don't know what I was thinking. I am not Fluffy. Fluffy is a character I invented. She would use weak little words like 'willy' and 'wee' instead of something stronger. She is sweet and silly, but she has standards and she speaks out. I thought of her message as urban activism for wimps.

I was fighting back, but I wasn't very brave. Take the chalk for instance. It would be washed away by rain or, yes, piss. I could have used spray paint but that would be vandalism and more permanent than the piss I was protesting about. Fluffy the activist was environmentally friendly in an unfriendly environment.

*

Harvey emailed to say that he'd checked with the court and they said they'd received no signed papers from me. Nowadays he always emails rather than rings because Alicia doesn't want him to speak to me directly. I replied five days later saying that I hadn't heard from the court. Well, I owe him a few lies, don't I? See what I mean about corruption? *His* lies are now in *my* mouth.

4

A week after that a duplicate set of papers arrived – recorded delivery. It was Alicia's handwriting on the envelope. But inside was a note from Harvey. He'd thoughtfully filled in the form for me, placed pencilled crosses where I was to sign my name, and included a stamped envelope.

I signed with the single word, 'Fluffy', drew a smiley, winking face under it where the date should be and sent it to the court. I hadn't yet saved enough money for a down payment on a divorce lawyer.

Mark said, 'Do that thing you do with the wax strips and the elastic band.'

Fluffy wrote on the pavement, 'Please don't wee here. I hate getting my new shoes wet.' She's such an innocent, but I couldn't help noticing that nobody had pissed on her previous message.

I met Pearl and Suzette at Blacks Burger Bar. Suzette looked as if she'd been crying. Her mascara crawled down her face like millipedes and she was shovelling chips into her mouth, one after another, and swallowing them without hardly chewing.

Pearl said, 'It's Suzie's Danni. She turned thirteen yesterday and didn't come home to sit with baby Steve. So, one, Suzie had to stay home last night and can't make the rent. And two, she's feeling very old cos she's got a teenage daughter.'

'Where's Danni now?' I asked.

Suzette's mouth was too stuffed to answer so Pearl said, 'Still not home. And she wagged off of school today. Suzie wants to call the cops.'

Pearl and I looked at each other long and hard. I said, 'Where does she hang out? Who with?'

Suzette almost choked, but said, 'She goes to George Park with a bunch of boys too old for her. The cops brung her back last time.'

'Let's go,' Fluffy said. Success had made her swollen-headed.

George Park is up the hill from the harbour. The kids sit on the harbour wall and get their older friends to buy them strong cider.

Then they walk up to the park. There's a lovely view over the bay from there, but smashed kids don't look at views.

We found three boys, two girls and six cider bottles. Danni was lying underneath one of the boys with her skirt up and her eyes tight shut. Suzette started shrieking, 'I knew it. I knew you was a lying little tart, getting into trouble. I said it over and over. Din't I say it? Well, din't I?'

'Wasser matter?' Danni shrieked back. 'You afraid I'll turn out like you – you filthy ol' sow?'

The boy didn't even look up, so Fluffy went over and kicked him in the ribs with her pointy new shoes. Then he rolled off Danni and looked at me with such surprise and venom that I got scared.

Suzette was squawking, 'I told you these boys was too old. I told you they was trash. Now you're trash too.'

Pearl marched over, grabbing Danni by the arm and hauling her up.

Danni screamed, 'At least they like me. That's more than my own crappy mum does.'

'Here's the truth,' Pearl told her, 'they don't like *you*, you silly little mare – they like *it*! Nother truth – you think your mum don't like you? Well, look at her.'

Everyone turned to look at Suzette with her face all red and scrunchied and her teary mascara creeping down towards her bra.

'See that?' Pearl said calmly. 'That's what love looks like. And don't you ever forget it.'

Yes, I thought. She's telling it straight. That's exactly how *my* face looked when Alicia sat me down opposite her and said, '*Someone*'s got to tell you the truth. Harvey doesn't want to hurt you, but you need to know…'

Fluffy fumbled in my bag and found a handful of condoms. I gave one to each of the kids except Danni. Danni was Suzette's job.

We staggered back down to the harbour, emotion and high heels making us clumsy. Pearl still had her scarlet tipped claws clamped around Danni's wrist. None of us trusted a teenager on heat.

'Don't you dare diss your mum,' Pearl said. 'Every scrap of clothes you wear, every mouthful of food comes from what she earns.'

Danni was cowed by Pearl but she mumbled, 'I don't want nothing from that old slag.'

Fluffy said, 'Then charge those boys fifty quid per quarter hour and buy your own.' Pearl, Suzette and Danni stared at me. So I said, 'Or go to school and learn stuff. Either way, shut up about it.'

The old harbour-side clock chimed three o'clock. I walked away wondering what on earth Fluffy thought she was saying. A huge chunk of chalk slid into my hand and I found my way to the sweet and swanky apartment block where Harvey and Alicia laid their treacherous heads. I wrote, 'Fluffy says, Be kind and don't tell lies.'

I was on my way home when a little silver car drew up beside me. Mark rolled down the window and said, 'Looking for a job?'

'What you got in mind?' I stooped to see him properly and saw that this Mark was Oliver D, my old manager from the bar-restaurant.

He said, 'It isn't what I got in my mind, it's what I got in my trousers.' Like no one ever said *that* before.

I stepped away, hoping. But he said, 'Effing-ell! Is that *you?* You on the game now?'

'What game?' I asked, as stiff and respectable as I knew how. I thought, maybe I could get in his car and beat his eyes out with the heel of my shoe.

He said, 'Oh wait till I tell the others. This is just too good.'

I thought maybe I could persuade him to drive us somewhere secluded, wrench the steering wheel out of his hand and kill us both against a concrete piling, mangling our faces so badly that I'd never be recognised. Because I worked for him for five years. He knows Harvey and Alicia.

But I stayed calm enough to say, 'You could regret telling anyone anything about me. You've got more to lose than I have.'

He said, 'Like I'm a stud but you're a whore?'

I said, 'I'm just walking home minding my own business. *You* are kerb-crawling. Which is a cop-calling offence.'

'You threatening me?' he asked, angry.

'You threatening *me*?' I asked, not showing I was scared.

I walked away, clutching the chalk so tightly it bruised my fingers.

*

The next night, just before dawn, Fluffy went to the bar-restaurant where I used to work and wrote on the pavement outside in large letters, 'The manager of this eatery consorts with prostitutes, and he doesn't wash his hands – signed, Fluffy.'

Fluffy uses words like 'eatery' and 'consorts'. I don't, but I seem to have her patter at the tips of my fingers.

Unfortunately it started to rain at about mid-day and Fluffy's words were washed away. My environmentally friendly revenge turned out to be environmentally temporary.

It rained for three days straight so all the piss and Marks were washed away too. I put my cash in the bank and went to see Emma, a solicitor who Pearl recommended.

She said, 'Sign nothing. You paid for your husband's studies, his qualifications, his living expenses, for five years. You are *owed*.' She said, 'He's taking gross advantage.' And she said, 'Leave it with me. I'll write to him.'

I went home and sobbed solidly for thirty-five minutes because I wasn't alone any more.

*

Then the weather improved. Mothers took their kids to the beach again. Suzette said Danni was going to school every morning. Mark was generous with his wallet and didn't ask for anything weird. Fluffy wrote, 'Real men can wait to use real loos.' She's so much more polite than I am. But she has the moxie to write to drunken yobs. I don't. Maybe it's because she's hasn't been corrupted by Harvey, Alicia and Mark. Maybe only the innocent have the right to be confident.

Emma, my lawyer in shining armour, told me she'd written to Harvey demanding half his earnings for the next five years as fair settlement for the past five years.

I nearly told Mark not to count on me any more, but a couple of evenings later, before I went out to work, Police Constable Josh Manvers knocked on my door. He said that my ex-husband and his fiancée had made a complaint about me for harassment.

He said, 'You've been writing disgusting, threatening messages on their doorstep. They want you to stop. Your ex says that if you cease and desist, and if you stop kicking up a fuss about a simple divorce, he won't press charges against you for harassment and criminal damage.'

I said, 'Disgusting?' Because Fluffy is the opposite of disgusting.

He said, 'You called his fiancée an evil troll, a slag, a slapper and a sow. You wished her death by...' he checked in his note book, '... suffocation, cancer and, er, strategically placed explosives.'

'What on earth makes him think I wrote any of this?' I asked, stunned. Was I going mad or did Fluffy have a life of her own?

He consulted his notebook again. 'The threats are signed "Fluffy", and apparently you defaced some official papers in the same way.'

'Oh,' I said. I'd forgotten about the divorce papers. Then I decided to set him straight. I said, 'Don't keep calling Harvey my

9

"ex". He isn't my *ex*. That's why his fiancée wants him to get a divorce. That's what this is about, isn't it? She's making up crazy stuff because she doesn't want him to pay his debts. Now that he's worth gazillions she wants it all for herself.'

He said, 'You're telling me Alicia invented this? You never signed anything as "Fluffy"?'

Heart pounding, I asked, 'Is this an official complaint? Because if it is, you should contact me through my solicitor.' And I gave him Emma's card.

Later, before the evening rush, I met Pearl in Blacks Burger Bar. I said, 'He called her "Alicia" which he didn't get from me. So how did he know? I don't believe he's a real cop. Or if he is, he's doing this as a favour to her. She used to be manageress of Sharp Bay Sports Club, and every fool knows cops go to sports clubs.'

Pearl said, 'Are you taking your tablets regular?'

Suzette said, 'I know Danni's *going* to school, but how do I know she's staying there?'

Pearl said, 'How should *we* know?' She walked out with her cheeseburger in one hand and an unlit cigarette in the other.

NelliAnne said, 'I think Pearl's back on K. I saw her with my dealer last night.' Usually NelliAnne's so strung out she never says a word.

'What's K?' I asked.

Suzette and NelliAnne looked at me as if I was three years old. But the burger-flipper said, 'Ketamine, horse aspirin.'

Suzette said, 'But she suffered with her bladder, which ain't a good thing in our line of work, so she packed it in.'

I wished I hadn't heard. This was more corruption sticking to my good shoes, I thought as I walked down to the harbour.

Mark said, 'I can get you some if you want. We can take it out in trade.'

But I didn't want curiosity to be my downfall. Or to be dependant on Mark for more than Emma's fee. My head felt strange. Pearl was my guru in my new life. I was as lost as I'd been when I heard my mum had muscular dystrophy and Harvey was away 'on a course' so there was no one to talk to.

I leaned on the harbour wall and the salt in the air stung my eyes and made them water. The boats did slow curtsies in the swell like old ladies at a dance class. A bunch of teenagers sauntered past. One of them turned to look at me.

I meant to keep Fluffy quiet, but she said, 'Who's looking after baby Steve?'

Danni said, 'I did my homework already. All I need is a little break.' She had a nasal whine like Suzette's.

'What if there's a fire?' Fluffy asked reasonably. 'Could baby Steve escape without you helping?'

'I'm going, I'm going,' Danni said furiously. And she went.

The other kids wasted a few minutes insulting me until one of the girls asked for a spare condom and the others slunk off up to George Park.

*

Mark said, 'It's my car, after all. Maybe you should pay me rent.'

I decided that I'd move to another town.

*

Emma's office was above a holiday rental agency on the High Street. She had a big desk next to the window and I couldn't read her expression because she had her back to the light.

I said, 'Yes I did sign the divorce papers "Fluffy", and Fluffy did write a message on their doorstep, but only to tell them to be kind, and yes, it's true, I *am* on antidepressants. But I'm not Fluffy and if I'm on antidepressants it's not so surprising.'

'Okay,' she said, but her voice didn't sound okay.

I said, 'Alicia's vicious and malicious. This is her way of making sure Harvey won't feel he owes me anything at all – let alone half his income for five years. That's like asking *her* to give away half *her* income.'

'She's writing all these things about herself?'

'Clever, isn't she? She was a really competent manageress. She manages people.'

'I think,' Emma said, 'we'll get along faster if we don't speculate. Our case is with Harvey.'

That night Fluffy wrote on the wall above the piss-drenched steps, 'Incontinence is unbecoming in a man.'

I didn't see Pearl, Suzette or NelliAnne that night but Mark said, 'Can I have your phone number?' I was so lonely I almost gave it to him.

While waiting at the bus shelter for another job, a woman in a pretty spring coat said, 'It's women like you give this town a bad name.'

I said, 'Men are physically, emotionally and sexually incontinent. Why are you blaming me?'

'Because you're a woman and should know better. You're exploiting their weakness.'

'Well, they're exploiting my poverty.'

'Get a job,' she said.

'This *is* a job,' I said. 'Anyway I had a job and now I need expensive legal advice because many men, including my husband, exploited my good nature and capacity for hard work.'

'Your capacity for *hand* work?' she asked.

I wanted to explain but the bus came so she sniffed loudly and got on it. I didn't suppose we'd ever see eye to eye, but it was a conversation.

Two years ago, while Harvey was still pretending to be my husband, he persuaded me to re-grout the kitchen tiles even though it was my only day off that month. 'You're so good with your hands,' he said. I should've remembered the last time he said that we were in bed. I should've seen it as a clue, but I was so starved of compliments that I failed to see anything but the compliment.

'You know what your problem is?' Alicia said, while she was still pretending to be my friend. 'You're a doormat. You should ditch him.' She tilted her head to show me the graceful silver earrings her 'boyfriend' had just given her. I still had grout under my nails and my hands smelled of garlic from making Harvey's favourite curry but I smiled because I was married to the guy I loved and I thought I had the better deal.

Mark read poetry to me on the beach while the waves sounded as tired as I felt. He had lost his university job and was trying to make ends meet by coaching. He said no one ever listened to him. The poems were amazingly long, and so were the words in them. He was old and his wife died three years ago.

He said, 'Why do you do this for a living? Isn't it dangerous?'

'I think I'm in more danger from just one man than I am from many.' I didn't know I thought that until the words popped out of my mouth. I was thinking about Harvey.

The people in this town are very lonely. It wasn't a belief I had when I worked as a hostess and greeter in a bar-restaurant.

*

The next night I saw Pearl get into a Land Rover parked illegally near the sea front. Usually, when we're sociable, we keep an eye on each other. This time, Pearl was on her own. The car looked familiar so I thought it might've been one of her regulars.

She didn't come back for over an hour – which is a long time when you're in a car, believe me. This time though, she saw me and came over. She was limping, her lip was cut and her frock was torn.

'I was stupid,' she said. 'He didn't want to pay so I tried to nick his wallet.'

'He didn't have to hit you.' I was shocked. It was the kind of thing that happened to NelliAnne but not to Pearl.

'He's one of the angry ones,' she said.

'I thought he was one of your regulars.'

'Never seen him before,' she said. 'Gotta go find a loo.' So I thought it must be true – what NelliAnne said about K.

But later that night when I looked at my old wedding ring and realised that the marriage had been as thin as the gold, I suddenly thought – that was Harvey's car! When we were together he drove a second-hand Astra. But one time I saw him and Alicia drive by in a Land Rover. Alicia always wanted a Land Rover.

I imagined sitting Alicia down in front of me and saying, '*Someone's* got to tell you the truth…' and then telling her about Harvey and Pearl. I slept without bad dreams for over eight hours.

But when I woke up I had a scary thought. What if Oliver D, my ex manager, talked to Alicia and told her about my new job? What if Alicia told Harvey? And then, suppose Harvey sought out Pearl for more information. He could have walloped Pearl to make her talk. She wouldn't have been able to resist so she would have spilled the beans and confirmed Oliver D's story. Then of course she couldn't tell me she'd betrayed me so she made up the story about pinching Harvey's wallet.

Emma said, 'Did you note down the registration number of the Land Rover?'

'No.'

'Then we have nothing to act on.'

'Suppose,' I mused, getting ideas, 'suppose it was *Alicia* driving? Pretending she wanted girl action…'

'Speculation. But, look, it is not uncommon, when you've been deceived every day for five years, to think that *everyone's* lying to you *all* the time. Now, excuse me, but I must get on.' She sounded tired when she hung up.

After dark I looked for Pearl but no one had seen her. It was a quiet night in spite of many stag parties. But of course that meant the steps down from Paragon Hill smelled like a urinal. So Fluffy wrote, 'Are you bed wetters too?'

I felt so comfortable with Fluffy's chalk in my hand that when I went to bed I kept it beside me on the pillow. Whenever Harvey went away I used to keep one of his worn t-shirts next to me while I slept so that the bed would smell of him. Nowadays it just smells of the launderette and shampoo. The scent of chalk is comforting.

But at 4.23, only an hour after I'd gone to sleep, I was wide awake and short of breath. There was a pain in my chest and I thought, 'Is this heartache or just a heart attack?'

The feel of chalk in my hand calmed me. So I got up, dressed in sweater, jeans and sneakers and snuck out into the pre-dawn chill. I walked to Alicia and Harvey's sweet and swanky apartment block. I ambled slowly up and down the street looking for the Land Rover until I realised there was residential parking behind the block and it was guarded by a security gate. I would not be able to check for Pearl's blood on the front seat. Unfortunately, too, it looked as if there were at least three Land Rovers. It was that sort of area.

I crossed the road and looked back at the block. Everyone seemed to be asleep behind clean windows and tidy blinds. What if Fluffy wrote, 'Alicia consorts with prostitutes' in large letters? Would she send Police Constable Manvers round to make more threats about official complaints and restraining orders? Or would she split my lip and tear my frock like she did to Pearl?

While I was wondering what Fluffy would do, a woman in a hoodie appeared in front of the building. She looked carefully up and down the street, then crouched down and started to write.

'Gotcha,' Fluffy thought. Quietly she rummaged in my pocket for my phone. Stealthily she crept up behind the woman.

'Hey Alicia,' Fluffy said, and when Alicia turned, startled, she flashed off a photo of her and what she'd been writing. Then I legged it as fast as I could.

I got as far as the seafront when a hand snatched at my shoulder and spun me. A boot hit my knee, buckling my leg. A fist hit my guts so hard it nearly shot through to my spine. I fell. My phone clattered down with me. A chalky hand grabbed it. I rolled, just in time to avoid a boot in my face. Car headlights suddenly glared, harsh and blinding. The chalky hand hurled my phone over the sea wall. The lethal feet ran away.

After a long time while I couldn't breathe Mark said, 'Can you sit up?'

'No,' I said, but he pulled my arm and propped me up against the sea wall. 'I'll call police and ambulance.' He had his phone out.

'No. Please don't. I'm okay.'

'The guy was assaulting you. All that violence for a phone.'

'A woman – it was a woman.'

'Looked awfully big and tough for a woman,' Mark said. 'If you won't let me call an ambulance, at least let me take you to casualty.'

'She used to run a sport's club,' I said. 'She's pretty fit.'

In the end, even though it's against all my principles where Mark is concerned, I let him take me home. I was too woozy and achy to resist.

*

My knee grew into a tender watermelon overnight. And there was a fist-sized bruise under my ribs. I couldn't go out. Pearl brought me a bar of chocolate and a copy of Hot Gossip Magazine. We turned on the telly to see a soap about bright and shiny American teenagers who could sing, dance and wear pretty clothes. It was so unlike real life as we knew it that it was the only thing we could bear to watch.

After a bit, Pearl said, 'Me little bruvver just got banged up for five years for robbing a handbag off of an old bird. He was in court last week. That's why I ain't been around much.'

'I thought it was something,' I said.

'It was something,' she agreed.

Later she said, 'I been a bit down. Y'know?'

I told her I knew.

'But I'm better now.'

I asked her to describe the person who hit her. But she said she couldn't remember anything about that night.

She didn't ask how I got my injuries. She just assumed she knew. We shared the chocolate and watched the rest of the programme in silence.

Her lip didn't look as if it was healing very well. Probably it was the sort of corruption that makes a woman lose confidence in herself. We all *know* we can be hit but we don't want to remember it or we'd never have the guts get up out of bed. But when you've been hit recently you don't have much freedom of choice about what you remember. You feel very small and alone. And you really, *really*, don't want to think about it. I knew that now.

*

Emma said, '*Alicia* hit you? Were there any witnesses?'

I told her about Mark in the car. But she said, 'What's his name, where can I find him, will he talk to the police, what's his car registration number?' All the stuff I hadn't asked. She rang off in disgust.

I thought about Alicia and wondered just how many times I could be defeated by the same person.

Hours after Pearl left, when the round electric moon was rising over the bay, someone rang my bell. It took me a while to limp down to open up. I put the safety chain on and squinted out.

It was Mark from last night. I said, 'You're a witness. Will you talk to my lawyer? Can you give her a description...?'

'Hang on,' he said, 'I don't want to talk to any lawyers. I just came to see how you are.'

He had a nice safe smile, so I took the chain off and let him in. He was the first guy ever to sit on my sofa since I moved. He looked at all the boxes.

'Unpacking's stressful,' he said politely.

I was too ashamed to tell him how many months it'd been since the move, so I said, 'I'm waiting for my friend Fluffy to give me a hand. Would you like a drink?'

'Don't get up,' he said. 'I can see how painful it is to walk. I just came to give you your phone.' He must've registered the dumbstruck look on my face because he hurried on. 'I know the guy threw it over the sea wall but I went back. The tide was going out, see, so I thought there might be a chance you could, you know, save your address book or something. It's such a bastard – starting from scratch.' He took my little pink phone out of his pocket and handed it to me.

I stared at it and I stared at him.

'Don't cry,' he said, showing manly fear of tears. 'I thought you'd be pleased.'

It was still warm from his pocket. I said, 'Thank you so much. I can't tell you what this means.'

'The battery's dead. We could see if it takes a charge.'

I told him where the charger was in the kitchen and said there was beer in the fridge. But to my amazement he put the kettle on and made two cups of strong sweet tea.

'Your phone beeped and a little light winked,' he said. 'You may be lucky.'

Later that night, before taking the painkillers Pearl gave me for my knee, I unpacked a box of books and put them on an empty shelf above the telly. I noticed that once I'd been interested in window-box gardening, and remembered that last summer, before Alicia sat me down and said, '*Someone's* got to tell you the truth…', I'd grown tomatoes, thyme and a productive little bush-bean plant. It felt a hundred years since I'd been that person. I don't like the truth anymore. It sticks to the soles of my shoes like corruption.

*

18

I slept for ten hours. The doorbell woke me up. I rolled out of bed. The K Pearl had given me made my head wallow and I felt seasick. But my knee was still quite numb so I made it to the bathroom before throwing up.

The doorbell kept ringing.

I put the chain on and peeped out.

Alicia was leaning on my door bell.

'Let me in,' she said.

'Wait,' I said, sick and suddenly dizzy.

I limped to the kitchen and picked up my heaviest frying pan. My little pink phone was snug in its charger. I was too scared to find out if it was dead or alive.

Alicia looked at my clouds and kittens pyjamas and laughed. 'Get rid of the kitchen-ware,' she said. 'You look ridiculous.'

She waved the sheaf of divorce papers at me. 'Sign,' she said. 'You don't listen to warnings, do you? And now you've played straight into my hands.' She sat in my armchair even though I hadn't invited her to.

I limped over to her and Fluffy smacked the frying pan down on the arm of the chair, just missing her elbow. I said, 'Get up. No one told you to sit down.'

Alicia smiled her mean-girl smile and didn't flinch.

'Last night,' I began, 'who played into whose hands? You're busted but you don't even know it.'

She has a cruel mouth, like a doll's, and she kept smiling as she said, 'You wrote, "Bitch Alicia, you'll die soon, broke and alone. I'll see to it," outside my front door. I can't believe how stupid you are.'

I said, 'You think you're so clever, but… '

'I can bring the law down on you so hard…'

'What sort of woman are you?' I cried. 'Pretending to be my friend and stealing my husband…?'

'He never loved you. He just felt sorry for you.'

I felt bubbles bursting in my chest like champagne in a glass. At last there was a living, breathing enemy in front of me and a weapon stronger than chalk in my hand. I could swing it like a bat and watch her head smash like a ripe tomato. It would fly across the room and pulp itself on the window.

'Mark brought my phone back,' I said. 'You couldn't even drown it properly.'

'Drown?'

'Destroy the evidence.'

'Why would I do that? I *want* evidence that you're threatening me. And *you* keep giving it to me. Does the name Fluffy ring a bell?'

'I'm not Fluffy,' I yelled. 'But you have no right to use her name for your own spiteful reasons.'

'You're pathetic.'

'You want Harvey to think I'm as spiteful as you. You're writing those messages yourself to make him believe everything bad you say about me. So he'll intimidate me into giving up my case against him.'

'I wish I'd thought of that,' Alicia said, rummaging in her luxury handbag. 'But it shows how your devious little mind works. Harvey will love it.' She held up a menacing black pocket recorder and showed me the winking light that proved it was still recording. 'You want to go to the police and repeat those "spiteful" accusations?'

There was nothing left to do but fetch my pink phone from the kitchen. *It* didn't look menacing, or half as business-like as Alicia's recorder. And I knew it wouldn't work. Nothing worked against Alicia. She wasn't even afraid of my frying pan. I would have to kill her to defeat her. Then Fluffy would never forgive me. Killing people isn't environmentally friendly.

Alicia looked at my phone with that superior smile I'd learned to fear. She said, 'You know what? Harvey was so fed up with looking after you. How long do you think a man like him can last without intelligent conversation?'

So I took a deep breath and started thumbing.

Mark, Mark, I love you. You rescued my pink phone from drowning. You saved her from a watery grave and me from further humiliation.

My fluffy pink phone looked bedraggled but she flickered into life, winked at me and showed me a picture of…

'What?' Alicia leaped out of my armchair. '*What?*'

I showed her the picture. She tried to snatch the phone. I whacked her hand with the frying pan.

'You *hit* me,' she said, as if she'd been expecting a hug and a kiss.

'Sit down Alicia,' I said. '*Someone's* got to tell you the truth…'

*

'At last,' Emma said. 'Something I can use.' My pink phone and Alicia's pocket recorder sat on her big desk. Proper evidence. The recorder hadn't been switched off so I was able to give Emma Alicia's own voice saying, 'It's *Harvey!* Why did Harvey write all those dreadful things about me?'

But it's pictures that speak louder than words, and although he was bleached by the flash and had red eyes like an albino rat, I'd taken a recognisable picture of Harvey.

'Why didn't you know it was him?' Emma asked.

'The phone was between our faces,' I told her. 'I was as startled by the flash as he was.' Actually I think it was because I was so *completely* certain it was Alicia. I'd blamed her for everything, including Harvey's incontinence and cruelty. I was so deluded I just saw her face instead of his.

*

On the drenched and stinking steps between Paragon Hill and Sharp Harbour Fluffy wrote, 'Do you know what you look like? Do yourself a favour – keep it zipped!'

We took our burgers down to the seafront and leaned against the wall watching the lights of a tugboat and a tanker cross the horizon in slow-mo. Young Danni had baby Steve on her hip and a sulky expression on her face. Suzette stuffed fries into his mouth like tokens into a slot machine.

'He weighs too much already,' Danni complained.

'Do you want him bawling in your ear all night?' Pearl asked. Fries shut baby Steve up. Pearl shuts Danni up. It's a knack.

'I want to thank you for introducing me to Emma,' I told Pearl.

'Yeah, but I'll miss you.' Pearl gave me a hug. She was looking a lot healthier – almost herself again.

'One day I'll get out and move away too,' NelliAnne said. This made me feel sad because she was the only one of us without any hope.

'Wish *I* had a rich ex to pay me off,' Suzette said.

'He's paying her *back*,' Pearl said. 'Not off.'

'Tell us again,' Danni pleaded, because she's young enough to think this was a story with a happy ending.

'She busted her husband,' Suzette said. 'Her lawyer's got him by the nuts. He's paying her *back* big time. The end.'

'Her Harvey is just a piddly-arse who can't stand up to a demanding woman,' Pearl told Danni. 'Our little friend here signed his divorce papers "Fluffy". And then his bastard twat-faced mate found a message about him going with tarts and not washing his hands outside that crappy bar he works at. Which caused all sorts of shit and was also signed by "Fluffy". Harvey got the idea from that. He was using Fluffy against Fluffy.'

'He's a pig,' she added after a moment and I had to agree.

'Pearl?' I asked. '*Was* it Harvey who bashed you up?' I'd asked before but she always said she couldn't remember. Emma told me that Harvey categorically denied ever going with prostitutes. 'But he would, wouldn't he?' she said. Harvey claimed he frequently lent his car to his friend, Oliver D.

Pearl ignored me. She says she can only look forward. If you look back, she says, you're buggered. There's too much corruption in the past and it's so heavy you can't stand up under the load. 'You just got to let it go,' she said.

Danni sat baby Steve on the sea wall so that he could look at the moon-spattered sea too. 'I want to hear about Alicia,' she said in her nasal whine.

'I broke her little finger,' I said. 'It's all taped up to her other fingers. But Emma says it was self-defence.' I still didn't know what to think about that. *I* felt triumphant but Fluffy felt guilty. Or was it the other way round?

'If my best friend done what she done with *my* boyfriend, I'd of smashed her face in.'

'Get yourself a boyfriend first,' Pearl said. '*Then* tell us about it.'

We laughed, but Danni said, 'It won't never happen to me.'

The rest of us looked at her but no one put her straight. She's too young to be put straight yet.

I said, 'I showed her a picture of her fiancé with piece of chalk in his hand and the words "Bitch Alicia" on the ground behind him. And she realised that the guy who said he loved her was calling her a bitch behind her back, and had wished cancer on her and all sorts of other painful humiliating deaths.'

'Harvey's one of the weak angry ones,' Pearl explained.

'I'd of wanted to see Alicia's blood,' Danni insisted. 'I'd of wanted to see her in little bits on the floor.'

'I sort of did,' I said. And Fluffy agreed with me.

23

THE OLD STORY

It was a sharp, clear autumn day, and as afternoon turned to evening Harold and I met by appointment outside QuickSave. No sooner had we met than I had my first shock.

'Move yer wrinkly bum'oles,' a kid yelled at us. And I moved hastily, pulling Harold with me. I was amazed at the kid's good manners. Normally they skate right through us without warning, like we're fallen leaves scattering in a high wind.

Harold took a swipe with the wrong end of his cane, trying to hook the board's back wheels.

Three things about Harold: one, he's hot-headed; two, he won't admit he's deaf as a bathroom door; and I've forgotten number three.

The boy whooshed away unharmed and unaware he hadn't even come close to being upended. He zigged and swerved and zagged and curved along the pavement scaring oldies, youngies and in-betweenies.

Harold said, 'Spotty little turd,' and banged his cane on the ground. 'He doesn't know how close he came.' Harold mimed the murder of a spotty little turd. 'I could've done for him. He doesn't know who he's messing with.'

'Let's keep it that way,' I said, taking Harold's arm.

'Huh?' said Harold, and I gave his elbow a pacifying pat. Sometimes I think I was only included on this enterprise to pacify hot-headed Harold. Because clearly it has been many, many years since I heated any one's head, and therefore my two old friends, The Gent and Wiggy, gave me the job of keeping him cool. He boasts that when he was young he ran with one of the famous South London gangs, but neither Wiggy nor The Gent believes him. I'm uncertain. We don't usually work with outsiders.

I kept walking and wondering why the three of us had fallen for Harold's pitch. It isn't as if he is charming and clever like The Gent or clever and funny like Wiggy. And it wasn't as if it were a particularly good plan. In fact it was downright crude when you consider the slickness of our usual operations.

But when I say usual… I have to admit that nowadays we don't plan much, and the last operation was Wiggy's – for nasal polyps.

Speaking entirely for myself, I wonder if my reluctance is due to the technicalities of modern banks and building societies. All the intelligent work is done by computers. Modern operators who want to rob a bank have to flip a switch and rattle around on a keyboard. They don't even have to visit the premises anymore. As Wiggy says, 'You can rob without even leaving your own home. All you need is your own five-fingered girlfriend.'

'And a little more know-how than we possess,' confessed The Gent.

I kept my mouth shut: technical stuff confuses me and I don't even own a computer. My contributions to our joint enterprises used mainly to be in the planning stage, and as a distraction when the operation went live. I could scream, faint or suffer epi-fits better than any RADA-trained actress.

'Elsie's scream is world-famous,' The Gent used to say. But it hasn't been employed for nearly five years, and my skill in planning is thwarted by security and surveillance I no longer understand.

Which explains why, on a sharp, clear autumn evening, I was calming Harold, and walking as fast as his hip would take us towards Preston's betting shop at the corner of Grosvenor Road and High Street. My hand was firmly clamped on the crook of his elbow. Our reflection in the coffee shop window showed me that we looked frighteningly like an old married couple.

We should be retired and living by the seaside, I thought. But how do you retire from a business like ours? There isn't a company pension. Besides, The Gent is having to remortgage his house because his son's in debt again. As is my daughter, but I try not to think about it. And early this month Wiggy was released from his last vacation at Her Magesty's pleasure to find that his precious Airstream had been repossessed by the finance company. During his absence his sister, who should have been dealing with the payments, took a dippy turn and handed all his money to a donkey sanctuary. We are all, in our separate ways, dogged by the choices we made when we were young and thought we would always stay ahead of the game.

My recollections were interrupted by someone calling, 'Mrs Ivo. Hey, *Mrs Ivo!*'

I would have walked on, but Wiggy appeared from the Bell pub doorway and said, 'Oh bloody hell, she's forgotten her own codename. Elsie, you'd forget your own family if you didn't carry photos.'

'You pronounced it wrong,' I said stiffly. 'It's Ee-vo. You said Eye-vo.'

'Ee-vo, Eye-vo, Nee-vo, Nye-Vo, let's call the whole thing off.'

'Eh?' said Harold. 'No one's calling nothing off.'

'It's just one of Wiggy's jokes,' I said, patting his arm. 'What are you doing here?' I asked Wiggy. 'We're not supposed to meet till…'

'Come inside,' Wiggy said, looking past my shoulder. 'Hurry, the CCTV camera's swinging in this direction.'

'Huh?' said Harold. Wiggy took one arm, I tugged the other and we whished him into the pub before he became visible and bellicose.

'We've run into a problem,' Wiggy explained, pointing to the slumped figure of The Gent at a table in a dark corner of the room.

'I'll have a pint since you're offering,' Harold said. 'One won't hurt.'

I hurried over to The Gent.

'It'sh my tooth,' he said, covering the lower part of his face with his hand.

'Not his wisdom tooth, obviously,' Wiggy said. 'He was supposed to go to the dentist last week but he funked it.'

'I don't think I can do the job,' The Gent said. And indeed he looked yellow and extremely unwell.

'Oil of cloves,' I said, rummaging in my handbag.

'Now's not the time for your portable pharmacopoeia,' Wiggy said. 'He's already rattling – the number of pills he's necked since lunch.'

'I don't want to hold you back,' moaned The Gent. 'I really am sho shorry.'

'What's wrong with him?' Harold said, sitting down heavily, slopping his pint.

'Tooth rot.'

'Eh?'

'Forget it,' Wiggy said. 'The only way I can see out of this is if The Gent waits in the car and does the driving instead of Elsie, Elsie is lookout instead of Harold, and Harold comes up to the betting shop with me instead of The Gent.'

'Huh? Say again.'

'The Gent waits in the car...'

'Shut up,' I said, 'anyone could hear you.' Except Harold.

'So what's going *on?*' And that's another thing about Harold – even before his hearing failed he never listened.

'Are you quite sure you want Harold on shtage with you at show-time?' The Gent was speaking through considerable pain.

'Eh?'

'Do we have any alternative? Or should we just abort?'

I would have pressed for standing us all down – it's what any sensible woman would have done. But I didn't want to spend the rest of my life eating at the YMCA cafeteria. I'd rather go back to choky. At least there, bad food comes free. Because when times were good, Wiggy, The Gent and I had often lived high in the sky in foreign cities where hotel suites were more spacious than English houses. Rhubarb and custard at the YMCA isn't the worst thing life can throw at you, but if I thought it was *all* life had to offer from here on in, I think I'd want to top myself.

As it turned out, *I* went onstage with Wiggy, The Gent waited in the car and Harold kept his job as lookout. It wasn't possible to explain a change of plan to him without a bullhorn. And shouting your plans through a bullhorn when you're making changes to a heist on a betting shop is not advisable.

'Take my coat,' The Gent said, 'the mashk ish in the left pocket, the plashtic gun ish in the other.'

Wordlessly, I took his coat and gave him my small bottle of oil of cloves in return. Wordlessly, Wiggy handed over the car keys.

'Show time,' The Gent said with a brave smile. 'Shparkle, guysh. I know you'll be shplendid.'

We left him in the car park behind Cristette's Kitchenware and Novelties. The great thing about Cristette's is that the main door opens onto the High Street and you can walk all the way through to the car park at the back. The shop is hugger-mugger with too many shelves and stacks, and there are no surveillance cameras. It's an excellent place if you want to get off the street in a hurry.

Preston's is a small betting shop above a newsagent at the corner of Grosvenor Road and High Street. We reached the newsagent five minutes before the betting shop was due to close and left Harold pretending to read the small ads in the early evening paper. He seemed edgy.

Halfway up the narrow flight of stairs Wiggy and I paused to put on our masks and raise the hoods of our coats. It was only then that I realised how much condition Wiggy had lost during his last spell away. For a big man he was always fit and pretty fast, but now his breathing sounded like a hinge that needed a squirt of oil.

'What's up?' I muttered, trying to make the coat of a much taller man zip over a much fuller bosom.

'Just an allergy,' Wiggy wheezed back. 'These stairs haven't been swept.' His mask was an elaborate affair that could have graced a Venetian ball.

'Decongestant?'

'Not now, Elsie,' he said patiently. Which was just as well – I'd left my bag in the car with The Gent.

The Gent's mask was a simple but elegant balaclava his wife had knitted for him from a silk and wool mix. I pulled it over my head and topped it with the hood.

'Let's get this over with,' I said. 'The hood's ruining my hair.'

'Let your coat hang open,' Wiggy wheezed. 'You still look too much like a woman.'

'And you look like a real hunk,' I snarled back.

'Let's go. And leave the talking to me.'

But after climbing to the top of the stairs he didn't have enough breath to blow out a birthday candle, and the staff behind grilles didn't even look up as he stood there panting and swinging his baseball bat. So I took over.

'Everybody freeze!' I yelled. Instantly everyone stopped what they were doing. Oh the power! No one had taken this much notice of me since my daughter was too small to talk back.

'The money!' I shouted. 'Give us the money and no one gets hurt.'

'The gun,' Wiggy hissed, his chest heaving. 'It's still. In your. Goddam pocket.' To cover for me he strode to the counter and whacked the baseball bat against the grill. The man and woman behind the counter cowered in shock. The portly manager started towards the back.

I fumbled the plastic gun out of my pocket and pointed it at him. 'Don't move a muscle,' I bellowed. 'Instruct your people to fill our bags or I'll put two bullets in your fat gut. Believe me, I can't miss.'

Out of the corner of my eye I saw Wiggy push a bunch of crumpled plastic bags through the grille. They came from Safeway and I swear they're the same ones we used on our last job. Wiggy never throws anything away.

By now he'd recovered his breath enough to say, 'Fill the bags. Quickly. Unless. You want. To see. Your boss. Shot.' He sounded eerily like an automaton. The woman started to cry, but she began to stuff bundles of money into the bags.

The manager stood, feebly protecting his paunch with his hands. I kept the gun trained on him while I screamed at the other, younger man. 'Help her! Now!' and he suddenly jerked into life and started stuffing bags too.

I was jubilant. Energy surged through every cell of my body. I had no idea what a sense of self-worth there was to be gained from pointing a plastic gun.

'Tie the bags,' Wiggy growled, 'and throw them. Over. The grille.'

Bags sailed over the grille and dropped at our feet.

We'd done it. All we had to do was pick up the bags and leave. Or not.

The door at the top of the stairs swung open and a man in SecureCorps uniform walked through humming a tune from Guys and Dolls.

'Hi there,' he said. 'Cashed up everyone? Ready to go?' Then he saw Wiggy. Then he saw me. Then he heard thunderous crashes from the stairs below.

He drew his weapon.

The young man behind the counter started to cry loudly.

Harold charged through the door.

Wiggy swung his baseball bat.

I picked up as many bags of cash as I could manage.

Harold fired his gun. A huge lump of plaster detached itself from the ceiling and fell on the SecureCorps guard's head just as Wiggy's bat connected.

'Oh farkin 'ell,' yelled the SecureCorps guard who was wearing protective headgear but went down in a pile of rubble anyway.

Harold fired his gun at the manager who seemed to be making for his panic button. The manager went down.

I said, 'That wasn't supposed to happen.'

'Don't just stand there,' Wiggy said, grabbing a couple of carrier bags in the hand that wasn't wielding the bat.

'Huh?' said Harold. And for once I could see what he meant: a real live gun, with real live ammo, going off twice in a confined space leaves you with real live tinnitus. It had never happened to me before. But then I'd never worked with Harold before.

We scrambled for the door. On the stairs Wiggy remembered to remove his mask. He pulled mine off too. And snatched the plastic gun out my numb fingers. Harold stumbled down after us, picking up his walking stick from where he'd left it at the bottom, and unwinding his scarf from around his head.

I didn't even want to look at him. Wiggy, The Gent and I had never, in all of our long careers, *ever* used live firearms. No one had ever been hurt except for the odd whomp with a baseball bat when persuasion didn't work. Harold was supposed to be the look-out. He was supposed to have warned us about the SecureCorps guard and not charged in afterwards firing a real gun.

I wanted to drop everything and run away from all of them. A lifetime of YMCA lunches didn't seem so bad anymore. I tore off The Gent's coat and carried it over my arm, hiding some of the Safeway bags. As I'd feared, my hair was a mess.

We stepped out into the bright autumnal street and Wiggy spun round to face Harold. 'What. The fuck. Did you. Do that for?' he wheezed.

'Say again,' Harold said. 'Come on, we got to get back to the car. Elsie, give me a hand. My hip's knackered.'

'I'd like to knacker your thick skull,' I said. I wanted to leave him but I couldn't without endangering the rest of us. 'Why the hell didn't you warn us?'

'Huh?' He leaned heavily on my arm and we limped up the High Street towards Cristette's Kitchenware and Novelties.

Wiggy started shouting, '*Why the hell didn't you...*'

'Shut up,' I said, 'anyone could hear.' Except Harold.

Harold didn't even hear the police sirens as three cars raced past us to the betting shop. My heart was staggering and my vision went speckly. I heard the gunshots and saw the manager tumble all over again.

I'm not quite sure what happened then because the next thing I remember clearly was The Gent helping me out of the car next to my block of flats. He carried a large Cristette's bag which he gave me when we got to my door.

'What's that?' I asked, and The Gent sighed diplomatically.

Apparently I'd had a funny turn in Cristette's and insisted on buying three baking trays, a set of glass candle-holders and a large wok. He reassured me that I'd paid for them with my own money. He said that the staff in Cristette's were very nice to batty old ladies and had thought nothing of it.

'I'll make you a cup of tea,' he said sympathetically.

'No, no, I'm quite alright,' I said, wondering what on earth I'd do with another wok. This wasn't the first funny turn I'd had in the last year, and for some very odd reason I always seemed to buy a wok. But I didn't want to tell The Gent about it. 'How's the tooth?' I asked to distract him.

'Your oil of cloves worked a treat,' he said. 'I tried it in the car while I was waiting. The tooth's nearly stopped hurting. You're more use than a pharmacist, Elsie.' Which, of course, is why we call him The Gent – he lies to make other people feel good. But he did look better.

'Wiggy'll be along when he's dropped Harold and dealt with the car.' He made sure I was sitting comfortably and then he went away to make the tea.

I sat and wrestled with my wayward mind, trying to figure out what had gone wrong. Why had I felt so wonderful with a plastic gun? So dismal with a live one. Had I drawn attention to us in the shop? What would happen now we were guilty of robbery with violence, maybe even murder? But most of all I wanted to know what went wrong.

I didn't find out until Wiggy showed up when The Gent and I were on our third pot of tea. He turned on the TV for the local news before dropping like a rock onto my sofa. His face was grey with fatigue.

'Harold,' he said. 'Not my favourite. Person. Big mistake. Working with him.'

The Gent poured him a cup of strong tea and we waited while he recovered his breath. 'Where's the money?' he asked first.

'Ah yes,' The Gent said, 'we need to talk about that.' He gave me a sidelong glance and then spoke directly to Wiggy. 'At the moment it's in Elsie's laundry hamper. I know she usually keeps it in her chest freezer, but when I looked in there I found there wasn't enough room. Elsie, do you know you have four woks in your freezer? Wiggy, she's got four woks in her freezer. I know it's where she hides stuff, but why hide four woks?'

'It's none of your business what I keep in my freezer,' I said. 'Why aren't we talking about what went wrong at the betting shop?'

'Hold on,' Wiggy said, turning up the volume on the TV. 'This is about us. Look.'

What we saw was black-and-white grainy footage from a surveillance camera somewhere in the ceiling of the betting shop. We watched fascinated as two shadowy figures entered and then one of them skipped around like a goat pointing a gun in all directions.

'That can't be me,' I said. 'I don't jump around.' The Gent and Wiggy said nothing.

Jerkily the two behind the counter began filling bags. The film froze while the newsreader said, 'Witnesses describe being threatened by two men wearing masks. The third member of the gang only made his appearance after the arrival of an employee from the security firm who should have transported the day's takings to the night-safe.'

'Two men?' I said. 'That's wonderful. We're home free.' Again The Gent and Wiggy stayed silent.

The film continued with the leisurely entrance of the man from SecureCorps, shortly followed by the muffled figure of Harold. The newsreader said, 'As you can see the footage ends abruptly when the third man shot out the security camera. The manager of the betting shop only survived what he describes as certain death by a trained marksman because he ducked behind the countertop. He said, "These men were armed to the teeth and very violent. They terrorised my staff in what was clearly a meticulously planned raid." Police are asking anyone who witnessed three men fleeing from the scene to contact them immediately.'

'Fleeing?' Wiggy said, turning off the TV. 'Harold flees at the speed of a rocking chair. What's up, Elsie?'

'I thought Harold shot the manager,' I sobbed. 'I thought...'

'I know, I know,' Wiggy said. 'Have you got a handkerchief, Gent? The old broad needs mopping.'

The Gent passed me his handkerchief, politely pretending not to see my streaming eyes and nose.

Wiggy said, 'Who knew Harold even had a real gun? Maybe he wasn't lying about the South London gang after all.'

'It's unforgivable,' The Gent said. 'We made it quite clear to Harold – no real firearms. He knows how we work. We have a reputation.'

'He wasn't supposed to be there,' I said, blowing my nose on The Gent's immaculate linen. 'He was supposed to be the lookout, but where was he?'

'Ah yes,' Wiggy said. 'Don't think I didn't ask him about that. Very loudly. Guess what?'

'What?'

'He had a beer in the pub, remember? So he's standing outside the newsagent waiting and watching and, stripe me pink, his bladder starts playing up. So the silly old bugger goes to take a leak. On his way back he sees the SecureCorps guy disappearing upstairs and all he can think of to do is follow him up and shoot him.'

'He was aiming at the *man*?' The Gent asked, horrified.

'That's what he said.'

'I'm too old for this,' I sniffed.

'I have to take the blame,' The Gent said. 'If I hadn't been too much of a wimp to go to the dentist we wouldn't have gone to the pub. If Harold hadn't drunk a pint of bitter his weak bladder wouldn't have been a determining feature of this fiasco.'

'Don't let's talk blame,' Wiggy said firmly. 'Because I might have to admit that I'm not fit enough for this kind of life any more. If I hadn't been out of breath Elsie wouldn't have had to take charge – which she's obviously unsuited to do. I feel directly responsible for her whatchamacallit.'

36

'*What?*'

'Don't get arsey with me, Elsie. You had a… er… an emotional episode in Cristette's.'

'Just a momentary confusion,' The Gent put in tactfully. 'You were splendid in the betting shop.'

'Thanks,' I said. 'But Wiggy's right. I have been having, well, memory lapses. I'm taking St. John's Wort and fish oils and something else I can't remember. But I should have told you.'

'Told us what?' Wiggy asked. 'That you're a mad old bat? Gee, what a surprise.'

'Maybe all three of us should think again about the active approach,' The Gent said. 'Maybe the way to go is technological.'

'I haven't got a computer,' I said. 'It's too late for me to learn, and anyway I can't afford it.'

'Yes you can,' The Gent said. 'As well as what we took from the betting shop you've got…' He turned to Wiggy. 'In her freezer she's got dozens of oddly shaped packages labelled "Leg of lamb" and "Ham hock" which, believe me, are not legs of lamb or hocks of ham or even sides of beef.'

'You're mistaken,' I said. 'I'm a vegetarian. I don't buy ham hocks.'

'We know,' The Gent said. 'You've got a freezer full of cash under all those woks. You're like a squirrel who's forgotten where she hid her nuts.'

'She's certainly nuts,' Wiggy said. 'But she may be right, Gent: we might just be home free. No one saw us.'

'Of course they saw us.' I waved at the TV. 'They called me a man.'

'Exactly,' said The Gent. 'They called two doddery old men and one dotty old lady "Three very violent men." Longevity makes us invisible and prejudice renders us incapable.'

'Apart from ripping off a betting shop,' Wiggy said, 'our second most serious crime was to get old.'

'But it saved our asses,' I said.

'Maybe,' The Gent said, 'but not for long.'

'Don't worry.' Wiggy consoled me. 'He doesn't mean the cops. He means the Grim Reaper.'

'Oh, that's alright then,' I said.

WHOLE LIFE

If eyes were knives she'd have cut me stone dead. Instead she gave me that look and then spat. I hate passing the bus shelter. But I have to pass it by because I can't wait for a bus there any more.

They took the shoe off of the roof of the shelter, but they still haven't mended the crazy crack where Jamie's board hit the safety plastic. It was a drenching night, that night, so when the Law arrived they say there was hardly any blood left. It gurgled away down the gutter as fast as it spilled out of Jamie's body and there's not even a stain left. Poor ginger lamb.

That's what I'd tell the woman with the eyes – poor ginger lamb. He was red-headed, plump, gay, and that night he was carrying a new skateboard. If she was even talking to me she'd tell me he was a sweet kid who never did anyone any harm. And she'd say he had 'his whole life ahead of him'. That's what they always say: 'Whole life ahead…'

What's a whole life? Is my life without my son a whole life? Is it a whole life when I can't use the nearest bus stop? My life, minus my kid and a bus stop; my life minus respect, my reputation, two of my three jobs and all my friends isn't a whole life, is it? It's a life full of holes.

Jamie's whole life ran red – from his eyes, mouth, ears, nose and groin. It ran away from him down a storm drain never to return. And Ben came home and said, 'Can you wash my shirt,

Mum? A kid had a nosebleed and it went all over me.' It was his school uniform so I stuffed his clothes into the washing machine and he had a hot bath because he was shivering from the rain and cold. I left him alone to do his homework with half a pizza in the oven and some chocolate pud in the fridge. His whole life was ahead of him. Then I went to the Saracen's Head to serve drinks to drunks.

You see, I thought I was a good mother. I washed Ben's clothes and I left a hot supper for him – I didn't just bung him a couple of quid and expect him to go back out into the rain for a takeaway.

The Law said, 'Your son comes in covered in a murdered boy's blood and all you do is wash his clothes? You must've known something was up. We could charge you as an accessory.'

Mary Sharp didn't wash her twins' shirts. The Law found their clothes in a soggy tangle under the bunk beds. Roseen Hardesty didn't even come home that night. Rocky Hardesty tried to wash his own uniform but the machine was bust. He ate his beans cold, straight from the can, and stayed up till five in the morning playing computer games.

There wasn't even a speck on Jamal's clothes. I think cleanness is part of Jamal's mum's religion, but I don't really know because her English won't stand up to an ordinary conversation.

Me? I was home by half past midnight. I asked Ben if he'd done his homework and he said, 'Yes – why do you always go on at me?'

I told him to go to bed and I transferred his clothes from the washer to the dryer because he'd forgotten. Then I tidied the kitchen and was in bed by a quarter past one myself. I was tired and I had to be up and out at six-thirty to clean three offices by nine.

That's when I saw the police tape at the bus shelter. The one purple and white trainer was still on the roof. At that point no one knew it was Jamie's. So I still thought I had my whole life ahead of me, whereas I'd already lost it hours ago. So had Ben, although most folk round here would say he didn't lose it, he chucked it all away and got what he deserved.

'What happened here?' the bus driver asked when I got on.

'Search me,' I said. 'Kids?'

'Someone got knifed,' a woman said. She works part time. I see her on the bus three mornings out of five.

'Not round here,' I said. 'They're good kids round here.'

'I heard it on local radio,' she said. And we all turned to look at the crazy crack on the plastic shelter as the bus pulled away.

Later, this same woman went round telling everyone that I was playing the innocent but she knew beyond the shadow of a doubt that I was lying. Do doubts have shadows? I think they must do. My whole life has been about doubts and shadows ever since.

That morning I went straight from the office block to Moby's Café where I worked during the day. I did the food preparation, waitressing and cleaning up.

Mr Moby was there when the school rang to say that Ben was with the Law. He looked daggers at me because I wasn't supposed to take personal calls while I was at work.

'It's a mistake,' I kept saying. 'Ben's never been in any trouble.' But I had to go to the police station to find out what was wrong and Mr Moby said he'd dock my wages. He'd been on my case since that time I slapped his face in the mop cupboard.

On the other hand he spoke up for me to the Law. He said I was a hard worker and as far as he knew I was honest. But he also told them I wasn't very bright. Then he fired me because of the boycott the Friends of Jamie Cooke people organized.

The Friends made Kath and Ed Majors at the Saracen's Head fire me too. But Pauline Greenberg said I could go on cleaning offices because I wasn't working with members of the public. She said nobody cared who cleaned for them as long as they didn't have to see me. She also gave me more hours on the nightshift, so I can keep up with the rent.

I remember Pauline from school. She was a couple of years older than me but she was famous for beating up two boys and Roseen Hardesty when they called her dad a dirty Jew. She did well for herself. She employs twenty women – but never Roseen Hardesty.

She likes us to be on time so I walked quickly through the estate to Kennington Road to catch the number 3. There was no one at the bus stop but me and a gang of screaming urban seagulls. They'd torn a rubbish bag open and made a mess of the pavement. At first I thought they were fighting over a chicken carcass, but then I saw they were plucking the eyes out of a dead pigeon and stabbing their cruel beaks into its throat and breast. Seagulls have such clean white heads. Their beaks are a beautiful fresh yellow. You wouldn't think, would you, that something so clean and fresh lived on city garbage and carrion.

I just waited for my bus and minded my own business. I didn't try to shoo the gulls away because they never take a blind bit of notice, and, truth to tell, I'm a little bit scared of them. They eat, fight and shriek, and if anyone gets in their way they attack – a bit like…

I didn't know Ben was in a gang. I just thought he had mates. He'd known the Sharp twins and Rocky since they were in Juniors together. When it all came out, he told me he'd only joined to stop the others picking on him. Jamal said the same thing too. The Law believed Jamal because Jamal's mum forced him to talk. But they didn't believe Ben. They took away his mobile phone and said they could prove that the gang members had been talking to each other non-stop all night.

But Ben is quite small; he hasn't had his growth spurt like the others. His skin is still fresh and peachy without spots and open pores. His voice hasn't broken, but he tucks his chin in and talks as low in his throat as he can. I think he was telling the truth – maybe the bigger kids would have picked on him for being not manly enough. The Law said that was probably why he wanted to prove himself and that's why he turned on Jamie.

But how can such a beautiful boy do ugly things to a poor gay ginger lamb? He can't, I know he can't. He's too innocent to be guilty.

He's sensitive. He cried when his dad forgot his thirteenth birthday and didn't even send him a card from Hull or wherever he and his new family are living now. I can't believe a boy who cried about his own father would do anything so cruel to Jamie Cooke. But the Law never saw him cry so they said he was guilty and 'showed no remorse.'

A white van pulled up to the bus stop and a man leant over to open the passenger door. It was Ron Tidey who lives on the estate. He drank regularly at the Saracen's Head, and he drank a lot. But he said, 'I saw you waiting all by yourself. Hop in. I'll give you a ride to work.'

I don't much like Ron Tidey but I got in because no one had spoken to me for weeks.

He said, 'I don't care what they're all saying. It isn't your fault. It'd be even more unnatural if a mother didn't stand up for her boy.'

'He didn't do it, Ron,' I said, feeling suddenly so tired I could've lain down then and there and slept for a hundred years. The cab was warm and smoky.

'You aren't doing yourself any favours, Cherry. You should just shut up about it and keep your head down.'

'I am doing,' I said. 'I'm always shut up cos there's no one to talk to.'

'Tell you what, Cherry, why don't you and me go out for a drink later? Somewhere no one knows you. It'll take you out of yourself. You're still a young woman, more or less, and you got your whole life…'

'Don't say it, Ron,' I interrupted. But I agreed to meet him. I was that lonely.

I suppose you could say that loneliness was always my downfall. Ben's father wasn't much of a catch. But I did get Ben out of it, and I thought, if I had a baby, there'd always be someone for me to love who'd love me back. But I suppose just loving a child isn't a whole love. I wasn't living a whole life, according to Roseen Hardesty. 'Get yourself a man,' she said. 'At least, get yourself a shag. A grown woman can't go without for long, Cherry, or she'll turn sour and grow rust on it.'

'Use it or lose it,' Mary Sharp agreed.

'Mary Sharp's in no danger of losing it,' Roseen said later. 'Her problem might be overuse.'

'Meow!' I said, because I wasn't taking anything they had to say seriously. They both had new boyfriends every week as far as I could see while their kids had holes in their shoes. Yes, I was a bit snooty back then. Now, when we meet sometimes outside the Young Offenders Unit on visiting days we hardly exchange a word.

Tomorrow they're moving Ben to someplace in darkest Wales and I don't have a car. I can still send him sweets and toothpaste but I won't hardly see him, train fares costing what they do.

'Cheer up,' said Ron Tidey later that night at the Elephant and Castle. 'Have another voddy and talk about something else. You're like a broken record.'

So I had some more vodka and then some more after that, and at about midnight when we were in the back of Ron's van and I couldn't find my underwear Ron said, 'There, you're more relaxed now, ain't ya? Don't never say Ron Tidey can't show a lonely woman a bit of sympathy.' He was busy spraying himself with deodorant and chewing peppermints so's his wife wouldn't rumble him.

I felt like crying, but I didn't because Ron has a van and if he thinks I'm a miserable cow he won't want to see me again or maybe even give me a lift up to Wales.

Also, last time I did anything like this I got Ben. Maybe I'll get a whole other life out of Ron, and if I do maybe this time it'll be a girl. They say girls are better company than boys. I hope it's a girl.

ART, MARRIAGE AND DEATH

When you're young you don't know what's going to be important later on. Things happen and then other things happen. Some of it jars your mind, some of it grasps your heart, but it takes time to decide which is which and how you really feel about it. You don't even recognise some of the really big events as big until later when you talk it out to yourself – make a narrative of it.

It was like that when I first met Gail. I went to pick up Alastair at his shared flat in Notting Hill and I walked in on two women. One had a pair or scissors in her hand, and the other had a towel around her shoulders. They turned towards me with the kind of bright curious eyes that made me want to account for myself.

'I'm looking for Alastair.'

'He'll be along in a minute,' Gail said, or her friend – I don't, to this day, know which was which. They looked at me, waiting, while I fought the urge to cough up my life story.

Then Alastair appeared and we left.

'That's Gail,' he said.

'Which one?'

'The one I'm going to marry.'

'In your dreams,' I said, shocked because now I knew finally that he meant more to me than I did to him. But equally, it didn't occur to me that I had just met one of my future best friends. And in the long run that was what made the day important.

For a while I assumed she was a hair-dresser. Of course I was wrong. I often am. Then I got a job at a small liberal arts college in Canada and didn't see any of my friends for three long years.

*

The next time I met Gail we were both wearing black. She was with Alastair and he was wearing black too. They had married while I was away, and I was too poor to come back for the wedding. Now, slightly richer, I was home for the funeral of a mutual friend, a woman both Alastair and I had been close to – the way students are, for no reason at all except you went to the same movies. Moselle was exotic, secretive and had rich parents. She was the one, early on, who introduced me to the word *recherché*. 'Searched out, rare,' she explained loftily. 'Far-fetched.' And Alastair nodded wisely. Words were his thing too. I didn't want to recognise it then but they shared far more than just a sophisticated vocabulary. Of course that was before he met Gail.

While a rabbi mumbled banalities about Moselle, who clearly he had never known, I studied the sparse crowd looking for other old friends, especially looking for her rich parents. I'd never met them but they were famous for bailing Mo out. She had much more money than the rest of us but she was always in debt.

Gail nudged me. 'Her father can't leave Simla. Apparently he's too ill.'

She nudged me again. 'That's her mother.' She pointed with her chin towards a large black hat in the front row. The large black hat was flanked by two young men, also wearing hats. Some guys knew how to dress in the presence of a rabbi. Alastair was bare-headed.

'Who're the guys?'

'I don't know.' Gail was obviously annoyed. I recognized the gleam of curiosity in her bright eyes. If the two guys were important enough to be in the front row they were important enough to be known by Gail. 'We'll find out later,' she promised.

I was only beginning to understand that the Gail I was getting to know needed, almost viscerally, to satisfy her curiosity. It was as much a part of her as her brilliant eyes.

I was glad to be whispering with Gail. It took my mind away from the grotesque thought of Mo, dead and nailed in a wooden box. The last time I saw her she was dancing in the mud at Glastonbury Festival, flinging the rain out of her hair, slender arms reaching for... well, everyone, everything.

She was the first of our group to die and it was as if the grim reaper stretched across her coffin and touched us all with his chilly finger. 'You may be young,' he hissed, 'but you are not exempt.'

Alastair, on the other side of Gail, stared stonily ahead. I wondered how he was taking it. Gail intercepted my glance and breathed, 'He's expecting her to leap out from behind the flowers and yell, "Ha-ha, can't you take a joke?" Like this was one of her Performance Art events. He doesn't believe it. He's still in shock.' She had an enigmatic expression on her face and I wondered, not for the first time, what Alastair had told her about the past.

There was nothing personal about the service: not one of Mo's friends had been asked to speak; there was no music or poetry. It was as if the grown-up world, as well as death, had claimed her and extinguished every individual spark. And there were so few of *us*. Where were all the friends who could have given her back some identity?

'Where is everyone?'

'In the last three years Mo fought with loads of people,' Gail said. 'You know Mo. She wasn't backward about confrontation.'

'With you?'

'Oh no. She tried, but I wouldn't let it happen.'

That didn't surprise me at all. Since I left England there had been two reluctant letters from Alastair. The correspondence and the friendship would have wilted from sheer neglect if Gail hadn't taken it over. Words might be his thing, but using them for communication and story-telling was definitely hers, and I'd come to rely on her for news of friends back home. At first I thought of these e-mails as a substitute for Alastair, but lately I'd looked forward to and welcomed them as a connection with Gail. I was at the crematorium only because she told me where to go and when.

'Where's Jay?' I murmured.

'Somerset,' said Gail. 'They had a really nasty bust-up. I wrote to you…'

'But all the same…'

'Still angry.'

'Christine?'

'Angry too. Something about money.'

That sounded like Mo, the rich girl, always over-spending, always borrowing from poorer friends and then not quite understanding when they became desperate to be repaid.

'Drew?'

'Couldn't stand her.'

'I thought he fancied the pants off her.'

'Oh Liza.' Gail sighed. 'You don't know much, do you? They had a little scene a couple of years ago and she went around telling everyone he couldn't get it up.'

'All the same…'

'Still angry. And he married Sha-sha and she's angry too. I *wrote* to you.'

But this was what Moselle was all about. No one was ever indifferent to her. She was infuriating. You loved her or you hated her and sometimes you did both at the same time. But you *cared*.

Now it seemed as if her mojo was still operating because just as the mumbled ceremony was droning to a close Moselle's mother's large black hat flew into the aisle and a scuffle broke out between the two guys in the front row. The service ended with fists and fury.

'Thank God,' Gail said, standing on tip-toe and craning her neck to see. 'Something Mo-like at last.'

The first to leave was a guy nursing a bloody nose. He strode to the door, raging and humiliated, not looking at anyone.

Gail shoved me. 'Go *on*. Find out who he is.'

'Me?'

'Don't be such a wimp, Liza. You're a writer now – go do some research.'

Reluctant to admit that I was more at home in libraries than real life, I ran, and when I caught up with him the man with the bloody nose was already unlocking his car – a brand new Volvo. I did the first thing to come into my jet-lagged head: I thrust a handful of tissues at him and said stupidly, 'Are you alright?' I have always despised people who say that when things are so clearly not alright. The man with the bloody nose distinctly felt the same way. He glared at me and grimaced – showing his bloody teeth. He did, however, grab the tissues.

'Am I alright!' he snarled. 'That arsehole hit me. At her *funeral*. What a brilliant time to meet her boyfriend! Oh yeah, I'm alright.'

He might've been quite fit if it weren't for the blood and the fury. He fumbled the Volvo open.

I said, 'Wait. You can't drive like that. Some of us are going for a drink or a curry. Come with us.'

'I never want to see any of you arty freaks again. You and your stupid stunts are what killed her.'

'What're you *talking* about?'

'North Camden Art Exhibition. Does that ring a bell?'

'I was in Toronto till last night.' Far away the sound of an ambulance rose and fell like a sigh.

The guy with the bloody nose said, 'Moselle was *not* a tart. She did *not* take drugs.'

'What are you talking about? Of course not.' I wanted him to calm down but he wasn't listening.

51

'She was my *wife*,' he shouted. He wadded up the reddened tissues and hurled them across the car park. I was too stunned to say anything. The guy climbed into his car and started the motor.

'Wait!' I cried. 'I didn't know Mo was married. Who are you?' But he didn't hear me. He just drove off, tyres screaming. He was Mo's *husband*? And he'd just met her *boyfriend*? I stood for a second with my jaw hanging.

The others were waiting in the Garden of Remembrance, looking perplexed. The woman in the large black hat turned out not to be Mo's mother after all. 'But I *am* married to her father, dear,' she told Alastair. She was redheaded, stick-thin and she was hanging on his arm as if being the deceased's step-mother entitled her to support. 'Actually, I'm the third Mrs Joffe, but I've never felt like a Mrs, so do call me Bekki.' The invitation seemed to be extended solely to Alastair.

Gail gave me an evil grin but didn't intervene. The second man from the front row, the boyfriend, was nursing a bruised hand and a swelling eyebrow; otherwise he was quite fit too. That was no surprise: Mo always picked lookers. It was a characteristic we shared. Sometimes we even picked the same lookers, except she was better at catching them than I was – which was one of the reasons I'd exiled myself in Canada.

The third Mrs Joffe was saying, 'You can imagine what a shock this has been, having to cope with all the arrangements on my own. Her father never leaves his precious air-conditioning at this time of year. Weak lungs, you know.'

'Where's her real mother?' I asked. I'd come all the way from Toronto but her blood relations were absent. Poor Mo.

Bekki ignored me and informed Alastair, 'Of course I tried to contact everyone in Moselle's address book but, there was so little time. Maybe she's abroad. She's quite *old* now, you know. She was the *first* Mrs Joffe after all.'

Alastair threw Gail a silent plea for rescue but she drew me aside instead. 'Well?' she said. 'Who's the guy with the bloody nose?'

'I don't know his name, but Mrs J must: he's Mo's husband and...'

'Oh Liza, no, you must have misunderstood.'

'No, no, he said...'

Gail pulled me even further away from the others. She nodded towards the boyfriend. 'Don't let him hear you. He's devastated. He's Woody, and Mo was married to *him*.'

'No way. My guy said he was the boyfriend.'

We stared at each other. Gail, who had been married for eighteen months, said, 'Surely even Moselle couldn't manage two husbands.'

I, who was not married, said, 'How the hell did she manage to marry two men?'

'Sheer bloody talent, I suppose,' Gail said, in a tone of such sardonic scepticism that she drove all my feelings of desolation away with one acid puff. Maybe Alastair had told her more about the past than was wise.

'But Gail,' I said hurriedly, 'bloody-nose husband said something about a North Camden Art Exhibition and that it was us "arty freaks" who killed her. What did he mean? I thought you told me she died of pneumonia.'

'Oh lord. Woody-husband said something about that too. All I know is that Mo was exhibiting with the North Camden Arts Group. It's a loose association of visual artists – NoCArGo they call themselves. Mo was the only woman – surprise, surprise.'

'Aren't any of them here?'

'I didn't actually know them. You remember I wrote and told you Mo had gone into Installation? Well, she got in with a bunch of, I don't know – wankers describes it pretty accurately. Their first exhibition opened a week ago and that's when Mo died.'

It started to rain and we all ran to the car park. Alastair tried to organise us so that Gail and I would ride in his car. He failed because Gail had other ideas. Bekki and I rode in his car. Gail went with Woody-hubby. We were going to The Star of India for a curry wake. Gail was satisfied with the arrangement, but Alastair looked miserable. Bekki sat in front with him and every time she spoke she squeezed his knee with her jewelled claws.

To distract her I asked quite bluntly about the two husbands.

'Well dear, yes.' Bekki squeezed Alastair's knee as if he'd asked the question. 'I suppose I did know.'

I met Alastair's shocked gaze in the mirror. It was the first he'd heard of it.

'But my step-daughter was so melodramatic. We couldn't make it over for the first wedding. We sent a cheque, of course, but Moselle was furious. She said she'd set her heart on us coming over for her big day. She said it wasn't a proper wedding without her father giving her away.'

'So much for Mo's feminism,' I muttered.

Bekki might not have heard me. 'I'm glad now we didn't make the effort,' she told Alastair, 'because hardly a year later, we received an invitation to the second wedding. That was during the rainy season and my husband refuses to fly in the rain. He sent a cheque again, but you know how ungrateful Moselle could be. I assumed she'd divorced the first one before marrying the second. But unfortunately that detail seems to have slipped her mind.'

'So who are they?'

'Well, dear, the first one, I think, was Joss who owns a house in Wentworth and pots of money. Quite a good catch we thought, because however grown-up Moselle was she could never manage to be self-supporting. Such a worry to my poor old husband. And all that artiness had to stop sometime. What's attractive in the very young becomes such a bore in later life.'

'And the second one?'

'Oh dear me, what a come-down! I'm sure Woody's a very sweet boy, but I'm afraid there's no money there. I'm told he has oodles of potential, but what good's that? Dear, aren't you driving a little fast?'

Alastair threw me a look of total despair and slowed down.

Bekki went on, oblivious. 'The third invitation arrived a month ago...'

'*Third!*'

'Yes dear.' She patted Alastair's knee. 'We thought it very odd too. That's partly why I'm here.'

'For the wedding?'

'I probably missed that, but I really felt... well, the cheques were for such very large amounts and my poor dear husband's so very gullible when it comes to the ways of young women.' She paused for a moment, leaning confidentially against Alastair's arm, and then added, 'And young women are so very clever about how to manipulate men – speaking of which, dear, isn't that your little girlfriend waving at us? I wonder what she wants now.'

'Wife,' Alastair said through clenched teeth. 'That's my *wife.*'

Woody-hubby was doing something no one should attempt on congested North London streets – he was overtaking. Gail, with the passenger-side window rolled down, was making frantic hand signals.

'Do you think she's being kidnapped?' Bekki asked hopefully.

Woody cut in ahead of Alastair to a chorus of furious horn-blowing and abuse. He then took the next available left turn and we followed. There was nowhere to park so he braked in the middle of a one-way street. Gail was out of the car almost before it stopped moving. She came towards us, dark hair flying, and I thought, No one has the right to look so alive on the day of a funeral.

She said, 'We're just two blocks away from the NoCArGo exhibition and I think we should check it out. Alastair and I would've gone last week if Mo hadn't died.'

'What about lunch?' Bekki asked.

Gail took in the jewelled claw on Alastair's knee and smiled sweetly. 'If you're that hungry... *dear*... we wouldn't dream of holding you up. There are plenty of taxis. Shall I call one for you? It's no trouble.' She fumbled in her bag for her cell phone. To me, she mouthed something that looked suspiciously like 'Hideous old bag.'

But Bekki didn't want to be alone and she was still hanging on to Alastair's arm when we trailed into the yard in front of St. Margaret's, a disused chapel just off Murray Street. A plastic banner advertised the exhibition but a handwritten note pinned to the door said, 'Gone for a pee, back in 5.'

'Typical artists,' Gail said, 'all genius and no loos. Where's the nearest pub, I wonder?'

'Drinkies?' said Bekki.

'No. I'm betting it's where the genius who's in charge of this exhibition will be. Coming, Liza?'

We left the others standing disconsolately in the tiny damp graveyard in case the genius showed up. Gail said, 'Well? What's the story?'

'How d'you mean?'

'What did you get out of Bekki?' My new best friend seemed unstoppable when her curiosity was roused. 'There was absolutely no reason not to run her over in the crematorium car park – except she knows stuff. Haven't you been pumping her?'

'Er...'

'You're supposed to be a writer, Liza. You're supposed to be good at research.'

All I'd done was to sit passively in the back of a car listening to Bekki. It wasn't research exactly but I couldn't disappoint Gail so I repeated as much of what Bekki had said as I could remember.

'A *third* wedding?' Gail said, stopping dead outside a grim little pub called The Sun in Splendour. 'Who to? Oh, don't tell me you didn't find out.'

'That's when you pulled us over. And anyway Bekki was more interested in the size of the cheques Mo's father sent than in the number of husbands. What about you? What did you find out about Woody?'

'Tell you later.' Gail pushed open the pub door. 'But talking of Bekki – if I dress like that or behave like that when I'm her age you have my permission to take me out to the country and shoot me.' She narrowed her bright eyes and searched the shadowy interior of The Sun in Splendour.

'The pub that time forgot,' she murmured, picking on the only man there with a sense of style and all his own teeth. He was nursing half a pint, a hand-rolled cigarette and a hangover. 'Go on, Liza, or do I have to do everything?'

I steeled myself. Talking to attractive men always leaves me short of breath.

'Yeah,' he said when I accosted him. 'I *am* supposed to be at the chapel but we've had practically zero visitors in since we opened.' He was tall, fair and older than us. His antique Armani suit hung raffishly over a purple granddad vest.

'Hmmm?' said Gail, flicking an eyebrow at me as we followed him along the narrow pavement. He moved well and she could see I was hyperventilating.

'He might be Mo's third husband,' I said gloomily. Men I liked often liked someone else more.

'Trigamy,' Gail said. 'Is there such a word?'

'We'll have to ask Alastair,' I said, even more gloomily. I was supposed to be the writer but he was still better at words than me.

57

The fair guy wielded a key as big as a tyre-iron. 'Don't come in till I see to the lights and music.'

'What do we call you?' Gail asked.

'Mick,' he told her as he disappeared into the chapel.

'Mick, eh?' Gail looked at me to make sure I was paying attention. She was the only one who didn't seem cold or depressed. Bekki was still clinging to Alastair like a magnet to a fridge and Woody stood, hands in pockets, with his head bowed.

And I thought, Today is one of the weirdest days of my life, and when I go back to Canada I'd like to be able to take with me a coherent narrative of all these improbable elements.

Just then the music started, and I cannot begin to describe how inappropriate it was – the voice, Morrissey's, was like a cat being neutered without anaesthetic; and the words hit me in the heart like a hammer: 'Take me out tonight, where there's music and there's people, and they're young and ali-i-i-ivve.' Drawn by the strangulated voice we stepped one by one into the chapel, into a series of compartments.

Mo's installation was in the first compartment. It began with a tumble of boxes wrapped in silver, gold and white. Some were torn open revealing the presents inside: a toaster with burnt toast already popping out, a steam iron crusted with limescale, china with dried-on food, stained and crumpled bed linen. Congratulatory cards were tossed around. It was all about wedding presents several years after the wedding when the shiny new gifts had become symbols of servitude.

'I don't understand,' said Bekki. No one bothered to explain.

A screen suspended from the ceiling came to life and there was Mo, stepping out of a church in a pearl embroidered white dress, holding Joss's hand, posing for a photographer. She looked archetypal and triumphant. She was beautiful and alive. And for the first time on that awful day Alastair looked as if he was holding back tears. Then the tape went into reverse – Mo and Joss were

58

sucked back into the church. There was a jump cut to another church door and Mo came out in a far more elaborate dress with…

'That's me,' Woody said unnecessarily. 'That's *my* wedding video.' But he too was sucked backwards into the church, still with the stupid but proud expression on his face that bridegrooms always seem to adopt.

Mo, however, emerged from what, this time, looked like a small cathedral. She was floating in clouds of lace and froth accompanied by a small plump man in full morning suit, grey top-hat, with ownership on his mind and stunned disbelief in his eyes. He was not Mo's usual type. Or rather, he was not mine. But I'd had too many surprises that day to be certain about anything Mo did.

'What a lovely dress,' said Bekki.

'Who the hell is that?' said Woody.

'It's art,' said Mick. 'It's a statement about marriage as a Performance Art in the 21ˢᵗ Century.'

'No it bloody isn't,' said Woody. 'It was *my* wedding. My marriage. I *loved* Moselle.'

The video looped back to Mo and Joss, and I noticed that the soundtrack was also stuck on a loop where Morrissey was singing, 'To die by your side – well, the pleasure, the privilege is mine.'

'Can you turn the sound off?' Gail asked. 'It's freaking me out.'

'It's meant to.' But Mick moved away to the sound-desk.

When I could hear myself think I said, 'Is she equating marriage with death? Isn't it time someone told me how she died?'

'Pneumonia, dear,' said Bekki.

'Then why did bloody-nose Joss say arty freaks killed her?' We all turned to look at Mick.

'Don't look at me,' Mick said. 'I'm not a freak. All I can tell you is what the police told me. They found her, in her wedding dress, chained to the railings outside the chapel with a pair of those fluffy pink handcuffs you pick up at sex shops. She was soaking wet and suffering from hypothermia. They cut off the cuffs and rushed her to the Royal Free Hospital but, you know…'

Woody said painfully, 'They told me it was some sort of publicity stunt gone wrong. There were broken eggs and posters and stuff written on the pavement all the way from the main road to the chapel.'

'The posters were for the North Camden Art Exhibition,' said Mick. 'Only someone added a T to Art.'

'North Camden Tart Exhibition,' Bekki said, slowly explaining it to herself. 'What were the eggs for?'

'Hen party, I suppose,' Gail said.

'And "This way to the TArt," and "Only 50 yards to the TArt." Which is why she was found by a bunch of drunken bastards who were actually looking for action.'

'Where were you while all this was happening?' I asked. I would have liked to ask all the husbands that but Woody was the only one available.

'You think I should've stopped her? She was in London to set up the exhibition. I was at home in Weymouth. She'd been gone for a week. How was I supposed to know what all this was about?'

'It's about *art*,' Mick insisted.

'It was a real marriage,' Woody said. 'But now I think maybe they were *all* real marriages. I shouldn't have hit that guy.'

'Who's the third man?' Gail said. 'Does anyone know who he is?' Again we all looked at Mick.

'Don't ask me.' He shrugged his elegant shoulders. 'I thought they were all actors. I never imagined she'd go so far as to actually *marry* anyone.'

'I don't understand,' said Bekki. 'Are you saying that it was all a joke? Because in that case it was a very expensive joke. Those were real cheques her father sent. And by the way dear,' she added to Woody, 'I don't know what you mean by being at home in

Weymouth – my step-daughter lives in St. Johns Wood. Her father pays the rent on a two bedroom flat there.'

'Well I knew she had a *pied à terre…*'

Gail nudged me and whispered, 'Three homes and a *pied à terre?*' Aloud she said, 'What about drugs? Didn't Joss mention drugs?' I nodded.

Mick said, 'C'mon! A little E and a little weed? That's not drugs. That's just relaxing.'

'Well, with daddy paying the rent,' Gail muttered close to my ear, 'and three husbands supporting her, I guess she could afford to relax.'

I said, 'At college they always ask if you can make a living out of art and I usually say "no" or "not for years and years".'

'You agree with Mick? This is art?'

'Female self-reference has been recognized as serious art for years now.'

'Bugger self-reference,' said Gail. 'There's something really worrying about handcuffing yourself to railings on a cold wet night and calling yourself a tart – even to publicise your own exhibition. It just doesn't sound like Mo. She didn't rough it even at Glastonbury. Remember her deluxe Caravette?'

'I think she felt she needed the exposure,' Mick said, and then blushed and squirmed. The rest of us stared awkwardly at our shoes.

Gail recovered first. 'But you said the police had to cut her off the railing. If she cuffed herself, where was the key? That's what I mean – she might do it to be dramatic, but she'd be damn sure to undo it if it got uncomfortable. This is *Moselle* we're talking about.'

'Good point,' said Woody.

'I thought it was a grand gesture,' Mick said. 'She liked grand gestures. It was another feminist statement about marriage – women going like slaves to the altar, loving their own chains, throwing away the key, just for the theatre, the spectacle, which is all that a wedding is these days.'

'Is that what she said?' I was interested.

'Did the police look for the key?' Gail was somewhat more practical.

'She said a wedding and a marriage were polar opposites.' Mick swung his arm to draw our attention back to the installation. 'Princess for a day, a servant for life.'

I nodded. I have always thought the Cinderella story was back-to-front – or, at least, ended the wrong way.

'I just don't see Mo as a servant,' Gail said, 'even with three husbands.' She turned and was watching the silent footage of the short plump man almost eclipsed by Mo's bridal crinoline. 'I want to know who the last poor sucker was.'

From the doorway behind us a voice said, 'I rather think you must be talking about me.' Dwarfed by his own cashmere coat, he came forward saying, 'I'm Charles. I got to the crematorium too late. I'm sorry.' His eyes behind the little round glasses looked weak and weepy but his voice was plumy and vigorous. 'They're still talking about you all there. I gather there was some dispute about who was the widower.'

'Er, how do you do?' Woody made a great effort and held out his hand. 'I'm Woody, one of the widowers, I suppose.' He introduced the rest of us except for Mick who'd gone outside for a smoke. I'd seen him fumble in his pocket for his tobacco and make for the door. He really was a pleasure to watch.

Charles said, 'Mine was a proper marriage and I have the certificate to prove it.'

'Me too,' said Woody. 'And I promise there was no divorce.'

'I don't remember speaking to anyone called Charles,' Bekki said. She assessed the quality of the cashmere coat and transferred herself to Charles's side. Alastair looked as though ten tons had been lifted from his shoulders and Gail whispered, 'Who put the cash into cashmere?'

'It was on her website,' Charles was explaining. 'I was in Paris on business…'

'Ooo, Paris.' Bekki sighed.

'Obviously we kept in touch while she was setting up the exhibition but she warned me things might get frantic, so I didn't worry when she stopped answering her messages. I went to her website to see if there'd been any critical reaction to the installation on her interactive. But Mick had put in the death notice instead. Of course I came straight over.'

'Of course you did, dear,' Bekki said, stroking the cashmere as if it were a thoroughbred horse.

I was conscious of Gail and Alastair drawing together and away from the rest of us. I followed them.

Gail was saying, '…three husbands none of whom knew anything about the others.'

'So they say.'

'Don't you believe them?'

'I've had an absolutely bloody morning,' said Alastair, 'and I don't believe anyone.'

'Alastair thinks one of the husbands found out about the others and decided to punish Mo,' Gail told me. 'He thinks the handcuffs and the TArt stuff demonstrate male anger and violence.'

'Which one?'

'Alastair thinks Joss was both the most angry and the least in control.'

'That's fair,' I said, 'but surely the whole thing was self-generated. I agree with Mick: I think it was art and publicity that lost control.'

'You would,' Gail said.

'Well, what do *you* think?'

'I think I want to talk to Mick again. You'd agree to that, wouldn't you, Liza?'

But when we went outside into the cold drizzle we couldn't find Mick.

'I've had it,' said Alastair. 'I'm cold and hungry and I want to leave before anyone notices we're gone.'

'Anyone?' said Gail. 'Who *can* you mean, *dear*?'

'I'm serious.'

'Well, you warm up the car. Liza and I want to see if Mick's gone back to the Sun in Splendour.'

But Mick was not at the pub.

'Shame,' said Gail. 'I don't suppose you asked for his phone number, did you, Liza?'

'What d'you take me for?'

'A wimp,' said my new best friend, 'a nice wimp, an arty wimp, but you don't take life by the throat exactly.'

'And do you?'

'I sort of have to – not being arty.'

We trailed back to the car, each in our own way disappointed.

Half an hour later at the Star of India, we ordered chicken tikka and lamb jalfrezi, aloo gobi, pilau, riata and paratha: hot food to warm our frozen hearts. The beer came and we began to thaw out. Alastair grabbed a napkin, borrowed a ballpoint and started a list. Gail and I craned our necks to see. He wrote, Woody: too nice. Charles: too fat. JOSS.

I said, 'Oh bloody hell, Alastair. You're assuming someone wanted to hurt or humiliate Mo. We don't know that. And lists don't work unless you know everyone involved, which we also don't. Besides, you're supposed to list suspects – not non-suspects.'

'Alastair's good at cutting out the crap,' Gail said.

'A list of non-suspects doesn't make it non-crap.' For some reason I was quite cross and depressed. 'And what about the non-husbands? Bekki for starters. As far as I can see she only came over to protect her husband's money because she thought Mo was getting too much of it.'

Alastair gave me a pitying look and wrote, Bekki: too stupid.

'But she's greedy enough,' Gail said.

I said, 'And Mo herself? Isn't it far more likely that self-promotion went horribly wrong?'

Alastair wrote, Mo: too sybaritic.

'What about Mick?' Gail said. 'I'm sorry Liza. You're going to hate me for saying this when you're so obviously smitten, but I've got a bad feeling about Mick.'

'*Mick*? Why?'

'Well, he's a liar.'

'How can you say that?' I protested.

'He said he didn't know any of the husbands and he thought they were all actors. But Charles knew him. Without being introduced. He said, "Mick left a message on her interactive." Also Mick slunk out as soon as Charles turned up. You know he did, Liza. You were watching him.'

'Was not – well, sort of.'

'Then you *know* he snuck off as soon as Charles appeared. I think he didn't want us to know he'd lied. And he didn't want Charles to accuse him of not informing him about Mo's death, except on the website several days later.'

'So Mick knew at least one of the marriages was real. So what?'

'He lied about it. Why? He wasn't surprised that Woody was a real husband either. He should've been as astonished as we were. What if he knew all the marriages were real? He'd be aiding and abetting... Trigamy. Is that a real word, Alastair?'

Absently, still circling Joss's name, Alastair said, 'Strictly speaking it's polyandry.'

I liked trigamy better.

'And,' Gail went on, 'he kept avoiding the question about the key – had the police found it? Why didn't Mo unlock herself when it got cold and wet? As soon as we brought that up he started droning on about Art. He wants us to think it was all about Art and promoting Art.'

Alastair looked up and said, 'Did any of us look at his work? Did any of us look at anything that wasn't Mo's?'

'Hers was nearest to the door,' I said. 'The music – it was so gob-smacking – "To die by your side, well the pleasure and privilege…" It drew you straight to her installation.'

'Did it, though? Mo despised that kitsch '90's retro. Her thing was Extreme Dance.' Alastair looked down at his list and hesitantly wrote Mick's name. 'If you ask me, the music didn't go with her work at all. She'd never have chosen it.'

'That's it!' Gail said.

'What?' I said.

'The music was *wrong*. Mo wouldn't have picked it. So *Mick* had to.'

Gail seemed to be obsessing about Mick just to wind me up. And yet, now that I thought about it, although the music spoke to *me* that bizarre morning, Alastair had a point – it was utterly wrong for Mo.

But Gail moved on. 'And it was Mick who turned the music on when we went in to see Mo's installation. The music was Mick's choice, not Mo's. And the only reason he'd have done that was…' She looked at Alastair and then me, her eyes gleaming, inviting us to catch up with her train of thought. I didn't know about Alastair, but I was thinking so slowly I was unlikely to catch up with a coat hanger.

'Mick was Mo's boyfriend,' Gail declared.

'Boyfriend?' I slumped in my chair. '*Boyfriend*? But…'

'Both Joss and Woody *thought* Mo had a boyfriend – they each thought it was the other. But it wasn't. It was Mick. Think about it. He didn't go to the funeral. Why not?'

I glanced at Alastair, then shrugged. There are plenty of reasons not to go to a funeral, but they didn't seem compelling in the face of Gail's enthusiasm.

'Because he *knew* Mo's husbands would be there,' Gail said. 'I think Mick was in love with Mo. I'll bet to begin with he really did think the "husbands" in the installation were actors – like he said – until he found out somehow.' She turned to Alastair.

'What?' he said.

'Charles. Charles is the answer. Where is he?'

Alastair looked at me. I said, 'Isn't he with Bekki? Or rather isn't Bekki with him, and his cashmere?'

'Mick didn't duck out when Woody showed up,' Gail said, 'but he vanished as soon as Charles arrived. I'll bet Charles will confirm that Mick knew he was Mo's husband. One of Mo's husbands.'

I said, 'And finding out one of the husbands was for real meant they all were?'

Gail said, 'All we have to do is talk with Charles to prove it.' She turned to Alastair. 'Call Bekki.' She dug out her cell phone and handed it to him. 'I saw her slip her card into your pocket.'

'She did?' Alastair felt in his pockets and discovered a card. 'Why the hell would that silly woman think I'd want her phone number?' He turned to Gail without knowing he was already defeated. 'No way, no *way* am I calling Bekki.'

'Mick's responsible,' Gail said. 'Maybe he didn't mean for Mo to die, Liza. I'm not saying he's a cold killer. He probably just wanted to teach her a lesson – leave her *chained* to her husbands in her wedding dress till she was really uncomfortable. Went for a drink, perhaps, but then had another and another and by the time he went back... Well, it was too late.'

67

'Three husbands,' I said, 'and yet it was her *boyfriend* who killed her? Gail, you can't mean it. She married three men for her installation and had Mick on the side for love?'

'She didn't marry for Art, Liza; she married for money.'

'But Gail, she already had money.'

'Her father had money but he married a greedy woman. Why do you want everything to be about Art?'

'Because Art's the only thing that makes sense of life. Otherwise it's all random and horrible. And Mo was an installation artist who had witty stuff to say about marriage. She was our friend. I don't want her death to be about clichés like jealousy and money.'

'*Love*, jealousy and money,' Gail corrected me. 'Love isn't a cliché.'

'It is, in this context,' I said, miserable.

'Don't argue with her, Liza,' Alastair said. 'You know she's always right.' He started circling Mick's name. 'Always, always right.' He began to draw hearts and pound signs around Mick's name. It was a detail I could fit into a narrative – the story about this day which I would tell myself sometime in the future; like the detail about the music – something I had not recognised as important at the time – which was that the soundtrack to Mo's life was Dance music because Dance is music for the party people in the pretty dresses, the people who don't care.

With astonishment I realized that I had never liked Mo and that I despised her taste in music. And with sadness I accepted what Gail probably knew instinctively, that Mick was a man who hid depression and destructiveness behind wit and irony – just like Morrissey. His taste in music gave him away. Just as the other big give-away was my taste in men. There had to be something wrong with Mick if I liked him.

Gail crunched into a popadum. 'Make the call, please, Alastair,' she said.

And I started to remember all of us as if it were already long, long ago. We are young, drunk, howling but essentially happy. The grim reaper hasn't chosen *us*. Yet. We have theories but no experience, no proofs. We're too green for that. In thirty years' time, who knows – Mo's death may mean more to us than it does now. It might even have become some sort of art. But until then there is hot food to eat and life to live and a story to construct.

MR BO

My son Nathan doesn't believe in God, Allah, Buddha, Kali, the Great Spider Mother or the Baby Jesus. But, he believes passionately in Superman, Spiderman, Batman, Wolverine and, come December, Santa Claus. How he works this out – bearing in mind that they all have super powers – I don't know. Maybe he thinks the second lot wears hotter costumes. Or drives cooler vehicles, or brings better presents. Can I second-guess my nine-year-old? Not a snowball's hope in Hades.

Nathan is as much a mystery to me as his father was, and as my father was before that, and who knows where they both are now? But if there's one thing I can congratulate myself on, it's that I didn't saddle my son with a stepfather. No strange man's going to teach my boy to 'dance for daddy'. Not while there's a warm breath left in my body.

*

I was eleven and my sister Skye was nine when Mum brought Bobby Barnes home for the first time. He didn't look like a lame-headed loser so we turned the telly down and said hello.

'Call me Bo,' he said, flashing a snowy smile. 'All my friends do.'

So my dumb little sister said, 'Hi, Mr Bo,' and blushed because he was tall and brown-eyed just like the hero in her comic book.

Mum laughed high and girly, and I went to bed with a nosebleed – which is usually what happened when Mum laughed like that and smeared her lipstick.

Mr Bo moved in and Mum was happy because we were 'a family'. How can you be family with a total stranger? I always wanted to ask her but I didn't dare. She had a vicious right hand if she thought you were cheeking her.

Maybe we would be a family even now if it wasn't for him. Maybe Nathan would have a grandma and an aunt if Mr Bo hadn't got his feet under the table and his bonce on the pillow.

I think about it now and then. After all, some times of year are special for families, and Nathan *should* have grandparents, an aunt and a father.

This year I was thinking about it because sorting out the tree lights is traditionally a father's job; as is finding the fuse box when the whole house is tripped out by a kink in the wire.

I was doing exactly that, by candle light because Nathan had broken the torch, when the doorbell rang.

Standing in the doorway was a beautiful woman in a stylish winter coat with fur trimmings. I didn't have time for more than a quick glance at her face because she came inside and said, 'What's up? Can't pay the electricity bill? Just like Mum.'

'I am not like my mother.' I was furious.

'Okay, okay,' she said. 'It was always way too easy to press your buttons.' And I realised that the strange woman with the American accent was Skye.

'What are you doing here?' I said, stunned.

'Hi, and it's great to see you too,' she said. 'Who's the rabbit?'

I turned. Nathan was behind me, shadowy, with the broken torch in his hand.

'He's not a rabbit,' I said, offended. Rabbit was Mr Bo's name for a mark. We were all rabbits to him one way or another.

'Who's she?' Nathan said. I'd taught him not to tell his name, address or phone number to strangers.

'I'm Skye.'

'A Scottish Island?' He sounded interested. 'Or the place where clouds sit?'

'Smart *and* cute.'

'I'm not cute,' he said, sniffing loudly. 'I'm a boy.'

'She's your aunt,' I told him, 'my sister.'

'I don't want an aunt,' he said, staring at her flickering, candlelit face. 'But an uncle might be nice.' Did I mention that all his heroes are male? Even when it's a woman who solves all his problems, from homework to football training to simple plumbing and now, the electricity. I used to think it was because he missed a father, but it's because you can't interest a boy in girls until his feet get tangled in the weeds of sex.

I fixed the electricity and all the lights came on except, of course, for the tree ones which lay in a nest on the floor with the bulbs no more responsive than duck eggs. Nathan looked at me as though I'd betrayed his very life.

'Tomorrow,' I said. 'I promise.'

'You promised tonight.'

'Let's have a little drink,' Skye said 'to celebrate the return of the prodigal sister.'

'We don't drink,' Nathan said priggishly. He's wrong. I just don't drink in front of him. My own childhood was diseased and deceived by Mum's drinking and the decisions she made when drunk.

'There's a bottle of white in the fridge,' I said, because Skye was staring at my second-hand furniture and looking depressed. At least it's mine, and no repo man's going to burst in and take it away. She probably found me plain and worn too, but I can't help that.

She had a couple of drinks. I watched very carefully, but she showed no signs of becoming loose and giggly. So I said, 'It's late. Stay the night.' She was my sister, after all, even though I didn't know her. But she took one look at the spare bed in the box room and said, 'Thanks, I'll call a cab.'

When the cab came, Nathan followed us to the front door and said goodbye of his own free will. Skye was always the charming one. She didn't attempt to kiss him because if there was one thing she'd learnt well it was what guys like and what they don't like. She said, 'I'll come back tomorrow and bring you a gift. What do you want?'

Now that's a question Nathan isn't used to in this house, but he hardly stopped to think. He said, 'Football boots. The red and white Nike ones, with a special spanner thing you can use to adjust your own studs.'

'Nathan,' I warned. The subject of football boots was not new. I could never quite afford the ones he wanted.

But Skye grinned and said, 'See you tomorrow, kid,' and she was gone in a whirl of fur trimmings.

*

Mr Bo used to buy our shoes. Well, not buy exactly. This is how he did it: we'd go to a shoe shop and I'd ask for shoes a size and a half too small. Mr Bo would flirt with the assistant. When the shoes arrived I'd try to stuff my feet in and Mr Bo would say, 'Who do you think you are? One of the Ugly Sisters?' This would make the assistant laugh as she went off to find the proper size. While she was gone, Skye put on the shoes that were too small for me and slipped out of the shop. Then I'd make a fuss – the shoes rubbed my heels, my friends had prettier ones, and Mr Bo would have to apologise charmingly and take me away, leaving a litter of boxes and shoes on the floor. It worked the other way round when I needed shoes, except that he never made the Ugly Sister crack about Skye. I hated him for that because although he said it was a joke I knew what he really thought.

The only time he paid hard cash was when he bought tap-shoes for Skye. He'd begun to teach us dance steps in the kitchen. 'Shuffle,' he'd yell above the music, 'kick, ball-change, turn… come on girls, dance for Daddy.'

*

The next day Nathan didn't want to go out. His friend came to the door wanting a kick-around but ended up playing on the computer instead. I didn't say anything but I knew he was waiting for Skye.

At the end of the day there was nothing I could do but make his favourite, shepherd's pie, and read Harry Potter to him in bed. I could see his heart wasn't in it.

I wasn't surprised – Skye had been taught unreliability by experts – but I was angry. She'd had a chance to show him that a woman could be as good as Batman and she'd blown it. All he had left was me and I was not the stuff of heroes. What had I done in the past nine years except to keep him warm, fed, healthy and honest? Also, I made him do his homework, which I think he found unforgivable. I thought I was giving him solid gold, because in the end, doing my homework and passing exams were the tools I used to dig myself out of a very deep hole. But how can that compare to the magic conferred upon a boy by ownership of coveted football boots? At his age he thought the right boots would transform his life and give him talents beyond belief. Magic boots for Nathan; dancing shoes for Skye.

*

Mr Bo tried to teach us both to do the splits. Maybe, at eleven or twelve, I was already too stiff. Or maybe, deep down inside, I felt there was something creepy about doing the splits in the snow-white knickers and little short skirts that he insisted we wear to dance for him. Either way, I never managed to learn. But Skye did.

75

She stretched like a spring and bounced like a ball. She wore ribbons in her crazy hair. Of course she got the dancing shoes.

One evening he took us to the bar where Mum worked, put some money in the juke box and Skye showed off what she'd learnt. Mum was so impressed she put out a jam jar for tips and it was soon full to overflowing.

Now that I have a child of my own I can't help wandering what on earth she was thinking. Maybe she looked at the tip jar and saw a wide-screen TV or a weekend away at a posh hotel with handsome Bo Barnes. Or was she just high on the free drinks. Once, she said to me, 'Wanna know somethin', kid? If you're a girl, all you ever got to sell is your youth. Make sure you get a better price for it than I did. Wish someone tol' me that before I gave it all away.' Of course she wasn't sober when she said that, but I don't think sobriety had much to do with it; it was her best advice. No wonder I did my homework.

*

Skye showed up when Nathan had stopped waiting for her. 'C'mon, kid,' she said, 'we're going shopping.'

'You're smoking.' He was shocked.

'So shoot me,' she said. 'You have dirty hair.'

'So shoot me.' He grinned his big crooked smile.

'Needs an orthodontist,' she said. 'I should take him back to L.A.'

'Over my dead body,' I said. 'Nathan, get in the shower. Skye, coffee in the kitchen. Now.'

She wrinkled her still pretty nose at my coffee. I said, 'What're you up to? What's the scam?'

'Can't an Auntie take her nephew shopping?' She widened her innocent eyes at me. ''Tis the season and all that malarkey.'

'We haven't seen each other in over fifteen years.'

'So I missed you.'

'No you didn't. How did you find me?'

76

'Were you hiding?' she asked. 'How do you know what I missed? You're my big sister, or have you forgotten?'

'I wasn't the one who swanned off to the States.'

'No, you were the one who was jealous.'

'I tried to protect you.'

'From what? Attention, pretty clothes, guys with nice cars?'

I said nothing because I didn't know where to begin.

She stuck her elbows on the table and leant forward with her chin jutting. 'It all began with Bobby Barnes, didn't it? You couldn't stand me being his little star.'

'He was thirty. You were nine.'

'A girl doesn't stay nine forever.'

'He ended up in prison and we were sent to a home. He robbed us of our childhood, Skye.'

'Some childhood.' She snorted. 'Stuck in that squalid little apartment – with no TV or anything.'

'And how did Mr Bo change that? Did he stop Mum drinking? Did he go out to work so that she could look after us? Okay, he brought us a flat-screen telly, but it got repossessed like everything else.'

'He gave us pretty clothes and shoes…'

'He *stole* them. He taught us how to steal…'

'But it was fun,' Skye cried. 'He taught us how to dance too. You're forgetting the good stuff.'

'He taught *you* to dance. He taught me how to be a look-out for a pickpocket and a thief. You weren't a dancer, Skye; you were there to distract the rabbits.'

'Why're you two quarrelling?' Nathan said from the doorway.

'We're sisters,' Skye said. 'If you're good I'll tell you how a pirate came to rescue us from an evil wizard's castle and how your mom didn't want to go and nearly blew it for me.'

'No you won't,' I said.

'Is it true?' He was as trusting as a puppy.

'Do you really believe in wicked wizards and good pirates?' I asked.

'Next you'll be telling him there's no Santa Claus or Tooth Fairy.'

'I know there's no tooth fairy,' he said. 'I caught Mum *putting* a pound under my pillow and she pretended she'd just found it there, but she's a rubbish liar.'

'She is, isn't she? Bet you took the cash anyway. Now let's go shopping.'

'I'm coming too,' I said, because I didn't know my own sister and I was afraid she might have inherited Mr Bo's definition of buying shoes.

'You'll spoil it,' my loyal son complained. 'The only thing she ever takes me shopping for is school uniform.'

'What a bitch... sorry, witch.' Skye dragged us both out of the house with no conscience at all.

A big black car, just a couple of feet short of being a limo, was waiting outside – plus a driver with a leather coat and no discernable neck.

*

Oddly, Mr Bo was not sent down for anything serious like contributing to the delinquency of minors or his sick relationship with one of them. No, when he was caught it was for stealing booze from the back of the bar where Mum worked. Of course she was done for theft too, thus ensuring that we had no irresponsible adults in our lives, and forcing us to be taken into Care.

By the time I was fifteen and Skye was thirteen we'd been living in Care for two and a half years. Foster parents weren't keen on me because I didn't want to split up from Skye, and foster mothers didn't like Skye at all because she was precocious in so many ways.

Crockerdown House, known for obvious reasons as Crack House by the locals, was a girls' care home, and judging by the number of non-visits from social workers, doctors or advisors,

78

and the frequency of real visits by the cops, it should've been called a No Care Home. No one checked to see if we went to school or if we came back. Self-harm and eating disorders went unnoticed. Drugs were commonplace. There was a sixty percent pregnancy rate.

I was scared rigid and spent as much time as I could at school. Teachers thought I was keen – most unusual in that part of town – and they cherished me. After a while I *became* keen.

Skye was the opposite.

It was only when a strange man turned up at the school gates in a car with Skye sitting smug as you please on the back seat that I realised she'd stayed in touch with Mr Bo while he was inside .

I knew that she and some other, older, girls regularly went to the West End to boost gear from shops and I lived with my heart in my mouth, fearing she'd be caught. She was never caught and she always had plenty of money. What I hadn't been told was that she supplied an old friend of Mr Bo's with stolen goods which he sold in the market. This friend kept Mr Bo in tobacco and all the other consumables that could be passed between friends on visiting day.

'He's coming out today,' she told me excitedly. 'We're going to meet him.'

I looked at her in her tight jeans and the trashy silk top which would've cost a fortune if she'd actually bought it. I burst into tears.

'We're not going back to Crack House,' she said. 'It's over.'

'What about school?' I wept. 'What about my exams?' I was taking nine subjects and my teachers said I had a good chance in all of them.

'We never have to go to bogging school again. We're free. He's taking us abroad.'

'What about Mum?' Mum was still inside. She wasn't just a thief; she was a thief who drank, and she was a bad mother who drank and thieved. Three strikes against her. Only one against Mr Bo. Classic!

'Oh, she'll join us later,' Skye said vaguely, breathing mist onto the car window and drawing a heart.

*

'Is this your car?' Nathan asked the driver, impressed.

'Huh?'

'It's mine,' Skye said, 'for now.'

'Will you have to give it back?' Nathan was sadly familiar with the concept of giving a favoured book or computer game back to the library.

'Where are we going?' The last time she and I were in a car together was a disaster.

'Crystal City. I heard it was the newest.'

'It's the best,' Nathan breathed. 'We don't go there.'

'Why not?'

I said, 'It's too expensive and too far away.'

'I know, I know,' Skye said, 'and you got a mortgage to pay and your tuition fees at the Open University. Studying to be a psychotherapist, aren't you? And both your lives gonna stay on hold till you qualify and hang out your shingle. When's that gonna be – 2050?'

'How the hell do you know that?'

'*You said "hell".*'

'You'd be surprised what I know. Some of us use technology for more than looking up difficult words.'

'You've been *spying* on us.'

'Cool,' Nathan said. 'I want to be a spy when I grow up.'

'You can be a spy now,' Skye said. 'Don't look back, just use this mirror and if you see a car following us, tell Wayne. Okay?' She handed him what looked like a solid gold compact.

'What sort of car?'

'Black Jeep,' no-neck, leather-clad Wayne said, 'Licence plate begins Sierra, Charlie, Delta.'

'That's SCD to you, kid.'

'Clever,' I said. 'Have you got kids of your own?'

'Do I *look* like a mother?'

'No need to sound insulted. It's not all bad.'

'Coulda fooled me. Do you do *all* your shopping from Salvation Army counters?'

'Bollocks,' I muttered, but not quietly enough.

'*You said b...*'

'Okay Nathan,' I said. 'Haven't you got an important job to do?'

'Of *course* I looked you up,' Skye said. 'How the hell else would I find you? You're my big sister – why wouldn't I want to? I didn't know about the kid when I started. And I must say I'm surprised you felt ready to start breeding, given the mom we had. But I guess you were always kinda idealistic – always trying to right wrongs.'

'No one's ready,' I said.

'Hah! Got caught, did ya?'

That was an incident in my life that I didn't want to share with Skye while Nathan's ears were out on stalks.

Crystal City is five enormous interlocking domes. It's a triumph of consumer architecture and weather-proofing. You could spend your entire life – and savings – in there without drawing one breath of fresh air.

Wayne dropped us at the main entrance and Nathan, who can smell sports shoes from a distance of three and a half miles, led the way.

Walking with Skye through a shopping centre was strange and familiar. We both looked around in the same way as we used to. Searching for good opportunities, I suppose – only nowadays all I was looking for were half-price sales.

Skye bought football boots, flashy beyond Nathan's wildest dreams. They had ten differently coloured inserts for designer stripes, extra studs and a tool kit. She threw in an England strip for nine-year-olds and paid for everything with a credit card in the name of Skye Rosetti. She caught me looking and said, 'I had to marry a Rosetti for the Green Card. But I liked the name so I kept it.'

I called on all my nerve and asked, 'What happened to Mr Bo?'

'Oh look, *shoes*,' she cried and flung herself through the door of the fanciest, most minimal shoe shop I'd ever seen.

'Do we have to?' Nathan whined. He wanted to change into his England strip.

'Ungrateful little toad,' Skye said cheerfully. 'Here kid, take your mom shopping.' She handed him a roll of twenty-pound notes.

'Wow!' he said.

'No,' I said. 'Absolutely, no.'

'Fuck off,' she said. 'Have a good time. Meet me at the Food Court on the ground floor in an hour. Don't be late. And kid? I want to see at least one strictly-for-fun gift for your mom. Don't try to scoop it all – I know you guys.'

'*She said fu…*'

'Nathan,' I warned as we walked away, 'grown ups say stuff. And don't think we're going to spend all that money. You don't want your aunt to think you're greedy, do you?'

'I wouldn't mind.'

All kids are wanty – they can't help it. But I love the way he's shocked by swearing. I melt at his piety. He wouldn't believe it if I told him what I was like at his age. And I was the goody-goody one who crawled away from a smashed up childhood via the schoolyard.

An hour later he had the hoodie jacket he'd wanted for months. He also bought a notebook and the complete range of metallic coloured gel pens. I chose the Best of Blondie CD for myself because for some reason I can't listen to Blondie without wanting to dance. There was still a thick wedge of money to give back to Skye.

She was ten minutes late, and when she turned up she was followed by Wayne who was carrying enough bags to fill my spare room from floor to ceiling.

We sat in the octagon shaped food court which had a carp pool and a fountain at its centre. Wayne took most of the bags back to the car.

Skye said, 'C'mon over here, kid, I got something else for you.'

'Skye.' I held my hand up. 'Stop. We have to talk about this. You're putting me in a very awkward position.'

'I *knew* you'd spoil it.' Nathan's mutinous lower lip began to shake.

Skye said, 'Look at it this way, Sis – how many birthdays have I missed? How many…?'

'Nine,' Nathan interrupted, 'and nine plus nine Christmases make, um, eighteen.'

'See how smart he is? He's a good kid who goes to school and learns his times tables, and I got a lot of auntying to catch up with. Right, kid?'

'Right.'

'But I understand your mom's point of view. She doesn't want me to spoil you. Your mom likes to do things the hard way, see. And I don't want to spoil you either 'cos I think you're perfect the way you are. So here's what we'll do. Do you have a cell phone?'

'We call them mobiles over here.' Nathan said bossily. 'Mum's got one but it's old and she says we can't afford two.'

'I can't afford two sets of bills,' I said. 'Skye, you would not be doing me a favour if you're thinking of giving him one.' I put the roll of twenties we hadn't spent into her hand. 'You've been very kind, but rich relations can be too expensive.'

She stared at the money in astonishment. Then she closed her hand over it and tucked it safely into her handbag. 'Okay, okay.

But I've got two phones and they have lots of cool applications. Want to play a game, kid?'

I watched them poring intently over the phones, two curly heads close enough to touch. Nathan's love of technology has been obvious since he first tried to feed his cheese sandwich into the VCR slot, so he didn't take long to master Skye's phone. I kept my mouth shut, but I was proud of him.

Suddenly I was content. I was drinking good coffee and eating a fresh Danish with my clever son and my unfamiliar sister. I was not counting pennies and rationing time. Worry went on holiday.

'Can I go, Mum?' Nathan was tugging my sleeve, his eyes alive with fun.

'What? Where?'

'Just down the end there.' Skye pointed to the far end of the mall. 'He'll have my phone and be in touch at all times. You don't need to worry.'

'I'm Nathan Bond, secret agent.'

'I don't know,' I began, but exactly then Skye turned her face away from Nathan, towards me and I saw with dismay that she'd begun to cry. So I let him go.

'Gimme a minute.' She blotted her eyes on her fur-trimmed cuff. 'That's a terrific kid you got there. I guess you musta done something right.'

'What happened to you, Skye?'

'Mr Bo died a year ago. He was shot by some country cops in a convenience store raid. Stupid bastard. I wasn't with him – hadn't been for years – but we kept in touch. That's when I started to look for you. I thought if he was dead, you could forgive me.'

'Oh Skye.' I took her hand. Just then I heard my son's voice say, 'Nathan to HQ – I'm in position. Can you hear me?'

She picked up her phone. 'Loud and clear. Commence transmission. You remember how to do that?' She held the phone away from her ear and even in the crowded food court I heard the end of Nathan's indignant squawk. She gave me a watery smile but her voice was steady.

He must have started sending pictures because she forgot about me and stared intently at her little screen. Then she said, 'HQ to Nathan – see that tall man in black? He's got a black and red scarf on. Yes. That's the evil doctor Proctor.'

'Skye?' I put my hand on her arm but she shook me off, got up and moved a couple of steps away.

I got up too and heard her say, '… to the men's room. Wayne will be there. He'll give you the goods. Can you handle that?'

'No he can't handle that,' I shouted, grabbing for the phone. 'What're you doing, Skye?'

She twisted out of my grasp. 'Let go, stupid, or you'll wreck everything. You'll put your kid in trouble.'

I took off, sprinting down the mall, dodging families, crowds, balloons and Santas, cracking my shins on pushchairs, bikes and brand new tricycles.

I arrived, out of breath and nearly sobbing with anxiety, at one of the exits. There was no Nathan, no tall man in black, no Wayne. I saw a security uniform and rushed at him. 'Have you seen my son? He's wearing the England strip, red and white boots and a black hoodie. He's nine. His name's Nathan.' I was jumping up and down. 'I think he might've gone into the Gents with a tall man in black and a black and red scarf.' Terror gripped the centre of my being. 'I don't know where the Gents is.'

'Kids do wander off this time of year,' the security man said. 'Me, I think it's the excitement and the greed. I shouldn't worry. I'll go look for him in the toilets, shall I? You stay here in case he comes back.'

But I couldn't wait.

He said tiredly, 'Do you know how many kids there are in England strips this season? Wait here; you aren't allowed in the men's facility.'

I couldn't wait there either. I pushed in behind him, calling my son's name. There were several boys of various ages – several men too – but no Nathan, no Wayne and no man in black.

'Don't worry,' the security man said, although he was himself beginning to look concerned. 'I'll call this in. Natty…'

'*Nathan.*'

'We'll find your boy in no time. Wait here and…'

But I was off and running back to the food court to find Skye. She had the other phone. She knew where Nathan was.

Except, of course, there was no sign of her.

I found our table. No one had cleared it. Under my seat was the carrier bag containing Nathan's old shoes, his ordinary clothes, his gel pens and my CD. I lifted his sweater to my nose as if I were a bloodhound who could track him by scent alone.

My heart was thudding like heavy metal in my throat. I couldn't swallow. Sweat dripped off my frozen face.

The most fundamental rule in all the world is to keep your child safe – to protect him from predators. I'd failed. My family history of abuse and neglect was showing itself in my nature too. Whatever made me think I could make a better job of family life than my mother? Neglect was bred into me like brown eyes and mad hair. There could be no salvation for Nathan or me.

*

I was fifteen when I lost Skye.

'We'll start again in the Land of Opportunity,' said ex-jailbird, Mr Bo. 'But we'll go via the Caribbean where I know a guy who can delete a prison record.' Skye sat on his lap, cuddled, with her head tucked under his chin.

'But my exams,' I said. 'Skye, I'm going to pass in nine subjects. Then I can get a good job and look after us.'

'You do that.' She barely glanced at me. 'I'll stay with Mr Bo.'

'Looks like it's just you and me, kid,' he said to her, without even a show of regret.

I was forced to borrow money from Skye for the bus fare back to Crack House. I had a nosebleed on the way and I thought, she'll come back – she won't go without me. But I never saw her again.

*

I sat in a stuffy little office amongst that morning's lost property and shivered. They brought me sweet tea in a paper cup.

Skye lent Nathan her sexy phone and I'd watched him excitedly walk away with it. It looked so innocent.

She was my sister but I knew nothing about her except that childhood had so damaged her that she experienced the control and abuse of an older man as an adventure, a love story. Why would she see sending my lovely boy into a public lavatory with a strange man as anything other than expedient? She'd been trained to think that using a child for gain was not only normal but smart.

I was no heroine – I couldn't find him or save him. I was just a desperate mother who could only sit in a stuffy room, drinking tea and beating herself up. My nose started to bleed.

'Hi Mum – did someone hit you?' Nathan stood in the doorway staring at me curiously.

'Car park C, level 5,' the security man said triumphantly. 'I told you we'd find him. Although what he was doing in the bowels of the earth I'll never know.'

'Get *off*,' Nathan said crossly. 'You're dripping blood on my England strip.'

'Nathan – what happened? Where have you been?'

'Don't *screech*,' he said. 'Remember the black Jeep – Sierra, Charlie, Delta? Well, I found it.'

'Safe and sound,' the security man said, 'no harm done, eh? Sign here.'

Numbly I signed for Nathan as if he was a missing parcel and we went out into the cold windy weather to find a bus to take us home. There would be no limo this time, but Nathan didn't seem to expect it.

On the bus, in the privacy of the back seat, Nathan said, 'That was awesome, Mum. It was like being inside of Xbox. I was, like, the operative except I didn't have a gun but we made him pay for his crime anyway.'

'Who? What crime?'

'Doctor Proctor – he hurts boys and gives them bad injections that make them his slaves.'

'Do you believe that?' I asked, terrified all over again.

'I thought you knew,' he said, ignorant of terror. 'Skye said you hated men who hurt children.'

'I do,' I began carefully. 'But I didn't know she was going to put you in danger.'

'There hardly wasn't any,' said the nine-year-old superhero. 'All I had to do was identify the bad doctor and then go up to him and say, "I've got what you want. Follow me." It was easy.'

I looked out of the window and used my bed-time voice so that he wouldn't guess how close I was to hysteria. 'Then what happened?'

'Then I gave him the hard-drive and he gave me the money.'

'The what? Hard…'

'The important bit from the inside of computers where all your secrets go. Didn't you know either? You've got to destroy it. It was the one big mistake the bad doctor made. He thought he'd erased all his secrets by deleting them. Then he sold his computer on eBay but he forgot that deleting secrets isn't good enough if you've got enemies like me and Skye. She's a genius with hard drives.'

'I'll remember to destroy mine,' I said. 'What happened next?'

'*You* haven't got any secrets, Mum,' Nathan Bond said. 'After that I gave the money to Skye and hid in the bookshop till she and Wayne went away. Then I followed them.'

'What bookshop?' When I ran after Nathan to the end of the mall there had been shops for clothes, cosmetics, shoes and computer games. There had not been a bookshop. I explained this to him. He was thrilled.

'You didn't see me. Nobody saw me,' he crowed. 'I did what spies do – I went off in the wrong direction and then doubled back to make sure no one was following. You went to the wrong end of the mall.'

'Is that what Skye told you to do?'

'No,' he said, although his eyes said yes. He turned sulky so I shut up. I was ready to explode but I wanted to hear the full story first.

When the silence was too much for him he said enticingly, 'I know about Sierra, Charlie, Delta.'

'What about it?' I sounded carefully bored.

'You know I was supposed to look for it but I never saw it? That must've been a test. You know how I know?'

'How do you know?'

'Cos Skye knew where it was all along. She and Wayne went down to level 5 in the lift, and I ran down the stairs just like they do on telly. You know, Mum, they get it right on telly. It works.'

'Sometimes,' I said. 'Only sometimes.'

'Well anyway, there they were – her and Wayne – and they got into the Jeep and the other driver drove them away. I looked everywhere for the limo, but I couldn't find it. I thought maybe it was part of the game – if I found it we could keep it. I wish we had a car.'

'We couldn't keep someone else's car.' I put my arm round him but he shrugged me off. He was becoming irritable and I could see he was tired. All the same I said, 'Describe the man who drove the Jeep.'

I was shocked and horrified when he described Mr Bo. But I wasn't surprised.

*

Later that night, when Nathan had been deeply asleep for an hour, I crept into his room and laid his bulging scarlet fur-trimmed stocking at the end of the bed. Then I ran my hand gently under his mattress until I found the shiny new phone. Poor Nathan – he was unpractised in the art of deception, and when he talked about wanting to keep the limo, I saw, flickering at the back of his eyes, the notion that he'd better shut up about the limo or I might guess about the phone. I hoped it wasn't stolen the way the limo and Jeep almost certainly were.

I rang the number Skye gave him. I didn't really expect her to answer, but she did.

'Hi, kid,' she said. Her voice sounded affectionate.

'It's not Nathan. Skye, how could you put him at risk? You're his only living relative apart from me.'

'Did he have a good time? Did his little eyes sparkle? Yes or no?'

'If you wanted him to have fun, Skye, you could've taken him to the fun-fair. Don't tell me this was about anything other than skinning a rabbit.'

'Well, as usual, you've missed the point. It was about making a stone bastard pay for what he'd done. Nathan was the perfect lure. He looked just like what the doctor ordered. And he's smart.'

'If I see you anywhere near him again I'll call the cops on you – you *and* Mr Bo. You're right Nathan *is* smart. He followed you too.' That shut her up – for a few seconds.

Then she said, 'Tell me, Sis, what present did you buy yourself with my money?'

She'd probably looked in the bag when I went running after Nathan so there was no point in lying. I said, 'A CD – The Best of Blondie. What's so funny?'

She stopped laughing and said, 'That was Mr Bo's favourite band. He taught us to dance to Blondie numbers.'

I was struck dumb. How could I have forgotten?

'Don't worry about it, Sis,' Skye said cheerfully. 'On evidence like that, if you never qualify, and you never get to hang out your shingle, you can comfort yourself by knowing you'd have made a lousy psychotherapist. Oh, and Happy Holidays.' She hung up.

Eventually I dried my eyes and went to the kitchen for a glass of wine. I sipped it slowly while I opened my books and turned on the computer. I will be a great psychotherapist – I can learn from the past.

Lastly I put my new CD on the hi-fi. It still made me want to dance. Mr Bo can't spoil everything I love.

TURNING IT ROUND

I keep a huge ball-peen hammer behind the door. It's one of those elementary precautions a single woman takes when she's feeling insecure. I did not feel exceptionally secure at 3 o'clock this morning when I heard someone trying to break in, which is why I nearly brained my older brother.

He *said* he knocked and rang the bell before attacking my lock with his credit card. Hah! Breaking and entering is about the only thing his credit card's good for.

'If I don't answer, maybe I'm out.'

'At 3 in the morning?'

'I might have a date.'

'Hah!'

'I *might* have. I mean, locked door, no one answers when you ring. What does that say to you? Come on in? Make yourself at home?'

'You might have been sick or lying injured at the foot of the stairs…'

'It's a *flat*, Robbie. Doesn't the word "flat" sort of imply no stairs? And don't turn it round. You weren't breaking in for my benefit, were you?'

'Okay, look, I'm here now. Couldn't you just pretend you're pleased to see me?'

Actually, in a primal way, I'm always pleased to see him. He's my older brother: he's been my Robbie forever. It's different for him. I was the cuckoo in the nest. Mum told me when she first brought me home from hospital he burst into tears and screamed, 'Take it away.' But somehow, after years of traumatic childhood, we forgave each other. Of course I let him in. I even sat him down on my sofa and checked his head for bruises. But I didn't let him off.

'You in trouble again? Girlfriend chucked you out? Lost your job?"

'No. Well... no. This isn't even about me. It's about Dad.'

Oh, right: the sins of the father – Robbie's last refuge. He'd have been alright if Dad had stayed around to encourage him. Okay, okay, but doesn't a girl need a father's love and approval as much as a boy? *I don't* use Dad as an excuse, and no one in his right mind would want him as a role model. What's even more pathetic is that Dad is dead. He died of a dirty needle ten years ago.

'Don't start, Paula, just *don't*. You've got your Ms Perfect Preacher face on, and I'm so tired of it. I just want one serious, quiet conversation about Dad, with nobody blaming anyone. I want to ask you, honestly, do you believe Dad was innocent?'

'Taboo subject, Robbie – I'm not listening.'

'You've got to now. We say, "There was no evidence," as if that proves something. And we say, "Dad was an addict, not a killer," as if being an addict is proof of innocence. And we say "Dad was too stoned to be competent enough," like incompetence and innocence are the same thing.'

'Hah! If it was, *you'd* be as innocent as a newborn babe.'

'Hah, yourself. You're too scared to make anything but jokes. You're always accusing me of not meeting life head-on, of not growing up and taking responsibility. But you're the one who'd rather make smart remarks than have a proper conversation.'

I didn't want to talk about the past. Nothing changes there. I wanted to say, 'Move on. I have.' I work in a bank for God's sake. I can't afford a murky childhood. But Robbie had that strung-out look – sometimes he needs soothing more than anything else.

'Of course I believe Dad wasn't guilty. We were just kids at the time, but Mum would have known. And she always said it couldn't possibly have been him.'

'Paula, she hadn't seen him for a week. We talk as if we had a normal family life when we both know Dad was hardly ever home. Any legitimate income came from Mum. I played hooky all the time, and you…'

'Shut up, Robbie. Everyone nicks something from TopShop sometime in their lives.'

'Right, Sis, shoplifting's normal. Persistent shoplifting, therefore, is super-normal and really, really healthy.'

'You're doing it again – turning things round to get at me.'

'I'm just saying we weren't as normal as you make out.'

'Well, *I* do all right.'

'You keep a giant ball-peen behind your door, for gawd's sake.'

'Okay, so I've been a bit unlucky with some of the men I've been out with.'

'You're a magnet for every loose screw in a ten mile radius. What is it with you and violent, unreliable freaks?'

So there we were, sitting, one at each end of my sofa, dissing each other, dissecting the family – a game everybody can play. But I don't blame my doomed love life on Dad. It's not as if I've got an irresistible urge to date junkies.

'I've never dated a junkie.'

'I said, "violent" and "unreliable" and "freak".'

'He was an addict, Robbie, of course he behaved weird.'

'*Weird?* He used to hit Mum. He robbed petrol stations. Weird! I think you're letting him off lightly. You want him innocent so *you* can be respectable.'

'And *you're* being hard on him so you can let yourself off lightly. You want him guilty so *you* can be irresponsible.'

Then it struck me – Robbie had never been in my flat for this long without asking me for money. What's going on? He's always on the cadge. Then it occurred to me – all this talk about Dad. What if Robbie is doing drugs? We always swore up, down and sideways we'd never do drugs. But something had changed. I reached across Robbie to turn on another light.

'What's up, Sis? Why are you staring at me?'

'I'm not staring at you.'

I was checking him out for the signs I was so familiar with when I was a kid. Let me see your eyes, Robbie, your arms, your receding gums. Are you scratching or nodding? How about the mood swings? Comatose one minute, rampageous the next? Oh, and I forgot to ask, are you keeping antisocial hours. Would you frighten a child?

'Robbie, I'm tired. I want to go back to bed and I want you to go home.'

'I can't go home yet. There's someone out there.'

'Who?'

'A girl – Nadine Meneer. Does that name ring a bell?'

'No, should it?'

'Oh yes. She's twenty years old and she picked me up in the Ha-Ha Bar.'

'Bit young for you.'

'Her decision. She's very decisive. And gorgeous. And I'm thinking, woh-oh, my luck's changing.'

'Hah!'

'Yeah. So a few drinks and a couple of clubs later, and we end up at my place. I'm, like, getting my moves together and hoping the sheets aren't too horrible, when, zap, it goes all pear-shaped. She takes out her wallet and shows me her driving licence. She tells me she's got two friends sitting in a car outside. And she's shoving her licence in my face and shouting, "Don't you know who I am?"'

'Robbie...'

'Yeah – because I didn't know either. She was pretty and sweet, and I thought I'd scored. But she'd played me all evening just to find out where I lived. That way, when she confronted me, I'd have nowhere to run to.'

I didn't want to ask because I was afraid I already knew the answer. Nadine Meneer must be what's-her-name's daughter. What *was* her name? Why can't I remember? Dad was suspected of beating her to death and I can't remember her name. Did I ever know she had a daughter? Suddenly I was furious.

'How the hell did she find you?'

'She hired a private detective.'

'What's the point? What gives her the right?'

'Hush, Paula, calm down. Her mother was murdered...'

'What's that got to do with us?'

'That's why I asked if you believe Dad was innocent.'

'He was never even charged. Of course he didn't do it. This Nadine has no right to stalk us, badger us... And what about the other suspect? He had a green van too. He didn't have an alibi either. What about him? Is your precious Nadine stalking him too?'

'As a matter of fact...'

'What does she *want?* We can't do anything about *anything.* We couldn't then – with all the neighbours staring when the cops came and took Dad away. Or when they came back for his clothes, in yellow polythene bags – could they have chosen a more eye-catching colour? Yoo-hoo neighbours – look what's happening to *our* family!'

'Paula, come on, take it easy...'

'How can I? Why are *you* so calm?'

'I'm not. I freaked and came here.'

'You broke in.'

'And you hit me with a hammer. Paula, listen. Nadine wants me to take a test. She wants a swab of my DNA. She says, "Don't you want to know the truth?"'

'Dad wasn't the only one. What about the other suspect?'

'Paula, the other suspect already gave her a swab. It was negative. He didn't kill anyone. But Dad's dead. He was cremated. She can't test him.'

'But we didn't murder anyone.'

'But half our DNA is his, and half is enough.'

'She expects us to provide her with evidence against our own father?'

'Only if he's guilty. She's so, I don't know, torn up. She has been for years. I want to help, but, oh God, Paula, he was my dad.'

'You're not actually considering this, are you, Robbie? I mean, the *nerve* of this woman!'

'She said she *had* to know.'

'And you have half the answer and you're prepared to hand it over?'

'No. Yes. All the time she was talking, I was thinking, yes, the truth is just a swab away. The truth's important to me too.'

'Since when?'

But he wasn't listening. With a hungry look on his face he added, 'Did I mention that Nadine is stunning?'

I couldn't believe it – my older brother fancied the daughter of the woman his father might or might not have killed. For this reason he's prepared to betray the family. Well, me actually; I'm the only one left.

But if I calm down and think rationally about this, *I'm* the one who must turn it round.

Because I cannot let Robbie risk my peace, my reputation, on a fifty-fifty chance. Do I really think Dad was innocent? Has Robbie got 50% of innocent DNA, or 100%? He's the son of an addict, a terrible father and a worse husband. That's enough for him when he's excusing his own faults and failings. But what about the other 50% – the 50% he ignores? His patient, masochistic, hard-working mother goes unnoticed, unacknowledged. And yet his mother's genetic contribution is the only one he can really count on. We're sure of our mother, Robbie and I. We could always rely on her.

But Dad couldn't. Not always. There is a way out, provided I ignore the truth. I take a deep breath…

'Robbie, calm down. If you're that screwed up about the truth, I'll take the bloody test. Bring Nadine here. I'll do whatever has to be done with her swab. Then it won't be your fault. After all, I'm the one who's positive my father's innocent.'

'But are you really? And, honestly, do we want to know if…? It's different for Nadine. She wants to close the case – she can't let her mother go unless she finds out who killed her.'

'Or who didn't. What will she do when I come up negative?'

'But then, see, it won't be *my* fault. I'll have done my best for her.'

Robbie smiles at me hopefully. This, for him, is the most successful outcome he could have wished for: I'll have taken the responsibility and he will get the credit. Did I say Robbie has a very sweet and feckless smile? I wonder who he reminds me of. Can it possibly be the man we both call Dad?

It's a good thing easy DNA tests weren't around when I was born, that's all I can say. But they are now. And as long as Nadine doesn't think of testing both me *and* Robbie and comparing the results, I think I can prove the man we both call Dad was not guilty. I'm as sure as our mum could be when she told me about it just before she died.

She said, 'Look after Robbie – I know he's older, but you're stronger.' And then she told me that the man we both call Dad was, almost certainly, not *my* father.

Yes, Robbie has a sweet smile – much sweeter than mine. He looks way more innocent than I do. But there's a strong probability that my DNA is way more innocent than his. I'm being true to my mother's last wish – I'm looking after my brother. I can't be bothered about the truth.

A HAND

One rainy night I was sent to an address in Whitby to investigate a complaint by a police helicopter pilot. He claimed that while on an operation he was almost blinded by a beam of green light. He radioed in the location and flew back to base.

My sergeant said, 'Okay Shareen, you'd better take a look. It could be a case of Endangering an Aircraft.'

'Eh?' I said, because this was not a crime mentioned at any course I'd ever been on.

The sergeant and the custody officer winked at each other. I always get the silly call-outs. I'm the new girl, so until there's a newer girl I'm all the fun they've got.

Up on the hill, where the holiday-makers don't go, a decrepit early Victorian building called Sutcliffe House has been turned into a tangle of bed-sits. Men with problems live there – the unemployable with no family, no money and nowhere better to go. Social Services call it a 'half-way house'. Cops call it the Tip.

I rang the bell marked 'Supervisor'. When there was no answer I used an old brass knocker that looked as though it would splinter the door. No one responded to that either. I knew there were people inside because the Tip is always crowded and I could feel eyes crawling all over me. But to the residents a police car and a uniform mean trouble.

Using my torch, I walked slowly to the back through nettles and bindweed. The old red brick was diseased with green slime, the paintwork had flaked off like dead skin and cracked guttering let dirty water leak into pools on the path.

I banged on the kitchen door. No one came. I was beginning to suspect I'd been sent out on a wild goose chase. Nightshift has a way of turning on me like a cornered rat.

Speaking of which, I was sure I could hear small animals scuffling in the weeds. I shone my torch but all I saw was a mess of empty beer cans, plastic bags and soggy cardboard boxes.

I used to dream of being the best detective in the CID – the one who noticed the tiny crucial clue and made the link everyone else missed. But there I was outside a house full of inadequate, tragic men who behaved stupidly when they forgot their medication. Where were the bad men? I was fed up with sad ones.

I backed across the muddy weeds and looked up at the house. In spite of the rain, two windows on the third floor were open. One was unlit and empty. A young guy with shaggy fair hair hung out of the other. There was a flickering light behind him – a candle, not a good idea in the Tip.

I called to him, 'Come down and let me in, eh?'

'Why?'

'Because it's raining and I'm soaked to the bone.' I could've said, 'Because I'm a police officer and I'm ordering you to.' But that never seems to work for me when I'm alone.

I was about to give up and radio in for further instructions when I heard a rusty bolt being scraped and worked in its keeper. The door opened about six inches and the young guy poked his nose out.

'You're foreign,' he said.

'You're drunk,' I said.

'You're pretty,' he said.

'You're *blind* drunk,' I said.

'I'm schizophrenic, not stupid.' He pulled the door open for me and stood swaying, backlit by dim institutional lighting in a grubby communal kitchen.

'Have you taken your meds today?' I asked as my uniform boots squealed on sticky vinyl flooring.

'Still not stupid.'

'Were you at your window about half an hour ago?'

'I'm a poet,' he said. 'I look at the moon. Any law against that?'

'It's raining,' I observed in my most unthreatening tone.

'So?'

'No moon. I'm not stupid either. Show me your room, please.'

He led the way up a staircase that grew narrower the higher we went. There were tacky handrails on either side for the infirm and white rubber treads on the stairs to aid the poor sighted. At every landing doors opened half an inch. Eyes I couldn't see saw me.

'What's your name?' I asked, wishing I'd made a different decision at the kitchen door.

'Tim. What's yours?'

'PC Manasseh.'

'PC Manasseh's very, very sassy,' he sang as he started to climb the last flight. There was a smell of rotting meat.

'Not my fault,' he said when he noticed my watering eyes. 'It's next door. He's a pig and a nut job. That's why my window was open. His stink seeps in from the corridor.'

I followed him into his room.

'I saw two open windows. Is that his next door?' I was asking questions in a casual way, but I was looking keenly round his room while speaking. His walls were covered from floor to ceiling with bits of paper. The paper was covered with writing so small that in the candle light I wasn't sure it was writing.

I flicked the light switch but nothing happened.

'No money for the meter,' he said cheerfully. But there wasn't a light bulb in the socket and no visible meter. I wondered if he lied about absolutely everything.

I said, 'Candles are dangerous – especially with all this paper.'

'They're Institutionally Approved Safety Candles,' he said.

He was taking the piss for sure.

'Tell me where the light bulb is,' I said, feeling I should make him realise I represented the law.

'The rats ate it,' he said. 'No, I tell a lie. There's illegal trade in stolen light bulbs here. You should investigate.'

Frustrated by candle light, I shone my torch in his face. He blinked and turned away, but not before I saw a freaky intelligence gleaming in his blue eyes.

Blue eyes – they always look so clear and transparent to me. I feel as if they can hide nothing. Yet blue is a cold, secretive colour.

I turned the torch beam onto the wall. With my nose three inches from the writing I read, 'In god's grey kitchen/ I see the ultimate power /cooking up the deformed/the lame, unlucky soul.'

'It neither rhymes nor makes sense,' I said to provoke him. But he flopped down on his back-breaker bed with an exaggerated sigh and blew alcohol fumes at the ceiling.

On a chipped Formica-topped table by the window I saw a mobile phone in its charger. The mug on the shelf above his hand basin held an electric toothbrush.

I should've walked away but I get pissed off when guys with blue eyes treat me like an idiot. I have to suck it up on the job, but I don't have to in the Tip.

'Where's the fricking light bulb?' I said loudly, shining the torch straight into those mockingbird eyes.

'That's a CIA torture technique,' he complained, staring straight into the light. 'But since you're using it, I'm forced to tell you that the light bulb blew and is in the wastepaper basket.'

There was no light bulb in the trash. What a surprise! But there was an empty package which told me it had once held an Anser 3.0, 5.0mW green laser pointer.

I put on my rubber gloves, lifted the packaging out of the trash and stowed it in an evidence bag.

After a methodical search by torchlight I found a light bulb in his three-shelf book case. It was nestling between Leonard Cohen and Lord Byron like an Easter egg, half hidden, where even a stupid child can find it. I did not see an Anser laser pointer but I stood on a chair and screwed the bulb into its socket. The light came on immediately. I stepped off the chair and blew out his candles.

'You're wasting my time,' I said. '*Now* tell me what you were doing at an open window with a laser pointer on a moonless night in August? I don't want to arrest you but you're acting like you want me to.'

'Do you know how sexy you look in rubber gloves?' he asked with what he probably thought was an innocent twinkle. '*Robber* gloves,' he added. 'You're here to steal.'

He had no right to be so handsome, given the circumstances. I unclipped my radio.

He said quickly, 'I don't know anything about a laser pointer. The guy in the next room comes in here. He breaks and enters. He breaks the poetry when he enters. He leaves his shadow behind when he goes. He cooks for the rats and says *I'm* insane.'

'What's that smell?' I asked

'Could be a laser pointer. You'll never know if you don't use your eyes.' He got up off his bed, unwinding his slim length in one athletic movement. He went to the window, leaning dangerously far out. If he'd been a friend or brother I would've caught his belt to hold him safe.

'Use your eyes,' he said again. 'Use them before someone sucks them out and swallows them like the black olives they resemble. Your eyes are food for thought.'

Maybe it was the smell from next door, maybe it was vertigo. I felt dizzy. There were tiny sparklers blurring my vision, and I couldn't breathe. How could I arrest someone who said my olive eyes were food for thought?

I stood shoulder to shoulder with the mysterious shaman-like lunatic I should be taking into custody, wondering how I'd feel about him if he hadn't introduced himself as a schizophrenic.

'Is *that* one of your robber gloves?' He pointed down into the toxic turf. 'Did you shed it like snakeskin in the garden? Shedding a glove doesn't make you less of a robber, you know.'

It *could've* been a rubber glove. It *looked* like one – lying there in the weeds. I shone my torch on it and saw the sly darting of rats' tails escaping the light. Do rats nibble on rubber gloves?

'Oh shit,' I said. I ran out of Tim's room and clattered downstairs.

What I found in the muddy weeds was a left hand, grey by torch light, shrunken, gnawed around the edges.

'A body part,' I said into my radio through frozen lips. 'A human hand. A left hand.'

'In the back garden of Sutcliffe House?' My radio didn't have a human voice. Whoever took the call sounded unreal through hiss and crackle. 'Is someone having you on?'

'I think it's real. But it looks…'

'What does it look like?' the radio asked.

I was about to say it looked mummified when I saw Tim, who'd crept up behind me staring down at the hand with great interest. He furtively nudged something with his foot into a denser patch of weeds.

'Don't touch anything,' I said sharply. 'Stand over there.' I pointed at the kitchen door. And saw for the first time the shadowy outlines of men gathering at the doorway. Watching.

'You're supposed to preserve the integrity of a crime scene,' my radio told me.

'I'm trying.' I caught Tim's elbow in my rubber-clad hand and turned him towards the kitchen. 'Go in,' I said, 'shut the door, and keep the others out of the garden,'

He responded by cupping my face between his hands, running his thumbs gently over my eyelids and planting a kiss as light as a moth on my forehead.

I sat down suddenly. On the radio.

'What…crackle…what?' asked my radio.

'Remember to pervert the integrity of the crime scene,' Tim advised me. He closed the door, but I could hear laughter.

As I got to my feet, a loud voice from the side of the house said, 'Did that arsehole push you over? You can do him for assaulting a police officer. I'll be your witness.'

I brushed wet weeds off the radio and my backside and said, 'Who are you?'

'Barry Seymour.' He had a slight lisp because of his pierced tongue. 'I'm in charge here.'

'The supervisor?' I asked.

'No, the dogcatcher,' he said with insulting patience. He had seven piercings in one eyebrow, three in his nose, three in his lip, and two in his tongue. His hair was in a ponytail.

'Mr Seymour, please would you go inside and prevent anyone from leaving or coming out here till my colleagues arrive.'

'What's going on?' he demanded.

The radio crackled and cackled but I couldn't make it work. My phone bleated instead.

The sergeant said, 'Oy, Shareen, why did you break radio contact?'

'My radio's playing up. Get someone over here? I need help.'

'I'll come meself,' he said.

'Come quickly,' I said, trying not to beg. 'It's getting out of hand.'

'What hand?' Barry Seymour said. 'Who put *that* there?'

He was pushing at the hand with the toe of his boot.

'Stop that!' I said sharply. 'Go inside and…'

'I'm the supervisor here,' he said. 'You can't tell me what to do.'

'Yes I can.'

'Police officer trumps supervisor,' Tim said, materialising outside the dark house.

'I might've known,' Seymour said. 'This one's a trouble-maker – a loony.'

'Sarge!' I yelled into my phone. But he'd rung off.

Two elderly men, holding hands and wearing night-shirts, crept up behind Tim. One said, 'Is it the Witch's Hand?'

'The Hand of Glory?' the other said. He began to giggle – hee-hee – high pitched and irrational.

'Get your arses indoors,' Seymour said.

The two old men shuffled off a few paces. The ghosts of Sutcliffe House were gathering in a circle around me and the Hand. The grass rustled with slow drugged footfalls. Even the rats ran away.

'Mr Seymour,' I said hopelessly, 'would you *please* send the residents inside. This is a crime scene and they're trampling all over it.' But what really concerned me was the presence of so many men who wouldn't listen to a word I said. I seemed to be invisible. I might as well have been a dream for all the difference I was making.

I thought about drawing my baton, but weapons don't prevent violence. They serve it.

All I could do was to stand astride the deformed human relic hoping I wouldn't have to touch it. I prayed that no one would come close enough to touch *me*. I wanted to look powerful, but I worried I was going to faint.

A lumpish guy in a jogging suit said, 'This is *my* house and I don't want you here any more. Go on – bugger off or I'll call the police.'

'I *am* the police,' I said. But I wasn't. I was a non-presence in their private fantasy worlds.

A guy in blue denim said, 'It's a Halloween mummy hand.' He rocked from side to side like a caged bear. 'It's plastic,' he assured everyone. 'It wouldn't scare a three-year-old.' He looked terrified.

'It's the Hand of Glory,' said one of the night-shirt twins.

'Did you know,' Tim interrupted, 'that skin, hair and body parts from hanged felons were considered to be lucky? Like a rabbit's foot. Unlucky for the rabbit but lucky for the pot and whoever ate the rabbit stew. Stew... mmm.'

Blue denim guy said, 'I think I'm going to barf...'

Barry Seymour grabbed him by the arm and marched him away into the kitchen.

'Yes,' Tim said, as though someone had asked him a question. 'Criminal body parts are thought to have magical powers. Some copies of the French Revolutionary Constitution are bound in human skin ripped from executed enemies of the revolution. Relics from public executions used to change hands for large sums of money.'

'You do come out with the rankest shite,' said a man with thick spectacles on his nose and nothing but underpants on the rest of him. He knelt in the mud to get a closer look at the Hand.

'Move away,' I said loudly and with all the authority of a budgerigar.

'It's the Hand of Glory,' said a night-shirt twin.

'There's one of them in the Whitby Museum,' said the wearer of underpants, kneeling at my feet.

He laid his hand on my right ankle and slid it up to my thigh. It was like rats were running up my leg. I kicked out.

I should know better – I'm trained for a measured response. But I kicked a sick guy on medication. He lay on his back among the wet weeds and started to cry.

'Tim,' I said – a trained officer of the law turning to a schizophrenic for help.

He laughed. 'Don't worry,' he said. 'This isn't really happening. *Something's* happening, but it isn't this. Think of this as folklore. We're the folk, and you're the law.'

He went over to underpants man and helped him up. 'She doesn't hate you.' he said. 'She's just frightened.'

And then my sergeant turned up with his sidekick, PC Nobby Redland.

Everyone melted away like sea mist. My Sarge said, 'You've lost control of a crime scene, Shareen. Your next assessment's going to stink. Like these drains.' He wrinkled his nose and smelled the rancid air like an old bloodhound.

The smell of rotting meat had indeed drifted down from the open windows on the third floor.

'Is it real?' he asked, shining his touch on the hand.

PC Nobby Redland bent down for a closer look. 'I think it's real, Sarge. But it's not right. It's sort of… um… pickled.'

'Pickled?'

'The rats think it's real,' I put in. 'They've been eating it.'

'Go indoors,' the sergeant told Nobby. 'Keep everyone there. Talk to the supervisor…?' He looked at me.

'Seymour,' I said, 'but…'

'Mr Seymour. See what he's got to say. Ask for the house records. Take the names of all the residents. I'll get some more bodies out here.'

He called for Scene of Crime Officers and forensics. He strode purposefully into the house to find witnesses and take statements. Simple, rational acts, easily achieved.

I remained in the rain guarding the Hand. I was glad to be alone and to have the chance, while no one was looking, to search in the undergrowth for what I'd seen Tim trying to nudge out of sight.

I hoped I wouldn't find anything, but I did – an Anser 3.0, 5.0mW green laser pointer was almost buried under the mud where the ghosts of Sutcliffe House had been milling around me.

Suddenly I didn't know what to do about it. It was evidence, and it should be treated as evidence. But it was evidence that someone I... *liked*... was at best an idiot and at worst a criminal. Wasn't he just a sweet damaged guy who would be even more damaged if the weight of the law fell on his tangled, beautiful head?

I sighed, picked up the laser pointer and slipped it, mud and all, into my inside pocket with the box I'd found in Tim's wastepaper basket. I didn't want the Scene of Crime Officers to grab it and bag it.

SOCO arrived in a blaze of arc lights, police tape and men in white coveralls. They looked at the back garden of Sutcliffe House with expressions of dismay.

My sarge gave me the list of house residents and told me to use my car radio to check the names for criminal records.

I was not surprised to discover that of the twenty-seven residents, eleven had been in trouble with the police – pathetic stuff: shoplifting two cans of lager from the Co-op, sleeping in a dumpster by the harbour, shouting obscenities outside the Magpie restaurant, begging, drunk and disorderly, running naked on the beach.

Tim Gordon had one entry. About fifteen months previously his sister rang us for help when he wouldn't leave her house. She hadn't pressed charges. I happened to know, because I'm sometimes seconded to the Domestic Abuse Unit, that her husband had been arrested four times for assaults against her. Tim Gordon's sister was a battered wife.

I sat in my car imagining Tim trying to protect his little sister from violent domestic abuse and her calling the police, for his protection as much as for her own. Why should having schizophrenia mean that a guy can't try to do the right thing?

The Hand was bagged and driven away for analysis. The Medical Examiner said it was real and recently severed, but certain 'procedures' had been carried out on it.

I followed her back to her car, helpfully holding an umbrella to keep her dry while she packed her kit into the boot.

'What's a Hand of Glory?' I asked.

She gave me one of the looks I'd become accustomed to recently. So I told her what the night-shirt twins said.

She sighed. 'I don't actually know what a Hand of Glory is, Shareen. But if you're interested in spooky twaddle there's a Ghost Walk every evening up on the West Cliff. All about Bram Stoker and Dracula too if that's what rocks your boat. But I deal in facts, and as a police officer, you should too.'

Off she went in her safe, efficient, Volvo, leaving me in the rain at the Tip where things were unsafe, inefficient, unscientific and irrational.

Nobby Redland came outside for a smoke. 'Bloody nutters,' he said. 'Either they're loopy cos they're on medication or they're paranoid cos they forgot 'em.'

'What about the supervisor?'

'One word from him and all the twats run to their rooms.'

'Scared of him, are they?'

'These guys are one step away from living rough. Piss Seymour off and he can probably get you evicted or have your benefits stopped.'

I said, 'Has anyone found out what's causing that rancid stink on the third floor?'

'What stink?' Nobby asked, dragging smoke into his lungs.

A commotion in the kitchen led to the SOCO team coming out of the house to open up the inspection pit and take unbelievably revolting samples from the drains.

'Can't you smell *that*?' I asked Nobby. But he just shrugged and went back inside.

No one told me anything. Nobody asked me anything. When I looked up at the third floor Tim's window was closed and his blinds were drawn.

*

Next day, an hour before dusk, I went to the West Cliff, to the Whalebone Arch where most of the Whitby tours gather. Tour leaders feel compelled to dress bizarrely and Cat Calloway, a rangy blonde woman, wore a man's frockcoat and top hat.

She said, 'If you want to know about the Hand of Glory join the tour. It'll cost you five quid.'

I showed her my identity card and she sighed.

'Okay,' she said. 'The Hand is cut from a hanged man while he's still on the gibbet. A witch boils it down and gets rid of the flesh and blood. Then she pickles the skin and bones in narcotic herbs and spices. Then it's stuffed with the fat of a hanged man, and made to hold a candle. A witch could sell a hand like that for a small fortune.' She spoke in a rapid monotone.

'Why?'

'The Hand was worth a lot to a thief, or even a rapist, because when he broke into a house and lit the candle, all the residents would fall into a deep sleep and not wake until the house was ransacked and the thief long gone.'

'Or the rapist.'

'Yep,' she said cheerfully. 'It isn't just a story, y'know – there's a Hand in Whitby Museum if you want to see one. What do you want to know for?'

'Sorry, it's police business.'

'I gave you my best material for free,' Cat said disgustedly. 'Well, bugger off – I've got paying customers.' She turned away to the people who had money in their hands.

Clouds were blooming like bruised roses in the gathering dark behind the abbey ruins on the other side of the harbour. I was going to be late for my shift if I didn't hurry. So I hurried. But I couldn't help wondering – if the Hand had such a powerful narcotic effect why didn't the thieves fall into a deep sleep too?

Unanswerable questions – I joined the Force because cops always seem so certain. I was young enough to hope that when I put on the uniform I would put on the certainty too. Nowadays I don't believe *anyone* knows what they're doing; they're just following rules and pretending they do.

*

The sergeant said. 'According to the medical examiner, we're talking about a hand that's maybe a couple of weeks old – not Victorian remains. So unless there's someone walking around minus a left hand, we're looking for a fairly fresh male cadaver. Savvy? No point digging up the garden of Sutcliffe House or the basement. Neither one's been touched for years.'

Nobby gave me a list someone on the day shift had made of all the churches and cemeteries within a fifteen mile radius that had reported any kind of vandalism. 'I hope that's not too tough for you,' he said, grinning

He was following up last night's enquiries at Sutcliffe House. Two of the residents had gone missing. Rob Wallace, 45, an illiterate, alcoholic, ex con, hadn't been seen for a while. His social worker hadn't visited him for nine weeks and his probation officer thought it had been five months since Rob had last checked in.

Patrick McArthur, 34, junky, ex con, with a reputation for wandering off to Leeds for weeks at a time, had apparently wandered off again. Nobody, even his social worker, could recall when they'd last seen him.

'No help from the Tip,' Nobby said. 'That lot can't remember when they tied their shoelaces or took a dump.'

I disappeared smartly before anyone remembered to ask why I'd been sent to the Tip in the first place. What was a green light in the sky compared to a pickled body part?

I parked the car next to St Stephen's church. The graveyard was small and it seemed that the last burial had taken place there in the 1950s. I was looking for a fresher, fleshier cadaver. I crossed St Stephen's off my list.

St Mark's vandalism consisted of an angry piece of graffiti comparing Shayne Haver's genitals to worms – not what I was looking for either.

I drove slowly past the Tip on my way to St Michael's, certain nothing good would come from looking for freshly disturbed new graves in old churchyards. Most legitimate corpses these days were cremated or buried in the big out-of-town cemeteries. The day shift had already investigated them and found nothing.

St Michael's was a ruined shell of a church, beautiful in its decay. Ancient graves of sea-faring folk were embroidered by lichen and guarded by overgrown black yews. Wild flowers, heavy-headed with rain, drooped and seemed to peer into the depths of the earth as if searching for the dead. Nothing looked up to the sky.

The vandalism here was a missing gravestone. It had been hauled out of the ground like a rotten tooth. Chips of grey Jurassic stone showed that someone had taken a sledge hammer to it, broken it beyond repair and removed the bigger pieces.

I put stones on my grandmother's grave whenever I go there. But she was buried in the old way, with just a shroud, unprotected by a coffin.

My skin tingled and I wheeled round quickly.

Tim said, 'Sad people always end up here. I knew you'd come. Those macho, bash'em cops think you're funny. They think I'm incomplete.'

'*I* think there's too much of you.'

'So do I.'

I picked up a stone chip, black and green on one side, fresh grey on the other.

He stooped too. 'Look,' he said, 'an ammonite.' He picked up the broken curve of a fossilised sea creature, millions of years old, released from its stony prison by theft and violence. He warmed it between his palms and then gave it to me.

No man had ever given me so gentle a gift. This warm piece of stone would not be placed on my grandmother's grave.

My eyes felt heavy with water. I said, 'Why did you point the laser at a police helicopter?'

He said, 'It's rude to point – even at deep space.'

'Who occupies the room next to yours?'

He smiled at me, a sudden ray of light and lightness.

'Rob Wallace or Patrick McArthur?' I asked.

'I was pissed,' he said, sitting down on the tomb of a long gone sailor. 'How else could I meet a girl with olive eyes? I called and you came.'

'Inappropriate,' I said. 'I'm on duty, Tim, you know that.'

'Dotty duty. Dirty duty. Be on datey duty. It's more fun.'

How could the mind behind such clear blue, intelligent eyes not understand me? He smelled of rum. I felt more lonely than I'd ever felt in my life. I said, 'I found the laser pointer. It can be linked to you.'

'Take me in,' he said. 'Arrest me, jail me. Give me freedom or give me death.'

'Pick one,' I said, defeated.

He looked at me. I thought, 'He's not trying to understand me. He's trying to make *me* understand *him*.'

I said, 'You want me to arrest you?'

He sighed impatiently. 'I have erred and strayed from your ways like a lost goat. I have done those things I ought not to have done and there is no health in me. That is my confession.'

The beautiful man was insane. I said, 'You *so* need someone to look after you.'

'I've just quoted from the General Confession. You think I don't know police procedure backwards? Although,' he added sadly, 'I confess there was a little mix-up between sheep and goats.'

'But Tim, I can keep you out of it, keep you safe. I can say I found the laser pointer in the garden. I can lose the box. All you have to do is say nothing. Do you understand?'

He stood up abruptly, frowning. 'This is the kiss of death,' he said. He held my face between his warm palms and kissed me with a mouth that smelled of toothpaste, tobacco and rum. My bones dissolved.

He slid his hands down, oh so gently, till they circled my throat. Slowly, oh so slowly, he tightened his grip.

I was completely engrossed in the kiss. I almost ignored the death. Then something in my ears popped and roared.

I hit him.

He fell down and lay still.

I clamped the cuffs round his wrists. 'You effing numpty,' I said. 'That's assaulting a police officer. *Huge* tariff.'

His head drooped till his shaggy fair hair hid his eyes, but he said nothing.

There were tears in my eyes as I guided him out of the graveyard towards the car. All I could think was, 'You fool. He was only pretending to like you, and you fell for it like a dumb little girl who's been offered chocolate by a pervert. You let a resident of the Tip kiss you. Twice. What on earth can I tell my sergeant? What can I write in my report?'

Waves of humiliation started in my gut and rose like vomit into my throat. My throat still felt the scalding touch of his hands.

I could hear the jeers and laughter. The story would be passed around the whole of North Yorkshire. Shareen Manasseh's so easy she let a loony strangle her while she was snogging him. If I was a joke before, I'd be a dirty joke now.

What could I reply? That something strange and narcotic had gone wrong with my mind from the moment I went into Tim's room at the Tip? I would have to leave the Force. The years I'd spent training, trying to be a good cop, trying to fit in, would count for nothing.

The sheer weight of wasted time fell on my shoulders like a burden too heavy to lift. I stopped the car a quarter of a mile from the station.

'Tim Gordon,' I said, twisting round to look at him sitting uncomfortably behind me, 'forget about Assault – I'm arresting you for Endangering An Aircraft.'

*

The Custody Sergeant, Don Dear, took Tim's shoes, his belt, a packet of rolling tobacco and his mobile phone. He accepted my evidence bags containing the laser pointer and its box. 'Write out your report, Shareen,' he said, without even looking at me. 'Someone else will conduct the interview. You can go back to cemetery patrol.' He laughed his snarky laugh.

I said, 'Tim needs an Appropriate Adult and a solicitor.'

Tim spoke for the first time since confirming his name and address. 'No solicitor.'

'Tim...'

'Not your call, Shareen,' Don Dear interrupted. 'Now bugger off. It's so busy tonight – the Inspector will probably just bail him to appear next week.'

Tim turned his charming smile on Don Dear and said, 'Thanks very much. So when can I have my Hand back? It has magical powers, you know, and it's worth a lot of money to me.'

'Eh?' said Sergeant Dear, who isn't the sharpest knife in the drawer. Then he caught up. And the custody suite got *really* busy.

I became so fed up with people coming to look at me that I went to the women's changing room to write my report. Even then people poked their heads round the door and said, 'Is it true you brought in a murderer by mistake? Classic, Shareen, classic.'

What could I say?

I couldn't say anything truthful in my report either except for the time, the date, and what I was doing in the graveyard when Tim Gordon approached me. I wanted to reproduce his voice, to think of something he might say that was suspicious enough for me to bring him in but not rational enough to sound as if I'd made it up.

In the end I wrote, 'He had in his possession an Anser 3.0, 5.0mW green laser pointer which he freely handed to me. He said he'd found it in the garden of Sutcliffe House on the previous night. He said, "It's my finger and I pointed it." When asked if he was the owner of the pointer, he replied, "I am the rightful owner of my own finger." So I decided there was enough cause to bring him in for questioning about yesterday's incident of a green light endangering a police helicopter.'

I'd never lied in a report before. Tim could contradict all of it. He could say he'd kissed me. My career would be over. Who'd want a lying cop? Especially one stupid enough to snog a psychopath. Because that's what everyone was saying: only a psychopath would dismember a corpse. Tim had coughed to being the owner of the dismembered hand. Therefore Tim was a psychopath.

Before I was hustled out of the custody suite to make way for the detectives, Tim caught my eye. He gave me the sweetest blue-eyed smile, as if things were going very well for him. I wanted to slap him. Things had gone tits-up for me from the first moment I clapped eyes on him.

No one bothered to give me fresh orders so I escaped into the rain and drove to another church close to the Tip. It didn't have a proper graveyard, just a paved area with a few stones laid flat around a solid Victorian church. It was too public and respectable to have been vandalised. It wasn't even on my list. But I sat in my car and looked at it.

I don't like churches – their unnecessary height and sharp, Gothic angles make me feel small and excluded. So do self-righteous, self-certain police officers.

I turned the car round and drove to the Tip.

The kitchen door was open so I walked straight in. The frightened guy who'd been wearing blue denims last night was making toast.

'I need to talk to the supervisor,' I said. 'Where can I find him?'

'He's gone.'

The toast popped up.

'Where's he gone?'

'All the other cops left. They got their man. That's what they said.'

I said patiently, 'What pub does Barry drink at?'

'The Kings Arms. Arms, Hands, what's the difference?' Denim man started to butter his toast.

I left and walked through the rain to the Kings Arms.

'I don't know a Barry Seymour,' the barmaid said. She turned to the landlady. They both shrugged.

'He's got loads of piercings.'

120

'I don't know his name,' the barmaid said, 'but there's a guy like that over there.' She pointed to a shadowy corner.

'Thanks,' I said and went over.

Barry Seymour was sitting with a very stoned red-headed woman. She said, 'Sod off – I haven't done anything. Yet.'

I said, 'Can I have a word, please, Mr Seymour?'

'Eh?' He stared up at me blearily. 'Haven't you lot had enough yet? There's vulnerable people at Sutcliffe House. Know what that means?'

'So could we have a word now while there's no one else around?'

'There's *me*,' the red-head protested. 'I'm not no one.'

'You're right,' I said. 'What's your name?' I watched while she got up, tripped and stumbled away as fast as jelly legs would take her. The uniform has its uses.

'Tell me about Rob Wallace and Patrick McArthur.'

'I already did. They're missing. People go walkies. They come back. I'll inform your fucking highnesses when they do.'

'No. Tell me *about* them. Describe.'

'What for? You got your man – they said on the news. Can't a guy have a drink without a cop in his face?'

I was so tired of blokes treating me like a loser. I snapped, 'We got the perp but not the vic. Vics are important too. Describe Rob Wallace.'

He got up. He wasn't very tall, but he had big shoulders and long arms.

'Outside,' he said. 'I'm not supposed to talk about the clients in public.' He walked lopsidedly to the door. I followed him out into the dark.

The rain had eased into a penetrating mist. A chill wind blew in from the North Sea.

'Turn back,' I said, catching him up. 'Sit in the car.'

'Gotta clear my head,' he said. 'You people shouldn't talk to me while I'm hammered.'

'Just a chat.'

He sneered and kept walking. 'Rob Wallace,' he said eventually. 'Sad life. Came from a crap family so no help there. Slipped through the net. Made some bad decisions.'

'Patrick McArthur?'

'Smokes too much bush,' he replied. 'Fried his brains. He calls it "paranoia", but he's a lazy sod.'

I stopped and let him get a couple of paces ahead. Then I called, 'Hey Rob…'

He wheeled round towards me. His face in the fine rain was glistening and contorted.

I took a deep breath and said, 'Rob Wallace, I'm arresting you for the murder of Barry Seymour. You do not…'

'Run,' he said, 'you stupid bitch, *run!*'

I nearly did. But my legs wouldn't budge.

I said, 'I can't run – I'm a police officer.'

'Then you're a dead bitch.'

'Two murders?' I said. My jaw was clenched so tight it was making my head tremble. 'They're already calling you a psycho down at the cop shop.'

Street light bounced off the metal in his lip. The man had mutilated himself. He'd endured pain to look this weird.

'Psycho, eh?' His eyes flicked from right to left and back. There was no one else in the street. I'd already checked.

He stuck a hand behind his back and pulled out a knife. It made the piercings look lame. An eight inch blade strobed light into my eyes. It was serrated on one side.

'Don't,' I said, reaching for my baton.

For a couple of seconds, hours, years, we stood staring at each other. Then he spun away on his toes and ran. I hadn't expected that.

I chased.

The bastard ran uphill.

Body armour is heavy. I had my baton in one hand and I was fumbling for my call button with the other. He sprinted round a corner. I tripped over a raised paving stone.

While I was on the ground I radioed in my position. I thought I'd lost him but when I rounded the corner I saw him standing about two hundred yards away. He turned, saw me still following, and ran again.

It didn't occur to me that he was waiting for me to catch up until, chest heaving from the uphill run, I stumbled onto the cliff top road. He leaped out behind me from between two parked cars.

He wrapped his long powerful arms round my body, pinning my hands to my sides and swinging me off my feet.

I threw my head back, trying to nut him but he was ready for that. He hustled me across the road and rammed me against the cliff wall with such ferocity that the weight of his body knocked the air out of my lungs.

While I was choking for breath he crossed my wrists in front of me, trapping my hands against the stone with so much force that I thought they'd smash. The weight of his body and the stone wall made a perfect restraint. I couldn't even let go of my baton.

'There,' he said, 'that's better, isn't it? Now you can stop pretending to be a cop and relax.' His hot beery breath tickled my ear. He shifted his weight and suddenly I felt the artery in my throat pulsing against cold metal. Something wet and hot began to leak through my frail skin, soaking my collar.

'Just a pin-prick,' he whispered, 'and then you'll bleed out.' I could barely hear him above the roar of the cold North Sea. 'Hardly any pain – I don't make them suffer. Think of it as a lovely deep sleep. You know it's what you want.'

He was an evil creature with super-human strength – a thief who could steal my breath and blood, who could command the elements. He called for the thundering wind to deafen me – thumping, booming wind that plucked the hair from my head and detonated the last of the air. He summoned a pillar of fire that burned white hot around us.

I was dying. The voice of an Ultimate Power howled in my head. It said, '*Give up. Surrender. Throw away your weapons. Lie down on the ground.*'

'I want to,' I whispered. But there was no breath in my broken lungs and no voice could escape from my throat. Only blood.

*

'*Shareen?*' said the Ultimate Power. '*Shareen Manasseh?*'

The Ultimate Power sounded like a senior police officer. They get in everywhere, I thought. They'll want my report now. Nobody makes any allowance for death.

There is no heaven and no hell – just a lonely walk through a cold dark night on a cliff top in Whitby, a tiny thread of a path – step off it and you'll fall for ever. I didn't want to spend eternity falling.

'You died trying to save me,' Tim said. He sounded more puzzled than grateful.

'Where are you?' I asked, turning round.

My foot slipped. I dropped into a warmer place among the walking skeletons of giant crocodiles and other beasts so huge you could shelter from the rain under their bellies. They smelled of rotten things hidden in caves deep under the earth.

'*Wake up.*'

'Are you the Ultimate Power?'

'Er, no, just a helicopter pilot. You can call me Hal.'

He had jet black eyes and flawless brown skin. My heavy eyelids fell. When I levered them up again he was still there.

He said, 'They said I could only stay a minute. Can I come back tomorrow?'

I like dark eyes. I nodded.

A nurse changed the bandage on my neck. Someone else encased my left hand in plaster. My right hand, distorted and blue with bruises was attached to a drip. Everyone told me how lucky I was. I was too tired to talk. Except in the end I had to.

Inspector Carole Sinclair sat on one side of the bed and a WPC sat on the other, taking notes.

'We need a statement.' Carole Sinclair was big and butch and was said to be very clever. She spoke softly and patiently.

'There's a problem, Shareen,' she said. 'We have two men in custody. One of them informally confessed to being responsible for the severed hand. The other was arrested while running away from the scene of your assault. What can you tell us?'

'Tim needs a solicitor and an Appropriate Adult,' I whispered. 'I don't think he had anything to do with the hand. But I'm pretty sure he endangered the helicopter because he was calling for help. The laser pointer was the only thing he could think of.'

She held a water glass for me and let me sip through a straw. 'Go on. What about the other man – Barry Seymour?'

'Not Barry Seymour. I think he's Rob Wallace.' I rested for a few minutes while the WPC looked through the case notes and told Ms Sinclair that Wallace was one of two men missing from the Tip at the time of the inquiry. Then I said, 'I think the hand belongs to the real Barry Seymour.'

Ms Sinclair turned to the WPC. 'We need photographs, Get on to Social Services, please.'

I closed my eyes and drifted for a bit, then woke to the touch of her hand. She said, 'Try to stay with me for a few minutes longer, Shareen. What were you doing alone with this man on a cliff top?'

'My head's gone weird,' I said. 'I can't remember.' Half of that was true. 'I was sent out to check vandalised graves. Then I was talking to him in the mist.'

'Okay,' she said, not sounding okay. 'But what makes you think he isn't Barry Seymour?'

'Tim.'

'The man who confessed?'

'*Because* of that. He only confessed after Sergeant Dear said he'd be bailed and could go home. That's when I realised he'd been begging to be arrested from the first minute I met him. Only I thought he needed protection *from* the law. It's true he was frightened – but not of us. I got everything the wrong way round.'

'Okay, Shareen, you're tired and you're not thinking like a police officer. But I'll check what you've said.' The nice thing about Inspector Sinclair was that she didn't sound as if she was criticising me even when she was.

'Don't talk to anyone but myself about this. There are some funny stories circulating.'

A nurse showed me the local paper. The headline read, 'Vampires Live?' Whitby papers love a reference to Dracula. According to this one a Woman Police Constable had been found on the cliff top exsanguinated nearly to the point of death with fang marks in her throat. She had survived only because of the heroic intervention of a police helicopter pilot and an emergency transfusion of nine pints of blood.

'An exaggeration, that,' remarked the nurse. 'It was only three. Where do they get this shit from? They say you were investigating the Severed Hand Case.'

'Not really,' I whispered. 'I'm very junior. Not a detective at all.'

'They say it was a Hand of Glory and there's witchcraft going on in Council funded sheltered housing. They say the Council can't control what goes on since they closed the asylums.'

'Have I got fang marks on my neck?' I asked.

She raised an eyebrow. 'I suppose you could call it two wounds if you want. But fangs… gimme strength! I'd say it looks like the knife slipped.'

Everything was upside down. There were two men; both of them wanted me to catch them. Tim wanted me save him. The other wanted to kill me. He knew he could turn the hunter into the hare.

I felt again the humiliation that I'd felt on the cliff top when I understood that far from fleeing, the other was leading me away from safety, seducing me into an act of complete stupidity. He was too clever for me. And I was too stupid to be a cop.

Then I thought about Tim. He kissed me. I thought he liked me. But in his tangled mind he wasn't kissing me – he was assaulting a police officer, hoping she'd arrest him and take him to a safe place. But I was too stupid for that too. And too stupid to be a woman.

Inspector Sinclair woke me with a hand on my shoulder. She said, 'Your suspicions would seem to be correct. The residents of Sutcliffe House and someone from the Social Services confirm that the man claiming to be Barry Seymour is in fact Rob Wallace. DNA should tell us who the hand belonged to. Meanwhile Wallace is being transferred to the secure facility in Middlesbrough. My assistant, Gina, will be along in a minute to write your statement up.' The inspector eyed the puffy lump of bruises that was my right hand. 'Why were you suspicious, Shareen? Take your time. I can see you're still tired.'

I tried to think. 'The smell of cooked meat gone bad. It came from the room next to Tim's.'

'Why didn't you tell anyone?'

'I did.'

'Who?'

'I can't remember. But when I was guarding the Hand and all the residents were milling around, Tim mentioned stew. And almost immediately the man who said he was the supervisor went inside. I wasn't thinking properly at the time but I think the word "stew" reminded him to pour the water he boiled the Hand in down the toilet. And Tim said the guy in the room next door cooked for the rats. But there's a communal kitchen. The residents aren't supposed to cook in their rooms.'

'Correct,' she said. 'It's a fire hazard.'

'And Wallace seemed genuinely shocked to see the hand in the garden so I think *Tim* put it there for us to find. I'd been sent because of a green light in the sky. But Tim wasn't playing silly buggers, he was signalling for help. Only he was unlucky. They sent me.'

'He wasn't clear, Shareen, don't beat yourself up. More of a concern to me is what you were doing alone with a man you suspected of violence.'

I frowned and tried to look like someone too sick and muddled to remember. In fact I knew that I decided that "Seymour" was Rob Wallace and not Patrick McArthur because he'd shown a smidgeon of compassion for Rob but not an ounce of empathy for Patrick. So I confirmed it by calling him Rob. That was when he turned on me. But it was too airy-fairy a thing to have broken the rules and risked my life for.

Suddenly I didn't care. I wanted to resign from the police force. I wanted a job where I didn't stand out, a job my family might approve of, something that didn't constantly make me feel like a failure.

'I can't remember anything except a church and then talking to Rob Wallace in the mist. Maybe I saw him on the street. Or he saw me.' I closed my eyes. I was lying to my superior officer in a particularly stupid way. If anyone bothered to trace Wallace's movements that night they'd know he was in the Kings Arms and that I went there to find him.

'Ma'am?' I said. 'I want to resign. I handled this badly. Stupidly.'

'Is this because I said you weren't thinking like a police officer? That may be true, but you *were thinking* – which is more than most junior officers do.'

Just then Gina skidded into the ward looking flushed and stressed. She handed her mobile phone to the inspector.

'What?' Ms Sinclair said into the phone. 'How did that happen?' She listened for a few moments more, then snapped the phone shut.

She turned to me. 'Well, Shareen, we'll have to postpone your statement. It appears that, while in transit to Middlesbrough, Rob Wallace escaped from police custody. Now we have a full-scale man-hunt on our hands.'

Away they went – two strong, competent women full of purpose. I could hear their sensible shoes squeaking down the corridor.

I lay there aching and bruised by the humiliation of being weak and wounded. In a weird way I was glad that Rob Wallace had escaped. I was now not the only one he'd outwitted.

*

Hal said, 'Have you ever been up in a helicopter, Shareen? I always wanted to fly, to be separated from the earth. Free from the muck and mess.'

'Was it you who reported the green laser?' I asked.

'You know, only *green* lasers are illegal. If the idiot had used a red laser pointer he'd have saved himself a lot of bother.'

We were talking at cross-purposes, but comfortably. He was so happy with his skill and his status that he made me hopeful. He wasn't judging me. He wanted to talk about rescuing me.

'It's such a buzz when you find what you're looking for down there,' he said. 'You turn your spotlight on it. It's like a freeze frame. There's some tiny little idiot below you and you can pin him like a bug to a rug.'

'It's more like a pillar of fire,' I told him, 'when you're the one pinned.'

'Pillar of fire,' he said. 'I like that.' His dark eyes gleamed at me. I smiled back, and when he said, 'I'd like to take you out flying when you're better,' I nodded in agreement. Maybe I too needed some of the perspective you can only enjoy from a distance.

*

I slept raggedly for nearly twelve hours. A nurse removed the drip. Apparently my blood was back to normal.

'Aren't you scared?' the nurse asked, 'with that psycho on the loose?'

'No,' I said. But I'd dreamed about him and his long arms, his freakish strength and all the metal in his face.

Nobby Redland appeared after lunch. 'The Sarge made me come,' he said graciously. He was twitchy, obviously needing a smoke. 'He said you'd want up-dating. No one's seen the psycho, but hospital security has a pic of him in case he comes here to finish you off. The transportation guy who lost him's been suspended. We're all on overtime cos of the man-hunt. Anything else you want to know?'

'What happened to Tim Gordon?'

'The brass decided it was a waste of police time to charge him with wasting police time. Funny thing – he was trying to get us to come to the Tip without alerting the psycho. They was all scared rigid of the arsehole.'

'I know,' I said, 'But why did Wallace do it? What had the supervisor done to him?'

'He's an effing psycho,' Nobby said, looking more than ever as if he wanted me to turn into pure nicotine. 'End of story.'

But it wasn't. Tim came to see me later with his fair shaggy hair newly washed and a tub of black olives in a supermarket bag.

'That's not a Hand of Glory,' he said, staring at my plaster cast and the thunderstorm colours of my bruises. I smiled at him wearily. He pointed his forefinger at the space between my eyebrows. 'You're thinking you don't have the energy for me and my games. You're thinking you want factual answers to simple questions. You're exhausted by madness, the occult and dreams of violence. But the limbic portion of your brain, the ancient part, still believes in the supernatural, you know. It's survived for millions of years. Survival is always for a purpose.'

'You should've just asked for help,' I said. 'You shouldn't have kissed me.'

'Oh.' He looked surprised. He opened the tub of olives, fed me one and kept the rest for himself. 'Don't you like being kissed? I do. I just don't get enough of it. Girls don't mind me being crazy but they want to understand a guy. Whereas I don't understand myself.'

'Or women,' I said bitterly.

'*That's* not a symptom of mental illness.' His bright blue eyes reflected light but no compassion.

'Why're you here, Tim?'

'I dreamed you fell off a cliff and I didn't like it.'

I stared at him, horrified. '*I* dreamed I fell off a cliff.'

He didn't look surprised.

'What happened at Sutcliffe House, Tim? Why did Wallace kill Barry Seymour? What was the point of The Hand of Glory?'

'You want to see more Seymour? Then check out why some kinds of guy want to work with vulnerable men – especially the young ones. Georgie Porgie puddin' and porn, kissed the boys and made them wish they'd never been born. Rob thought he was the instrument of revenge, a dark power.'

'But revenge isn't justice.'

'Maybe it's the *only* justice when the law won't look at the sin.'

'But why the Hand? What did he do with the rest of the body?'

'Seymour, see. Sea more. Sea. See no more. I don't know, but that's what I think. The Hand was his reward. It puts people to sleep. It's about the triumph of his will over sleeping men. Sutcliffe House was supposed to be his Kingdom of Lost Souls.'

'He told you that?'

Tim hesitated. 'He's not a poet. What he actually said was, "I'm in fucking charge now so you losers gotta do what I say or I'll cut you down with Spike here." That's what he called his knife: Spike. You met Spike. Spike speaks.'

I was tired but I wondered hazily whether Wallace and Spike's reign of terror had been more effective than the Council's rule of indifference? Because what was the Tip if it wasn't Whitby's very own garbage dump for guys who had no one to protect them. Out of mind – out of sight.

'Barry Seymour must've had a clean Police Record,' I said in the end. 'There are supposed to be safeguards.'

'Will you be my girlfriend?' Tim asked. 'Can I come and live with you?'

I was gob-smacked. 'What would my family say?'

'Are there lots of Manassehs?'

'Enough to make my life a misery.'

'There'll be an enquiry,' Tim said. 'They'll close Sutcliffe house. Then I'll be homeless. I have a sister but she's in thrall to a dark power too.'

Yes, the sister, the battered wife. 'You should run away together,' I said without thinking. 'Save each other.'

'You don't know what "in thrall" means, do you?' He gazed at me with those translucent eyes.

'Did you really dream I was falling off a cliff? What happened?'

'You broke,' he said with his charming, playful smile.

Sleepy, I imagined living with a blue-eyed boy with rock-star hair. I imagined a tall slender man, pearly skinned, in my bed. What would I do? Feed him his meds, love him and hide the matches? Never see my family again? Would all our conversations be random and poetic? Would I try to learn his logic, and then ditch him if I found there was none?

Because, whatever the limbic portion of my brain was trying to tell me, I really do need rational thought.

*

They sent me home next day in a police car driven by Inspector Sinclair's assistant, Gina. She gave me a handwritten note from her boss which read, 'I'm ignoring your verbal resignation. Work-related traumas affect judgement. You have a lot to offer.'

'But you need to toughen up,' Gina added helpfully, seeing me read the few words for the third time. She prowled my one-bedroom flat checking window locks, deadbolts and the entry system to the block. They were all fairly modern, but she sniffed and said, 'Keep your eyes open, eh?' before clip-clopping efficiently down to her car.

I was alone. The flat was cold and smelled abandoned. Rain beat mercilessly on my windows. I closed the blinds, turned on the heat and wrapped myself in a blanket in front of the TV. My hands and ribs throbbed. My neck itched. I wanted to call my mother but she'd have panicked. My father would've come to drag me home as if I didn't have a life and a home of my own.

I watched an American cop show where clever people cut up tiny pieces of material evidence, examined them under microscopes and made logical deductions that fit neatly into theories. All the women were blonde, bronzed and tiny. They wore skin tight jeans, had guns and blue eyes.

When the itching and throbbing became unbearable I took painkillers and went to bed. But three hours later I woke from a nightmare where a man hovered outside my third floor flat, tapping on my window. Even awake I was sure that I could hear tapping. No one could actually tap at the window – it was too high and there was no balcony. I got up and went to the door. Squinting through the spy-hole, I saw nothing and nobody.

I took some more pain killers though I should've waited another hour. Then I turned off the light and raised the blind. The only things tapping on the glass were raindrops.

But down below, on the opposite side of the street, was a shadow – the shadow of a not very tall man with long powerful arms. I jumped away from the window and went for my phone. My broken hands were trembling so violently that I dropped it. By the time I'd picked it up and controlled my stiff, shaking fingers enough to attempt to punch in a number, the shadow had gone.

I stood dithering, staring at the dark empty street. I couldn't call for help. I checked the window locks, the door, the dead bolt. I locked myself in the bedroom and, with the phone still in my hands, I crawled into bed, and pulled the duvet up over my head.

*

I was on sick leave but I didn't feel safe at home. So towards evening I went out to join Cat Calloway's Ghost Tour on the West Cliff. They gathered in front of the house where Bram Stoker rented an apartment and began to write 'Dracula'.

'Here are some facts about the Irish author that you might find interesting,' she said, executing a dance step, and twirling her black top hat on the silver knob of her cane. 'He died, raving, of tertiary syphilis. I see you're shuddering.' She whirled suddenly and pointed at a woman in the front of the group. 'Madness and disease should be avoided if humanly possible.' She emphasised the word 'human' with a ghoulish laugh. 'Next: one of Bram Stoker's ancestors was the legendary Sheriff of Galway who hanged his very own son.' She whirled to face a man in a big thick anorak. 'You, sir – would you hang your own son?'

'Me?' The man said, startled. 'I don't believe in capital punishment.'

'The Sheriff of Galway did.' Cat Calloway circled her own throat with a hand gesture and pulled an imaginary rope. Her head jerked sideways. My hand was throbbing violently. I hid it between the buttons of my coat.

'Oddly,' she said in a more normal tone of voice, 'the Irish author was also distantly related to Sir Arthur Conan Doyle, writer of the Sherlock Holmes mysteries.' She narrowed her eyes and surveyed her group. 'Have any of you actually *read* Dracula?'

There was a silence until one woman reluctantly raised her hand.

'There was a shipwreck,' Cat said to the cowering woman. 'Where?'

The woman pointed across the estuary to the shape of the cliff and the ruined abbey outlined black against the darkening sky.

'There was a ferocious storm,' Cat said, 'and the ship carrying Dracula's coffin foundered on the rocks. The coffin washed up on the shore just over there. This is a dangerous coast. Bram Stoker used reality in his work of fiction. Now I'll take you to the places where he liked to drink and talk of the myths and legends that so many local people still remember.'

She danced away, the tails of her shabby black coat flying, till she reached a genteel looking hotel. 'But first,' she said, as the rest of us caught up, 'I want to tell you another fact about this strange Irishman. One of his blood ancestors was an ancient king who ruled much of Ireland. His name was Manus the Magnificent. Manus, as the educated lady who's read Dracula, will tell you, is the Latin word for hand. By an odd coincidence, another chilling story I'll tell you later is all about a Hand, the Hand of Glory. And if any one of you is the type to sneer at stories of Hands and Vampires, we have among us someone who knows, to her cost, that truth is stranger than fiction.'

She didn't even look at me, but all the members of the tour glanced around trying to guess who she was talking about.

I'd had enough. Both my hands were hurting badly. I ducked into Bram Stoker's favourite watering hole and ordered a drink to wash down more painkillers. Then I had another to wash away the realisation that my own story had become a titbit to be used by Cat Calloway to scare the tourists. The third drink gave me the guts to go home.

*

Rob Wallace was never caught. There were many reported sightings – about five a week – till I transferred from Whitby to Bristol a couple of months later. Bristol's in the South West and a long way from Whitby in the North East. They have a lot of officers with foreign sounding names. There aren't any Ghost Walks that I've heard about. And even if there were, I wouldn't feature in any of them.

I haven't flown with Hal yet, but we text and email. I like him. He's good at his job. He doesn't read poetry or novels.

But sometimes I dream about Tim. Last night I dreamed that he beckoned and I followed him onto the cliff top. 'You shouldn't have come,' he said. As he turned to kiss me I saw that he'd tied his hair back in a ponytail and pierced his beautiful face with metal studs.

DAY OR NIGHT

I'm Shareen Manasseh. Sometimes I wish I had a plain name like Anna Lee which any fool can spell. Anna Lee is a good name – short, fits on a granite headstone in big gold letters. According to the date underneath she died two years ago. She's remembered – there were two fresh vases of daffodils and jonquils and a spray of yellow roses.

Rachel Silver said, 'I should have come before now. I feel terrible.' A slow tear rolled out from under her dark glasses and stuck quivering in the make-up on her left cheek. Her hands, in their beautiful suede gloves, fluttered. She seemed to be waiting for me to re-assure her so I said, 'It isn't easy for you.'

'No. I don't come to the UK often. I was ill when she died – a basket case.' Again she waited for me.

'You'd been through a lot,' I supplied.

'No one gets it.' She sighed. 'When I first saw her… Anna… she was the first human being I'd actually *seen*… they told me… in nearly five months.'

I said. 'They told me that too.'

'He kept me in total darkness. Can you imagine that, Shareen? I thought I was blind. You've no idea how badly light hurts the eyes.'

Now her eyes were shielded by dark lenses. Her perfect hair was raked by a breath of early spring wind but it soon settled back into its smooth shape. She hunched her shoulders as if she were freezing. Why, I wondered, was she putting herself through this? It was like watching someone poke at an unhealed wound with a fork.

'I almost forgot.' She took a round white pebble out of her pocket. 'From Atlantic City,' she said and placed it on Anna's black granite stone.

I followed her example. Before leaving home I'd picked up a mundane grey pebble from the stock I keep for my grandmother's grave. Even in the matter of stones this woman made me feel like a pauper.

I said, 'Shall we get out of the cold?'

'It *is* pretty bleak,' she agreed, surveying the grassy ground with its network of narrow paths – a crematorium at one end and a chapel at the other. There were no lichen-covered stones, no Victorian angels or whimsical mausoleums. All the trees and dead people had been planted less than a decade ago.

'Soulless,' I said without thinking.

She let out a sharp gasp and a brittle laugh.

We sat in her chauffeur-driven car with thick privacy glass between us and the driver. It embarrassed me. I wished my Chief Inspector had picked someone else to come to London for this assignment. I didn't know why it was a police job anyway. All he said was, 'You've heard of hush-hush? Well this is hush-hush-hush.'

Rachel Silver said, 'He kept me in the dark. I didn't know what time it was. He fed me through a letterbox in the door, shoving food through like I was a dog.'

The car had bullet-proof glass, a bomb-proof chassis and a security driver. I'd been issued with a regulation Glock side-arm. But Ms Silver did not look like a woman who would ever feel safe.

'First he gave me a ham sandwich.' She shuddered. 'I said, "I can't eat this." He said, "You'll eat what I give you or you'll starve." I made up my mind to starve. But I'm weak.'

'That's not weakness. That's survival.' I felt she'd put me in the place of her therapist or someone whose responses she could rely on for comfort.

But she rejected the comfort. 'It was the thin end of the wedge. He said, "You've been here a week" and I said, "Okay," even when I was sure it was only a couple of days. And then it got so I wasn't sure. He'd shove a sandwich through the door and say, "Lunch," waking me up from a sleep so long I thought it must be breakfast. I'd say, "Is it day or night?" just so I could hear a human voice. He said, "It's what I say it is, stupid, dirty woman." And that was better than when he said nothing at all.'

Kept in the dark and lied to. A bit like what my last boyfriend did to me. He too was the kind of guy who could convince a woman that day was night. But he wasn't a terrorist so I had no reason to believe he was torturing me.

'He wouldn't let me wash,' Rachel Silver went on, her head bowed. She seemed to be giving a speech she'd returned to over and over again. Maybe her therapist said, 'Keep telling the story till it loses its power.' You'd think if that was going to work it would've worked after two years.

I was uncomfortable sitting so close to a woman who'd been brainwashed and tortured. But the Chief Inspector said, 'Do whatever it takes. The Deputy Commissioner in London doesn't want the Americans complaining we can't do a simple job right.'

I tried to change the subject. 'How did an English private detective get involved with this?'

'Anna Lee?' Rachel sounded as if she'd forgotten that she'd come all this way to visit her rescuer's grave. 'She was working in the States and I guess my dad had her on salary. He likes the British. Maybe Military Intelligence kinda seconded her because she was an outsider. I don't know. The operation's still classified. Even from me. They think I'm a security risk.'

'That's a bit unfair.'

'They think I was "turned". They still monitor my calls in case *he* gets in touch. But he wasn't just one person. I think there were five of them but only one mattered. I had to call all of them "Friend". The real Friend escaped in the gunfire. They say he shot Anna Lee the next day. She was gunned down in the street, you know. It was like a regular LA gang drive-by, but they insist it was Friend because she was the only one who saw him and he was the only one who could possibly recognise *her*. He's still out there.'

She was beginning to sound like a tired little girl. I said, 'Do you want to go back to the hotel?'

'I'm exhausted.' She took off her dark glasses and I turned to look out of the window.

I knew, because it was in the notes I'd been given, that when she was rescued, Rachel had an eye infection so bad that she lost the sight of one of her eyes and eventually it was removed. I didn't want to see it.

I couldn't understand the resentment I felt – the toxic twin emotions of pity and impatience. 'Get over it,' I wanted to say. 'Your daddy's a Senator. You're rich. You can afford all the therapy, all the security you'll ever need. What about the woman who got tangled up in US politics almost by mistake and lost her whole life? Is that what you rich important people do – hire someone to stand between you and the bullet that's meant just for you?' Because today it was me and my stupid little side-arm that I'd never actually used outside a firing range. We'd been chosen to stand between Rachel Silver and her own personal bullet.

*

I spent the night at her hotel in London because she wanted an escort to the airport the next day. Then she was gone.

After that, to my surprise, I was sent to a newly built office in South London to talk to a quiet man who called himself Mr Franklin. I was warned that he would want to see my case-notes. He stood with his back to the window reading and turning pages. I sat on a hard chair embarrassed about my spelling and handwriting which I'm sometimes told is 'chaotic'. He didn't comment on either. Nor did he give me back my notebook.

All he said was, 'Thank you so much for your help on this one, Ms Manasseh. In the unlikely event that anyone should ever approach you about this matter I'd appreciate it if you'd report back instantly to Deputy Commissioner Mead in the Met – not anyone from your home station. Is that clear?'

He pushed some papers across the desk, and that's how I found out that the previous day's assignment was an Official Secret.

*

I don't know how it happened – I never said anything to *anyone* about my trip to London – but word spread all the way back to Bristol.

A few nights later I was in the Cat-Man-Do bar with a couple of women from work. Teresa said, 'We saw your ex last night, Shareen.'

'Al?'

'How many exes you got?' Jude said. 'You ain't *that* popular.'

'Yes, Al,' Teresa said. 'He said you were on Special Assignment to MI5 in London.'

I didn't know quiet Mr Franklin was MI5, so unless Al was bullshitting Teresa, he knew more than me.

I said, 'He's shitting you Teresa. It's what he does.'

Jude said, 'He was with Norm and Kill-Bill from the armoury. They said you were issued a side-arm.'

How did they know that? The Glock was issued in London, not locally.

'It's a joke,' I said. 'I passed the basic course, that's all. *You're* both more qualified and experienced than I am.'

Teresa said, 'They told us it was cos you were baby-sitting that Jewish Senator's daughter who was taken hostage by terrorists, remember? Because no one knows you in London.'

'Al said they always pick an "exotic" for a job like that,' Jude added.

'*Exotic?*'

'Don't get all huffy,' Teresa said. 'It doesn't mean you're more expendable.'

'Don't count on it,' Jude said with a malicious grin. She tipped the last of her pint down her throat. She still looked thirsty.

'Never mind her,' Teresa said, while Jude was at the bar getting the next round in. 'Al was talking about you and she hates that. You're supposed to be history.'

'I *am* history,' I said sadly.

'That's not how Al sounded last right.'

'Well, *he's* history,' I said even more sadly, because he'd been gone for six weeks and I was lonely. It was dark in the bar, and 'Fix You' was playing on the sound system.

Al used to like me. Now he likes Jude. Or maybe it was exclusively about sex, and liking had nothing to do with it. I don't understand men at all.

Deputy Commissioner Mead told me that when Anna Lee freed Rachel Silver she ran into the underground bunker while a fire fight was going on around her. He said that she had to dress Rachel in Kevlar and carry her out in her arms – not because Rachel was too weak to walk but because she didn't want to go.

As well as the eye infection, she was treated for multiple STDs. But according to the debriefing reports she never once, even to this day, described a rape. Deputy Commissioner Mead doesn't understand *women* at all.

Sitting in the Cat-Man-Do bar, listening to 'Fix You' and waiting for Jude who hates me to bring more drinks, I knew I should leave, phone Mead and tell him that the Official Secret wasn't a secret – that my colleagues, the men and women I'd been trained to protect and rely on, were asking questions.

Jude came back with a pint for Teresa, a pint for herself and nothing for me.

'*Jude!*' Teresa protested, laughing.

'She get's stupid and slutty when she's rat-arsed,' Jude explained sweetly. 'That's what Al told me.'

'Al would never lie to *you*,' I said. 'You remind him too much of his mother.'

Jude threw knives with her eyes. Clearly she knew as well as I did what Al thinks of his mother.

'We used to be mates,' Teresa said. 'There's way more interesting stuff to talk about than some twat-faced bloke.'

'Like what?'

'Like what Shar was doing in London. Like, how does Rachel Silver look now? She used to be one of the Ten Best Dressed Women in Washington. Like were the terrorists really behind that private eye's murder or is it just another conspiracy theory?'

'Is she even dead?' Jude said. 'Kill-Bill says she's prob'ly in some witness protection program somewhere. She's the only one who actually saw the leader. He was long gone by the time the military stormed the bunker.'

'They killed the other four,' Teresa said. 'Anna Whatsername can't be protected twenty-four-seven. Unless they fake her death and give her a new identity.'

'Don't look at me,' I said because they were both waiting for me to comment.

'You're involved.'

'I'm *so* not involved. Where on earth are you getting your gossip from?'

'Already told you,' Jude sighed impatiently. 'Al said you never listen.'

'Oh do shut up,' Teresa said, but added, 'Don't go, Shar. She's just trying to wind you up.'

'Failing,' I said. 'I'm bored.' And I left.

*

I should've rung Deputy Commissioner Mead. I should've said, 'Teresa, Jude, Norm, Al and Kill-Bill know where I was last week. Everyone's speculating. No sir, I never said a word. I'm not trying to call attention to myself by implying I'm part of an international operation. Possibly the leak started in the Armoury. Am I an exotic?'

I work with these men and women every day of the week. On duty, they watch my back and I watch theirs. Even Jude and Al. Rule number one – you don't rat on your mates. Never.

But a week later, at three-thirty in the morning, the phone rang. I wasn't even awake when I put the receiver to my ear.

A man's voice said, 'Shareen Manasseh? This is a friend.'

'Who?' I mumbled.

'A friend.' He sounded angry. 'We've got your number. We know your family. Believe that we can reach any of you any time we want. Your phones are monitored. We'll know if you contact anyone. Wait for our instructions.'

'Al?' I mumbled. But he rang off.

He wasn't Al, he rang on my landline, he sounded English – not like my idea of a terrorist, he…

I got up and dressed like a spook or a burglar, all in black. I left the flat, got in my car and drove randomly through Bristol streets for five minutes the way they taught us on the Security Driving course. I hardly needed to – it's easy to see if anyone's following you in a residential area at three-thirty in the morning. The streets were empty and dead.

What made me think the voice on the phone was Al's? Maybe I'd been dreaming about him. Maybe it was because he used to ring at odd hours, sometimes pretending he was talking to a sex line. I miss him.

I drove out to the motorway and kept driving till I reached Leigh Delamere Services. Then I stopped and, from a payphone, called the number on the card the Deputy Commissioner had given me. It connected to voicemail. I left a message.

I went home and waited. And waited.

No one called or came so I drove to work at the usual time and spent the day in the usual way, rushed off my feet, dealing with urgent trivia and writing it up afterwards.

'Come for a drink?' Teresa said as we went off shift.

I didn't want to go home alone so I accepted even though Jude and Al were among the crowd going to the Cat-Man-Do.

But when I got to my car I found Mr Franklin waiting quietly in the shadows.

We drove to the underground car park behind the Watershed near the docks. He didn't speak until we were facing the water. Then he said, 'Tell me everything, Shareen – verbatim if you can.'

When I'd finished, he said, 'Is that all?'

I was offended.

He said, 'I know, he told you he was a Friend and threatened you and your family in very few words – I mean, what else has been happening?'

I'd thought about this question all day and prepared an answer. I said, 'Everyone at my station and everyone at the Armoury knows about me escorting Rachel Silver in London. Everyone's speculating.'

'Everyone? I'll need names.' He looked at me. I looked at him.

He sighed and said, 'Ms Silver is still emotionally attached to the leader of the cell who kidnapped her. She was half blinded and so messed up inside that she will never be able to have children, but she's still loyal to him.'

'She's frightened.'

'So are you. Rightly. But because she persists in a bad choice there are some very dangerous people still out there. One of whom you spoke to last night.'

'She didn't have a fair choice.'

'Agreed. But choice about who you're loyal to should be re-assessed in the light of new information. Mindless fidelity to a person, a group, a policy or a nation... well, you, Shareen Manasseh, should know better than most what that can lead to.'

I was grateful to him for not naming the fascistic, extremist groups I might be afraid of. He gave me time to think.

In the end I said, 'Is this why you always choose "exotics"?'

'I beg your pardon?'

'Because we don't quite feel we belong? And so it's easier to persuade us that our friends aren't our friends?'

He looked me straight in the eye, holding contact till I looked away. His eyes were pale grey and his gaze was as frank and honest as Al's.

In the end I chose the family I'd left behind and I gave him the names he wanted. I gave up my friends.

As far as I know nothing at all happened to Teresa, Jude, Al, Norm or Kill-Bill. But I was transferred from Bristol to South London by the end of the month. I was given no choice.

I never heard another word from the so-called Friend. Why had I thought the caller was Al? It wasn't Al but it might have been a voice I'd heard recently. An English voice. Like quiet Mr Franklin's. So I began to wonder how 'Friendly' *he* was. Could the threat have been made just to manipulate me – to expose a leak? Was Mr Franklin another man who could convince a woman that day was night? I wondered about this for quite a long time.

I never saw or heard from him again. And I still don't know who to be loyal to, unless it's to family – even though I left them behind long ago.

GHOST STATION

Before that day I'd never been to Bath even as a tourist. There was something gentrified and bookish about the city which, I felt, excluded me.

Now, my supervising officer, McNabb, was driving the unit the wrong way up a narrow one-way street. He was swearing already, so I kept my mouth shut.

'Effing community policing, Shareen,' he snarled. 'Special Constables – they're crap. Why ain't Bath got a proper force any more? Eh – tell me that?'

Someone rapped on my window. A round pink face topped by a blue and white beanie grinned down at me. He blew cider fumes in my face and said, 'Lost your way, my lover?'

'How can you tell?' I asked, because it had been days since anyone grinned at me, and months since anyone called me his lover.

'They changed the sodding system,' McNabb said, making a five-point turn, almost causing a pile-up, and speeding back the way we'd come. 'This town's just a tourist trap – they got nothing to do but foul up the roads.'

This tourist town where nothing happens was the site of what we'd been told was a serious incident. We'd driven over five miles through heavy traffic and mean mizzling rain to attend: five miles on the A4, the most annoying road in the West Country, while

McNabb complained about his regular partner who was on paternity leave. 'Why can't they let the ladies have the babies? It's what they're good at. What's wrong with the way things used to be? Eh – tell me that?'

He was trying to provoke me into the sort of reply that he could repeat to his Neanderthal colleagues, which would've made me even less popular than I already was. I said nothing.

He solved the parking problem on Milsom Street by driving up on the pavement.

The serious incident was marked by a traffic cone, a faint smear on a bookshop window and a dripping wet Special Constable wearing a high viz bib and a pissed off expression.

'Ray Perkins,' he said. 'It's a knife crime.' He jerked his thumb at the rusty smear. 'It was a lot bigger half an hour ago,' he added pointedly. 'There's some more under the cone. Aren't they sending the Scientific Unit?'

'Why would they bother when we got Shareen? She's dynamite with bloodstains. Take some pictures Shareen.'

All I had was the camera on my smart-phone, and he knew it. He turned to Ray Perkins, and started to fire out questions.

My phone camera wasn't up to the job. The bloodstain didn't register at all, but I got a couple of great shots through the bookshop window of a display – a pile of hardback books, cunningly arranged in the shape of a diamond, that advertised an appearance by the author. The bloodstain never stood a chance.

'Useless,' McNabb crowed, confirming all his prejudices about me. 'This ain't no way to treat a scene of crime.'

'You be me,' Perkins countered, sneezing. 'I can't even tell you who the vic is – the paramedics carted her off to the Royal United before we could ascertain her identity. It wasn't even a proper ambulance – my mate Suzie had to follow them there in a taxi. We're supposed to be a *foot* patrol.' He sniffed and wiped his nose on his sleeve.

McNabb gazed at him contemptuously. 'No proper cops, no proper scene of crime, no proper ambulance. This town's proper rubbish.'

'Get real.' Perkins fought back. '*I* didn't close the Manvers Street station. Don't you bitch to *me*, mate, *I* ain't the effing problem.'

'You ain't the fucking solution neither.' McNabb was as good at establishing an atmosphere of trust and co-operation as a scorpion. Two prickly guys scoring points off each other – my favourite on-the-job amusement.

Trying to prevent a disaster from becoming a catastrophe I held out my hand to Ray Perkins. 'Shareen Manasseh,' I said. 'This is Sergeant McNabb. Pleased to meet you.' Perkins looked as if he'd prefer to stay prickly, but he was forced to shake my hand. Reluctantly he said, 'Suzie will call from the hospital when she knows anything. But I'm as frustrated as you are. Everyone had scarpered by the time we got here so there's no witnesses except an old couple waiting in the café upstairs. I don't suppose they'll be much use.'

'I'll be the judge of that,' McNabb said. And then to me, 'We're finished out here unless you want to take forensic pictures of a wet traffic cone.'

I opened the bookshop door, and let Perkins lead the way upstairs.

'Is she dead?' the old woman, Mrs Ovendon, asked. 'I hope she didn't die. I thought he punched her.'

'All she said was, "Oh dear",' Mr Ovendon said. 'She leant against the window, and then she went down on her knees.'

'She just toppled over sideways.'

'We didn't see the knife.'

'So we didn't understand why she started bleeding,' Mrs Ovendon told us, bewildered. 'Does it always take so long for them to fall down and bleed?'

'Maybe it was because she was wearing a waterproof coat,' her husband said. 'She looked as surprised as we were.'

'Thanks for the description,' McNabb said when at last he could interrupt. 'But I asked you about the man with the knife.'

There's something horribly shaming to me about a woman bleeding in public. It's probably a remnant of the old religion. I've seen surprisingly little blood since joining the police force, but even so, although they try to hide it, my family seems nowadays to treat me as unclean. I don't go home much any more.

'We didn't see the knife,' Mrs O said. 'Just the blood.'

'He must've taken it with him,' her husband said. Both of them wore thick spectacles with brown plastic rims.

I was tired of looming over their tea cups, cake crumbs and puzzled old eyes. I crouched down and said, 'Did you see the man who punched her?'

'Tall,' said Mrs O. She was very short – her feet dangled, like a child's, in mid air.

'Young,' said the very old man.

'Scruffy.' She was neat in her brown coat, matching shoes and handbag. 'We weren't looking at him. We were looking at her.'

'Anything else?' I could almost hear McNabb's teeth grinding.

They looked even more confused and shook their heads. When my grandparents were as old as this they never went out unless one of their children or grandchildren drove with them.

I said, 'What made you notice *her*?'

'She gave the girl some money and then she petted the dog. That's right, isn't it, dear?'

'And I said, "It'll be her own fault if that big dog bites her hand." You don't touch a strange dog. You always warned the children, didn't you?'

'Of course I did,' Mrs O said with a fleck of pride. 'And neither one of them ever got bitten.'

'*What* girl?' McNabb almost shouted.

'She was selling the homeless magazine,' Mr O said.

'Another witness,' Perkins said. And then his phone rang.

I could see that McNabb wanted to tear it out of his hands. He restrained himself, and instead grabbed me by the arm and pulled me to my feet. He nodded to the old people and hissed, 'These two are a waste of skin. Go down and talk to the manager. Someone must've seen *something*. Then find that beggar. Do something useful for a change.' He was watching Perkins. He hated it when someone had more information than he did. It was not a trait that made him good at taking witness statements.

Leaving the Ovendons unprotected I went downstairs to find the manager. She was getting ready for the Meet The Author session, measuring peanuts into a bowl and placing wine glasses next to half a dozen bottles. An assistant was setting out chairs. They seemed to be expecting a big crowd. No one had time to talk.

Outside, the rain was heavier. A traffic warden was writing out a ticket for the unit. It was too late to stop him. I did not look forward to driving back to Keynsham with McNabb.

The blood on the window was gone. So was the red stain under the cone. The scarlet essence of a victim had slid, unresisting, into a gutter outside a bookshop in a tourist town where nothing happened.

I scanned the street looking for CCTV cameras. They are usually attached to street lamps, but weirdly it was only when I started looking for cameras that I noticed that there were no lamp posts in Milsom Street. I was shocked – I am a trained observer but I hadn't noticed the absence of lamp posts. How then could I blame anyone for not noticing a knife? I could hear McNabb's hectoring voice, 'No proper cops, no proper scene of crime, no proper witnesses, no proper lamp posts. So where *are* the sodding cameras? Eh – tell me that?'

The streetlights, in fact, looked like large antique carriage lamps, and they were attached directly to the yellow stone walls.

The cameras would be too. I just couldn't find any yet. But somewhere, in a bunker, would be a covert observer sitting in front of multiple monitors. This would be why the bean-counters somewhere could persuade the authorities it was safe and economic to close the Manvers Street station.

Of course, the covert observer would not be a police officer.

I settled my cap more firmly on my damp uncontrollable hair and took note of all the umbrellas, rain hats and hoods. Maybe even now a trained observer was manually tracking the man with the knife from camera to camera, plotting his route, noting into which rubbish bin he threw the weapon. A cop can dream, can't she?

Meanwhile, on the other side of the street a Big Issue seller was hawking his magazines from the shelter of the NatWest Bank. 'All the news, views, blues, do's and don'ts you could possibly want – for less than the price of a cuppa cappuccino. I ain't begging, I'm working. Homeless but not hopeless… '

I crossed the road. He saw me coming, took in the uniform and the patter stopped abruptly. He was quite burly but sunken-cheeked.

'Don't go,' I said, and held out a few coins. He gave me his wettest magazine in return. 'The stabbing outside the bookshop? Were you here when it happened?'

'I'm always here,' he told me. 'I live here and when I die, I'll die here, and when I come back as a sodding ghost, I'll haunt here.' He had speedy, damaged eyes. 'I've never killed nobody except when I was serving my country, so don't you try to pin shit on me just cos I'm a rough sleeper.'

'Wasn't going to.' I smiled – a sad attempt to pacify those eyes. 'I just wanted to know if you saw what happened.'

'Someone pushed the lady down. It's her own fault – she shoulda been over here, buying from me. If she'd been in her proper place, over here, nothing woulda happened to her.'

'*Proper?*' I was becoming allergic to the word.

He stuck out his chest. 'See this here badge? I'm legit, on the up and up. I'm who she shoulda given her bunce to.'

'There was another seller… '

'That's where you're wrong, lady!' He thrust his head forward so aggressively that I nearly stepped back. 'What they do is pick up a mag from somewhere and *pretend* to be legit. That's stealing. You should stop them. What's that uniform for if it's not to stop thieves, eh?'

'Okay,' I said. 'But there *was* a girl selling, and the woman who got stabbed gave her money and patted her dog.'

'You don't know sod all, do you? Only time you show up is when a member of the posh class gets hit. The dog's bogus too. There's a bloke lives up the top of Broad Street got three dogs with blue eyes he hires out. You can make a load more dosh with a dog.'

The last time I saw my old nan was when I took her out to buy winter boots. There was a small black poodle tied up outside the shoe shop, and I couldn't persuade Nana to go inside until the owner came out to take it home. My nan had a very soft heart for small animals, but she didn't make it through the winter in spite of the boots.

'You look like you missed lunch,' said the man with the speedy eyes. 'I get like that meself – it's low blood sugar.'

'I had lunch,' I said, collecting myself and lying.

'Must be the weather then. I bet you come from somewhere hot?'

'Yorkshire,' I said flatly.

His eyebrows shot up. 'I saw women looked like you in Iraq. You got war-zone all over your face.'

Suddenly I felt bone tired but I managed to ask, 'The girl across the road, has she got a name?'

He shrugged. 'I heard someone call her Dana. She's a meth-head.'

A big woman in a green hooded raincoat touched me on the arm and said, 'Did that poor lady die?'

'We don't know yet. Did you see what happened?'

'Oh no.' She blotted rain off blood red lips. 'But my friend told me all about it. She was over there texting me when it happened.'

'What did *she* see?'

'Nothing – she was texting. I came as soon as I could because if the lady dies I want to buy some flowers to put on the spot.' She pointed to the flower stall just a few paces away, protected from the rain under an archway.

I said, 'We're hoping she'll be okay.'

'I won't bother then. You don't put flowers on the pavement unless they die, do you?'

The Big Issue seller said, 'Now that you've saved yourself a bundle on flowers, why don't you buy a magazine?'

'Oh get a proper job,' she said, turning away.

'I got one,' he yelled after her. 'What do *you* do?'

He sighed. I sighed. Rain fell like a curtain between us.

He was almost right – a long time ago my people were desert people. They covered their dead with sand and placed rocks on top to stop animals digging them up and defiling their bodies. It meant too that they could find their relatives when they came that way again with extra stones to mark the place. That's how cairns are built – the first pyramids perhaps. Flowers, even if there were any, would have been useless.

'Eat something,' said the guy with damaged eyes. 'You're away with the fairies.' He wasn't concerned; just entertained.

'Dana?' I said to prove how sharp I could be. 'A dog with blue eyes? Anything else?'

'Nah,' he said. 'Now bugger off — you're keeping the punters away.'

I copied his name and badge number into my notebook – to punish him, I suppose. Cops need entertaining too.

The flower stall was very expensive. The arrangements were artistic and lavish – the sort that would look good on antique tables, pristine white tablecloths or brides.

The flower seller, more down to earth than her displays, said, 'I'm sorry, I didn't actually know anything had happened till the paramedics came. There was a big party of Chinese tourists, and the women wanted to take selfies in front of the flowers. It happens quite frequently. I couldn't see what was happening in the street.'

'But before that, did you notice a woman begging outside the bookshop?'

'There's *always* someone begging outside the bookshop – they try to use the loo in there – it drives the manager crazy. So, no. I didn't notice anyone in particular. They're part of the furniture here. But I wish someone would tell that chap outside the bank to shut up. He's got such a loud voice I can't hear myself think.'

There was a proper lamp post at the bottom of the street. I spotted a camera mounted on it with a 180° view up Milsom Street and around a higgledy-piggledy intersection. Which way would it have been pointing when a 'posh class' woman was pushed or punched?

A tourist came up and asked me the way to the Abbey. Of course I didn't know, but rather than admit I didn't belong, I pointed in the direction some other tourists were going. In fact I needed to ask the way to Broad Street myself, so reluctantly I made my way back to the bookshop.

'A beggar possibly called Dana, and a bloke up Broad Street who hires out blue-eyed dogs? You're wasting your time *Officer* Manasseh. Worse, you're wasting *my* time.' McNabb was staring in helpless rage at his parking ticket. He wanted to blame me – I could see it in his little red eyes. He didn't like me. There were many reasons but I couldn't do a thing about any of them. I would just have to struggle through this posting and then wait for the next. A homeless, refugee police officer – that was me.

Perkins, who was trying not to laugh about the parking ticket, gave me directions to Broad Street. 'There's two halfway houses on the corner of Broad and Bladud,' he said. 'And yeah, you do see some blue-eye dogs that look like huskies round here.' He might have been helpful simply to spite McNabb, but I thanked him anyway.

'What was the news from the hospital?' I asked.

'Her name's Imogen Bron and she's in surgery now. She doesn't seem too badly hurt. Suzie wasn't allowed to interview her. She'll stay there till the lady can talk. We're going down to the council offices to see if we can look at the CCTV footage.'

'Fat chance,' McNabb snarled. 'It'll be all data-protection this, and data-protection that. Like data-protection trumps police work. Do they think we can do this job with both hands tied behind our backs? Eh – tell me that?'

'Shall I try to track down this Dana?' I asked.

'Shareen couldn't track down pepperoni on a pizza,' McNabb said to Perkins. 'No, my girl, you are going to drive me and *Mister* Perkins here to the council offices, and then you are going to park this effing unit somewhere legal.'

The council building was called One Stop Shop and it housed a police 'desk', all that remained of a complete police presence in the city. I had to agree with Perkins – it was a 'bit of a comedown'. According to him the ugly yellow stone block opposite One Stop Shop, that once housed Manvers Street Police Station, would soon be turned into science labs for Bath University.

'What this town needs is a few ram-raiders smashing windows and nicking all the merchandise,' lectured McNabb. 'That'd have all the sodding retailers clamouring to bring us back quick enough. That's all the councils listen to these days – pressure from poxy retailers… ' He snorted. 'That's if the bleedin' villains could find their way through this stupid one-way system,' he added.

'It's the end of an era,' Perkins said wistfully.

For now Manvers Street was a ghost station with a No Parking sign in front of it. I had to go to the car-park next door and pay.

With no orders except to 'stay put', I sat behind the wheel and watched a stream of people with wheelie-cases and backpacks flow to and from the train station at the end of the road. I stole one of McNabb's peppermints, and then I stole a toffee. The rain rolled drearily down the windscreen. I was hungry.

I was on a case: assault with a deadly weapon. I knew nothing about it. McNabb and Perkins were talking to the high tech people who might or might not have watched the event, and who might or might not have recorded it, and who might or might not share the information. I had a low tech meth-head, Dana, pretending to be a Big Issue seller, drumming up sympathy with a blue-eyed dog, not her own. Imogen Bron gave her money, crouched to pat the dog and got herself knifed.

I was part of a half-hearted, overstretched police response, but would we pay even this much attention if it was Dana who took the knife instead of posh Imogen? If Dana had taken the knife, would Posh Imogen have stayed around to give a witness statement? Maybe she would – she patted dogs and gave money to beggars – both attributes of a responsible, caring citizen who we have sworn to protect and serve. We've sworn to protect and serve Dana too, but sometimes it doesn't work out that way for meth-heads.

The windscreen was fogging up. I put my cap back on and left the unit in search of a sandwich. I found one, only a hundred yards from the ghost station, in a tiny, sticky floored caff in an ally between Manvers Street and what looked like a new built retail citadel.

It's impossible for a police officer to eat on the job without breaking one ancient dietary law or another, and this place seemed to be the reason why – having not much more than ham, bacon, sausages and pork scratchings on the menu. I was about to get reacquainted with my old friends, cheese and pickle, when the woman serving me said, 'I wish you lot hadn't run out on us. Especially with all those homeless blokes at the shelter over the road. There's way more fighting than there used to be when you were next door to sort the buggers out. Now all you got is a couple of fat girls in the council office. I know, I seen 'em.'

Over the road, next door to the Ghost of Manvers Street, was a looming thunder-cloud of a church with its doors firmly closed. But leaning against them, trying to find shelter, were five ragged men. The one in front watched me cross the road. As I approached, he rolled up his sleeves and folded his arms. On one arm were tattoos of the name and insignia of a Welsh regiment; on the other was the hooded figure of Death gripping his scythe with skeletal hands.

'What?' he said belligerently, protected by tattoos, his long black hair rain-flattened against a cannonball skull.

'She brought us our tea,' said a scrawny, bearded bloke behind him. They were all staring at my cheese sandwich with the eyes of raptors.

I said, 'Do any of you know a young woman called Dana? She hasn't done anything, but she witnessed a stabbing while she was begging in front of a bookshop.' My voice, weaker than the sound of traffic, seemed to stop dead two inches from my mouth.

'Giss yer sarnie,' said someone else, 'or we won't say nothing.'

Five men; one woman's very overdue lunch. Another domination game. Hallelujah.

'Aw, starving?' I asked. 'Missed your lunch too? *All* of you?' I spoke to the bearded bloke because he had what looked like fresh ketchup on his moustache. A feeble way to fight oppression, I know, but then who was oppressing who? – bearing in mind that I was wearing the uniform and had a bed of my own to sleep in at the end of the day. All the same, I was pissed off. I went on, 'Judging by the pub smell, you made your choice. Cheese and pickle's *my* choice. Get over it.' I turned round and marched away, tired of fighting the same battles over and over again. But I was tired of turning away and refusing to fight too. A win might give me encouragement, but I hardly ever won.

The sound of sniggering followed me half way to the unit. Then the pounding of running feet stopped me. I spun round to face two of the younger men from the group coming to a halt in front of me. The shorter ginger one said, 'We decided to talk to you. Dana's gone and ain't no one gonna tell you where she went, so Taff said it was okay. See, she used to be a sweet kid, but the glass ruined her. Even her teeth's falling out and she ain't hardly over twenty yet. We drink, yeah, so *you* won't see the difference, but we despise synthetic drugs.' He himself wasn't much older, but already his skin was reddened and roughened by alcohol and weather. His teeth looked all right, though – scummy, but healthy.

His mate, shaven-headed and thin enough to be chronically ill, said, 'No names, right?' He wore a black hoody and the deep dark eyes staring out at me were like a younger version of Taff's Death tattoo.

I said, 'What am I going to do? Run you all in?' I gestured over my shoulder to the ghost station behind me.

He laughed and his teeth were like a skull's teeth. Ginger said, 'You and who's army?'

'Yeah,' I agreed, because I didn't even know if there were any holding cells over the road at One Stop Shop and I couldn't arrest them and drive them all to Keynsham.

Death said, 'We heard what happened at the bookshop. We talked it over and we're pretty sure what musta went down – no one wanted to carve the *lady*. It's obvious – the knife was meant for Dana. That is why she's fucked off without saying bye-bye to anyone.'

Ginger said, 'It's the Countdown King. There – solved your crime for you.'

'Thanks,' I said. 'Who's the Countdown King?'

'Glass dealer,' he said.

'He deals more than crystal meth,' Death told me. 'But what he does, like, when people owe him money, see, he puts a knife to their necks and says, "Gimme everything you got." And he goes, "Ten, nine, eight, seven … " and that really freaks especially the girls. So they give him, like, even their rent money.'

'Has he ever actually cut someone?'

'Course he has,' Ginger said. 'They wouldn't be so shit scared otherwise.'

'There's no one can make a bad time worse like a dealer,' Death said.

I thought, You should know. Because he reminded me so strongly of a heroin addict I knew up North when I was just a cadet. 'Who… ?' I began.

'No names,' Death reminded me.

'And I've *got* to ask – sorry – where's Dana running to?'

'And I gotta *not* tell you,' said Death with his death's head grin.

'Well, thanks,' I said. 'Do you still want my lunch?'

'Nah,' Ginger said. 'We was just rattling your cage. We had fish fingers and chips at the shelter. And we'll be having chicken curry and rice tonight. All for free.' He fumbled in his pocket, brought out a pack of tobacco and retreated to the shelter of the church to roll his cigarette.

Death said, 'I'll take half.'

'Want to sit in the unit?' I asked, opening the wrapping.

'No. The others are watching.'

I handed him half my lunch. 'Anything you want to tell me?'

'No.' He took a big bite. 'Except I wasn't always like this.'

'What happened?' Because sometimes all you've got to give is five minutes.

162

'I was a nurse,' he said with his mouth full. 'I burned out. Something went wrong with my head. And then I got cancer.' He coughed. 'My mates call me Lucky.'

'I'm sorry,' I said, rather than stand silent like an idiot. 'Well, I certainly got you wrong. I thought you were a junky.'

'That's one bullet I ducked,' he said. 'I meant what I said – I fucking hate dealers. Nothing you can do about the Countdown King, is there?'

'Not without a name,' I said.

'You'll be gone by nightfall,' he said. 'I gotta live here.'

I waited while Death walked away before finishing my own half of lunch. It wasn't as soggy as I was.

'Where've you been?' McNabb said. 'Who's the junky? You were supposed to wait in the car. Can't you do *anything* right?'

'Probably not,' I murmured sadly, wiping pickle off my upper lip. I noticed that McNabb had a dusting of fine white sugar on his tie. Conclusion: he'd been offered doughnuts at One Stop Shop. He never refused doughnuts.

'Well, you're driving me to the hospital,' he said. 'You'd better get that right. Mrs Bron's just come out of surgery. So maybe we'll get an answer or two from a reliable source. I don't want to leave it to Perkins' mate, Suzie – she'll be an even wetter shower than he is. I hate community cops. Did I say?'

'Might have,' I said, turning the key. Two sodden cops sitting side by side in a confined space gave the unit the smell of mouldy bread. The windows steamed up immediately.

I found my way out of central Bath by following the Bristol signs. McNabb was right about the traffic system. Bath was a town designed for horses. Cars always seemed to be facing in the wrong direction.

He wasn't going to give me any information voluntarily. Information is power in his world, and power is to be kept tucked inside a clenched fist.

'What about the CCTV?' I asked in the end. 'Did you get to see anything?'

He grunted disgustedly. 'Didn't even get inside the bunker. Had to kick our heels till the supervisor deigned to come out and talk. Know what? I bet their famous system was down. I bet they fucked up royally and no one wants to admit it. No one wants to admit they should never have moved us out of Bath. They need us and they're too busy covering their arses to say so.'

Maybe I should leave the force and train to be a CCTV observer. Then I could deal with pictures, not personalities. Or blood. But I'd have to rely on unreliable technology and sit in a dark room watching TV all day. Which sounded quite restful compared to a car trip with McNabb. And at least I'd know when lunchtime was. But maybe I wouldn't know who I was working for. Because I suspected that the kind of penny-pinching city that cut its police force to the bone would farm out its surveillance to a penny-pinching private security firm.

McNabb said, 'So what did you do while I was getting nowhere at sodding One Stop Shop?'

Reluctantly I told him what Death and Ginger told me.

He said, 'I thought you people were supposed to have a reputation for brains. Instead you put the Ass into Manasseh.'

My brother's a history professor, my sister's an architect – while I am trying to find a hospital, trapped in a unit that smells of mouldy bread, with a man who gets off on making me crazy. Brains? Who needs 'em? Eh – tell me that?

They'll never forgive me in this area for the one time I put family before the force.

Bath's parking problems extended to the Royal United Hospital. McNabb ordered me to let him off at the main entrance, and then find somewhere legal to park. But before he could open his door a sleek silver grey Audi bristling with antennae pulled in beside us.

'Oh crap,' McNabb said. 'CI-fucking-D. All I needed to make today perfect. Stay here.'

I watched as he bustled over to the two CID men – two hard-arses I recognised from Keynsham – huddling with them under the overhang in front of the hospital's automatic doors. They didn't seem overjoyed to see him either. The doors slid open and a tubby woman wearing a Special's high viz bib came out to join the group. She had greying blonde hair and no-nonsense body language which began to crumble after only two minutes in their company. I recognised the posture.

Five minutes later, having failed to make herself heard over the roaring testosterone, she approached me and let herself into the passenger side.

'Suzie,' she said, holding out her hand. I took it and introduced myself.

'Looks like we're surplus to requirements,' she said. 'Your boss says you're going off shift anyway. He said you're to give me a lift back to town.'

'Okay,' I said, starting the engine.

'I could catch the bus,' she offered without conviction.

'You're okay,' I said. As I drove off, out of the corner of my eye, I saw McNabb waving urgently at me. I pretended not to see him and accelerated away, saying, 'So, what's the story? Did you get to talk to Imogen Bron?'

'Lordy, what a mess!' She sighed. 'Know what? Some idiot rang in to say it was a mad Jihadist who stabbed Mrs Bron. That's why the big boys came over double quick.'

'They'll love that,' I said.

'Oh, they did. Bath was on some terrorist hit list someone found. Paranoia reigns supreme. Which is why they didn't want to listen to me. I know Mrs Bron was out of it, but her sister turned up and said we should arrest Imogen's ex-husband. They're recently divorced and he went dipsy-doodle about her getting custody of the kids, and him paying too much maintenance. He'd been threatening her. Oh no, said the big boys – that's just a *woman's* story – always concentrating on small personal fears when there's big important man-stuff to be scared of.'

I said, 'Everyone's scared of something.' I was thinking about Death's hatred of drug dealers.

'Me, I'm scared of losing my job and not being able to feed my dogs,' Suzie said. 'You've no idea how insecure everyone in Bath is feeling right now.'

'I'm beginning to get a hint,' I said. 'Have you heard of a drug dealer called the Countdown King?'

'Heard of him; never actually come across him. It's shameful – Bath's such a rich city, and beggars cluster round wealth. Sometimes I think that all we do is enforce parking regs and stop beggars hassling tourists. But can we afford the time or manpower to stop predators hassling *them*?'

'Apparently not,' I said. And we drove along in companionable silence for a few minutes.

Then she said, 'Your boss is awfully rude, isn't he?'

'If you believe what's written on the wall of the ladies' bog in Keynsham he's a "massive twat".' We smiled sympathetically at each other.

'Well then,' she said, after a short pause, 'maybe I won't tell you that he ordered me to instruct you to turn round and go straight back to pick him up after dropping me off.'

I could hear his voice ranting about the CID shoving him off his case. 'No proper information, no continuity. All I got is you. Why? Eh – tell me that?'

'You forgot,' I said, 'because… '

'Because I still have a report to write,' she said. 'Besides, I'm in a hurry. No, really. Can you drop me back at Milsom Street? I want to catch that Meet The Author event at the bookshop. He's my favourite writer – tells a cracking story. So, y'know, your boss's orders went clean out of my muddled little head.'

'What a shame,' I said.

So I drove back to Keynsham in peace, by myself.

Three weeks later I was transferred back to London. This was a great relief, but it meant that I never heard the end of the Bath story. Or stories. Because there's always more than one – it depends on your view point which one you accept.

At least, I thought, I'd never have to visit Bath again unless it was as a tourist.

HEALTH AND SAFETY

It was a warm August afternoon and the sun fell like a lover's hand on the back of my neck. I was walking away from the kitchen of a party-house, hoping for a couple of hours rest before a flock of bridesmaids showed up to make life hell.

My backpack was heavy because I carry all my kit with me. You can't trust hens even with a second-class stamp. After a few cocktails they're all thieves and vandals.

I cannot tell you how much I hate chief bridesmaids. They are anxious and peppy. They try to force booze into the others as quickly as possible, ensuring that their judgement will vanish along with their inhibitions. They are the ones who ring me in the middle of the night because they 'forgot' to tell me that two of the hens are gluten intolerant, one is sensitive to lactose, and the bride's little sister will die if she so much as sniffs a nut. Everything, in fact she should've told me at the planning stage.

I ask up front if any of the party has food allergies or religious prohibitions. There's even a form to fill in and sign. But does she? Oh no. She's so keen to acquire the services of a reasonably priced personal caterer that she keeps information about difficult eaters to herself.

'No problems,' she'll say, all perky and peppy.

I can't tell you how much of a problem the 'no problems' people are.

I am a professional. It's my job to deal with food allergies. But tell me about them while discussing menus, not at two in the morning when you've woken up depressed and anxious about a party for ten beginning in three days time.

So, I was thinking about Margie 'No Problems' Dawson in a mood of simmering fury while walking away from the hated henhouse. To distract myself I watched my own shadow. The low afternoon sun stretched it out ahead of me, and for a while I could kid myself that I was super-model tall and thin. I fantasised that there was a companion shadow walking beside mine – a broad-shouldered shadow so close to me that our hips merged.

My companion shadow's name was Axel – which distressed me in a different way: Axel had departed with most of my client list and my whole heart only three months ago. That was why I couldn't afford to give Margie 'No Problems' Dawson the push for lying to me.

No, there was only one shadow – mine. And there was only the illusion of height and a slender shape.

And then, out of nowhere, another shadow suddenly appeared to join mine. I heard nothing – no footsteps behind me. I felt nothing – no touch, no jostling. But I saw clearly on the pavement in front of me the shadow of someone seeming to interfere with my backpack.

I swung round fast, letting the backpack fall from one shoulder. I saw a woman. No. All I focussed on was a skinny hand, a claw, grasping my wallet and my phone.

The front flap of my pack gaped wide. Without thinking, my hand flew to my most precious possession – my set of Damascus knives. Almost of its own accord the handle of the santoku knife came out of its holster into my right hand. Not wanting to drop the fine blade on the stone paving, I gripped it tightly as I lashed out.

It's so weird what's crucial in a crisis. It wasn't the wallet holding cash, credit cards and driving licence, or my phone with its vital contact list. It was my insanely expensive set of knives. Did I want to save myself from harm, or worry about injuring another human being? No, I was protecting the blade and tip of a santoku knife.

And when I saw the thin red line on a human wrist split and blossom into a gush of blood my instinct told me to wipe the blade clean rather than to help the human being. What kicked in was a Health and Safety rule about never allowing human blood to contaminate food. So before even *seeing* the real problem, I was registering the fact that I'd used a vegetable knife on meat.

Then I saw a young woman with the body of an eating disorder.

Enormous, hollow eyes, wide with surprise, met mine. She looked down at her bleeding wrist, dropped my wallet and phone, and sank to her knees.

Someone erupted from a nearby car. A man shouted, 'What the hell you done? You kill her!'

At last my brain started to work. I shoved the knife into its holster, dropped the backpack on the ground and tore off the cotton scarf that was binding my hair. The woman was cradling her left hand in her right arm as if protecting a baby from bad weather. I grabbed her and started to wind the scarf around her wrist. She resisted me. But her wrist was hardly bigger than a pair of chopsticks.

'I'm trying to *help*,' I yelled at her.

'You attacked her,' the man said. 'She's afraid of you.' He snatched the scarf out of my hand and tried to wrap it tightly around the wound. But the woman struggled against him too. She scarcely had the strength of a day-old chick. He was clumsy and even though he was wrapping fast, he couldn't beat the blood.

Someone else said, 'Call an ambulance.'

Where was everyone coming from? One minute I'd been alone with my shadow, and now there were two men shouting at me and an anorexic woman at my feet, bleeding to death.

I picked up my possessions and tried to open my phone, but my fingers were slippery with blood, and shaking with shock. I dropped it. The glass cracked.

'Oh, for Chri'sake,' the new man said, and whipped out his own phone.

'She's a thief.' I found my voice at last. 'She was stealing…' I held out my wallet and broken phone as if they were evidence.

'I didn't see stealing,' said the kneeling man. 'I saw attack.'

'Honestly,' I babbled. 'When I turned around she had my things in her hand.'

'Be quiet,' said the second man. 'We must stop the bleeding. Hold her arm up, up, up, up.' He pulled his tie off and wrapped it tightly round the woman's arm above the elbow.

My hands were bloody. I took my dish towel out of my backpack and tried to wipe them. My phone and wallet were sticky. So was my precious santoku. The blood wouldn't come off without soap and water.

'Give me that.' The second man held his hand out for my dish towel with such authority that I gave it without question.

I always take my own dish towels to a job. They're boiled for at least half an hour as well as being bleached and ironed. If someone got ill because I'd wiped up with a dirty towel my reputation would be wrecked.

Now I watched the first man wad it into a pad while the second man held the thief's arm perpendicular, and I saw him secure it tightly over her gushing wrist with my blood-soaked headscarf. It's another law of hygiene: keep your hair out of your clients' dinner.

My teeth were chattering and my mind was running in circles while I stood, paralysed, watching two strangers trying to repair the damage I'd done.

'It was an accident,' I stammered. 'I was shocked. I hit out.'

'With a knife,' the first man said. 'You tell cops, eh? This is a knife crime.'

I hadn't thought about the police – just the ambulance. If the second man asked for help with a knife wound then of course the police would be informed. I was even more frightened.

'But she was stealing,' I whispered.

'Were you stealing?' The first man spoke directly to the skinny woman.

She said nothing. She gazed at me through strands of lank hair that looked as if it were dying too.

'Tell them,' I pleaded. But she just stared at me. Panic rose from my chest to my throat and tears began to slide down my cheeks. I sat down on the kerb to stop myself falling over.

The second man said, 'Don't you dare faint.'

He was helping. Maybe he would help me too. He was more comfortable-looking than the kneeling man.

He said, 'She hasn't run away.'

'She can't run,' the first man said. 'She's weak.'

'No, *her*.' The second man jerked his chin at me. 'She's going to be sick. She's a problem.'

'She should be sick. She should pay for this.' The thin aggressive man had been angry with me from the start. If he thought I'd attacked the woman for no reason he could only have seen half of what happened.

'I was protecting myself and my property.' I tried to make both of them believe me. 'Especially my knives. I'm a caterer – they're the tools of my trade.'

'What's your name?' The comfortable man looked hard at me.

'Becky Elias.'

'I don't think she's lying,' he said to the angry one. 'She can talk to the cops later. Now we must deal with this one.' He gestured to the woman. To me he said, 'You are allowed to protect yourself if you use reasonable force.'

The angry one butted in, 'This is reasonable?'

His hands and clothes were wet with the woman's blood.

'I want to do the right thing,' I said feebly.

The comfortable one said, 'The right thing is to save this one here. Write down your address, Becky Elias, and give it to me. Then leave. You are not helping.'

'You trust her?' The angry one turned on the big one.

'The police will find her,' he said.

I was crying now. I wanted him to put his arms around me and tell me that I would be forgiven. I fished in my backpack. Underneath the knife holster and the sticky santoku I found the notebook I write all my lists and instructions in.

'She won't stay,' the angry man said. 'She's a tourist – she carries a backpack.'

The softer one looked in my bag. 'She's a cook,' he said. 'She carries the tools of her trade.'

I tore a sheet out of the book and wrote the address of the B and B on it. I handed it to the man who trusted me.

'Go,' he said. 'We'll deal with this.'

'Will she be alright?' I thought maybe I shouldn't leave.

'You better hope so,' the angry one said.

'An ambulance is coming. Let us worry about her. You're in the way.'

That was the permission I needed. I scurried away like a rat in a gutter. The sun was still behind me, but now my shadow looked hunched and mean.

*

Margie 'No problems' Dawson had ordered asparagus sushi for finger food, with homemade mayonnaise and champagne. The main course featured venison escallops with pureed potatoes, served with a Barolo 2006. Last, I'd made a strawberry cream (lactose-free) sponge (gluten-free) with more champagne – the bride's favourite foods.

I'd been pleased because a lot of it could be made in advance and chilled. I was more grateful now because my usually orderly mind had turned feral. Images of knife and blood, blame and denials, bared their teeth and tore my neat to-do list to shreds.

I concentrated on trying to reconstruct the timings Margie had given me. Party games would take place between courses but the meal had to finish at eleven sharp because the limo would arrive at eleven-thirty to transport the hens to the first city-centre club. As soon as they'd gone I was to make humus and Mediterranean vegetable wraps for when they got home. Also I would prep brunch. That would be between midday and two when the masseurs and reflexologist were due.

I looked at my lists. They were lying on the bed because my hands were shaking too much to hold them steady enough to read. Was there any point in studying them? I was waiting for the police.

I'd scrubbed my knife and hands. I stared at the santoku. It was a thing of beauty, but would I ever be able to chop carrots again after seeing how easily it sliced through human flesh?

My phone's screen was cracked, but it worked. Should I ring Margie 'No Problems' Dawson, or Kath, the event planner who'd recommended me? What would I say? That their caterer was in danger of arrest for murder? But I couldn't bear to tell anyone what had happened. So I showered and washed my hair. When the knock came on the door I wanted to look clean and innocent.

I dressed in my work clothes – a tailored grey trouser suit and a white shirt, decorated only by some discreet pin-tucks. I tied my hair back and bound it with a silver-grey scarf. I wanted to look sober and professional while also seeming warm and approachable. An hour passed and then it was time for me to leave.

I looked at my phone. It hadn't rung, so I told Mrs Landlady the approximate time I expected to return. I did not tell her the address of the hen house. The police would have to wait till I'd finished work.

Mrs Landlady gave me a key saying, 'I'll be asleep by the time you get back so I'll thank you not to slam doors.'

'What's the name of the nearest hospital?' I asked.

'St Stephen's. Why?'

'A young woman was hurt in, er, an accident. I was just wondering what happened to her.' It's so despicably easy to tell the truth dishonestly.

I left the lodging house and hurried back to the hen house. I didn't look at my shadow, and it was a relief to fall straight into work mode.

Kath turned up with armfuls of flowers and nets full of pink balloons. As the sun went down and she lit the lamps the reception room began to look festive and childish.

'All parties resemble children's parties these days,' Axel told me once when we were catering the 80th birthday party of a successful barrister. We'd spent nearly a week making and icing a cake that looked like a steam train circa 1935. The cake drew a standing ovation. It took the two of us to carry it. We worked well together. We created together, we shared the load. Then he met Estelle, an 'actress' filling in as wait staff. Now I carry the load alone.

Anger isn't helpful when you're setting out champagne glasses. It used to be pure grief, but grief isn't helpful when you're trying to rebuild your business almost from scratch. There's more energy in rage; more destruction too. I saw the dead-eyed woman again. Had I been thinking about Axel when her shadow appeared on the pavement in front of me? Had I been wishing I'd hurt him as much as he'd hurt me? If only I'd just hit her. I might have cracked her wrist, but I wouldn't have had to watch her life-blood drain away.

'Are you okay?' Kath asked. She's just as perky as Margie but she's better at it – she's been running this, and four other party houses, for over six years.

'I'm fine,' I said.

'Have you eaten?' And then, distracted by a wayward balloon, 'I say, those asparagus thingies look simply yummy.' She took one.

'Perfect.' She smiled, relieved she'd recommended me to Margie. 'I know everyone says "save the best till last" but in our business it pays to start with the best. By the time they get to that beautiful sponge pudding no one will be sober enough to tell it from a pot of cold tapioca.'

In the ten quiet minutes before Margie was due Kath and I systematically ran through our lists. At one moment I looked up and saw her shadow on the kitchen wall. I thought of the angry man. What had he told the police? When would they come? The accusation – you slashed a woman with a sharp knife, cutting her to the bone, and you stood there wasting precious seconds until two strangers showed up and fought to save her life.

But the police hadn't come. Did that mean Ms Hollow Eyes was still alive? I felt my phone in my pocket. I should ring St Stephen's and find out.

I watched competent Kath. She'd know what to do. But Kath was not a friend. She was a client. She would not recommend a suspected murderer to her chief bridesmaids. She's a party planner, not a charity.

Margie rolled in on a blast of night air with the photoboard. We set up the easel and helped decorate it with floating balloons and swags of fairy lights.

In the middle was a studio portrait of the nearly-bride, Cheryl, smiling angelically, maybe aged eighteen, looking forward to uni. Around this innocent image were smaller photos following her descent into drunken depravity: stoned on the floor of a Student Union bar; dancing with three drunk guys in Magaluf wearing only a feather boa above the waist; topless and hungover at someone else's hen party – pictures of a young woman having a good time. All the good times involved sex, drink and humiliation.

The first guests arrived and Kath left. A little later the last hen led in the bride-to-be, blindfolded, giggling, disoriented. They gathered around her, a perfumed, joyful coven helping her to squeal with delight and surprise at the arrangements. I opened the fourth bottle of champagne.

*

Walking back to the lodging house in the small hours of the morning, I took no notice of the shadows cast by street lamps. But I kept turning to look over my shoulder. I was convinced someone was following me.

The lodging house was dark and silent. There was no note from Mrs Landlady on the hall table, no note pushed under my bedroom door. I showered quickly and quietly. The white easy-iron sheets clung, cold, to my damp skin, and the artificial fibre-filled pillow accepted my guilty head without protest. But when I closed my eyes I saw a woman bandaged from hand to elbow, attached precariously to life, transfused blood dripping into her veins to replace what she'd lost in my moment of panic.

I turned on the bedside light again, took my phone off its charger and looked up the number of St Stephen's Hospital. Then I found my earphones and plugged them in, comforted myself with Leonard Cohen and woke to the alarm at nine-thirty.

This was too easy. I hated my cowardice. So after brushing my teeth I called St Stephen's. There was an interminable wait while someone with an accent I couldn't recognise put me on hold. I was halfway to work before a brusque voice with a Midlands accent told me that unless I could supply him with a name and convince him I was a blood relative he could give me no information.

At the hen house Zahara, Kath's cleaner, was sighing and trying to put the reception room to rights without using the vacuum cleaner. Hens need peace and quiet on a morning after.

The room was now festooned with party poppers, toilet paper and dead sparklers. Three posing pouches hung from the light-fitting – one gold, one silver and one scarlet. The no-smoking rule had been ignored.

Zahara showed me the downstairs bathroom. A quantity of last night's skilfully cooked dinner was now on the tiles and porcelain. It was one of those sights that convinces me that my life has no purpose whatsoever.

We sighed in unison. It says something about party culture that neither of us was shocked.

I went to the kitchen and saw that the hens had played cricket with the wraps that hadn't been gobbled. Humus and Mediterranean vegetables were smeared over floor, window and walls.

I rolled up my sleeves and got busy. When the surfaces were hygienic again I made a pot of the strong mint tea Zahara likes and set a few custard creams on a plate.

She washed her hands and sat down at the kitchen table. She lives in this city, so I said, 'Is St Stephen's the only hospital with an emergency room in this part of town?'

She thought for a moment. 'Yes. Only one. But serious cases sometimes go to United. Why?'

So I looked up United's number. And told her a version of yesterday's story that didn't make me look as despicable as I'd actually been.

She blinked at me. 'This woman was stealing? You hear nothing, feel nothing?'

'I know I don't pay enough attention,' I began.

But she waved a hand to stop me. 'This woman is, how do you say? Yes, professional. An artist.'

It was my turn to blink at her. But at the same time we heard a door bang upstairs and a pitiful voice began to wail, 'Coffee, coffee.'

Zahara grimaced and took her tea and biscuits through to the dining room to begin work again.

I put beans into the coffee grinder. There's no finer method for keeping hungover hens out of the kitchen than turning on a coffee grinder. I made two large thermos pots of strong coffee and set them out with milk and sugar on trays in the reception area.

'Oh God,' said Margie Dawson, who had managed to exchange her party dress for a pair of pyjamas but hadn't cleaned last night's makeup off her face.

The bride, Cheryl, was still in her purple satin dress. She looked down her own cleavage and said, 'It's when you find your mascara's dripped into your bra that you know you had a good time.'

'Oh God,' groaned Margie. 'Did you have a good time?'

'The bra says "yes". I can't remember a thing.'

The rest of the hens trailed down one by one looking like unwashed laundry. They'd seemed as sleek as seals when they went out last night, bouncing with anticipation and bubbling with champagne. Now they collapsed and sprawled over the chairs and sofas.

After the afternoon massage and reflexology the hens were booked into a West End musical. There was a pre-show snack to make – shrimp tartlets with a quinoa salad. And a post-theatre pudding – *tarte aux apricots* – although how you make good gluten and dairy-free *tarte aux apricots* is a secret I will take to my grave. I certainly never told Axel. That's one piece of my ingenuity he couldn't steal. He nearly stole my knives. I caught him at the door with my holster in his hand. 'Those are mine,' I said coldly.

'Oops, sorry,' he said. 'Honest mistake.'

'There's nothing honest about you.' I hugged my knives to my unloved chest. 'And as for your mistake, her name is Estelle and you deserve each other.'

'Ooh, bitter,' he said.

'Like your mango sorbet,' I said. 'We had complaints about that. You don't know a ripe mango from oven cleaner.' I didn't begin to cry till he slammed the door.

The limo left early for the West End so I was able to get back to the lodging house before Mrs Landlady's bedtime. She scurried into the hall at the sound of my key.

'A plainclothes police officer came to see you,' she said, jagged lines of anxiety scraping at her eyes and mouth. 'I didn't know where you were. I could've looked in your room for the address, but I don't suppose you'd want him turning up at your place of work, would you?'

'That's very thoughtful,' I said, as calmly as I could. 'What was it about?'

'I think it was that accident you witnessed.'

'Okay,' I said as if my heart hadn't jolted every time I thought about it.

'He was hard to understand,' she went on. 'Honestly, you never know who they're going to take into the police force. Half the teachers at the school up the road are from Somalia or somewhere.'

Mrs Landlady thinks she has old-fashioned values. She doesn't realise she's a racist, and because I'm not very brave, I have never told her I am a Jew. She runs a clean orderly house that I can afford, but one day she'll force me to stand my ground. And then I'll have to find somewhere else to stay when I'm working for Kath.

'He asked when I expected you home and he wanted your phone number. I hope I did the right thing.'

At that moment my phone rang, making us both jump. I didn't want Mrs Landlady to overhear so I turned away and took the call while going upstairs. But it was only Kath, who was organising a reception for a tenth anniversary in December. Might I be available?

I was just scribbling the date in my diary when the phone rang again.

'Miss Becky Elias?' a deep male voice asked.

'Yes.' My heart sank. I looked at my watch. It was after midnight. No one but cops and event planners would ring so late. No one but freelance cooks with guilty consciences would answer.

'I will come to your house.'

'No. Wait.' I said, panicking. 'Are you the police?'

'Of course.'

'Then I'll come to the police station tomorrow. You can't come here – people are sleeping. How is the young woman who I... who was cut?'

'She is dead,' he said flatly. 'This is a crime.'

A fist hit me in the stomach. 'It was an accident. I swear. I never meant to hurt anyone.'

'I come now. This is murder. Witness saw.'

'I'll wait for you outside,' I offered, defeated. This was terrible. I was responsible for a hollow-eyed woman's death. Me! She was a pickpocket. But so what? I caused her to bleed to death. I saw the santoku knife in my hand. I saw the lovely blade flash in the afternoon sun as I struck out. A scared, thoughtless act of self-protection. Two seconds later, the damage was done and I watched the scarlet flowers bloom.

Axel doesn't look after his knives. I do. A few quick flicks with the sharpener before and after use keep the blades razor-sharp. It only takes a couple of seconds. Axel doesn't realise what a waste of time and energy it is to work with a dull blade. Or maybe he does, and that was why he was stealing mine.

If only he'd succeeded. If only the santoku I'd laid my hand on yesterday afternoon had been Axel's blunt one. If only I wasn't so proud of my knives.

Sadly I took the knife holder out of my backpack and laid it gently on the dresser. I packed a clean shirt, my sponge bag and two pairs of knickers instead. If I was going to spend the night in police custody I didn't want my knives with me.

On the street outside I thumbed through my contact list and found that I didn't know any solicitors. I'd never needed one before. I'd have to ask for the help of a duty solicitor at the police station. And that raised other questions, like, would I qualify for legal aid? And if I didn't, how could I afford representation? I'd been doing fine, well, *Axel* and I had been doing fine. His charm with clients, his talent at cutting a deal, coupled with my... My what? Reliability, knowledge of health and safety rules and sharp knives?

'No!' I said out loud. 'Don't do this to yourself. You're a good cook. You have flare, and a feel for food.'

But the woman Axel left three months ago replied, 'Yeah, so *that's* why you're working for a woman with a degree in Event Planning, while Axel walked off with the banking contract. That's why you're waiting for the police outside a cheap lodging house, while Axel's sleeping between my sheets in a king-size bed.'

A car door slammed and a man crossed from the dark side of the road to where I stood under a street lamp. I hadn't noticed him arrive so I was startled. He was in plainclothes – a lightweight windbreaker over jeans. The brim of his baseball cap was pulled low over his eyes which made him tilt his head back and look down his nose at me.

'You are Becky Elias?' he said as he approached.

'Yes.' I held my hand out.

'Get in the car,' he said, ignoring my hand.

'What's your name?' I asked following him across the road. 'Where are you taking me?'

'Where do you think I'm taking you?'

'Yes, but which police station?'

'You'll find out.' He opened the back door for me.

I got in. I wanted to make a connection with him, to break down this angry indifference and show how helpful and well-meaning I was. I wanted him to realise that someone as inoffensive as I was couldn't possibly, with anger and malice, have sliced through the wrist of a sneak-thief. Just a few seconds before I became a killer I was the helpless victim.

And yet, I recalled, the first man who had run to help the thief didn't think so. I felt his contempt and anger all over again as I sat in the back of a car that reeked of cigarette smoke. Obviously he hadn't seen the thief reach into my backpack, but he had seen my fury as I spun round and lashed out with the santoku.

He knew I'd meant to hurt her.

'I didn't mean to hurt anyone,' I said now. 'She was stealing from me and I was frightened.'

The policeman didn't even look at me in the rearview mirror.

I thought that if I'd spun round and seen Axel with his hand in my bag I'd have used the point of the knife. I'd have pierced his heart – revenge for smashing mine. That's what the first witness saw – rage and revenge.

I *was* guilty. Strangers like this plainclothes cop who wouldn't meet my eyes could see through my calm competence to the knife-sharp anger and grief beneath the skin.

The smell of cigarette smoke was making me sick. I twisted in my seat to open the window.

'Stop that!' the cop snapped. He'd been watching me after all.

I withdrew my hand as if it had been burned, and as I did so I saw, by the light of a shop window, a piece of cloth that I thought

I recognised. Stealthily I hooked a finger round it and drew it closer. Yes! There was no doubt in my mind at all.

'Stop the car,' I cried. 'I'm going to be sick.' I retched. I wasn't pretending.

'Don't dare to be sick.' The cop turned for an instant, and what he saw made him pull over to the kerb.

I tumbled out onto the pavement – my backpack in one hand, my headscarf, so stiff with dry blood that it felt starched, in the other.

Instead of being sick I scrambled to my feet and started running back up the road we'd just driven down.

There was an ominous whine behind me. I looked round. The plainclothes cop was reversing after me.

I ran faster. But I'm a cook, not an athlete. The cop caught up.

Thank God this city never sleeps: traffic was passing sporadically in both directions. I ran into the middle of the road, jumping up and down, windmilling my arms. Cars, vans, lorries hooted, yelled, swerved around me. No one stopped. But at least they noticed me. The plainclothes cop just rolled down his window and waited.

'What's going on?' I yelled at him. 'Where were you taking me?'

He didn't answer. Either he couldn't hear or he was too disgusted to answer.

'What's my scarf doing in your car?' I shouted. Surely that was all wrong? And this road – didn't it carry on South, straight across the river? Why was he driving me from North of the city all the way to South of the river?

At last I saw a taxi with its For Hire light lit. I would've lain down in front of it to make it stop, but dancing and flailing my arms like a lunatic worked.

'Are you mad?' the driver yelled at me.

'I'm scared,' I yelled back. 'I'll pay you double.'

'If you're *meshuga*, that won't help.'

The cop was getting out of his car.

I said, 'I'm not *vild* or *dul* either. Please… '

'Okay, okay,' he grumbled. 'So you know a little Yiddish. Get in.'

I got in. 'Would you do a U-turn and go back North?' I asked.

He nearly stopped the cab to throw me out. 'It's after two in the morning. Against my better judgement I stop for a mad woman who knows some Yiddish, but will she let me go home to my wife and kids who all think I'm made of money, which I'm not, and if I had any I'd spend it on a holiday in Malta or a therapist, because I'm telling you if anyone deserves to be *meshuga*, *dul,* or *vild*, it's me, lady. Are you listening?'

But I was watching the car behind, which had done a U-turn and was following the cab back North.

'I'm very, very grateful,' I said. 'But did you notice the car that did a U-turn just after you did? He's following me.'

'What's his game?' the driver said. 'Do you owe him money?'

'No. He said he was a plainclothes policeman, or I would never have got in his car but there's something wrong.'

'No shit,' the driver said. 'If that's a cop's car you can wrap me in brown paper, stamp me, and post me to Blackpool. What do you want me to do?'

I scrabbled in my bag for my notebook and wrote as much of the following car's number plate as I could see. Just in case, I copied down the driver's name and cab licence number. Harry Greene was right – the following car was too old and shabby to be credible. The radio antenna was bodged from a wire coat hanger.

Eventually I said, 'Well, if he's in the police force he won't mind if we go to a police station, will he?'

'Now you're talking,' Harry said. 'So alright – you're legit. Let's see if we can find a cop shop that stays open all night. I'll call the dispatcher.'

But the dispatcher came up blank. 'Effing hell!' Harry said in wonder. 'You should've been kidnapped during banking hours. That was your mistake. Find a cop awake and out of his kip at two in the morning? Tell you what, send him an email and he'll get to it by lunchtime. Or how about you friend him on Facebook? That'll do the trick. Cops nowadays? Don't make me laugh – they're as much protection as a cardboard bomb shelter.'

In the end we drove to Scotland Yard. There were lights on in the building, but the entrance and the lobby didn't look open for business. It didn't matter. As soon as we turned the corner and it was obvious where the cab was setting me down, the grungy old Honda overtook us and shot away.

Harry watched it go. 'Looks like our boys in blue got a reputation they don't deserve no more. Your knight in shining armour was a tired, old taxi driver with a bad back who needs to lose some weight.'

I couldn't disagree. I gave him fifty-five quid which was all I had on me and he gave me five back in case I needed it for the tube. I gave him my business card and promised I'd cater his twentieth wedding anniversary for free. He gave me his card in case I needed a witness for the night's events.

I sat down, out of sight from the road, behind the concrete bunker blocks that protect the Metropolitan Police headquarters from the public. I tried to tell my own story to myself in a way that sounded reasonable-ish, and didn't make me look too stupid. But I couldn't think properly. So I got my phone out and dialled 999, although there wasn't an emergency any more – as the woman in the great call-centre in the sky told me. She was sympathetic but advised me to go back to my lodging for a few hours sleep. She'd make sure someone would talk to me in the morning.

'This time,' she said in a teacherly way, 'ask to see their warrant cards. And if you're in any doubt, ring and check. Okay?'

I felt like a total dip-brain: I'd been expecting the police. Mrs Landlady said a policeman was looking for me. The guy said he *was* the police. So as far as I was concerned any contrary evidence could be ignored. But given what I now knew, someone claiming to be a cop working outside normal business hours was only the first clue I'd missed.

So I leaned against my backpack, closed my eyes, watching for the hundredth time the thin line of cut flesh well up and spill its scarlet waterfall.

Three months ago I would've called Axel to come and get me. Who could I call now? Not Kath or Mrs Landlady. Not my parents in Leicester, not my sister in Australia. They may care but they have no power to help. Not the police who have the power, but don't care anymore. Like Axel. Although I'd paid for half of it the car was in his name so he took it.

When I began to see office cleaners arriving I got up and took the tube north to Mrs Landlady's house.

I wasn't due at the hen house till ten so I showered and lay down for an hour, sliding stealthily into sleep.

I went to work early and was grateful to find that the hens had been more continent than the night before. Zahara, who unlike the cops, works overtime and weekends, was having an easier job too. She's been through a lot and seems to be as unjudgemental as a woman can be, so I told her about my blundering into a strange man's car. She drank her mint tea and listened closely.

'Is he English, this man?' she asked.

'He just sort of barked orders,' I said. 'I was so alarmed that I didn't notice an accent. But Mrs Landlady did.'

'What accent?'

I tried to remember. Put me down in the fruit and veg section of any market and I'll notice what's fresh, what's ripe and juicy. But accents?

'Describe,' Zahara said, not very hopefully.

'It was dark.' But I did my best.

'Your scarf was in the back seat of his car?'

'Yes. But it shouldn't have been.'

'No.' She nodded. 'It should not.'

I said, 'If it was of no account it should have stayed in the hospital or the ambulance. If it was evidence the police would've kept it properly.'

'The man who was helping the woman took it?'

We stared at each other. She went on, 'This man – was he the man in the car?'

'The angry man? No.'

Zahara shrugged impatiently. 'And the other one?'

'The nice one?'

'The one you trusted to tell your name and address?'

'No, it wasn't him either. Oh… I see what you mean. How did the so-called plainclothes policeman get hold of it?'

Zahara almost laughed at me, so I knew she thought I was missing something obvious. Not for the first time I wished I spoke her language, or that she spoke mine more fluently. She was way too intelligent to be cleaning up after incontinent hens for less than minimum wage. But Zahara was an illegal immigrant with a child to support. She worked three jobs.

Now she said, 'This man you told him your name… ' She frowned in frustration and took a breath to start again, but we were interrupted by the hens emerging from their nests and coming down in a riot of nightwear demanding tea, coffee and freshly squeezed orange juice.

*

The last party event took place at the brunch. They had each bought Cheryl a piece of underwear, and a prize would be given to the most obscene.

It was while the women were squealing with raunchy laughter, and Cheryl was being festooned with peek-a-boo bras, crotchless panties and see-through teddies that two fresh-faced uniformed constables knocked on the door, asking for me. Even after it was explained that they weren't strippers, the hens, over-excited by more champagne, kept intruding into the kitchen shouting, 'Get 'em off'.

The constables seemed to enjoy the situation. I fed them an early lunch of crispy bacon and egg sandwiches because I wanted to keep them happy till the guests had packed up and gone. Until then I was forced to remain attentive to one nearly-bride and ten demanding hens.

But I told the whole story as best I could. 'I'm not good with the unexpected,' I said. 'I can deal with kitchen crises just fine. But thieves and kidnappers?'

They nodded and watched while I reloaded the cappuccino machine, buttered a gluten-free teacake, sliced and juiced three more oranges.

I hoped I was impressing them with my strengths, because otherwise my story was a catalogue of my weaknesses. Over-reaction, panic, cowardice, dithering, passivity and stupidity were just a few of the finer points.

They looked like brothers, Kyle and Sean, and they were both soft-spoken and polite. If I'd know that was what real policemen were like nowadays, I would never have got in a car with a man who barked at me so rudely. But what I know about the police is what I receive from films and telly where cops are often the enemy.

'So,' Sean began gently, 'the woman was very thin, with lank shoulder-length dark brown hair. You can't remember what she was wearing, but it might have been jeans?'

'She was very good at what she did. I never heard her, or felt her unzip my backpack. If I hadn't been looking at my own shadow I wouldn't have noticed a thing till I got home.'

'But as it was, you took a knife out of your bag and –'

'It wasn't like that.' I fetched my knife holster and laid it reverently on the table in front of the two constables. It was made of leather. There was a pouch for each knife and the knife handles protruded. It was designed to roll into a neat bundle which would protect the blades. I showed them where each knife went and where the sharpening steel was placed.

'These knives cost a small fortune,' I explained. 'They're the best I could afford, but more than that – I chose them because they're balanced and weighted almost as if they were designed just for me.' I held my strong, competent right hand up. 'I'd be lost without them. I thought the woman was stealing them.'

'Was she?' Kyle asked.

'No,' I admitted. 'She had my purse and my phone in her hand. But I didn't see that till later. I was just afraid for my knives.'

'Show me which knife,' Kyle said.

I showed them the slender, shallow-curved santoku. 'I didn't *choose* this knife. It was just the first thing under my hand when I was scared.'

'That's a very dangerous weapon,' Sean said.

'It isn't a weapon. It's a tool.'

'In the wrong hands,' he said.

For an answer I took a carrot out of the fridge and chopped it into nineteen perfect roundels before either of them could blink. Their eyes widened in surprise.

'Mine are not the wrong hands,' I said.

'They were on Friday,' Sean said. 'But I really can sympathise with your point of view.'

'Why didn't you call 999?' Kyle asked.

'Because one of the men said he'd already done it.'

Absently, Kyle picked up a carrot disc and put it in his mouth. It had been chopped by the knife that sliced the thief. But I didn't remind him of that. He said, 'No such call was received.'

'And,' Sean added, 'we've checked the hospitals and private ambulance services and no woman suffering from a knife wound was picked up, or admitted to a casualty department at the relevant time.'

I stared at them both, astonished.

'No act of violence was reported,' Kyle persisted. 'So as far as we're concerned, no crime has been committed.'

'But *I've* reported it.' I turned away to wash carrot juice off the santoku hoping they wouldn't see the relief on my face.

'But there's no evidence for what you've told us,' Kyle said.

'Maybe we should be looking for a body,' Sean said, eyeing me carefully.

I sat down heavily, only to leap up again when a hen dressed only in hot pink underwear poked her head around the kitchen door to request Sean and Kyle to strip for her, and to ask me to provide her with soda water. Not to drink, she explained, but to remove a red wine stain from her white jeans. Stain removal isn't my job, but Zahara had left just two minutes after the police arrived. So I went upstairs and helped. It wasn't a wet stain, so soda water didn't work. Luckily there was plenty of vodka in the fridge – the theory being that strong alcohol will dilute weaker alcohol. It does, and I made quite a good job of it.Downstairs again, I laid the bloody scarf, carefully sealed in the sort of Ziploc bag I usually use for freezing chopped vegetables, on the table in front of the two constables.

'Isn't this proof that someone lost a lot of blood?' I was worried by their conclusion that they couldn't do anything because there was no evidence that anything had happened. 'That's my scarf. It was used to bind the woman's wrist. It turned up in the false policeman's car.' I gave them the page out of my notebook on which I'd written what I could see of his number plate.

'And this,' I went on, 'is Harry Greene's business card. He picked me up on Vauxhall Bridge Road after I'd escaped. He saw we were being followed to Scotland Yard. My landlady talked to the guy who claimed to be a police officer. Isn't this proof that something weird happened?'

'We'll write it all in our report,' Kyle said reassuringly.

But I suspected they'd only stayed as long as they had because I'd promised them some leftover *tarte aux apricots*. I sighed and divided the remaining slice between them.

'You really are a fantastic cook,' Sean said.

'Magic,' Kyle said with his mouth full.

It was heart-warming to be praised by someone sober enough to taste my work. But I wished they would take some action and not just write a report destined to moulder on someone else's desk.

I have not been very confident since the day Axel left me. It's as if I'd become over-lookable to *everyone*; not just him. He'd turned his back, so everyone else would too. He drained my value out of me by choosing another woman.

I had one last try. I said, 'Could you, just for a moment, look at my story and assume it's true?'

'We aren't saying you're lying,' Sean said, wiping his lips and gazing regretfully at his empty plate. 'It's just there's no evidence.'

'If you accept that the woman was an excellent thief, that the blood on the scarf is hers – but she wasn't taken to hospital by the two men who said they were helping her, and that the scarf turned up where it had no business turning up – what sort of story contains facts like that?'

'What're you saying?' Kyle asked.

I was thinking about Zahara. She hadn't said anything directly but she had from the beginning seemed to suspect something about the two men who were helping. She hinted she thought I was a fool to have told one of them my name. And she'd called the thief an artist. Something in her experience of the world was informing her – the same experience that today made her leave abruptly when the police arrived. I was beginning to accept her point of view. England was not a safe place for everyone, and society's defenders weren't as eager to defend as I'd previously believed.

But I trudged on. 'What about a story that's about people who, officially, aren't here? And the people who prey on them?'

'Are you talking about illegal immigrants?' Kyle asked.

'Or refugees,' I stammered. 'I don't know.' I hadn't wanted to know Zahara's story. I should've asked if she'd arrived in a container truck or on an overcrowded boat. Had she swum ashore with her daughter clinging to her back, terrified in the dark? How much had she paid for the privilege, and to whom? Did she still owe someone money? Was that why she had to work three jobs?

Of course I didn't say any of this out loud. I watched as Kyle and Sean glanced at each other with raised eyebrows. They were polite enough not to roll their eyes, so I filled a plate with homemade chocolate chip shortbread. But I was running out of sweeteners.

Then Margie Dawson breezed into the kitchen. 'We're leaving now,' she said. She was still acting perky, but I could see she was exhausted.

'I hope it all went well,' I said, shaking hands with her.

'No problems. I just wanted to thank you – the food was delicious.' She turned to Kyle and Sean, 'Are you sure I can't persuade you to give the girls a last treat?' she cajoled, twinkling naughtily.

'Sorry to disappoint,' Kyle said, grinning.

'Pity,' she said. In her world everything was entertainment and it was safe to tease policemen.

The hens straggled down from their bedrooms, bumping wheelie cases on the stairs, stumbling out into the afternoon sun and into taxis. I saw them off, wishing Cheryl a beautiful wedding because that was all she was thinking about, not the marriage.

I went back to the kitchen and found the two constables preparing to leave.

'Don't worry,' Sean said. 'Everything you've told us will go to the proper department.' He fished in his bulging notebook for a card which he handed me saying, 'But if you have any further concerns here is the helpline number for our Customer Liaison Office.'

Then they were gone.

As soon as I was sure they were out of sight I rang Zahara to tell her the coast was clear. Then I loaded the dishwasher, bagged up all the kitchen waste and started swabbing surfaces and mopping the floor. Zahara likes me is because she doesn't have to clear up after me too.

She appeared in a rush, having lost time because of the police. She couldn't stop for tea and talk so I pitched in and helped. She scrubbed bathrooms, dusted, wiped and vacuumed bedrooms while I stripped and made up the beds with clean sheets.

At last, when three bags of rubbish had been left out for collection on Monday morning, she allowed herself ten minutes for a cup of mint tea sweetened with a spoonful of clover honey.

I told her what the cops had told me, asked her what she'd been thinking when she'd called the pickpocket an artist, and what it was she suspected about the three men in the story.

She said, 'The man who say he call the ambulance? He did not?'

I nodded.

'These people do not want to be seen. If this woman is hurt, if this woman is dead, no one must know.'

'Because?'

'Because.' She spread her hands and shrugged as if to say, 'It's obvious, isn't it?'

But it wasn't obvious to me. 'They're in this country without permission?'

'Perhaps. But if this woman is making money for them, stealing for them… ' She broke off again.

'Are you saying they're like Fagin and she… ?'

'I don't understand,' Zahara said. 'If she pretty, she whore for them, yes? If she clever with her hands, she steal for them. Or maybe she begs. She is not the only one.'

'But they don't care if she dies?' I was horrified. 'Who are they?'

'If she cannot work, she is no use to them. They own her. Why should they care?'

'But… but that's slavery. This is England.'

'Not for everyone. Nobody knows she is here, yes? This woman, she is more frightened of them than of policemen or dying.'

'But why? She could report them. The police would give her protection.'

Zahara rolled her eyes at my stupidity. 'And who will protect her family at home?'

'At home? Where?'

She shrugged. 'Anywhere the people are too poor to live. They must escape and they are forced borrow money to travel.'

She and I were about the same age, yet I felt just then as if she had lived a thousand years longer.

I didn't want to ask the next question because I didn't want to be responsible for the knowledge. But I took a deep breath. 'Do you owe anyone any money, Zahara? Do you have family back home?'

She smiled briefly. 'I thank you for asking. There is my cousin, me and my little Beyza. We came together. All the old ones are gone. Beyza is the only little one left. We paid our fare. No hostages. We are lucky.'

Then Kath bustled in. 'Any more tea in the pot? I'm gasping.'

She didn't like mint tea so I made her a pot of Earl Grey. While it was brewing she and Zahara took a tour of the house. Kath took the inventory list she always checks after a party finishes.

This time she came back saying, 'You'll never guess, one of the little cows actually unscrewed the soap dish from the shower stall. She would've nicked the toilet paper holder too but her nail file broke. Zahara showed me the pieces.'

I pretended to be shocked, but my head was still full of the huge, shadowy tragedies and crimes that Zahara's information conjured. With all that swirling around behind my eyes, it was hard to get excited about a soap dish.

Kath sat on Zahara's chair. Zahara left quickly. Sometimes at weekends when she's sure that Kath won't turn up, she brings Beyza to work with her. The little girl reads her school books at the kitchen table. She hardly ever speaks, but I know for a fact that her English is already better than Zahara's, and when there's time they read the storybooks together. Beyza never laughs and she won't accept so much as a spoonful of homemade ice cream from me unless her mother gives her permission.

'She's a good worker,' Kath said, listening as Zahara closed the street door. 'You don't suppose she stole the soap dish herself and then blamed one of the hens?'

'Absolutely not,' I said, outraged.

'She's very secretive. I always wonder.'

'She's one hundred percent honest.' If she was a thief, she wouldn't be working two other jobs or bringing up her daughter to be scrupulous too. I didn't mention any of this to Kath because I didn't know what Zahara wanted spoken about. I'd never had such a long conversation with her before and I thought it had only happened because *I* had been in trouble.

Now Kath changed the subject and asked if I was available to cater a funeral reception the next day.

'Short notice,' I complained.

'It's Jewish,' she said, looking embarrassed.

'I see,' I said. 'But I don't do kosher.' In fact, I know the Dietary Laws almost as well as I know British Health and Safety rules. But the restrictions and proscriptions, coupled with the fact that I'd have to have two sets of everything, make kosher catering impossible. I could barely afford the one set of Damascus knives when I bought them. 'There are specialist caterers,' I said now. 'I can give you the numbers of several good ones.'

'It's not Orthodox,' Kath said. 'Actually it's barely religious. Remember the Sorkins? You did a private party for the grandson's A-level results. They asked for you. Provided you don't serve ham sandwiches you'll be all right.'

I was pleased to hear that it wasn't one of the nice old couple who'd died. I accepted the job even though I really wanted to go home. But I felt too vulnerable to go back to Mrs Landlady's Bed and Breakfast. It was as if a subterranean, dangerous England had opened up at my feet – a place where the rules I lived by didn't apply; where the safeguards I thought I could rely on were impotent. I looked again at the card Sean had given me: Customer Liaison Office. It looked about as useful as a sugar umbrella.

I didn't want to explain any of this to buoyant, bubbly Kath who was one of the few party planners I hadn't lost to Axel. I simply said I'd had to vacate my room, and she gave me another address. Then she rang old Mrs Sorkin, and after making her own deal, passed the phone to me.

The dead relative was very old, Mrs Sorkin told me. What she needed was a buffet for, at most, twenty. None of the young people would come, she said sadly. It was a pity that the young had been protected from the past because, as she put it euphemistically, this was the last member of old Mr Sorkin's family to have lived with a tattoo on his arm.

We discussed blinis, cheese puffs, cold roast chicken slices and potato salad. She wanted a three-layered chocolate gateau as well.

She was of the generation that survived a world war and a holocaust, for whom sherry trifle was a luxury. I understood her as well as I understood my own grandmother who had kept cupboards full of canned goods, rice and dry pasta. Emergency rations, she'd say, almost laughing at herself, but not quite. Grandpa kept candles, matches, torch batteries and a tiny camping stove in his office room. Because, as he put it, 'You never know.'

Quaint, I used to think. But not any more.

I wrote notes and lists while talking to Mrs Sorkin. Kath watched, nodding. She too was a note-taker and list-maker. We agreed that as I wasn't going home, and the party house would be vacant until Tuesday night, I would make the chocolate gateau and roast the chickens in the oven here. She would help me transport food, extra tableware and glasses over to the mansion block in St Johns Wood in the morning and leave me to work. She'd come back with the wine and flowers while the family were in Golders Green cemetery. She would help with the serving.

'Thank god Mondays are slow,' she said. 'Jewish funerals can be a nightmare.'

Kath seems to assume that because I'm not religious I'm not a Jew. I didn't want to hear any more so I rushed off to Waitrose to do the shopping. I had to cook and move digs. It would be a busy afternoon and evening.

*

The new place was an airbnb: an elderly woman trying to make her pension go further by letting out her spare room one night at a time. She was nervous of strangers and kept apologising for her furniture. Apparently someone had complained online. I reassured her as best I could, although I felt my need for reassurance was greater than hers. All my spare anxiety centred on one question – had I killed an impossibly thin woman, or hadn't I? Sometimes the uncertainty comforted me – 'She's fine,' I'd tell myself at those moments. Perhaps my shock made me exaggerate

199

what I saw as a gush of blood. I knew from many kitchen accidents that a little blood could go a long way. The two men would've stopped the bleeding and the paramedics decided there was no need to take her to hospital. But…

But while the chickens were roasting in the party house oven and I was making the mayonnaise for the potato salad, I thought the doubt would kill me. How could I live the rest of my life, no, how could I even tackle baking a three-tiered chocolate gateau not knowing whether or not I was a murderer?

She's fine, I thought, as I rolled out and refrigerated the puff pastry.

No she isn't, I thought, as I finely chopped a handful of dill to give depth to the cream cheese.

I went to the police, I thought, scrubbing out the oven. They're the law – *they* must tell me if I'm a murderer or not. I can't do it on my own.

I added a dash of Eldorado rum to the cake ingredients. Rum and chocolate are a magical mix. At that moment I made a bargain with the god whose existence I denied – I would make the very best chocolate gateau it was in my power to make if he or she would keep my victim alive. I wouldn't charge the Sorkins for it and I would save a slice for the rabbi who would probably come to the reception after the funeral. I promised as well that if I had time I'd talk to him or her with an open mind.

I used the best dark chocolate, muscavado, golden caster sugar and cocoa. I beat in the most beautiful free range eggs. When the layers were baked to perfection I spread a thin layer of my own raspberry jam before the generous coating of ganache. By the time I'd smoothed on the rich dark topping and arranged the chocolate curls I was sure that I'd never made a finer cake.

I care, I told myself. I try. This cake is proof that I'm a good person. I cannot possibly be a killer.

Then I cleaned the kitchen and sorted everything ready for transport to St Johns Wood in the morning. Only then, comforted by magical thinking, did I allow myself a tot of the magical Eldorado rum.

It was very late when I called a cab. I closed and bolted the shutters, set the intruder alarm, let myself out and locked the front door.

I was alone in a dark street, waiting for a cab, scanning shadows, flinching at the touch of the wind on my face, jumping at the rattle of paper in the gutter.

But the taxi came quickly and took me safely to my new lodging. I didn't have a key but the anxious landlady had given me the code to the key safe next to the front door.

The safe was mounted below knee-height. Crouching down to enter the code saved me – the blow hit my backpack instead of my head. I fell forwards cracking my nose hard against the door jamb.

'Help!' I shrieked, shocked at the violence, blinded by the pain of my nose. 'Someone, help me!'

Last time I tried to protect my knives. This time I tried to protect myself. Quiet, unobtrusive Becky Elias had only her voice as a weapon. 'Help!' I screamed at the top of my voice to the sleeping world. 'Police!'

The police wouldn't come. But I was shouting with all the power of my lungs – to wake up residential London to what was happening in the dark, on their own quiet streets.

I screamed with such force I made myself retch. I could taste blood and chocolate. I thought, 'I'll die here, curled up on the doorstep of a nervous old woman.'

'Get up!' a man said. He wrenched my right arm backwards and tried to heave me to my feet. 'You're coming with us.'

'*No*,' I screamed. I wasn't going to help him. I was rigid with fright but I made my legs wilt like sweated spinach. He'd have to carry my dead weight.

'Get up,' he yelled, kicking my legs.

Without any warning, the front door opened. Light poured out like spilled custard and my nervous old landlady appeared – dithery and ridiculous in a grey and white polka dot dressing gown.

'Sod off,' shouted the man.

'No,' she said shakily. With a trembling hand she pointed a gun at his head.

'Please don't get up, Ms Elias,' she quavered. 'I wouldn't want to shoot you by mistake.' Her white hair was cloudy on one side and pillow-flattened on the other.

The man just laughed at her and bent to drag me by the straps of my backpack to the street.

I was resisting with all my strength, but I heard the landlady say, 'Don't make me pull the trigger.'

I was jerked over backwards. There was a dry click. The man shouted with harsh laughter saying, 'You a stupid weak old woman…'

And then I saw the man's hair burst into flame. It flared, sparked, crackled, then shrivelled away to nothing, leaving the stink of burnt fat and pork rind.

He screamed.

The landlady crumpled to the floor.

I leaped to my feet, rushed indoors to the kitchen at the back, fumbling with my backpack as I went. I dragged one of my beautifully clean dishtowels out, soaked it in cold water and stumbled back to the front door.

My first thought was to revive my fainting landlady, but when I got back to her she was sitting up and pointing, horrified, at my attacker's burnt head. His skin was bubbling and smoking. I threw the sopping towel over his raw scalp.

We heard a car start as we scrambled indoors and bolted the front door.

*

There was nothing for the paramedics to do except swab my bloody nose and diagnose it as 'possibly broken'. The landlady, who urged me to call her Phoebe, resuscitated herself with a large dose of Armagnac, which she told me she usually only drank on her birthday.

We couldn't tell Sergeant Brewer what the violent man was driving but we could tell him that he was wearing jeans, a leather jacket and had a wet dishtowel on his head. He was not quite six feet tall, sturdily built and moaning in a language neither of us recognised.

With relief, Phoebe handed him the gun. He stared at it with an expression of total incredulity.

'I haven't seen one of these for years,' he said, pulling the trigger and watching the little finger of blue and yellow flame flick out of the barrel. 'A semi automatic M 459 – I think these things have been illegal for a couple of decades. And you set light to a guy's hair?'

'It was his fault for using cheap alcohol-based hair products,' I said, remembering the smell.

'I didn't know there was any lighter fuel left in it,' Phoebe said. 'No one in this house smokes anymore. My son gave it to me when he wanted me to give up. He said cigarettes were suicide and if every time I lit up it was with a gun I might get the message.'

'Did it work?' I asked.

'Actually, I lost a tooth and my dentist told me I'd lose a lot more unless I quit. He sent me to a hypnotist. That's what worked.'

The sergeant was looking from one to the other of us as if he couldn't quite believe what he was hearing. 'So you didn't intend to inflict first degree burns on the guy?'

'He had an iron bar with a hook at the end,' Phoebe said. 'I just wanted him to think I'd shoot him if he hit Becky again. But he laughed at me. So I pulled the trigger. I never meant to hurt him.'

I remembered her horrified expression, but now I wasn't so sure. She seemed to have grown and straightened in the last half hour. I couldn't swear that she wasn't enjoying herself.

'It was a very brave thing to do,' Sergeant Brewer said in the tone of voice that means stupid rather than brave.

'He was dragging Becky out to the road like a bag of garbage,' she explained. 'But she's my guest.'

'Is that what happened?' the sergeant asked. 'Why?'

So, wearily I told the whole story again. Wearily the young constable, who'd just come in from searching the path and pavement for clues, took notes.

'So this is already somebody else's case?' the sergeant interrupted me.

'Only if you count your Customer Liaison Office as "somebody",' I said acidly.

'Is that a joke?' Phoebe asked.

'Probably not,' Sergeant Brewer admitted sadly. 'Continue with your story, Ms Elias.'

I did, and the constable wrote notes. Then Phoebe told us what she saw. She started with the hesitancy of someone not used to being listened to but finished strongly. At the end she said directly to Sergeant Brewer, 'I hope you can do something better with this than the Customer Liaison Office.'

'So do I,' he said, but he looked doubtfully at her spectacles, polka dots and pillow hair.

She caught the look and said, seemingly out of nowhere, 'Do you know why old women smell of lavender, young man?'

He shook his head.

'It's because people your age keep giving us lavender soap. I have a drawer full of it upstairs. Keep an open mind, Sergeant, if you please.'

This made the two policemen smile politely and leave quickly. But I hoped they'd heard her. There is *so* much more to old women than meets the eye.

*

After barely two hours sleep I got up and looked in the mirror. I saw a panda with a shapeless, purple nose and blood-crusted nostrils. I showered and washed my hair. I put on my last crisp white shirt and, as an act of despair, added lipstick. Nothing helped.

Downstairs, Phoebe, who hadn't been able to sleep either, opened her first aid box and hid my nose behind a gauze bandage fixed with surgical tape. There was nothing she could do about the black eyes. In return I cooked poached eggs on toast for our breakfast. Then I went to work.

Although Kath and the Sorkins were appalled by my appearance they left me alone in the kitchen when I said I was okay. But my hands were shaky and fumbly, my head was aching and my brain jumped around like popcorn on a hotplate.

I was more comfortable when Kath went off for wine and flowers and the Sorkins left for Golders Green. I needed quiet. Confusion is the enemy of catering. I am not normally discombobulated but this time I took ten minutes to write detailed instructions to myself. It turned out to be time well spent. Mrs Sorkin came home early, distressed by the funeral, and tried to hide her emotions by 'helping' in the kitchen. Kath, noticing the problem, drew her attention to the flowers until Mr Sorkin arrived with the first of the guests. By this time the dining room looked lovely, there were plates full of cheese puffs artfully placed and I was dropping the first blini disks onto the hot skillet. Mrs Sorkin knew what her friends and relations liked. Kath ran around like a one-armed paper hanger keeping up with demand.

By now I'd got into my stride and was working like an automaton. But I stayed in the kitchen not wanting my broken face to put the guests off their food.

This worked fine until after Kath had served the chocolate gateau, when the rabbi forced her way in, to compliment the chef, she said, but in fact to steal my recipe. She wasn't in the least interested in my moral dilemma.

Then all the remaining guests trooped in to add compliments and medical advice – a well-meaning bunch of elderly people needing to take their minds off the inevitable end of their own existences.

It was during this interval that someone knocked and Mrs Sorkin opened the door to a young woman in police uniform. She looked middle-eastern, Syrian or Iraqi, but she said her name was Shareen Manasseh. The rabbi reminded us all that Manasseh was one of the tribes of Israel. Shareen assured Mrs Sorkin that, although her family was of the Eastern People who followed the old form of religion, she didn't herself keep kosher. So because there was no cake left Mrs Sorkin hesitantly offered her a plate of chicken and potato salad. Only the rabbi knew who on earth the Eastern People were.

More to the point, Shareen told me she was on a temporary secondment from a domestic abuse team to an organisation called the Counter-Trafficking Directory. She asked if we could have a private word after I'd finished work. She apologised to the Sorkins for intruding but said it was important that she caught me before I left London to go home. She'd already spoken to Phoebe and it was Phoebe who'd told her where to find me.

I cleaned and packed away all my equipment, boxed up the extra plates and glasses Kath had brought. After that I scrubbed the kitchen and made the exhausted Sorkins and the rabbi a pot of strong tea. Shareen Manasseh sat quietly in a corner, watching. She did not make the mistake of thinking she could hurry me by 'helping'. But as I stowed the last of my kit in the bulging backpack she put the kettle on and made a pot of tea just for me. She fished in her bag and silently offered me a choice of aspirin or paracetamol. I picked the latter and poured myself a glass of water.

We sat opposite each other at the Sorkins' kitchen table. She took out a small voice-activated recorder and placed it halfway between us. 'I can't think and write at the same time,' she told me apologetically. 'I'm here in response to what happened to you last night and the story you told the attending officers. It wasn't a robbery, or an assault motivated by sexual violence. Right? I gather that you're pretty sure it was linked to a previous incident when you lashed out at someone who was stealing from you. And that it was the second attempt at abduction in two days. Is that fair?'

'As far as it goes,' I said grudgingly. But I was relieved that someone had been listening sufficiently to provide Shareen even with this limited précis.

'I'm terrified I killed the thief,' I began. But I was interrupted by the rabbi choosing this moment to come in with an offer to find me a lawyer or to be my witness and adviser herself. She caught my last words, so now she knew the worst. I found that I was angry with her. When I'd wanted to talk about guilt and innocence all she'd been interested in was chocolate gateau. Meanly, I was glad I'd 'forgotten' to mention the raspberry jam and Eldorado rum. Now I was no longer in confessional mood where a rabbi was concerned.

But she might be a future client so I told her politely that I'd be alright with Ms Manasseh. Shareen had taken off her cap and her crazy unfettered hair made her look less official.

Alone again, she broke the silence by saying, 'If the thief died it would not be your sole responsibility. If, for whatever reason, she was denied medical treatment, responsibility is shared. I'm talking ethically, not legally. I'm working at the moment in a horribly grey area where people who might be guilty of something in law may have had no agency over their decisions and no choices. Therefore culpability is a redundant concept. I think you may have strayed into that area.'

'You aren't making me feel any better,' I said.

'Did you set out on that walk to your lodging intending to harm someone?'

'But it's what I did. I caught a woman with my wallet and my phone in her hand and I lashed out. I did intend violence.'

'Instinct, of course.' She shrugged. 'Look, I'm not here to accuse or excuse you of anything. I'm here to assess what you've told, er, how many officials?'

'Including 999 calls? Six. So you're not here to apply the law to me, or to help me? But I might be able to help you? Priceless!'

She smiled patiently at me. 'The police haven't caught up with the enormous consequences of people trafficking. You have whole communities living in underpasses or condemned buildings, working for traffickers. Begging is huge business. Prostitution, porn? Enormous. Agricultural gang workers? Populations shoved around, enslaved, exploited. And we simply don't know what to do about it. The law can't cope, partly because these things are organised internationally as well as domestically. There's some attempt to put charities and NGOs in touch with each other – to deal with the consequences to individuals. That's one of the things I'm involved with now. But I feel like a gnat nibbling round the edge of a whale.'

'You're still not making me feel any better.'

'So let's look at what the woman nicked from you – your wallet and your phone. Those would give someone a lot of information about you, your identity and your money, right?'

I nodded.

'Well, identity theft and fraud are very big business too. The two blokes who turned up, as you thought, out of the blue, you now think must've been associated with her?'

'Yes.'

'You found the scarf they used to stop the bleeding in the car of a third man who was pretending to be a plainclothes cop.'

I interrupted. 'Why were they trying to kidnap me?'

'I don't know. Maybe they think you can identify them. Maybe they think you'll be so scared of being charged with assault or murder you can be bullied into working for them. They have something on you.'

'Then you think she's dead?'

'It wouldn't matter as long as they could convince *you* that you killed her.'

'It matters to me,' I wailed.

'Sometimes,' she went on doggedly, 'the motive might be more primitive – punishment or revenge.'

'Oh brilliant,' I said, holding my aching head in my hands.

'But look,' she said, 'they know you went to Scotland Yard. That sent a message.'

'Obviously it wasn't enough.'

'No.' She paused. 'I've been ordered to ask if you'd be prepared to act as bait… '

I was outraged. 'I was kidnapped and the only person to help me was a taxi driver. You've got to be kidding.'

'Sadly not.' She looked me squarely in the eye. 'If you want my advice… ?'

Advice? 'You've got a nerve,' I said. But even so she was more use to me than any rabbi.

'How easy would it be to change your address?' she asked. 'Never to use the same bed and breakfasts? To work for a different employer for a while? It's easy to underestimate people because they seem rough, uneducated and their English is poor. But they know how to negotiate the internet and computers in ways that would scare the crap out of you. And life has taught them not to be afraid of violence and danger. They've lived with it since birth in some cases.'

'Are you asking me to feel sorry for them?' I was aghast.

'I'm asking you to take time to think. About how things are for people who have lived all their lives in the kind of poverty which you, I hope, can hardly imagine. There are some places where there's little difference between the lives of the victims and the criminals. All, in a way, are victims of their context.'

'Can't you protect me?'

'Do you want an honest answer?'

'No,' I said without a moment's thought.

*

Nowadays, when friends or clients want to get in touch with me they use my new name – Reb Elias, Reb L Catering, which is building a solid reputation. I moved to the other side of town where I'm no longer reminded so much of Axel.

I Skype with Phoebe every now and then. On her advice I spend three hours a week cooking at a women's refuge centre. Redemption, she calls it. And she's right, because while I'm cooking I hear the stories Zahara might have told me had I been a better friend. Phoebe says my bent nose is quirky. It gives me 'character'.

Shareen Manasseh emails me once a week without fail. She's checking that I've had no further contact with dangerous men. This is a comfort. Someone cares enough about my safety to spend five minutes on a Monday morning. She can also reassure me that nobody yet has found the body of a lank-haired, emaciated thief.

I ask her sometimes if she thinks the woman is alive or dead, and she always replies, 'Do you want an honest answer?'

I know I'm acquiring more 'character', but I'm still not strong enough to deal with an honest answer.

MY PEOPLE

I was standing with five other people, arms linked, protecting a man dressed as a giant cauliflower who had superglued himself to Lambeth Bridge. The vegetable needed our protection: we'd all seen on Facebook how rough the police had been to Climate protesters in the first two days of the action. Previous actions had passed off quite amicably, so no one had expected brute force.

While I was linked, I couldn't protect my possessions and I watched, helpless, while the cops confiscated my tent, my bedroll, my wash bag, my spare underwear and the thick woolly I wear at night. They broke my tent pole and my radio.

The irony was that the cops were damaging the equipment they had bought and paid for themselves. My name is Shareen Manasseh, Police Officer Shareen Manasseh, and I was employed by the Metropolitan Police to infiltrate a group of Climate Change Rebels. Six months ago we, the police, had been caught napping by imaginative, energetic Climate Rebels who had brought London to a standstill. Our bosses were left with egg on their faces as far as the media was concerned. And ever-sensitive to their public image they decided, this time, to take a much tougher stand and get ahead of the game.

'Expletive deleted!' yelled Boxer, shocked at the aggression. 'Can they do that?' He was almost as new to the game as I was, but much younger and far less cynical.

'They think they can,' said the cauliflower. 'And that's what counts.'

So the six of us protecting him watched, dismayed, as our temporary homes were destroyed. They even dismantled the kitchen tent and carried away the pots and pans that had fed nearly forty of us who had come to the capital from the West Country.

*

I hadn't asked for the assignment. As usual I was simply dropped in it a couple of months ago and sent, no argument permitted, to Bristol. The property officer said, 'I am issuing quality camping gear. Try not to get it wet. You *are* housetrained, aren't you Shareen?'

I glared at him.

He was pleased enough with himself to add, 'And here's your vegan cookbook. From now on it's aduki beans and tofu for you, my girl. Don't let anyone see you with a pork chop or they'll kick you out of the movement.'

This was insult combined with prejudice. I opened my mouth to protest but seeing his expectant leer, I shut it again.

'And them upstairs are suggesting you get a tattoo,' he went on. 'You want to fit in with the other crusties, don't you?'

'No,' I said flatly. 'No tattoos, no piercings. It's a cultural thing.'

The property sergeant looked genuinely surprised. This was not a familiar prohibition like the one against unclean meat.

'I didn't think you believed in all that rubbish,' he said.

'*Cultural,*' I repeated. He was right though: I'm not a believer. But my people are strict and I don't want to be more alienated from them than I am already.

'A nice Bengal tiger?' he wheedled. 'Just a little one on your bum?' He was delighted to have found something fresh to taunt me with.

'*You* get one,' I said. 'If it looks good on you maybe my culture will make an exception.'

*

Now I watched as my new rebel friends divided. The non-arrestable ones like me would allow themselves to be hustled off the bridge while the arrestables lay down.

I was pleased to see that all the arrestables went limp and it took four police officers to pick up and carry one limp body. It was exactly what we'd been taught at the non-violent training day. But the tactic irritated the cops and they were not gentle.

'Oh f…, I mean expletive deleted,' Boxer said, watching.

'You can still back out,' I said. 'You don't *have* to be arrested. You can live to fight another day.'

'That's right,' said Aurelia, one of our group's leaders. 'No shame, no blame.'

'I'm okay,' Boxer said. He sounded wobbly, but he was too young to realise he could change his mind without losing face.

About a dozen cops in their yellow and black high-viz vests advanced on us. Now that I was on the wrong side of the law, I could appreciate how very big they looked. And how extremely pissed off they were.

'You get the van numbers on the south side,' Aurelia said to me. 'I'll do the north side. Text me. I'll see you on Victoria Street.'

'Okay,' I said. We were supposed to have Legal Observers to witness what the police did, but there had been too many arrests in too short a time. All I could do was record the van numbers our people were carried off in. It was the only way we could find out which custody suites they'd been taken to.

Our people. I was beginning to have my doubts as to who my people were.

'Got your bust card?' Aurelia asked Boxer. 'Ring one of the numbers on it. Don't let them palm you off with a duty solicitor.'

I added, 'And you don't have to say anything to anyone until you're actually in custody.'

'I know,' Boxer said miserably.

Aurelia and I exchanged glances and I squeezed his hand before letting go and escaping to the south side of Lambeth Bridge.

We lost the bridge on only the second day of the protest. The police had too much information and had acted far too quickly. Their success was in part due to information received from snitches like me.

I walked south, diligently writing down van numbers and the names of people I recognised who had been bundled into them: Jen, Fiona, three Johns, James, Ash, Megan and Dot. Then I was shoved off the bridge and avoided more police presence by walking a long way before re-crossing the river by another bridge.

It was no more than I deserved. Double agents have to take their licks from both sides. The London sky frowned at me, granite-grey and heavy with rain.

'They're disrupting the whole city,' said my cop colleagues. 'Costing the country billions. Preventing ordinary working people from making a living.' I believed them. They had facts and figures to prove it.

'Tell the truth,' said my Climate Rebel colleagues. 'Ignorant society is sawing off the branch we're all sitting on. It's almost too late already. There is no planet B.' They had facts and figures to prove it. I was beginning to believe them too.

So the enemies of the movement were paying me to march behind a Climate Change banner – dance behind it actually, because the samba drummers we followed were so irresistible. And I had to admit that it was way more fun to protest than to arrest.

The Climate Change Rebels looked after me much better than my employers did. As word spread that the West Country rebels were homeless we received dozens of offers of food, clothing and shared tents from other groups. Meanwhile, our polluted, money-grubbing capital was crowded with colour, alive to the beat of the drummers and entertained by street theatre and graffiti.

I hooked up with Aurelia on Victoria Street. She had managed to find seven more of our original group. They were gloomily waving rebellion flags. I unfurled my own and joined them.

But, unlike them, I wasn't thinking about the danger of climate change. No – I was replaying in my mind the sight of the destruction of my tent-home and the confiscation of property. My people did that, I thought – the guys I'd worked with for five years.

I was looking at the insecure remnants of our group and thinking of my own family – the tight little self-imposed ghetto up in Yorkshire that was the pathetic remainder of a thriving group of families in Kolkata who had been split and dispersed from the East by the Second World War. I suppose this present diaspora was a bit of a game by contrast. But I was shivering even before the rain came.

Luckily the samba drummers arrived at the same time as the downpour.

"'If I can't dance to it it's not my revolution",' I quoted, perking up. I'd been encouraged to read some revolutionary literature in Bristol.

'Emma Goldman!' Aurelia exclaimed happily. "'The most violent element in society is ignorance".'

George, an ex-teacher and communist, said, "'If voting changed anything, they'd have made it illegal",' in a depressed tone of voice. But he picked up one end of the banner. I picked up the other, and we fell in behind the drummers dancing our way through the Rebel village camped outside Westminster Abbey. Our flags were soggy and sagging but the Lambeth Bridge survivors were heartened. We had Emma Goldman on our side.

We spent that night uncomfortably squeezed into Trafalgar Square alongside the original camp and the survivors of other camps, like ours, displaced from many sites around central London.

I knew what was happening: the police were corralling us into one giant ghetto. Tomorrow or the next day they would descend like wolves on a flock of sheep to disperse and arrest thousands of us in one operation. Disrupt the disruptors. Game over.

I was a police officer – I should have kept the thought to myself. But my sorry family history made my job as snake in the grass confusing. I'd been brought up on stories of camp survivors, escapees and relatives who were never heard of again. A few of us fled to England and were useful enough to work as medics in the army, nurses in a Yorkshire hospital and cartographers. After the war in the East ended so explosively in Hiroshima and Nagasaki it took years before the survivors gathered to form a protective huddle around my great-grandfather in Yorkshire. His house became their synagogue.

Squashed into a single occupancy tent with Aurelia and George I ignored a text from my so-called boyfriend who was actually my Liaison Officer. I whispered to Aurelia, 'We're sitting ducks here. We need to regroup somewhere the cops can't find us.'

'Where?' she said. 'The cops seem to know our plans before we do.'

'Is communicating by Telegraph as safe from hackers as everyone said it would be?'

No, it wasn't. That was my fault too. Treachery's name was Shareen Manasseh.

By texting we could all know where we were and where to go next at a moment's notice. But so could the police. There were too many double-dealers like me. It hadn't been hard: Climate Rebels were a welcoming bunch. They were absolutely convinced they were right and righteous. All they had to do was tell the truth and live in good faith with their people. Everyone who joined them would be in good faith too, wouldn't they? Well no, they wouldn't.

Aurelia, her little face creased with concern and pinched with fatigue, left our tent to talk to Dave and Julie, our area leaders.

George, who is over 50, sighed with relief as he stretched his legs into the space she'd left. I closed my eyes and tried to let my mind drift. But all I could see, projected like a movie on the back of my eyelids, was the sight of the West Country village of small tents, spread like acne on the face of Lambeth Bridge, as it was destroyed by scores of police officers, huge in their black boots destroying our homes. Black boots-jackboots, I thought, knowing I had a pair of uniform shoes exactly like them.

My phone hummed and George's beeped at the same time. Something was coming in on our group's special thread.

I looked at the message. It read, 'they said to trafalgar square where is everyone'. It was from Boxer.

Immediately about fifteen Rebels told him, 'outside Canada House.' And then the phones went quiet again.

I hugged my borrowed sleeping bag around my shoulders like a cloak and edged out of the tent, trying not to wake George who had dropped suddenly into sleep. It was almost impossible to move around the Square without tripping over someone.

I couldn't see Boxer, but somewhere in the Square, someone was playing 'Dream a Little Dream of Me' on a piano.

*

'Listen up,' our training officer said, 'we have to keep the traffic flowing, we have to maintain order, and stop the whole economy from grinding to a halt. *That's our job.* These people may think they've got God on their side but they can't hold the whole country to ransom.'

'They're just a bunch of hairy hypocrites,' said one of us.

'They eat at McDonald's like the rest of us,' said another.

'I've heard they eat babies,' said someone else.

Even if my idiot colleague was joking this sounded awfully like the old blood libel. I shivered while the rest of the group sniggered.

'Our job,' the training officer interrupted loudly, 'is to keep our country safe from extremist ideology and unwanted elements. We all know who I'm talking about.' He nodded vigorously and we did too.

Later when we were all having a beer and a curry together, the idiot who'd talked about eating babies sat next to me and said, 'I was only joking. You know I talk bollocks when I'm nervous, don't you, Shar? Well, I'm a bit edgy about this gig – I think I'll get rumbled as soon as I open my big gob.' I grinned at him. I was edgy too. But that was months ago, before the likes of Aurelia and George welcomed me into their affinity group.

When I first joined the force, it was because I wanted some of the black-and-white certainty I thought would come with the job. Now, in cold, wet Trafalgar Square, I wondered if it was more like a time at secondary school when I was sorely tempted to join the baddest, meanest girl gang. Better to be *with* the bullies than against them. I was tired of being picked on; I just wanted to belong.

*

I stood, cramped on all sides by sleeping Climate Rebels, looking across a square full of small tents and the stages erected for performances and speeches. I was still watching for Boxer.

Aurelia didn't come back. Maybe she'd found more comfortable quarters.

Boxer didn't show up either. Someone else must have scooped him up, fed and bedded him. The piano player moved on to 'Mr Sandman'.

I crawled back into the tent and lay down beside snoring George. It started to rain heavily again and there was a collective groan from all the neighbours.

Just before dawn the next morning, my phone was humming with instructions. We were to pack up, leave quietly by ones and twos and make our way to Vauxhall Pleasure Gardens. A new campsite had been found for us. As well, my 'boyfriend' texted that he was missing me terribly and wanted to know where the hell I was.

The sky was still dark but the early risers were beginning to move off to a friendly church hall for a wash and pee. I went too, stumbling between tents pitched far too close together. I had my head down, following the beam of my flashlight, watching where I put my feet, so I almost missed a small commotion on the steps of Nelson's column. Then someone grabbed my arm and said, 'Hey, bring your torch over here.'

'What's up?' I asked.

'Dunno mate,' the guy said. 'Someone's sick, I think.'

So I climbed the barrier and joined a group of rebels standing and kneeling beside a fallen man.

The woman who was holding his wrist looked up bleakly and said, 'Shit, I think he's croaked.'

'Does anyone know him?' another woman asked.

I knelt down beside her. *I* knew.

I said, 'He is Bobby Short, also known as Boxer. He's from Bristol. He was arrested yesterday.' I closed my eyes for a moment, thinking, am I a cop or a rebel?

'What happened?' I asked.

Several people said, 'I don't know.'

I played torchlight over Boxer's face. He looked scared and forlorn, exactly how he'd seemed when deciding whether or not he was brave enough to be arrested. He smelled of vomit, and it was smeared around his mouth and down the front of his waterproof jacket as if he'd been careless with his mushroom soup.

What time had it rained last night? If he'd been out in it before he died had it been heavy enough to have washed his face and wet his hair? Could I say he must've died after the rain stopped? I was thinking like a cop.

'What do we do now?' A woman asked. 'You said he was arrested yesterday?'

'Yes,' I said. 'Don't touch anything.'

But she was kneeling down feeling Boxer's dead head. She said, 'I think there's an injury. Help me turn him over.'

'No,' I said, holding out a hand to prevent a man, maybe her partner, from touching Boxer. 'If you move him the cops will lay this on us.' I was thinking like a rebel. But maybe he'd died in someone's tent and he'd been moved here after the rain stopped. I was thinking like a cop.

'You said he was arrested,' someone else put in. 'Who knows what the police did to him?'

'Which makes it even more likely they'll want to lay this off on us,' I said. 'But he could have tripped and fallen. It won't be any good for us if we get into an accusing match with the cops.'

'So what do we do now?'

'Call an ambulance?' suggested an older man at the back of the crowd.

'Yes,' I said. 'Do that. Say there's been an accident, but don't say he's dead or the cops will come too. And listen, everyone – tell your affinity groups and leaders. But don't use Telegraph – I'm pretty sure it's been compromised. Word-of-mouth would be safest.' I was thinking like a cop *and* a rebel.

And I was bursting for a pee. So I started to walk off sharpish. 'Someone stay with him, till the paramedics come,' I added over my shoulder. 'And don't let anyone touch him. I have to find his friends.'

I went to Charing Cross Station as quickly as I could. It's hard to think logically when you're anxious about wetting yourself.

After that I WhatsApped Aurelia, saying, 'Where are you?'

My 'boyfriend' texted, 'where the fuck are you?'

Aurelia texted 'leaders meeting.'

I texted, 'Station, ladies loo,' to my 'boyfriend', and, 'where? It's urgent,' to Aurelia. It was about 6.45, and I was tired already.

There was a pause and then my 'boyfriend' texted, 'stay there,' and Aurelia texted, 'Come to Costa, St Martin's Lane.'

I replied, 'can't,' to my 'boyfriend', and, 'I'll be there in 5,' to Aurelia.

At Costa Coffee I paused to catch my breath. My reflection in the window showed a wild unwashed woman with mad black hair and a coat covered with Climate badges. I looked unreliable. Well, all in all that was a pretty fair assessment.

I pushed the door open and saw Aurelia at a table at the back with Julie and Dave, who I knew, and another couple of guys I didn't recognise.

Aurelia got up and met me at the counter where I was queuing for a flat white and Danish.

She was as short as a twelve-year-old so I bent to whisper in her ear, 'Look, I'm really sorry, but you've got to know: Boxer died in the night – in Trafalgar Square. There's going to be a shed-load of hassle when the cops find out. And someone has to inform his girlfriend and family in Bristol.'

Her mouth fell open in shock. I said, 'Yes, as he would have said, "expletive deleted".'

'Are you sure?' she asked when she could speak.

'Absolutely. I just came from there. A guy was calling for an ambulance but not cops. We aren't saying he's dead yet. But the paramedics will when they see the situation.'

She tried to pull herself together, straightening and saying, 'What happened?'

'I don't know.'

'Is it something that happened while he was in custody?'

'We got a text from him, remember?' I thumbed through my texts till I found it. 'It came in at 9.23. Before the rain. A bunch of people replied.'

'Yes,' Aurelia said, remembering. 'Look, get your coffee, then come and join us. I have to tell the others. This is serious.'

I looked at Boxer's message again. Last night I'd assumed he was actually in Trafalgar Square when he wrote it, and he was as confused by the chaos he saw as I'd been. But he might have been drinking and taken a bad fall. Or maybe he'd suffered some sort of concussion while in custody. I didn't want to think about how that might have happened. And then there was the possibility that with several hundred strange men and women bedding down in a small space, not all of them would be as sane and well-intentioned as most of the others.

As I collected my coffee and pastry I realised that I had not seen Boxer's backpack. All I could say for certain was that he had texted at 9.23 before the rain. And this morning his hair was dry. He must have found some sort of shelter.

I made my way through the tables and sat down beside Aurelia. The hot drink tasted wonderful and I warmed my hands on the mug.

Aurelia said, 'Word seems to have spread. A lot of us are moving out.'

Dave, Julie and the other two were texting frantically and barely raised their eyes.

I said, 'Do you know which custody suite Boxer was taken to?'

'Walthamstow. I can't find out if anyone met him on release.'

'It could be important,' I said.

A tall guy with long dark hair, looked up and said, 'I was at Savile Row. They were so rammed I didn't get my phone call, but they kept me for five hours anyway. The Legal Observer was dealing with a whole bunch of us. I think the LOs were way over-stretched.'

'If you didn't get your phone call you weren't charged,' I said mechanically. 'So you're in the clear. Were you treated okay?'

'Yeah,' he said. 'They gave us vegi-burgers for tea. Are you a Legal Observer?'

'No.'

'You should be. You seem to know the right kind of stuff.'

'Not me,' I said. 'I just run with the crowd.' He was a little too sharp for comfort.

Aurelia said, 'Shareen, meet Zeke. So should I keep asking if anyone went to Walthamstow?'

'Yes.'

'Because we need to know if he was charged and if he was okay when released?'

'Yes.'

'Because?' asked Zeke.

'Have you guys had a fatality before?'

All five of them looked up now and shook their heads.

'Because there will be consequences. Because the cops are looking for any excuse to shut… ' I caught myself about to say, 'to shut you down,' but I coughed and added 'to shut us down.' It was a bad moment after a bad night. 'So proper legal advice may be needed,' I finished lamely.

'On it,' said Zeke, attacking his phone again.

Dave said, 'Shit, maybe you should have hidden the body.' Everyone gaped at him.

'Joke,' he said.

I let the others tell him how inappropriate it was both as a joke and as a suggestion. He was a leader. I thought he was an arse. I was thinking like a cop.

'What do you want to do now?' Aurelia asked me.

'Have a hot shower and eight hours in my own bed,' I said. 'What do you want me to do?'

She exchanged a glance with Zeke. I hoped he wasn't her boyfriend. I found him, well, more than likeable.

Zeke said, 'It's a big ask, but would you go back to Trafalgar Square and keep an eye on the situation for us?'

I gave him what I hoped was a neutral, helpful smile. 'You know the cops can surround the square at a moment's notice and treat the whole place as a crime scene – keep everyone there till they're all arrested.'

'It isn't a crime scene,' Julie said.

'You don't know that,' I murmured, and Aurelia said, 'That won't stop them,' at exactly the same time.

Zeke said, 'Have you got your burn-phone and your bust card on you?'

I patted my pockets.

'So?' he asked, and his chestnut eyes seem to smile back at me. He was expecting me to get arrested. In spite of that, I found myself striding back to the Square with a renewed sense of purpose, thinking like a rebel. Well, no: to be honest, I was thinking like a woman who felt she'd been noticed and valued after a long, lonely time in the wilderness. The first drenching rainstorm of the morning didn't spoil my mood.

*

To nobody's surprise the paramedics declared Boxer DOA. They carried him away in a bag, on a gurney. Everyone pushed their tents and belongings out of the way to give them space. A crowd of us formed a quiet corridor for the makeshift cortege to move through. Everyone looked stressed and sombre. One of our own was passing by.

The older guy who'd stayed with the body said, 'Those two…' he meant the two paramedics '… are going to catch an earful from the police for removing the body without permission.'

'Yes,' I said. Because Boxer's was an unexplained death and proper procedure had been breached.

'They understood without being told,' he said. 'The woman was on the big march on Saturday. They're both sympathisers.'

Any forensic investigation would have to take place at Charing Cross Hospital, and the Square would be torn apart when the Scene of Crime team arrived.

I watched the groups of Rebels part to let the ambulance through. Then they hurried away. The Square was emptying fast. It would now be safe to text my 'boyfriend'.

'Sweetie,' I thumbed, 'I really miss you. When can we get together? xxx' by which means Liaison would know I had something urgent to report.

While I was waiting for instructions, I went to a small huddle of Lambeth Bridge survivors. The others had moved on to Vauxhall Pleasure Gardens, but I found George, staunch old Communist that he was, waiting for me.

'Boxer?' He asked as soon as he saw me. I nodded.

'They say the cops roughed him up in custody.' He looked as though he believed this without question.

'Do they?' I asked, thinking, and so it begins. 'It looked to me as if he choked on his own vomit.'

'Really?' George looked disappointed. 'Ah, but throwing up can occur as a result of concussion, can't it?'

'I don't know,' I said, although I did. 'Poor Boxer. At least the hospital will know who he is and where he's from. Aurelia is informing his folks.'

'Sod it,' George said. 'He's too young to die. This puts a real damper on the day.'

As if the day needed a damper. It was still raining. George went on, 'I was afraid something like this would happen. The cops are so much more aggressive than last time.'

'Are you going to Vauxhall?' I asked.

'I was waiting for you.'

'Thanks,' I said. 'But Aurelia told me to stay here and keep an eye on the situation.'

I helped George pack up the last of our borrowed bedding and waved him goodbye as he set off.

A text came in from 'boyfriend'. We were to meet at Victoria Mainline Station in an hour. It would take me twenty minutes to get there. Meanwhile I watched the rebels leave and the police arrive. There were enough of them to surround the whole square but all that was left was a handful of tents, two pianos and a pile of unclaimed bags and belongings.

Again, I wondered where Boxer's backpack was. He had been lying flat on his back when I turned my torch on him and that wouldn't have been possible if he'd been wearing a backpack. The spot where he'd lain was completely clear, washed clean by recent rain. There was no evidence that I could see. And I watched without intervening as all the possible witnesses drifted quietly away.

Two cops in plain clothes walked over, looked at the base of Nelson's Column, then turned to talk to a senior uniformed officer who went off to instruct the troops. The troops fanned out to question any straggling rebels left in the Square.

This included me so I sloped off down to Trafalgar Square tube station and caught the first train that came along.

I texted, 'very few rebels left,' to Aurelia. 'Cops taking names and addresses. No witnesses or evidence. I'm out.'

She replied, 'thanks.'

I changed trains at the next station and went on to Victoria where I discovered that my 'boyfriend' was Sgt Lucy Jones in plain clothes. She was powerfully built and fast – famous for winning medals for the Met's women's sprint team. We went to sit in a Starbucks.

Although she began by saying, 'I see you haven't been checking in regularly,' she wasn't unfriendly.

I explained that since our efficient colleagues evicted us from our home base on Lambeth Bridge there had been precious little time or privacy for regular contact.

I handed her my burn-phone and she went through all my sents and receiveds. My urgent texts to Aurelia and her replies were already deleted, but anyone examining the phone properly would want to know about the deletions.

'So you spent the night at Crusty Central,' she said. Crusty Central as a nickname for Trafalgar Square was what passed for police humour. 'And you're off to Vauxhall now. We know that. Where's the fire?'

I told her about Boxer, about his arrest, custody and last text. And I told her I'd seen the body before the paramedics whisked it away.

'Describe,' she said. So I did.

'Couldn't you have stopped them removing evidence?' she said irritably.

'Not without breaking cover,' I said. 'But I texted immediately. I left when CID arrived with the troops. I wasn't supposed to make myself known to our people either. Remember?'

'You were supposed to use your judgement,' Liaison Lucy said curtly.

'I did.' I could do curt too. 'I judged you'd want me to go back in and keep collecting information.'

'Wait here,' she said, and hurried out of the café to make the sort of call she wouldn't want a lowly field operative to overhear.

I went to the loo. Rebels can't miss opportunities like that. Then I went to the counter to buy hot chocolate and a cheese and tomato toastie.

*

Lucy drove me to Earls Court Road for a proper debriefing and to give a detailed witness statement. No one was at all pleased with the huge number of things I didn't know. Lucy actually told me in no uncertain terms that I hadn't been thinking like a well-trained police officer. I told her she couldn't have it both ways. I hadn't been a particularly well-trained undercover cop either, but I *did* know that rule number one was to hide my official identity. I was not allowed to carry my warrant card on me or anything that would expose me. In any case, given my appearance, and unprotected by my uniform, I couldn't have expected much help from the police.

I knew what they wanted. They wanted me to say categorically that Boxer had been unharmed when he arrived at the Square and that he'd spent the night with rebels who somehow caused his death. They wanted me to give them something they could pass on to Public Relations, something to counter what they were sure the Climate Rebels would say about *them*. That seemed trivial and I didn't want to be involved with it, so I told them about where they might find Boxer's bag and phone. My spasm of spite, now I was with cops and thinking like them, seemed unprofessional and childish.

But I was as fed up with Lucy as she was with me. In fact, she didn't know what to do with me. She didn't want to admit she had no authority either to send me back into the action or pull me out. So she just sent me off, telling me to stay close. She'd buzz me when she got her orders. 'You certainly look the part,' she added, nobly keeping the contempt out of her voice.

I went to the cinema round the corner not knowing how I was supposed to feel. A long, violent Tarantino film filled the time. Warm and dry, I shut my eyes and went to sleep until my phone vibrated against my thigh. I left the movie in the middle of a bloodbath.

There were five texts: one from Aurelia asking if I was okay; the next three were news of various actions I could join; the last was from an Inspector I'd never heard of before. It told me, without reason or explanation, that my assignment had been terminated. I was to 'smarten myself up' and report for normal duty at my normal station at 08:00 hours tomorrow morning.

I phoned Liaison Lucy but she didn't answer so I just stood on Kensington High Street staring at my phone, wondering who I was. My bosses had just ordered me to stop being a Rebel. But the assignment they'd given me had changed me. My eyes were burning and I felt as if I was being strangled. Something was happening to me that I didn't understand. A huge weight squeezed the air out of my lungs. I crossed the road, cutting between poison-belching vehicles.

I thought the pollution that was killing the planet was killing me. Right here and now. I turned north and ran to the trees of Holland Park, my backpack whacking against my shoulders like a self-administered beating.

October leaves, like gold coins, dripped crystal drops of rain. I turned my face up and let them wash my stinging eyes. I thought I was gasping for breath. I thought I was coughing. But in fact I was crying and I didn't know why.

Eventually the storm passed. I phoned Aurelia. She said, 'How are you, where are you?'

'In the park,' I said, without specifying which park. 'I needed to get away. I don't know why.' I paused. 'I was thinking about Boxer.'

'Yes,' she said. 'Me too. Some of us are meeting this evening at sundown. Come, eh?'

'Okay,' I said. 'Thanks.' My assignment had been terminated. I told myself I could spend the rest of the day, in good faith, as a Rebel – a simple solution to a dilemma I didn't understand.

She told me where the drummers were and I found them in the City disrupting the financial district. I followed them wherever they went. It had nothing to do with nonviolent activism in a good cause. I just wanted to go wherever the music went. I did not want to see Boxer's dead face accusing me, at very least, of betrayal.

I thought maybe I should have myself checked for schizophrenia. Instead I followed the band. I sat and blocked roads, I lay down and joined the Die-In outside Barclays Bank, and I yelled when asked to, and waved my flag when everyone else did. I just wanted to be told what the right thing to do was. I was tired of failing to make it up for myself. The planet was dying and Boxer was dead. One of those facts could be reversed; the other could not.

I was not thinking like a cop.

That night we met in an overcrowded church hall near Limehouse. Some victims of yesterday's diaspora had given up on camping and banded together to hire the hall for a week. Someone was cooking vegetable curry in the very basic kitchen. People were sharing plates and cutlery. Someone else had rigged up lines where people could hang wet clothes and bedding. It looked like a refugee camp and smelled of food.

The drummers stood in the middle of the floor, joined by musicians from other groups. We gathered round them and sang 'Lean on Me'.

I took out my phone and looked at Boxer's last message: 'they said to trafalgar square where is everyone' – garbled and unpunctuated. Did that mean anything? Was he concussed, rat-arsed or, as most of us are especially when tired and stressed, just a sloppy texter? It came from his phone, but had it come from his hand?

We sat on the floor after the singing. Julie got up, tired but tall and said she was sure Boxer's group would like to say a few words about him.

It wasn't going to be a search for answers; it was going to be a goddamn wake. I wanted to leave. I was not thinking like a rebel.

Several hands shot up and James, David, Megan, Fiona and Ash took turns to tell small stories and say what a good bloke he'd been. Then it was Aurelia's turn. She said 'I was there when Boxer was arrested. He was scared, really scared. We told him he didn't have to go through with it but he wouldn't back down and he was arrested. That's brave.'

There were murmurs of sorrow and approval. Then staunch old Communist George got up and said, 'What happened in custody? Did someone meet him on release?'

Zeke got up and said, 'It's been a muddle, but here's what we know so far. He was taken to Walthamstow, quite a long way from the centre. We try to have someone to meet all the arrestees on release, but so far, we don't know if anyone met Boxer. We are still looking. So, if someone hears anything please tell me, or get in touch with your group leaders.' His eyes were the colour of toffee.

George, still on his feet added, 'What did the police at Walthamstow have to say?'

Zeke said, 'They say they can't comment about an ongoing enquiry but as far as they know Boxer was in perfect health when he was released. Blah, blah, blah.'

'Was he charged?' George again.

'No comment,' Zeke quoted, weary. This time there were murmurs of frustration and suspicion.

'Look,' Zeke said patiently, 'it's going to be tough. But our London legal team is on it. Can we hang fire with the paranoia till we hear from them? There will be an autopsy as well. We need facts but we have to wait.'

One of the Johns asked, 'Who took him in when he got to the Square? We all got the message. Did anyone see him? I know I didn't.'

We looked at each other. We shrugged. We shook our heads. No one raised a hand.

Dot said, 'Another group? There were so many of us there.'

Aurelia said, 'We're asking. Whatever we find out we'll share.'

I caught Zeke looking expectantly at me. I wanted to please him but I had no desire to describe what I'd seen that morning. I shook my head and he turned away.

We sang, 'No More Silence'. Then someone played a recording of Leonard Cohen singing 'Everybody Knows'. When he got to the line, 'Everybody knows the boat is sinking, everybody knows the captain lied,' we all got to our feet and raised jazz hands. We were together; we were making ourselves feel better and braver.

Food was ready and a crowd swarmed around the serving hatch. It was a good moment to leave. The 'wake' had not consoled me. Answers might have. Whatever mistake cops made, at least they searched for information and tried to evaluate facts. I picked up my bag and sneaked out into the dark.

Two figures detached themselves from the wall. Aurelia and Zeke were sharing a spliff. A couple of 'marijuana smoking crusties,' my cop colleagues would say, pleased to have their prejudices confirmed. Zeke offered the spliff.

I said, 'Thanks, but I'll fall over. It's been a rough day.'

'You look wasted,' he said. 'Where are you going to sleep tonight?'

'I want to go home for a day or two,' I mumbled.

'Another three hours on the coach?' Aurelia looked aghast. She assumed I lived in a Bristol suburb. But of course I didn't. I had a flat at the end of the Northern line. My time in Bristol had been bought and paid for by the promoters of law and order, capitalism, large cars and three flights a year to sunny resorts.

I noticed that Aurelia and Zeke, my temporary friends, were holding hands in the dark.

We said goodbye, sleep well, see you soon, and I trudged away into the night towards the Commercial Road. Cops don't cry. I can't remember which fool told me that.

*

The next morning, clean, with brutally tamed hair under my regulation cap, and my feet crammed into black boots/jackboots, I presented myself to the Station Superintendent. He said, 'I want you to spend the morning writing a detailed report to have on my desk after lunch. I appreciate you haven't been able to keep proper notes, but do your best. We have copies of your Liaison Officer's report but I'm looking for the worm's eye view – if you'll forgive the expression.' He smiled as if he'd made a witticism and hadn't really called me a worm.

With an effort I lifted the corners of my mouth and said, 'Yes sir.'

He studied me and then said, 'Make an appointment with the medic as soon as you've finished the report.'

I said, 'I'm all right, sir.'

This stiffened his resolve and he said, 'I'm sure you think you are, but this is an order. I can't use stressed out junior officers. Dismissed.'

*

The doctor diagnosed anaemia and exhaustion. He laughed and blamed the anaemia on a crusty vegan diet. Word of my secondment had got around. He gave me a sick note and two weeks leave.

'Your family's in Yorkshire' he said, his weak eyes only inches from the computer screen. 'When did you last go up there?'

'I can't remember,' I said, although I could.

'That's too long,' he said, smiling. 'Time to reconnect with your roots.'

'Okay,' I said without meaning it. I left quickly and quietly before anyone thought of taking my burn-phone away.

*

First, I went to Bristol to clear out my room.But instead of returning to London straightaway I went to the sad seaside town of Minehead. It was too depressing to stay more than a single night. However I used one solitary walk to throw my burn-phone off the pier. Messages from my affinity group were still coming in, including a couple from Aurelia and Zeke. They asked if I was all right, and did I want to talk?

I thought of them holding hands in the dark, sharing a spliff, looking like lovers.

233

'Talk to each other,' I said to the squawking gulls, trying to sound more sarcastic than disappointed. The phone hit the water.

It wasn't a real friendship, I told myself. However comfortable I'd been with Aurelia, Fiona, Dot, George, and the Johns it could never be true connection because one of us was lying.

My bosses had used my foreign name and outsider credentials when they placed me in a group *they* saw as outside law-abiding society. They thought I'd fit in with the weirdos. Which meant, that however hard I tried to assimilate into police culture, I now believed the police had always seen me as a weirdo too.

The phone sank. Now no one would see the evidence of how little I reported or how much I'd identified with 'the enemy'.

It wasn't that I'd been close to Boxer. He was too young and too idealistic. He was a trainee children's nurse and believed without question that being a Climate Rebel would save the planet for the next generation. The last time I'd seen him he'd been scared to death. No, that was the second to last time. The last time I saw him he really was dead and I didn't know why. Would I ever know? Probably not – unless there was unambiguous footage from CCTV cameras showing his release from Walthamstow or his arrival at the Square.

Had frustrated, overtired, overstretched cops mistreated him? Or had well-intentioned Rebels given him food, drink or drugs he couldn't cope with? Or had he fallen prey to a nutter disguised as a Rebel? Boxer trusted other Rebels implicitly, saying, 'We're on the side of the angels, aren't we?' I think he actually believed in angels.

But whoever 'we' are, we aren't angels, I thought, as I turned my car north for the long drive home to another group of people I didn't really belong to.

KALI IN KENSINGTON GARDENS

'Are you mugging me?' I always thought when this moment came, if this moment ever came, I'd be scared. I wasn't. I was insulted. Outraged.

'I'm robbing you.' She corrected me with bored contempt. 'Gimme your purse and your phone, oh and shut up.'

I hit her with my sandwiches. And woke up on a bench with a tanned, blond rollerblader bending over me, brow creased with concern.

'You okay?' He felt for my pulse in all the wrong places. I sat up groggily. My jaw burned and my teeth wobbled. There was a growing, soggy lump on the back of my head.

'You went down like a tree in a hurricane. He must've packed one helluva wallop.' He helped me to a bench dedicated to 'Harry – a great companion.'

'She,' I said.

'She? Wow. Good punch. No, look sorry. I called the cops anyway.'

Like being whacked by a woman didn't count. I said, 'Go home. I'll be all right now.'

'The cops say I'm a witness. I'm supposed to wait.'

Some witness, I thought. Can't tell a guy from a girl – fat lot of good you'll be.

'Erm, was she black?' The rollerblader looked uncomfortable enough to be a tactful, if unobservant, lad.

'Indigo,' I said. 'Tattoos all over her face.'

We sat in silence then. It was a beautiful winter afternoon: just right for the last picnic of the year. I looked around. 'Oh bugger.'

'What?'

'She stole my sandwiches. Bloody cheek!' There was painful drumming at the base of my skull and spasms of nausea. A nice salt beef, chilli and dill pickle sandwich might have settled my stomach or even my nerves.

'Which way did she go?' I asked my handsome rescuer.

He pointed towards the setting sun. I staggered to my feet.

'You can't leave.' He was shocked. 'The cops will be totally pissed with you.'

'I'm not too pleased with the cops. Where are they?'

The rollerblader looked up and down the avenue. It was remarkably empty of officers of the law. 'Where are you going?'

I limped southwards. 'I'm following a trail of breadcrumbs.'

'You should sit down,' he said. 'You were unconscious for one minute, forty seconds.' He was trying to be accurate now. Too late.

I said 'No one can eat my sandwiches but me.'

'Shouldn't you be more worried about your purse?' He was tagging along, crunching laboriously through dead leaves. A rollerblader trying to walk on grass is a heroic sight. But not a sensible one.

'Salt beef, chilli and pickle? Seriously, no one eats my sandwiches but me.'

One minute you are walking past the Italian fountains observing with amusement the statue of Jenner with a book in one hand and a seagull on his bonce, and the next you've been violently floored by an indigo-faced thugette.

236

'Cobwebs,' I said, remembering suddenly. 'Cobwebs and skulls.' I stopped. 'The design on her face was one dense spider's web and there were skulls tattooed round her throat like a necklace.'

My companion said. 'Then she's unmistakable. All you have to do is describe her to the cops. You don't have to find her yourself. Not at your age.'

'Oops,' he added, catching what was undoubtedly my most incensed expression. 'Not that you aren't great for your age... whatever that is – but she was big, strong and fast. And violent. Look, I know about girl gangs – they scared the brown stuff out of us boys at school. They don't seem to have any rules, see.'

'I don't see any gang,' I said. 'What rules? Are you talking about articles of war? The Geneva Convention? Those sophistries that are supposed to make brutality more palatable?'

'A pacifist as well,' he muttered. 'Could today be any more perfect?'

'As well as what?'

'I don't mean to be rude, and please don't jump down my throat, but you're a woman of a certain age, and you obviously don't dress to impress...'

'I dress to distress.'

'And you're, forgive me, gobby, and you can't cook for shit...'

'I have an ex-husband who knows less about me than you do,' I said.

'So most likely you're a feminist as well as a pacifist,' he went on as if l hadn't spoken.

'And you're young enough to make all that sound like an insult.' I looked up and saw three crows watching us from the bare, tip-tilted branch of a chestnut tree. 'Also you're trying to walk on grass with your skates on so you probably aren't in further education ...' I broke off, thinking, Why do I feel the need to retaliate? How many guys under thirty would stop to help an old pacifist feminist who can't cook for shit? I might have met the only one in Kensington Gardens.

'Harry,' I said, 'you're right, I'm gobby. I'm sorry.'

'Who's Harry?'

'A great companion, 'I told him. 'You should learn to read the backs of park benches. They're as good as books for feeding the imagination.'

Three crows screamed and rose as one, beating heavy black wings in the delicate blue air. A grey squirrel sat up, alarmed, and folded demure hands over her belly. I watched. The crows flew west and then circled twice. Beneath them was the little stone-built folly known as the Queen's Temple. They circled once more over the cupola and then dived behind it. After a few seconds they rose again, bickering loudly, competing. Then without warning they shrieked and parted, each flying off at top speed in a different direction.

I pointed. 'My sandwiches?' I suggested.

'Well, bugger off!' Harry said. 'Whatever they picked up, they couldn't get rid of it fast enough.'

'Definitely my sandwiches then,' I said, starting off towards the temple. 'If you're coming, Harry, for goodness sake use one of the paths.'

The setting sun was in my eyes, dazzling me. It reminded me that this was the shortest day and also the day of the longest shadows – they striped the green grass like the hide of a tiger. I squinted along the shadows and saw dogs as tall as ponies sparring clumsily. I saw walkers, and mothers with children. I saw another rollerblader and two skateboarders. But I did not see an indigo-coloured thuggette fleeing with my wallet and phone.

From the tiny temple came the sound of someone playing the banjo. I heard a high voice singing, 'It's not too far to India, the tour bus leaves at seven…'

The temple is only three small connecting rooms with no doors, all facing the rising sun. Like any other public place in every city in this country it smelled strongly of male pee and was decorated with graffiti and gang tags. The most aggressive piece of writing proclaimed, 'Kali Rocks & Rules.'

Sitting cross-legged on a square of cardboard was a girl, no more than eleven or twelve years of age. She was singing, 'And every nutter gets off at Calcutta…' The surrounding stone made her weedy young voice ring. She stopped when she saw me. A tattered blue beanie was pulled down over dirty hair and she regarded me with bright rodent eyes.

'Spare a little change?' she suggested hopefully, 'for a cup of tea and a sandwich.'

I said, 'Someone just stole my purse so I'm flat broke. She also stole my sandwiches so I can't give you anything to eat either.'

'They was your…?' She stopped abruptly, glancing shiftily from left to right. There was a crumb of pumpernickel visible on her chin. I was in no doubt now that this malnourished child had received and rejected my stolen snack.

'They was indeed mine,' I told her. 'Where did she go?'

'Who?'

'You know who. The girl with the big tats.'

'Dunno whachoo talking about.' But her eyes shifted automatically towards the wall which read 'Kali Rocks & Rules.'

I said, 'The cops are coming. Tell me which way she went and maybe I won't bring them here to you.'

The young girl laughed. It was not the politest sound I'd ever heard. She said, 'Whachoo gonna do then, old lady? You wind her up, she'll chop you down and lick your blood off of the floor. You don't want to meet her when she's off on one.'

'Your problem is that if I don't meet her I become your problem.'

Harry arrived then, out of breath. He was wearing trainers and his blades protruded from his backpack.

'Have you found her?' He was as sharp as a sofa cushion, was Harry.

'Yes,' I said. 'This girl assaulted me and took my purse and phone. Call the cops, Harry. Tell them it was robbery with violence and we've caught the perpetrator.'

'You lying old cow!' protested the girl with the banjo. 'I never touched you. I never even seen you before. Don't you call nobody,' she pleaded with Harry who had pulled his phone out of his pocket. 'Don't listen to her. She's picking on me cos I won't tell her…'

'Won't tell her what?'

'She won't tell me where Kali went,' I said.

'I swear I never even said her name.' The girl squeaked like a mouse. Harry crouched down next to her.

'Why not?' he asked gently. The girl stared at him. His fair hair seemed to glow in the dying winter light. He was a stunning lad, now I came to look at him properly. And much nicer than I was.

The girl obviously thought so because she leaned towards him confidingly. 'I can't say nothing,' she whispered. 'She protects me.'

'Who are you?' Harry asked. 'Who does she protect you from?'

'From people who hit me.' She turned huge eyes towards him. 'They call me Sara S.'

'Who hits you?' Harry's handsome brow was furrowed with sympathy.

'She does,' the girl said simply, glancing at Kali's writing.

I laughed and my headache went away. 'The classic protection racket,' I said. 'Give me your lunch money or I'll hit you. Only in my case she took my lunch and she hit me.'

'You don't understand,' the girl said. 'Everyone used to hit me till she came along. Now no one does, not even me bruvvers.'

I looked at Harry and Harry looked at me. He shrugged and we walked out of the temple into the dusky park. There was still no sight of any cops. We exchanged addresses, and Harry walked away. He looked a lot cuter on rollerblades.

I waited for a few minutes, listening. But the girl did not start singing. All I could hear was the sound of chainsaws as the park tree-surgeons lopped off dead branches.

*

The next day was Friday and I went to see my friend Min. The neighbourhood is infected with a creeping rash of cheap hotels. Min's house is one of the last to remain private but someone has bought the freehold and Min is worried.

She buzzed me in and I found the new landlord's son in the hall doing semi press-ups against the wall. He didn't move when I said, 'Excuse me.' I had to step over his feet. He said, 'Hey lady, wait till I finish.'

I said, 'Maybe you should do your exercises at a gym.'

He said, 'Maybe you should suck dick.'

Upstairs, Min said, 'That's Rak – I wouldn't suck an ice-lolly in a heat wave if he gave it to me. He's a hooligan and a mental midget.'

So I told her about Kali in the park because a trouble shared is a trouble doubled and we were both at the mercy of young toughs.

'The police weren't interested,' I said.

'Nobody's interested in Rak either,' Min said. 'But he's such an intimidating presence that Edith and Stephen downstairs have already moved out. We were all going to stick together but what can you do when people get scared?'

'I had to stop my credit card,' I told Min, 'and you know what, it was used within fifteen minutes of being stolen.'

'Where?' Min asked.

'The supermarket. She spent a small fortune on food – enough to feed a very large family.'

'How odd.' Min's kindly eyes creased in puzzlement. 'From your description I'd have thought her more likely to buy a Harley Davidson or a load of Gangsta music.'

'I was surprised too. But buying food for a family doesn't turn her into a good person. She robbed me and she hit me.'

Min got up and poured more tea for both of us. Her teacups are a harlequin set of pieces she inherited by being the last survivor of her family. Her furniture's like that too: it's good but mismatched and there's too much of it. She was hoping she would never have to move again, but that hope is looking more and more forlorn.

I said, 'We're giving up far too much territory to bullies. You don't want to leave your flat, and I want to keep on walking in Kensington Gardens without fear of violence.'

Min has a wayward streak which I've always found entertaining. She handed me a steaming cup of tea and mused, 'If there were a fight between your Kali and my Rak who would you bet on?'

I pictured the hulking tattooed mass of Kali and remembered the ferocious speed with which she retaliated when I hit her with my lunch. But Rak was an arrogant young man with a lot of muscle. I shook my head. 'What a good thought,' l said.

Min took a ladylike sip from her floral patterned cup and said, 'They could beat the shit out of each other and leave us alone.' She is a translator of novels from Spanish to English. I used to restore antique clocks and watches before my fingers got too stiff. By today's standards I suppose you could call us thinkers.

I said, 'It shouldn't be beyond us to arrange something of the sort.'

'Beware of old broads with brains.' Min smiled at me and I smiled back. Like a lot of people who work alone I'm attracted to a good conspiracy.

*

In the late afternoon I watched the Queen's Temple from a park bench fifty yards away. I wore my ex-husband's old raincoat which made me look poor, defeated and undeserving of attention from thuggettes. No one came or went. No song hung suspended on the cold air. An odd couple in white coats took a photo of the unnecessary little building, but apart from that and the furtive raids of squirrels through the dead leaves all was still and silent.

Just before sundown I crossed the grass myself and went into the temple. I took a can of scarlet spray paint out of my plastic bag, and in the room where the girl with the banjo had sat I wrote, 'Rak Rules, Kali Cowers.' Next, in girlie pink, I sprayed, 'Kali Luvs Rak 3:30 Monday xxx.' Then I hurried away for tea and toast at Min's.

'I was a bit more direct,' she said, proudly handing me a single sheet of typed paper and a plateful of hot buttered toast.

The toast was delicious and the writing on the paper was libellous. Both were just what I'd hoped for.

Min wrote, 'Theres a girl who plays banjo says you got good pecs and do it for money. She says you'll do that filthy thing with a soupspoon your famous for and it'll only cost a fiver. I like a guy whoos dirty and cheep. Meet me at Queens temple in Kensington Gardens 3:30 pm Monday. Roger.'

'Roger?' I said.

'I don't approve of anonymous letters.' Min took a prim nibble from her toast. 'If you're still up for it, put your stake money under the candlestick.'

'Ten pounds on Kali to win.' I flourished my money.

'Ten pounds on Rak. Winner buys supper.'

On my way out of the house I thumb tacked Min's letter to the front door where anyone could see it and even Rak couldn't miss it.

*

The next day was Monday. Min and I sat on a park bench watching the Queen's Temple. Min brought the sandwiches – tuna and cucumber; I brought the thermos. Soon we were surrounded by indigent pigeons and squirrels. Even the crows looked approvingly at Min's crusts. I have to admit she has a way with food.

It was very cold and the sky was white with unshed snow. From the temple came the chug-chug-chug of a banjo, and a thin young voice sang, 'You warned me, never linger when your eyes are red with anger…' Then the music was interrupted by the sound of a motor. A green van with City Suburban Tree Surgeons written on its side drove across the grass to a dead tree. Three men got out. Two of them used orange tape to cordon off an area around the tree. The third began to unload equipment.

There was no sign of Kali. Min looked at her watch and said, 'What happens if she doesn't show up and the kid with the banjo has to face Rak alone?'

'That'll teach her not to pay protection, won't it? She'll just have to get strong and look after herself.' I caught Min's expression and added, 'We'll intervene, of course. I brought my ball-peen hammer.'

I looked up at a sudden noise and there was Harry rolling towards us on a skateboard. He stopped when he saw us, tipping his board back and hopping gracefully to the ground. Automatically, Min raised a hand to fluff her hair. I couldn't blame her – Harry looked like a young god.

He said, 'Aren't you scared to come here again?'

'I brought a friend,' I said, and introduced him to Min.

'Sit with us and have a sandwich,' Min said.

'Who made them?' he asked suspiciously.

Min giggled like a girl and I suppressed an urge to wring her neck. 'Don't let us keep you,' I said. But he sat and munched a sandwich with obvious pleasure.

He said, 'I came to see if Sara S. was okay.' He gestured towards the song and its banjo accompaniment. 'I don't suppose you have a spare sandwich for her, do you? She's always hungry.'

I could see Min struggling between the twin snares of wishing to please and wanting to keep Harry by her side. I was horrified, because there, striding towards the temple, pectorals bulging under a thin t-shirt, was Rak in a foul temper. I couldn't let Harry take a sandwich to Sara S.

'Are you her protector now?' I asked rudely. 'How much does she pay you?'

'Excuse me?' Harry said.

Min looked shocked. 'Of course you can take food to the kid.'

I stood up between Harry and the temple. 'She receives stolen goods,' I said, 'she didn't give a toss about Kali hitting me.'

'She's just a kid,' Harry protested. 'She was scared.'

Min, the traitor, gave me a defiant look and handed the rest of the sandwiches to Harry. He kissed her on the cheek. A simple 'thank you' would have done just as well. Min blushed and cooed. I could've used my ball-peen on both of them.

As Harry started off towards the temple, Rak disappeared inside.

'You idiot, Min,' I hissed, 'you could get him killed. Rak's here.'

'Why didn't you say?' We went in pursuit.

Twin roars split the winter air.

The first was a chainsaw. The other was Kali erupting out of the temple in a full shoulder-charge. Sheer momentum forced Rak backwards. He was a big, bullisome man but he couldn't match Kali for ferocity. She was terrifying – indigo skin making her primitive and tribal, eyes staring and insane.

Rak rained blows on her face and shoulders but she ignored them. Some found their mark for her lips and teeth turned scarlet with blood.

Harry stopped, stunned. Min said, 'That girl hit you? And you survived?'

Harry sprinted to the temple.

'Don't!' Min cried. 'You'll get hurt.'

I wrenched my hammer out of my handbag and followed.

'Wait for me,' Min wailed. It's all very well for her to make a decent sandwich and receive kisses from handsome blond guys but she doesn't have a clue about action.

'Use your phone,' I called over my shoulder. The police didn't come the first time so they were hardly likely to come now, but it'd keep Min out of trouble for a while.

Kali grabbed and hauled Rak towards her. She wound her arms around him so that he couldn't raise his hands to hit. She ran him backwards into the dead tree and began to ram his head rhythmically against the trunk.

The tree surgeons scattered out of her way.

'Stop her!' Sara S. screamed as she came running out of the temple. 'Stop her or she'll kill him.'

We all rushed forward. One of the tree surgeons caught at Kali's arm but she brushed him off like a dead twig and he went spinning to the ground.

She snarled, 'This is Kali cowering!' Bash. 'This is how much I love you!' Whack.

'Kali!' Sara S. shrieked. 'Stop!' She pleaded with us, 'Stop her. She goes mad. She can't stop herself.'

Rak crumpled to the ground. Kali whirled and with one hand snatched the chainsaw out of a tree surgeon's grasp. The chain howled as she held it poised over Rak's throat.

We all yelled at once. But she didn't hear us. Blood was in her eyes, her mouth, her ears.

My plan had careened out of control. We were about to see Kali tear Rak's head off.

And then Harry, blond hair flying, threw himself on Rak's body. Clear blue eyes looked straight into Kali's. He said only one word.

I could hear nothing over the screams and the chainsaw. But Kali heard him. She stood stock still and for a second it looked as if she would kill Harry too.

He spoke again, and I could almost see the blood-rage drain out of her like water from a bottle.

She tossed the chainsaw aside and reached down to help Harry up. She looked almost human.

I was astonished and relieved. But I couldn't help myself: I was disappointed too. Under the blood-rage she had been terrifying. But she'd been magnificent as well.

Now she turned and ran. Huge, fast, she loped away from what was nearly a terrible murder and disappeared into the glare of the setting sun.

The rest of us gathered, shaken, around Rak's body.

'He's alive,' Harry told us, and Sara S. sighed and smiled through her tears.

'An ambulance is coming,' Min said. She drew me away from the group. 'This is our fault,' she said. 'We made this happen. I wrote it in a letter; you wrote it on a wall – the power of words. If Harry hadn't stopped her Rak would be headless.'

'A word stopped that too,' I said. 'One word.'

'I couldn't hear a thing,' Min said.

Harry came over to ask if we were all right.

I said, 'You were incredibly brave and incredibly stupid. What did you say to her?'

'Nothing.' Harry shook his beautiful hair out of his eyes and looked embarrassed.

'Oh God.' Min looked ill. 'We could've got you killed.'

'What do you mean?' Harry stared at her in surprise.

'Timing,' I hurriedly. 'She gave you a sandwich to take to your friend, which meant you were at the temple when Kali attacked Rak.'

'Who's Rak?'

'Oh dear,' Min said, her lip trembling.

'Yer busted.' Sara S. had crept up unnoticed and was standing close to Harry. 'You old witch.' She gave me a knowing malevolent glance. 'Couldn't deal with Kali yerself so you set her up. She went critical when she saw what you wrote.'

Harry's steady blue gaze fixed on me and made me blush. 'You should be ashamed of yourself.'

Min, I noticed, did not rush to my defence or explain her part in the near massacre. As I stomped away I said, 'You owe me supper. Your boy lost.'

Let her explain the bet to Harry, I thought angrily. But she was too busy batting her greying eyelashes at him to own up.

I wasn't as disappointed with Min as I was with Kali. Min has a well-known weakness for handsome men. Kali, on the other hand, in attack, looked like a warrior: female strength in full flow. I couldn't help being thrilled by it when it was directed at someone other than me.

But one word from a gorgeous guy and she chucked down her weapon and ran away, tamed.

What was the one word? Obviously I couldn't hear it, but I had been watching Harry closely, and from where I stood it looked as if his mouth formed the word 'Please'.

LIFE AND DEATH IN T-SHIRTS

I'm Ruth Hall and Sophia Mariam won me in a charity auction.

I have no glamorous talents. All I could offer was a free day of domestic help. This proved surprisingly popular. I made more for the new MRI scanner than dinner for two at a city centre restaurant. Chores for once beat romance.

'Clothes,' Sophia confessed as we exchanged details. 'They're out of hand.'

'Just clothes?' I asked. 'You've got me for a full day.'

She grinned with charm as well as a hint of embarrassment. And when a couple of weeks later, armed with a roll of black rubbish bags, I presented myself at Sophia's door she greeted me with the same charmingly embarrassed smile.

She had a lopsided faceful of character. Mad hair was caught up with a red plastic clip. I couldn't tell how old she was. Body fascists would've accused her of being overweight but she moved like a girl, running up three flights of stairs, leaving me panting behind her.

She occupied the top two floors of a five-storey house in a Georgian terrace overlooking Bath. The view might have been spectacular but I couldn't see it. A path between walls of bags and storage boxes led from the bedroom door to the bed, but I felt I'd need climbing gear to get close to the window.

Every box, every bag was stuffed with clothes. I felt my can-do smile wilt. The only hopeful sign was the bed itself which was neatly made up.

Sophia sat on it now and pulled me down beside her. She sighed. 'I sometimes imagine myself in a Nuclear Winter trying to live without heat, wearing layer upon layer of garments. Other people freeze to death but I survive.'

'Alone?'

'My lover's with me.'

'Wearing women's clothes?'

'In a Nuclear Winter I don't suppose he'd be fussy.'

Was there really a lover? What she'd said about Nuclear Winter sounded so whimsical that I wondered if she might be a fantasist. I shouldn't say this but she looked too old for a lover. But I hardly knew her so I pulled myself together and said, 'Where do you want to start?'

'Here,' she said, tapping her forehead between arched eyebrows. Then she laughed lightly and asked, 'Where do *you* think I should start?'

'Here?' I asked, grabbing a plastic bag next to my left foot.

'Don't touch that,' she said sharply. 'It's my daughter's wedding dress.'

I dropped it. 'But why is it here?'

'I bought it for her. She gave it back after the divorce.' Sophia looked sad. 'He was a nice man. We still text.'

Maybe she couldn't throw people away either.

'This then?' I asked, pointing with my toe to a blue storage box.

'Let's have a look,' she said doubtfully.

I put it on the bed between us. Opening the lid, I saw that it was crammed with t-shirts. The legends on the top four said, 'Rolling Stones, Voodoo Lounge', 'There's no crying in cribbage', 'Dorset Steam Fair,' and 'Let's eat grandma. Let's eat, grandma. Commas save lives.'

'Keepers!' Sophia cried, hugging Voodoo Lounge to her breast. 'Best stadium concert ever. I was with a gorgeous guy. He played a great game of cribbage too.'

'And had a thing for steam engines?' I asked.

'Don't be silly,' she said. 'That was just a two-week fling while I was feeling lonely.'

'So we can throw the Steam Fair T away?'

'Heavens no!' She looked shocked. 'It reminds me that I left the guy in the Dorset mud and drove to Lyme Regis where... ' She fished in the box and produced a weathered garment with an ammonite on it. The legend read, 'I Dig Fossils.' She smiled mistily. 'Olly – a palaeontologist and a mighty man. He fixed my washing machine too.'

A sinking feeling was grabbing my normal optimism by the throat and drowning it like an unwanted kitten. 'We should talk,' I said.

'Coffee?' She smiled brightly as if we'd been working hard all morning and deserved a break.

I won't describe the kitchen except to say I was glad Sophia was making the coffee because I wouldn't have found the kettle let alone cups.

We sat at a table where two places had been cleared between letters, bills, envelopes, magazines, newspapers, packets of pills, sunflower seeds, and paper bags full of walnuts and almonds. More hedging against a Nuclear Winter or evidence that Sophia shared DNA with squirrels?

But the coffee was rich and fragrant and she regarded me with a shrewd narrowing of her golden-brown eyes. 'I will be seventy-three at my next birthday.'

I was pleased to display genuine astonishment. She waved it away saying, 'Is seventy-three a prime number? I used to know. Now I don't.'

I opened my phone, touched an icon and asked, 'Is seventy-three a prime number?' A plastic voice recited all the prime numbers up to one hundred. The number seventy-three appeared on the screen in bold. I turned it so that Sophia could confirm what she'd just heard.

'Thank you,' she said. I was certain she was thanking the phone rather than me.

I began to feel spooked. I held the steaming mug under my nose, breathed in deeply and said, 'Sophia, what do you want me to do today?'

She said. 'Everything I've kept is a memory. I need to keep only what I *want* to remember.'

'It looks to me,' I began carefully, 'as if you've kept your whole life.'

'And that could be a problem. A person's whole life is not something she can be wholly proud of. I haven't a lot of time left, so I'd like to jettison the guilt and pain.'

'Freedom from pain?' I queried, just to be clear. 'I'm only here for one day.'

'Not all problems have a logical solution.' Her chuckle was throaty and infectious. But I wondered how a twenty-five-year-old could possibly understand the laughter of someone like Sophia?

I thought for a moment and then said, 'Isn't your daughter's wedding a painful memory?'

'That was pure theatre. She starred. It was her perfect Disney moment. Not everyone works for that, achieves it and then, bless her, enjoys it.'

'I'm not sure I believe in weddings,' I said sadly.

'I'm not sure I believe in marriage but Karine does.'

'So what counts as "guilt and pain"?' One of us, I thought, should stick to the point.

'I need to wipe out everything that has happened in the last year and five months.'

'A particularly difficult time?'

'It was the sweetest, most contented time of my life,' she said, a spasm of intense pain momentarily twisting her charming quirky face into an ancient, exhausted one. 'Sweetness and contentment turned out to be delusion. A bad mistake.'

'A lover?'

'What do *you* think? Oh, wait: first, at my age I was too old for a lover. Then, if by some remote chance I wasn't, an older woman would have enough experience to recognise a bad'un and she'd know what to do to save herself.'

'Nothing further from my mind.' I squirmed guiltily.

'I thought so.' She sipped her coffee, regarding me over the rim of her mug with fathomless eyes. I gazed back at her hoping I didn't look as flummoxed as I felt.

'Okay,' I said. 'You want help getting rid of everything that reminds you of a toxic time. To throw away a garment is to throw away a memory?'

'It isn't that simple, but sort of, so let's go back upstairs and start work.'

As we stood the doorbell rang.

The entryphone was outside the kitchen door. All I could hear was the squawk of someone shouting at her from the microphone by the front door. I couldn't see her face, but when Sophia spoke her voice was as withering as a hard frost. 'I've already told the proper authorities everything. You gain nothing by harassing me. Go away before I call the police again.' She snapped down the receiver.

She didn't come straight back into the kitchen so I waited, taking in the sight of more pots and pans than you'd find in a canteen. Because of overstuffing, the cabinet doors and drawers were all ajar. I wondered if she'd been a deprived, neglected child. But then I decided pop psychology and Sophia would be a bad fit.

Eventually she poked her head around the door and beckoned me back to the bedroom as if nothing had happened.

We attacked another two boxes of t-shirts, and she decided to give up Bob Dylan, Tears for Fears, The Chelsea Flower Show, Welsh Women's Championship Snooker, Bath Literary Festival, Twycross Zoo, Berthe Morisot at the Tate, and The Slits Reunion. She dithered and sighed over each item.

According to the t-shirts this woman had travelled all over the world – from a line dancing club in Arizona to a Naum Gabo exhibition at the Hermitage. She had an ochre shirt with the legend 'I Picnicked at Hanging Rock' and another from an archaeological site in the Orkneys.

'How did you find the time to travel so widely?' I asked, really meaning 'Where did you find the money?'

'I was a sound recordist working mainly on documentaries,' she said sadly. 'I had hearing that could catch the landing of a feather.' She brushed a hank of her crazy hair to one side displaying a hearing aid. 'Losing sharp hearing was like losing a limb. Suddenly I was unemployable. I think it was one too many old landmines. Percussion, you know – hearing never returns properly.'

'An adventurous life,' I said, feeling both admiration and envy.

'Shall we stop for lunch? There's a good pub up the road. I hate cooking.'

I almost asked about the mountain of kitchen paraphernalia and decided against it. Sophia had paid a hefty price for my help, not my criticism.

We went downstairs. I carried my meagre haul of discarded t-shirts to stow in my car before she could change her mind. I also needed to move the car and renew the parking sticker.

'I'll find us a table,' Sophia said. I watched her walk away. She moved lightly, but there was fragility too.

A parking space opened up outside her front door. I backed my shabby Kia into it. One day might someone envy *me?*

I was locking the boot when a guy with a tall black dog appeared from the house opposite. His haircut was aggressively short but he had a good-humoured smile. He said, 'I shouldn't stick my nose in, but you were talking to Ms Mariam, weren't you? The guy hassling her, I had to threaten him again today. She should ask the cops for help. He scares the kids.'

The black dog gently poked its nose into my hand, stole my car key and dropped it on the man's shoe.

'He's half retriever,' he explained, picking up the key. 'The other half is lurcher – he's a thief who always gives the swag back.' The dog licked my wrist and I stroked his velvet ears. I decided I liked them both.

'Who is the guy?' I asked. 'What's his beef?'

'It's complicated I think. She had an odd relationship with someone who was more my age than hers.' He grinned and shrugged tough shoulders. 'This is a small street and we try to keep ourselves to ourselves, but we look out for our neighbours too. Especially the older ones.'

'That's nice,' I said, not quite believing him. I'd spent my life in short-lease places where nobody looked out for anyone. 'The guy shouting at her is odd-relationship guy?'

'I think he's related. And you? I haven't seen you around before.'

'Not that you were looking.'

He laughed. I waved in a friendly way and set off towards the pub.

'Nice guy or nosey neighbour?' I asked Sophia. She'd found a small table and bought me a white wine spritzer.

'Nosey but nice – he's bringing up two pre-teens on his own. He likes to think it's a safe neighbourhood.'

'Why don't you ask the cops for help?'

'I have. They've spoken to the guy. It made no difference.'

'Who is he?'

'You know,' Sophia said, handing me a menu, 'they do a lovely avocado and lobster sandwich here. I think I'll have that.'

It was the perfect way to shut me up.

While we were waiting for the food she asked about my life as a paediatric nurse and my ambition to retrain as a children's therapist. She was so attentive and encouraging that I only realised she hadn't said a word about herself when we were walking back to her house. Seduced by being noticed, I thought ruefully. But I relished the inner glow her attention gave me.

Back in her bedroom Sophia said suddenly, 'Your first day off in three weeks and you've given it me?'

'I gave it to the Friends of the Cancer Ward,' I corrected.

'I must discipline myself. I'm resisting the help I requested.'

As if she'd flipped a switch Sophia became serious and determined. By suppertime although we'd hardly made a dent in her bedroom we'd filled five huge bin bags. What was a mountain of rubbish to me was history to her, and I suddenly thought about how my old nan would have reacted if I'd asked her to throw away half her photo albums.

The five bags were a big deal to Sophia and she thanked me over and over as I lugged them down to the street.

'One last thing,' she said. '*Please* don't donate my old clothes to charity shops – I'd be mortified to see another woman wearing my memories. Just take them straight to the tip.'

I'm a great believer in charity shops but I was about to reassure her when I noticed that I'd forgotten to move my car again and had been given a parking ticket.

'I'll take that,' she said, holding out her hand. 'You shouldn't have to pay for helping me.'

It was a kind act. I couldn't afford a parking fine.

I really liked her. I loaded my car with her discarded clothes and felt glad I'd told her to contact me any time she needed help again.

It began to rain. As I ran to the driver's door I saw the man with the black dog cross the street towards me. He held out his hand. 'Barney,' he said.

'Ruth,' I said, taking it.

He jerked his chin towards the dog who had followed him as far as the nearest lamp post. 'Archie,' he said apologetically.

*

It was three in the afternoon nine days later when the front door banged and footsteps pounded up the stairs. 'Shit!' Barney muttered hauling the sheet up over us.

The bedroom door hit the wall. 'Daddy!' It was Abbi, eleven, Barney's youngest. 'Police cars,' she shrieked.

'Out!' he roared in return.

'What're you doing in bed? Are you sick?'

'And shut the fricking door!'

'Now you owe a pound to the swear jar,' Abbi said primly. But I heard the door shut.

I emerged pink and breathless from under the sheet.

'Fricking is what I say when I'm *not* swearing,' he complained in a whisper. 'She wants to punish the intention as well as the commission. And what's she doing home so early?' Barney struggled into jeans and a flannel shirt. 'Do me a favour and make your mac-cheese for tea? You know, distract the girls from awkward questions.'

I sighed but he didn't notice. He ran his fingers through his buzz-cut hair as if it needed tidying and left the bedroom. He had great shoulders. I would make mac-cheese without complaint.

I pulled on a large grey t-shirt over my jeans. On the front it read 'Smoking Gun Club, Louisiana' in gothic lettering with three bullet holes instead of dots over the i's. I went to the window and peered out between curtains. Two police cars and an ambulance were double-parked outside. Sophia's front door was wide open. Archie appeared at my side. He was carrying one of Barney's slippers which he offered to me like consolation.

I saw the two girls cross the road and begin to assault the constable at the door with questions. Barney followed, hopping uncomfortably on bare feet.

I took the opportunity to scurry to the kitchen and begin the mac-cheese as if I'd been there all along. Dating a man with children was like dating a married man, I thought dolefully. There was the same horrid need for lies and secrecy, and first place in his heart was already irrevocably occupied. I'm ashamed to say I'd learned that lesson the hard way. Now I was learning it again in a different context. But I was lonely and Barney had great shoulders.

He rescued the constable so Abbi and her elder sister Gina camped out at the front window instead. As a topic for speculation Barney and I had been upstaged by the drama across the road. I worried about Sophia although her house was divided into three flats, and something could've happened in any one of them.

So far I'd avoided running into Sophia while visiting Barney. I was embarrassed about the speed of my hook-up with a man who lived so close to her. It wasn't just that I hardly knew him; it also felt like I'd intruded into her personal territory.

Gina said, 'Is that man carrying a doctor's bag?'

'Come away from the window and sit at the table,' Barney said. 'It's nearly tea time.'

'Why is that policeman just standing there?' Abbi asked.

'How come you two are home from school so early?'

'Flood,' Abbi said, her eyes glued to the window as if it were a screen.

'In the girls' toilets,' Gina explained. 'Dad, the Hobsons went on holiday. So something's happened to Mr Gooding or Mrs Mariam.'

'Mr Gooding's car isn't there,' Abbi added eagerly. 'So he's still at work.'

'Something bad's happened to Mrs Mariam,' Gina decided.

Barney glanced at me. He was anxious.

'Daddy, what's happened to Mrs Mariam?' There was a wobble in Abbi's voice.

'We don't know anything's happened to her.' Barney's voice was level and confident. 'Now stop being ghoulish and eat your tea.'

'It's the angry man,' Abbi said, taking his hand, allowing herself to be drawn towards a steaming dish of mac-cheese.

'He broke in and beat her to death,' Gina said delightedly.

'Stop it, you two,' Barney said in comfortable tones. But I knew, because he told me on our second date, that his wife had died of cancer when the girls were seven and eight. For a whole year they'd all had to sleep in the same room because the children couldn't bear to let him out of their sight after dark.

I thought about that now with a mixture of understanding and jealousy. I wasn't allowed to spend the night because Barney didn't think his daughters would accept me sleeping in 'Mummy's bed'. Or was he was sheltering his *own* reluctance behind what looked like parental care? Somehow an ordinary hedge against loneliness had become very complicated.

Archie sat on my foot while I served up.

We were still eating when Mr Gooding crossed the road for a quick chat with Barney. I didn't see him but the girls were listening behind the kitchen door and they told me that Sophia was dead. They cried. Barney looked grim – he seemed angry with her because he thought her death was reminding his children of losing their mother. I felt guilty.

In spite of this everyone gobbled up their food and held their plates out for more. There was almost no time for conversation because a policeman came knocking.

Barney, Gina and Abbi met him as a family, together on the sofa. I sat off to the side on the piano stool. Officer R. Nicholas perched on the edge of an armchair. He didn't give the girls any information but he wanted to know when we'd seen Sophia last. And, as we were directly opposite her house, had we seen any of the comings and goings in the past week? I was silent because I'd managed not to see her at all. My three visits to Barney were in the early afternoon. We went to bed and when the girls got back from school I cooked their tea. I didn't tell PC Nicholas this. Nor did Barney. We exchanged one glance before I said I hadn't seen Sophia. Abbi and Gina conferred in whispers before Abbi, as the spokeswoman, confessed to meeting her yesterday at the corner on their way back from the bus stop.

'What else?' Nicholas must've had children of his own; he was no slouch about devious body language.

Abbi's chin wobbled appealingly and a classic single tear rolled down her cheek. 'She gave us money to buy sweets.'

'Where's the money?' Barney asked sternly.

'Where are the sweets?' asked the officer who had more experience with the criminal mind.

The sweets of course were long gone. But as Barney encouraged the girls to carry shopping for Sophia, and sometimes to pick up milk or bread for her at the nearby Minimart, Sophia often let them keep the change – undeclared income which they shared and spent on the junk food Barney always avoided.

He gave them a 'This isn't over' look but said, 'Sophia was very kind. Is that really the last time you saw her?'

'Yes,' Gina said.

'But?' Nicholas had a good eye for children. I work with them myself and I'd caught the quick flick of Gina's eyes and Abbi's minuscule shoulder squirm.

'Daddy,' Gina said, 'the angry man was in Minimart.'

'He was buying whisky,' Abbi said. 'The same bottle you hid in your cupboard. Yukky. '

Gina kicked Abbi's ankle. Abbi said, 'Ow-ow-ow.' She started to cry. Barney looked mortified. His girls were spying on him.

He counterattacked. 'Why didn't you leave the shop and come straight home?'

'We couldn't,' Gina said. 'He saw us.'

'You shouldn't have been there.'

'He was wearing Ruth's t-shirt,' Gina said, pointing straight at my torso. Barney and PC Nicholas stared at my boobs, reading Smoking Gun Club, Louisiana there.

'Or Ruth's wearing his,' Barney said, his eyes hardening.

'Who is this angry man,' Nicholas asked, looking from one of us to the other.

'Oh crap,' I muttered, heat rising like flame from my toes to my nose.

'A pound for the swear jar!' both girls yelled in triumph. Abbi rushed to the kitchen and came back to shake it in my face, thrilled that I was now in more trouble than she was.

Of course I was in trouble. I'd done a bad thing.

'Who's the angry man?' Nicholas repeated.

'He's scary,' Abbi said, over her shoulder still shaking the jar of coins under my nose. 'I bet he murdered Sophia,' she added, excited to have a distraction from her own iniquity. Sweets and murder can get equal billing from the very young.

Barney got to his feet. His face was wooden but his voice was calm. 'Both of you go to your rooms. Do *not* come down until I call you. And no listening at doors.' He cut off the mutiny I was expecting by holding out a hand to each daughter. Then he firmly shooed them upstairs.

'Who is this angry man?' Nicholas's patient tone matched Barney's. 'And why are you wearing his t-shirt, Ms Hall?'

'I'm not,' I said. 'This is *my* t-shirt. And I don't know who the angry man is. I never saw him.' I sounded indignant even to myself.

'Bit of a coincidence.' Barney narrowed his eyes at me.

'You're jealous,' I thought, elated.

Barney turned to Nicholas. 'There's a guy who was hassling Sophia. Ringing her bell and shouting abuse through the entryphone. Sometimes, at night, he'd yell up at her window. Check your complaint records. I rang you three times. So did Sophia. Someone talked to him but no action was ever taken. He scared my daughters. Whoever he is, the police know more about him than I do.'

'Did either of you see this man today or yesterday?'

'No,' Barney said. I shook my head.

Then Barney said, 'Can you tell me what happened to Sophia?'

'I don't know myself,' Nicholas said. 'But the doctor was up there an awfully long time.'

Then they both looked at me again. I was going to confess, but the radio on Nicholas's shoulder started to chatter. He went out and it was almost time for me to leave for my shift.

Barney eyed me coldly, waiting. I was dismayed. He had said, 'Can you tell *me* what happened to Sophia,' not 'Can you tell *us*'. Such a little word, 'us'. An hour ago we'd been in bed together. Now I wasn't, even temporarily, part of 'us'. I picked up my coat and bag and walked out. I left him and the girls with the washing up.

*

Five days later, in the middle of my shift, an eight year old boy was sent up from post-op after an emergency appendectomy. He was groggy and uncomfortable. His name was Vaughn Gooding and he was the child of divorced parents both of whom wanted to stay. The usual smiling battle over which parent cared more was being waged in front of a sick little boy.

I told the parents it might be best if only one of them stayed. Mr Gooding won.

I made Vaughn as comfortable as I could, checked his temperature and gave him some ice shards to suck. Mr Gooding hovered even though there was a nearly comfortable chair beside his son's bed.

I went round the other beds in my two wards. When I returned to the workstation to complete my notes Mr Gooding was hovering by my desk.

He said, 'Aren't you dating a neighbour of mine – Barney?'

'Oh,' I said. The penny dropped: this was Mr Gooding who lived in the flat below Sophia's.

In fact I hadn't seen Barney or had so much as a single phone call from him since I'd walked out leaving him to clean up on the day Sophia died.

I said, 'Vaughn's doing fine, Mr Gooding. You should get some rest yourself.'

He didn't take the hint. He stuck out a neat, clean hand. 'Call me Murray.' His buttoned down collar suited him. 'Abbi said you were Sophia's cleaner,' he went on. 'But I never saw you go into our building.'

'I'm not a cleaner,' I said. 'I was helping her with some decluttering.'

'You're kidding!'

I didn't feel like sharing confidences about Sophia's hoarding so I said, 'I really need to write up my notes.'

'I won't keep you,' he said. 'But as you're a nurse, can you tell me why the police were so excited about my medication?' Then he told me he'd come back early from work, having left his car at a nearby garage for its MOT, and found a leak from Sophia's kitchen flooding his flat.

'I hammered on her door,' he told me. 'I know she's hard of hearing. And sometimes she forgot her hearing aids. So I let myself in with her spare key. We all know where the spare keys are kept in case of emergency.'

'You had access to each other's flats?'

'The police found that fascinating too,' Murray Gooding said dryly. 'But we live in the same house and we could suffer from one another's accidents or carelessness. We make a point of staying out of each other's business otherwise.'

'So you let yourself in?' In spite of myself, I was intrigued.

'I didn't want to.' The tidy, buttoned-down man pulled a face. 'I hate it up there. I live in fear of her ceiling collapsing and all her junk falling into my place. Anyway, I called to her. No answer. So I went up into her kitchen. Oh lord – I thought she was just another pile of clothes on the floor.'

His mouth turned down as if it had been pulled by strings. 'Her eyes were open but... ' He shrugged. 'I couldn't make myself touch her. I just called an ambulance. Apparently she'd been dead since the day before. Oh and I turned off the water. She had a leaky tap. There was too much crap in the sink and it got blocked.'

I looked down at my hands. How could someone so brim-full of kindness and character end up mistaken for a pile of old clothes? And what mischief made Abbi tell this man that I was a cleaner? She knew full well I was a nurse. Actually, I understood perfectly. The girls were still reeling from the loss of their mum. They were terrified of anyone who might threaten the bond with their dad.

Understanding didn't help. I was ashamed of my hurt feelings and my inadequate response to what Murray was telling me. 'Poor Sophia,' I said.

'Yes,' he said indifferently. 'But I wanted to ask you why the detective who interviewed me asked about the medication I'm on – specifically whether on not I take statins for cholesterol. He searched through my kitchen cabinets and fridge – most interested in what kind of tea and juice I drink. He took away my grapefruit juice. Why would he do that?'

The phone rang and I answered. Another child. Another bed to conjure out of thin air. They close wards to save money and then complain when we can't find space for the next emergency.

At least Murray Gooding had the sense to go and sit by his son's bedside. He was asleep when my shift ended and I was too tired to wake him to say goodbye or get the end of his story.

My two housemates had gone by the time I reached home. The heating was off so I went straight to bed. But before sleeping I checked my phone and found a message from Barney.

I should've deleted it without listening, but it always takes me longer than five days to get over a man.

*

He fell into one of those deep naps I envied so much. I tiptoed to the bathroom. By the time Barney woke I would be soapy fresh again. I looked at myself in the mirror and thought, 'If you act like a doormat, don't be surprised if someone wipes his feet on you.'

The girls were going from school to a birthday party. It was supposed to be a sleepover, but I'd bet myself that Gina and Abbi would ask to be brought home before bedtime.

Barney stretched and scratched his armpits. He yawned and said, 'Murray Gooding told me he saw you last night. He said you were frantically busy.'

I lay down beside him and smelled the drying sweat on his skin.

Barney said, 'He didn't get to ask you about his medication.'

'Do you think I should drop in on him later?' My lips were nearly touching his shoulder. I could bite it without moving more than an inch.

He rolled over, propping himself on one elbow. 'I don't want you talking to Murray – he's a gossip.'

'Maybe mention that to the girls,' I suggested. 'Abbi told him I was Sophia's cleaner.'

'Why would he tell *you* that?' I could've slapped him. There was a silence.

Then I said, 'Murray found Sophia, so he knows more than I do. But if Sophia took statins for high cholesterol she was probably warned about eating grapefruit or drinking grapefruit juice.'

'What's wrong with grapefruit?'

'Bergamottin – it's found in grapefruit,' I said. 'It's harmless on its own but interferes with the way some statins are processed by the liver. That causes a build-up. There can be dangerous side-effects. You'd have to drink a lot of juice though. If Murray was drinking grapefruit juice he was probably on one of the less reactive statins. I wonder about Sophia though. The police wouldn't be interested in any of this if she'd died of natural causes.'

'Maybe she didn't.'

Just then his phone warbled and he held up his hand to interrupt me. His daughters, I thought resignedly, although it was only midafternoon.

'Hello,' he said cautiously. Then he listened for a couple of minutes, sitting up and pulling the sheet over his lap. Eventually he said, 'Of course you can. Give me half an hour.'

I knew he was talking to a woman. He was using his 'I *like* you' voice.

I lay on my back, one arm behind my head. An odalisque pose I'd seen in one of his art books. I thought it made a woman look nonchalant.

He was waiting for me to suggest that I should leave. My stomach clenched. I smiled at him.

At last he said, 'I should go and pick the girls up.'

He was wiping his feet on me. I said, 'That call wasn't about the girls.'

Exasperation scudded across his face and disappeared. He said, 'I never promised you anything.'

'But you owe me something. I'm going to bed with you, cooking for you and your children, *coming when you call,* damn it. If that isn't ever going to add up to anything, respect me enough to tell me to my face.'

'I like you,' he said, and I could feel salt smarting under my eyelids.

'But?'

'But,' he said, as if the one word was enough. And because it wasn't I remained where I was – an unwanted odalisque in his bed.

I said, 'You invited me here today. You mentioned supper. But… '

This time the one word was enough. 'The woman who rang just now is Sophia's daughter, Karine. The police won't let her into her mother's house. No one will tell her anything. She wants to talk.'

'So? You asked me to cook cutlets and mash for supper. She can have some too.'

'I don't want to muddy the waters,' he said, breaking eye contact. 'She doesn't know I was seeing you.'

'*Was?*' I said. 'Is this your way of telling me you're seeing *her?*'

'Not exactly. But I like her and she has a daughter Gina's age. I thought it might simplify matters if the girls got together.'

'How did you get to be so stupid?' I asked. 'It's *obvious* that your girls aren't ready to accept the women you bring home. And now you want them to welcome a strange daughter too?'

'What am I supposed to do?' He almost wailed. 'Live like a monk till they have kids of their own?'

'Of course not. But recognise what's going on. Ask for advice. Otherwise every woman you ever fancy will be in a no-win conflict with your daughters. It won't just go away because you close your eyes.'

'How did *you* get to be so damn wise?' Sarcasm sharpened his voice.

'Being with you. I really liked your kids to begin with.'

'I thought I was dumping you,' he remarked. 'Now it sounds like you're dumping my kids.'

'Oh no,' I reassured him. 'You're dumping me alright. So are Abbi and Gina.'

'Yet here you are.' His bitterness matched mine.

'You called me!' I yelled. 'Soddit – I'm an *optimist*.' I jumped out of bed and threw on the black t-shirt with the word Escapism printed in gold on the front. Being dumped was not a suitable job for an odalisque. I squeezed into my jeans.

He was just ahead of me on the stairs when the doorbell rang. He turned as if he wanted to beg me to pretend I was the plumber but he wasn't brave enough.

Karine looked at my bare feet and drew her own conclusions. To Barney, she said, 'You should have told me you had company.' To me she said, 'Why are you wearing my mother's t-shirt?'

I thought, 'Oh crap', but said, 'I'll put the kettle on.' I pushed past Barney into the kitchen.

He and Karine followed. The atmosphere was not warm and snuggly.

I was such a push-over. A short while ago he'd made me believe he wanted me. Now I was the intruder.

Karine, I already knew, was in her mid forties. She looked spectacular – auburn haired, creamy skinned and slender. She had Sophia's golden-brown eyes, but not her strong chin or her humorous mouth.

I had my back to her, fussing with the kettle when she said, 'My mother had a dream about a rock star who was performing in a black t-shirt with Escapism written on it in gold. She took it as a message and had three t-shirts made exactly the same as his. They're unique.'

'And what about the Louisiana Gun Club?' Barney said, frowning at me – Mr Self-righteous. 'You'd better explain yourself.'

'Why are you wearing my mother's t-shirts?' Maybe her chin was stronger than it looked at first glance.

I said, 'She gave me her old clothes.' She gave them to me *to throw away*. I just left off the last three words.

'She did not,' Karine said.

'I was decluttering for her. She gave me five full bin bags.'

'She did *not*,' Karine repeated with complete conviction. 'Have you any idea how many times I offered to help clear her flat?'

I turned to Barney, but he wasn't going to support me against Karine. I put the teapot, milk and two mugs on the kitchen table and searched for my shoes.

'She's wearing the Large size,' Karine said to Barney. 'She's a big girl. My mother always wore Medium even when she shouldn't. Was the Smoking Gun Club large too?' When he nodded she went on, 'The large ones were Eddie's.'

'Who's Eddie?' I asked. Her face looked like a slammed door. I ignored it. 'Is he the "angry guy"?'

'No,' Barney said. 'I haven't seen Eddie for weeks.' He spoke to Karine even though I had asked the question. He went on, 'Do you know who was hassling Sophia?'

'I didn't know anyone was.' She spoke stiffly. 'All I know is that Eddie went missing. I haven't seen Mother for a while. I've been away.'

'Somewhere nice?' I asked in my chirpy small-talk voice. Because I didn't believe her.

Barney glared at me. Archie whined and licked my wrist.

I said, 'Don't worry, I'm leaving.' And as I was feeling too sad to be nice, I added, 'Next time you want a booty call, pick on someone who *doesn't* care.'

I left, eyes and cheeks burning, thinking I really wanted to talk to the angry man. I drove away, but only as far as the pub at the corner of the road where I had a good view of Barney's front door.

Sitting in my battered car I tried to transmute the lead of sorrow into the gold of rage. I couldn't sit inside: I'd already squandered tomorrow's lunch money on inner city parking. I'd paid hard cash for the privilege of being used like a sneezed-in tissue. I could learn something from an angry man.

Did his anger have something to do with the missing Eddie whose Large t-shirt I was wearing? One that I'd kept after promising Sophia I'd destroy her bad memories. Did he represent 'pain and humiliation' to Sophia the way Barney did to me? Barney and Eddie. Beddy. Why did I invest so much in an animal act, and he so little?

At last Karine came out and climbed into a neat silver Audi. She drove past and I was glad to see that she did not look happy.

Barney came out five minutes later. I checked my watch. Yes – suppertime – Gina and Abbi hadn't let me down. Unless he paid better attention to them they would never enjoy sleepovers. Nor would he.

He didn't see me as he drove away. But Archie did – our eyes met. His affection seemed genuine.

I drove home heartsick.

*

After that, whenever my shift allowed I haunted the pub. I knew the girls' school hours, and Barney's too so I could avoid the family. If I could afford a drink I sat at the table Sophia and I had shared when we had lunch together and I'd poured my heart out about my future.

I wore either the Escapism or the Smoking Gun Club t-shirts. If they were in the wash I wore one from Muscle Shoals, Alabama. I figured that as Louisiana and Alabama were nearly neighbours maybe this t-shirt represented a stage on the same trip. If I couldn't recognise the angry man then maybe he'd recognise Eddie's t's. The girls had seen him in the Minimart so, I reasoned, he might live nearby.

Why was I doing this? Was I stalking Barney one step removed? No, of course I wasn't. Yes, of course I was. Seriously, I don't know.

He'd treated me as if I had no value. Even my talent for mac-cheese was disposable. So I sat, hollow and lifeless as a zombie, waiting for something to animate me. This was not the first time my hopes had been trashed. What was different now? Straws and camels' backs came to mind.

Then, one evening when I was wearing Muscle Shoals, a big man with long hair and a short beard leaned over me and said, 'Where did you get that t-shirt?'

He was wearing plain denim although he was far too big to wear jeans elegantly, and his hair needed a wash. But he looked comfortable in his skin – not angry at all. I was so surprised I let him buy me half a pint of cider and sit at my table. He introduced himself as Dan Winfield, explaining that he had a Muscle Shoals t-shirt too but had never seen another like it. He asked me if I was a fan of Southern Soul music.

'No,' I said, perplexed. Now that the angry man was sitting in front of me, amiable and curious, I didn't know how to proceed. He started to tell me complicated facts about a famous sound studio. I thought about Sophia, loving music but becoming deaf. My ever-present sense of loss gathered and to my horror I felt my eyes begin to smart.

I decided to tell the truth. 'This t-shirt was supposed to go straight to the council tip with bagsful of others, but I'm in a low paid job so I took a few that fit. Sue me.'

He stared at me in astonishment. 'Are you Sophia Mariam's cleaner?'

'Who told you that?' I said, temper replacing tears. 'I'm a paediatric nurse at the local hospital.'

We both hurriedly re-assessed the meeting. He opted for frankness. 'Then you're the girl that prig Barney dumped.'

'Thank you, Mr Sensitivity,' I snapped. 'And I suppose you're the "angry man" who was stalking Sophia?'

'Who told you that?'

'Probably the same ones who told you I was a cleaner.'

'That would be Murray Gooding who has the flat below Sophia's. Are you the nurse who explained about statins?'

'Not the sort of information a cleaner would have at her fingertips?' I was still in a huff. 'And you haven't told me why you're interested in my t-shirts.'

'Okay,' he said. 'My half-brother, Eddie, brought me back the Muscle Shoals T after he and Sophia went on a Blues and Country tour of Southeast USA. I'm well into Wilson Pickett and he loves Willie Nelson.'

'Are you into Smoking Guns too?'

'I only wear that one when everything else is in the laundry bag. That was Eddie's little joke. He's into guns; I'm *so* not.'

'What size?'

'Eh?'

'What size t-shirts does he wear?'

'He's a Large,' Dan said grumpily. 'I'm Extra Large. Got any good diet tips, Nursey?'

I was equally grumpy. 'About the pot calling the kettle black? It looks as if I'm wearing your half-brother's discarded Large t-shirt.'

'On you it looks good.' He was shooting for gallantry and missing by a mile. He frowned. 'See, that's my point – Eddie would never get rid of that t-shirt. He'd wear it to a rag, then frame it and hang it on the wall. So why was Sophia chucking it? Why did she even *have* it? And where is *he*?'

'I don't know anything, unless he's the guy Barney said was way too young for Sophia – the one she wanted to forget.'

'Shit! Barney said she wanted to forget him?'

'No, Sophia said it.'

'Eddie said she was nuts about him.'

'She probably was,' I said. 'You don't reject a memory unless it's very painful. And you don't feel pain unless you're nuts about the guy.'

Dan looked at me like I was dippy. 'So,' I hurried on, 'he must've done something to hurt her.'

'He's forty-seven. She was *seventy* something.' He looked as if he was explaining arithmetic to a baby.

'How old is *your* girlfriend?' I asked.

'Twenty-one,' he said, puzzled. 'But I'm unattached now.' He paused. 'Oh, I see what you mean. I'm forty-five. ' He did not say, 'but that's different,' and he blushed as he went on, 'I get Sophia binning her own clothes, but how did she get hold of his?'

'Maybe she asked for them back. I'm assuming *she* bought them. She had the Escapism one made specially.'

'She paid for everything,' Dan admitted. 'He was always broke. He had some bad habits… Y'know, casinos. I was fed up with bailing him out. God help me, I was relieved he'd taken up with a rich old girlfriend. Let her carry him, I thought, maybe she can afford him. I sure as shit can't.'

'When did you last see him?'

'When they came back from the States. He was full of himself – gave me the t-shirts – in here, actually. She turned up after a while. I liked her. I could almost see the attraction. She was colourful. Alive.'

'Not any more.'

'I'm sorry about that. But she shouldn't have just blanked me when I started worrying about him. I registered him as a Missing Person with the cops. I know she was pissed off about that. And it's true that sometimes I drank too much and rang her doorbell. But, wouldn't you if it was *your* bro who just vanished?'

'If Eddie did something really cruel to her, why would she want to talk to his brother?'

We stared at each other. I said, 'Did he talk about… ' I was going to say 'relationships' but at the last moment changed it to 'women'. I hurried on, 'Perhaps he fancied someone else?'

Dan hesitated.

'Oh my god – he *did!*' I exclaimed. 'Someone younger.'

'Steady on! Eddie's just a guy, for gawd's sake. All I remember is, after he met Sophia's daughter and granddaughter, he kinda hinted he'd stuck himself with the wrong generation.'

'Eddie fancied her daughter?' I was shocked.

'He also kinda hinted that Sophia took him to the States to remind him which side his bread was buttered.'

'That doesn't sound like her at all.'

'Because you knew her so well? If you don't mind me asking, how old are you?'

'Twenty-five,' I said before I could stop myself. 'You're telling me – Eddie and *Karine?*'

'I dunno, but he said she was hot. Do you know her?'

'Why do you think I'm in here on my own?' A mudslide of depression fell on me.

'Because Barney's a prat, a twat and a fat-head,' he said, almost as if he meant it. 'But Sophia was a weird pick for Eddie, you know. He was always into the young ones.'

'Like his brother?' I said acidly.

'You haven't got a very forgiving nature,' he complained. 'I'd just broken up with my long-term partner so I went to Club XL with Eddie, to make myself feel better. I got wasted and copped off with Poppy. It lasted three weeks.'

'You and your brother, both forty-several, went to Club XL? *I'm* too old for Club XL. And yes, there *is* a t-shirt – someone gave it to me as a joke.'

'Exactly – Eddie's little joke on Extra Large me.'

'I don't think I like your brother much.'

*

According to the Chronicle the coroner's decision about Sophia's death was suicide: she'd washed down a four-month supply of statins and a heap of paracetamol with two big cartons of grapefruit juice and a pot of Earl Grey tea. Sophia, it seemed, knew that Bergamot is what gives Earl Grey its smoky flavour.

It took the police days searching to find her note in the tiny second bedroom she used as an office. It read simply, 'I did a terrible thing. I don't deserve to live.'

'I don't believe it,' I said passing the paper to Dan.

'I do,' he said. 'She had something to do with Eddie disappearing. That's why she wouldn't talk to me. She got so jealous she killed him and this is as close to a confession as I'll ever get.'

We were sitting side by side in Boston Tea Party, eating poached eggs on toast.

'You can't say she's a killer,' I said staunchly. 'She isn't the type. And there's no body.'

Dan was equally unmovable. 'Anyone can be a killer given the right provocation. And there *is* a body. I feel it in my bones. I'm not giving up, you know.' He gave me the same look he'd given me when he'd ordered a mound of crispy bacon and four pork sausages to go with his poached eggs. The look said, 'Don't even *start.*' Oh no, he wasn't the kind of man who'd give up – unless it was on his diet.

'And why *kill* him?' I asked. 'If being ditched for a newer model was a killing offence there wouldn't be many men left.'

*

Barney rang me after midnight two days later. I'd transferred to the day shift but my internal clock was still confused. I was awake and took the call.

'Ruth?' He sounded toasted. 'I shouldn't ask, but I need a favour. I mean Karine needs a favour.'

I thought, 'Dig a hole, crap in it, jump in afterwards.' But I said, 'You've got a nerve.'

'I know, but Karine needs help clearing her mother's flat. Everyone runs away screaming. Murray Gooding suggested you. I can't think of anyone else. You were always so kind… ' His voice trailed off. I yawned.

'Well?' he said.

'Well what? You haven't asked me anything.'

'Will you help Karine?' he said furiously.

'No,' I said, and let the silence between us harden.

He swore.

'Why didn't she ask me herself?'

'Oh, you know,' he said drearily. And I probably did although it made me ashamed of both of them.

I said, 'I won't do it for Karine and I certainly won't do it for you, but for Sophia's sake I'll meet Karine outside the house at six thirty tomorrow evening.' I hung up immediately. Whether he'd crow or grovel, I didn't want to hear it.

At six thirty I walked down to Sophia's house wearing my oldest jeans and rattiest sweatshirt. I knew I looked rubbish and that Abbi, Gina and Barney could see me from their front window.

'I'll give Karine exactly three minutes,' I thought. 'Not a minute longer.' I looked at my watch.

But she got out of her Audi a few houses down. The passenger door opened and a thin child stood in the middle of the road.

Karine and I approached each other like gunfighters. Just as we met, Gina and Abbi flew out of their house yelling my name. But the one who got to me first was Archie. He wagged his tail with enthusiasm, licked my hands and gently purloined my rubber gloves.

'Ruth!' Abbi screeched. 'I miss you *so* much.'

'Are you going to cook our tea?' Gina wheedled. This told me as clearly as a newsflash that Barney was serious about Karine. They didn't give a toss about me. They were just making a point to their father.

I sighed and greeted them amiably. It wasn't their fault. Barney looked relaxed but when he collected my gloves from Archie I noticed hidden tension.

'Come on, girls,' he said firmly. 'Say hello to Devon. I'm making popcorn and we're going to watch a DVD.' He held out his hands to his daughters but they stuck stubbornly to my side. Karine gave Devon a little push in his direction.

Devon said, 'I don't like popcorn.'

'Yes you do,' Karine said.

I stared at Barney with cutting eyes. He avoided my gaze.

Karine ignored her daughter's imploring whispers and led me through Sophia's front door.

'Where do you want to start?' I asked without a polite greeting.

'Kitchen,' she said. 'I had some flat-pack boxes delivered. A scrap dealer's coming in the morning.'

'You're keeping *nothing?*'

'There's some quite good china buried somewhere. When you find it please wash it and pack it separately. Otherwise everything goes in garbage bags or boxes. Carry them down to the street for collection in the morning. I want this kitchen empty. *Empty.*' She stood in the doorway, pale as peppermint. It was the room her mother died in.

In a monotone she added, 'Thank you for doing this,' and stumbled away into the living room.

I rolled up my sleeves. I'd have to clear the floor to make enough room to assemble the boxes. I realised from the smell that there were mice.

I hauled on rubber gloves and looked at the table, the place where Sophia sat when we drank tea. It had been partially cleared. I was guessing that pill boxes, juice boxes, the teapot and her mug had been removed to a lab somewhere for testing and comparison with blood samples and stomach contents. Without a doubt it was suicide. As instruments of murder, statins, paracetamol, fruit juice and Earl Grey tea were ridiculous. The amounts needed to do the job were phenomenal. I thought about Sophia, sitting there alone chugging down litres of grapefruit juice and pots of tea. Such determination. Such a long time to hold her nerve and not call for rescue.

*

Three hours later fifteen bulging garbage bags and eleven stuffed cardboard boxes sat in a row against the railings. Murray Gooding poked his head out of a window as I stood for a moment easing the muscles in my shoulders. He said, 'The Hobsons both took statins, you know. It isn't just me.'

I glared at him and went back up to the kitchen without a word. No sound came from the living room so I went in. Karine had managed to clear a path to one sofa. She sat with her head in her hands. She didn't look up but said, 'I'm so fricking angry.'

I said, 'I've found some Famille Rose china. Is that what you want saved?'

'There's newspaper to wrap it in…' She pointed helplessly to a stack of Times Literary Supplements that nearly reached the ceiling. I was tempted to hold my head too. In the kitchen newspapers actually did reach the ceiling. I'd knocked one column over and discovered a mouse nest.

At twenty to midnight Karine found me scrubbing out the rancid fridge which no one had thought to empty before turning off the electricity. Every surface had been washed. Two boxes of carefully wrapped china rested on the table.

Karine's jaw dropped. She said, 'I loathe my mother.'

I said, 'She kept your wedding dress.'

Karine burst into wracking sobs.

Because I didn't think I could make matters any worse I asked, 'Do you know what Sophia was wearing when she died?'

Karine looked at me with hate-filled eyes. 'What an awful question!' But then, maybe thinking she owed me, she said, 'She was wearing her Hillel t-shirt. Black with white lettering.'

Ignorance was written on my face. So she added, unable to keep contempt out of her voice, 'Hillel the Elder – a *very famous* Jewish teacher. On the front it said, "That which is hateful to you do not do to your fellow" and on the back, "If not now, when?" She was such a hypocrite.'

'Okay,' I said. 'But she still kept your wedding dress.' I was too bone weary to be clever.

So was Karine. All she said was, 'Same time tomorrow?'

The next day Karine said, 'I've taken a diazepam.' She looked stoned enough to have taken six. She remained in the living room and sent me up to the bathroom which was, amazingly, clean. Of course Sophia had hoarded hundreds of those slivers of soap that sane people throw out when they become transparent. And she'd kept squeezed-dry toothpaste tubes, old toothbrushes and even gum massagers. But the bath, basin and lavatory shone white with hygiene.

Two mirrored cabinets bulged with everything except statins, prescription drugs or over-the-counter medicines. I presumed they were either inside Sophia or confiscated by the cops.

The cupboard on the bathroom landing was stuffed with towels, flannels and bathmats. Compared to the kitchen this was easy-peasy, and I had three bags and three boxes filled and out by the railings in less than an hour. Some of the towels looked brand new. I was tempted, but I'd learned my lesson with the t-shirts.

Karine had cleared a path to the mantle shelf. Now she was back on the sofa with a half-filled box at her feet. She'd been sandbagged by photographs. 'I can't do this,' she said.

I went to the kitchen. Out of my backpack I hauled my own kettle, two mugs, a handful of teabags, a plastic bottle of milk and a packet of chocolate hobnobs. I made two mugs of strong tea, gave in to the lure of hobnobs, and carried everything in to Karine. My notion of comfort turned her into a weeping jelly.

She said, 'I've been such a bitch to you. I don't give a dry fart about Barney but he lives opposite my mother, so I'd been seeing him for weeks before you showed up. He thought he was so clever lying to two women.' She blew her nose on a 'Frankie Says Relax' t-shirt.

I felt something lurch in my chest. 'Barney was sleeping with you *before* he took up with me?'

She shrugged, indifferent. 'I hate her,' she said, shaking a framed photo of herself, Devon and Sophia in my face. Strikingly, Devon looked like a sturdy athletic child. Karine went on, 'Fricking hell, my mother was seventy-something. What was she doing with a man like Eddie? She said she was in love. Don't make me gag! Couldn't she see what he was? The great wise Sophia!' Karine was laughing and crying at the same time, so smashed that she nearly fell off the sofa.

I rescued the mug and said, 'Lie down.' Her bony face and wild red eyes scared me. I thought about texting Barney to come and look after her.

'A man Eddie's age? I was younger than him and *I* was too old. Couldn't she *see* how creepy he was? She wouldn't believe *us* – her own flesh and blood.'

I said, 'You *knew* Barney was cheating on you with me? *And* he was cheating on me with you? Why didn't you warn me?'

She flopped into a horizontal position, almost kicking me off the sofa. 'Don't be stupid. No one takes a chancer like Barney seriously.'

'I did.'

'More fool you.'

'Sophia did believe you,' I said harshly. 'Obviously I didn't know at the time but she must've been talking about Eddie when she spoke of illusion, delusion and treachery.'

'Too little, too late,' Karine slurred.

'What're you talking about?' I wanted to shake her. 'Your mother *killed* herself.'

She closed her eyes and turned her head away. 'Sometimes even Soppy did the right thing,' she mumbled.

'You're using Barney as a babysitter,' I shouted at her. 'He doesn't understand children at all.'

When she didn't answer I took both mugs to the kitchen and rinsed them. I packed everything in my bag and walked out of Sophia's house.

As Karine hadn't offered to pay me and I couldn't afford parking fees or fines I'd come by bus. To avoid crying in public while I waited at the bus stop I opened the packet of chocolate hobnobs.

I was crunching unhappily when Abbi tugged at my sleeve. 'Can I have one? We only had beans on toast for our tea.' Gina stood beside her, looking famished too. It was a few seconds before I saw Devon lurking in a charity shop doorway, insubstantial as a little grey ghost.

The sisters tore into the biscuits, taking three apiece. I beckoned Devon over because if Gina and Abbi kept up this rate of consumption there'd be none left. Devon shrank even further back into the shadows.

Gina said, 'She doesn't like food.'

'She spits it into kitchen paper and flushes it down the toilet when no one's looking.' Abbi looked self-righteous.

'Nothing gets past you two,' I said. 'Why?'

'Dunno,' Gina said with her mouth full. 'She doesn't talk.'

'Why?'

'Don't know,' Abbi said, her fingers in the hobnob packet. 'Don't care. Don't like her.'

'Daddy thinks we should be friends,' Gina said. 'He isn't very clever.'

I nodded and hid the hobnobs behind my back. 'Do me a favour? Tell your dad that Devon's mum is in Sophia's flat alone and she's sick. Wait till Devon's gone, then tell him about her spitting out food.'

'Can we have the rest of the biscuits?' Abbi said.

'If you promise.'

'If we promise,' said Gina, chief negotiator, 'will you make mac-cheese for our supper? Promise?'

'You first,' I insisted. Oh, I'd make a shit-hot child therapist alright.

*

Barney rang at one thirty that night. I was dreaming about ambulances. He was blasted. He said, 'I don't want you talking to my girls anymore.'

'And I don't want you waking me up in the middle of the night anymore.'

'Is Devon really anorexic?'

'What do *you* think?'

'Her gran'ma jus' died.'

'Is that how Karine's explaining it?'

'Karine's a mess,' he said as if being a mess was just peachy if you were Karine. 'I asked her to marry me, an' she says she'll think 'bout it.'

'Is she going to find help for Devon?'

'I thought, like, we could share expenses an' all go to family therapy together. So do you know any shrinks who won't cost an arm and a leg? I'm doing like you said, Ruth. My kids don't like Karine and Devon doesn't like me. If we're gonna get married… '

I was really tired. I said, 'Given the amount of shite you talk, God should've given you two arseholes – one at each end.' And I rang off.

But I couldn't sleep. I decided to go to the police and tell them that Eddie was probably a paedophile, and either Sophia killed him or, more likely, Karine had and Sophia was taking the blame. Then I decided the worst sufferer would be Devon who was suffering already.

I decided to ring the social services and report Devon as an abused child in danger. But even if I called anonymously everyone would know it was me. They'd tell the cops and the social services that I was a vengeful bitch Barney dumped for Karine. And how would I explain to Dan that his half-brother had abused Devon in some way?

I was convinced, but proof?

I couldn't stop thinking about Sophia's last t-shirt, 'That which is hateful to you do not do to your fellow', and 'If not now, when?'

Was she saying that killing was a hateful act; that she had committed a hateful act and therefore had to do the same to herself – to rebalance the world or at least her family constellation? Or was she saying that, as the matriarch of this trio of women, she was responsible for their sins *and* their suffering? And if she was to redress the balance she had to act against herself: 'If not now, when?'

Looked at yet another way, maybe the t-shirt was the only clean one Sophia could lay her hands on quickly.

But Sophia brought Eddie into Karine's and Devon's lives. Karine had said something revealing: '*I* was too old for him.' Did that mean she tried to entice him away from her ridiculous mother only to find that it was *her daughter* Eddie was interested in? If he'd done something unspeakable which turned Devon from a sturdy, athletic child into a mute grey ghost, how would she feel? What would she do?

What if they both thought he'd only got close to Sophia so he could groom Devon? How destructive to the family was that idea?

Mothers get blamed for everything. They keep therapists in business. There should be t-shirts to celebrate *that* concept. Had Sophia accepted the blame? Karine certainly blamed her. I wondered who Devon would blame in later years. I didn't really care as long as it wasn't herself. It's never the child's fault. Ever.

I got up and went to the kitchen. Out of respect for my sleeping housemates I closed the door and, without rattling too many pans, made a big batch of mac-cheese for Gina and Abbi. They must've kept *their* promise, otherwise Barney wouldn't have got drunk and called me. It wasn't their fault his emotional IQ was identical to a root vegetable's.

Then it was time to shower and dress for work. Children keep getting sick even when their nurse has a headful of razor wire.

*

The last time I saw Dan was three months later. We met at the pub on the corner of Sophia and Barney's street. He was waiting for me, already half-cut.

A broken, decomposed body had been found on the rocks off the Pembroke coast after a storm. It was unrecognisable, but Dan gave a DNA swab to help with identification and the answer came back immediately. He'd found his half brother Eddie.

I held his hand and listened while he became more and more incoherent.

Before it was too late, I said, 'The DNA result came back immediately? It usually takes weeks.'

'Huh?' Dan said. Then, 'Oh yeah, well, see, they already had Eddie's in their computer.'

'How come?' I was stroking his hand as if he were a dog who might turn nasty.

'Shshsh,' he hissed loudly. 'Don' tell anyone, but Eddie had a record. It's a secret. 'Bout five years ago this li'l bitch told the cops he followed her home from school and got her to… And the cops *believed her.*'

'No shit,' I said, sitting up straight.

'Y'know what else? They asked if I wanted his clothes back – a 'Wings' t-shirt. Ain't that a kick in the slats? When Sophia shoved him off the cliff, he couldn't fly.'

'Sophia shoved him?' I asked.

'Stands to reason.' He pushed his sweaty face into mine. 'But no one listens to me 'cept you. Gimme a kiss, eh?'

'In your dreams.' I got up and went to the door. The landlord's father had already promised to take him home for twenty quid, thirty if he threw up in the car.

That was the last time I saw him. I was accepted on an accredited therapy course and leaving Bath. Besides, my diet was working: I wasn't filling a Large any more. I was nearly a Medium. Maybe it was the revelation about Dan's brother's record that decided me: I wanted this chapter in my life to be closed. I deserved better.

WHEN I'M FEELING LUCKY

Every now and then, when I'm feeling lucky, I take a shot at unearned wealth by buying a National Lottery ticket. That evening, jazzed up for a public appearance, I was at Hanif's shop picking numbers. Sometimes my picks are completely random but this evening I was pretending to be an intellectual by choosing prime numbers: 11, 17, 23…

I was thinking about what to pick next when I heard the glass door open and felt a waft of damp night air. Nothing special about that. But then I heard Mr Hanif's voice raised in rage. An almighty crash silenced his voice. The boy who was collecting discarded wire baskets poked his head around to see what was happening. Another blast hurt my ears and the boy flung himself flat on the sticky floor.

He was wearing an apron. I thought, It's all right for *you*. I was wearing my best jacket. I was meeting friends at the Bell and Belly so I wasn't going to lie down on an unmopped convenience store floor.

There was a thump and a cascade of broken glass. I looked up at the mirror Mr Hanif has in the corner over the biscuits. It's angled so that he can see what is going on at the back of the shop without leaving the counter. Distorted, I saw his head, spread like a burst melon, slithering down from the cigarette shelf onto the smashed booze bottles below.

I stood, uncomprehending, still worried about my jacket, until I heard someone say, 'You killed him, fuckwit.'

Then, hoping for a relatively clean spot, I dropped to the floor. It wasn't real. I'd seen all this before in a dozen movies. The next scene would show a drug-crazed teenager leaning over the counter, scooping money out of the cash register. That was what happened on the endless rerun episodes of Hill Street Blues my father watched when he was out of work. He was out of work a lot. My mother left him when I was fourteen.

Now I was lying on the sticky floor of a convenience store in Streatham next to a puppy-man who was close to tears and trying to hold my hand.

Someone shouted, 'Lock the door, Donkey-dung, turn the closed sign, pull the blind down. Now! *Now!*'

Mr Hanif's blood and brains would be dribbling down to join the alcohol he wasn't allowed to drink – I'd seen it at the movies.

I thought, why am I here? I don't need bread, milk or eggs. I'm here because I thought today might be my lucky day. I might be the chosen one. Several thousands of pounds might be showered on my head like golden sunshine. Then I could give up working at Sally's Antiques and Vintage Vogue shop and write poems full time.

I was there because I'd been feeling lucky. And Mr Hanif was slumped somewhere without half his head. But it wasn't real. It was a scene repeated in thousands of movies. The foreign owner of a convenience store gunned down by druggies, gang members, crazies, anyone, for whatever reason. Mr Hanif was a bit-part actor, hired for one day to die a violent death. It had absolutely nothing to do with me.

I was a poet and a songwriter, or I would be when I made the right connections. I shouldn't even be here.

All at once a poem by the great haiku poet Matsuo Basho came into my head:

'Had I crossed the pass
supported by a stick I would have spared
myself the fall from the horse.'

It was unusual because it didn't have the traditional 'seasonal word'; instead it was the lament of a man who wished he'd made a different decision. I loved it because it meant that even the greatest poets have regrets.

'Don't just stand there,' the angry voice said. '*You've* got the fucking gun – search the back room.'

Feverishly I replied to Basho: 'Had I stayed at home
                                untempted by prize money
                                I might not have died.'

I knew I'd die because I could hear the squish of Donkey-dung's shoes creeping towards me on the tacky floor. But I was astonished that I could conjure up a five-seven-five syllable verse at a time like this.

What should I do? I thought, panic beginning to bubble up into my brain. What would the hero of this movie do? The hero would be armed with a bigger weapon than Donkey-dung's. Or a more ingenious brain.

Donkey-dung's footsteps passed by on the other side of the tinned goods shelf while I lay rigid breathing mouse breaths. The kid beside me was biting his sleeve to stifle sobs.

Donkey-dung yelled, 'The effing back door's locked.' I knew the stockroom was only a couple of yards away.

Angry-man shouted, 'Come here, turd-face, and go through the A-rab's pockets.'

'You do it!' Donkey-dung retorted. '*I've* got the bleeding gun.'

'Whatcha gonna do? Shoot me too? What would Big Boss Baz have to say about that, bollocks-for-brains?'

As the squeak-squeak footsteps retreated I thought, He's been called donkey-dung, turd-face and bollocks-for-brains. Angry-man, even under stress, likes words. Not poetic words to be sure, but I like words too. What on earth am I thinking about? Mr Hanif, from whom I'd been buying bread, halloumi, milk, aduki beans and chilis for years, has been savagely destroyed and I'm thinking about words and seventeen-syllable poems. What sort of psycho am *I*?

Donkey-dung said, 'I'm not touching *that*.'

There was the sound of a fight: grunts, blows, swearing, crunching cereal boxes. I buried my head in the crook of my elbow. Then, to my horror, the kid on the floor scrambled to his feet and yelled, '*Stop it, stop it*! Key on hook behind counter.'

He was, I realised, one of Mr Hanif's nephews – the slow one who only worked the late shift when business was light.

'Come here,' shrieked Donkey-dung.

It was way too late to stop him. Before I could reach out a hand to hold him back he was already plodding down the aisle he should have mopped. I didn't know his name. 'My nephew will get,' Mr Hanif said of many young guys who fetched and carried for him. I never saw Mr H leave the counter.

The plodding stopped. 'Uncle?' Nephew said in his odd monotone. '*Uncle*?' he repeated in rising hysteria.

There was the sound of a slap and Nephew started to cry. This was when the heroine would rise up in protective outrage and say, 'Leave the kid alone – he doesn't understand.'

I hugged the floor and thought, 'My duvet hugged me –
safe from September danger.
Foolish, I left home.'

Five-seven-five syllables. What was *wrong* with me?

After pie and chips at the Bell and Belly Keisha, Grant and I would climb the narrow stairs to the small events room on the second floor where the poetry slam would be beginning. I was ready. I had my notebook in my bag which was hanging securely across my chest. If I was popular at the Bell and Belly bash it wasn't because I was talented but because haiku is one of the shortest poetic forms on the planet. But I can say right now that never in a million years would I recite something that began, 'My duvet hugged me...' The correct number of syllables does not make a good poem.

I knew why Nephew had screamed, 'Stop it, stop it.'

No I didn't, but I remember screaming, 'Stop it,' at my parents when they were fighting because I couldn't stand the violence anymore and there was nowhere to hide. If I were at home now I'd have a pillow over my head and I'd still hear the screaming.

Sobbing, Nephew said, 'Nail behind rolling tobacco.'

'Get it,' Angry-man ordered.

'But, Uncle,' whimpered Nephew.

'Bugger Uncle, fetch me them keys.' This was someone else. Not Angry-man or Donkey-dung. No blood on *his* shoes, I thought.

Nephew was quite hysterical now. He was making animal sounds as if he couldn't breathe for tears and snot. Mr Hanif always spoke to him in simple sentences, usually in Arabic, and always in a quiet, even tone. He never shouted at this nephew, which he did with others in his family, calling them, 'Lazy boy,' 'Idiot,' and 'Waster'.

Three men, one gun – at least one gun. It was way too much violence to deploy for Mr Hanif's meagre night-time cash register. Didn't everyone know Mrs Hanif or Elder Daughter Hanif emptied it after rush hour and took the money away?

Someone must've hit Nephew, because he shrieked.

'Give me that fucking shooter,' Angry-man yelled. 'You can't be trusted.'

There was a scuffle. Then the man with clean shoes said, 'Give me the sodding gun or I'll carve "twat" on your face.'

Three men, one gun and a knife.

Two pairs of footsteps walked down the next aisle. A key entered a lock. The door opened.

'Storeroom,' said Angry-man. 'Where are the stairs?'

'Stairs?' This was Donkey-dung.

'These buggers always live upstairs with their six wives and twenty kids.'

'No stairs,' Donkey-dung decided after a pause for the sound of rummaging.

'No safe,' Angry-man said. 'But, hello, we got a back door. At least we won't have to go out the way we came in.'

Clean-shoes joined them saying, 'So we're cushty. No cameras, no witnesses.' I hadn't heard his footsteps.

Donkey-dung said, 'What about boo-hoo boy?' And I realised that Nephew, a witness, had stopped crying.

Clean-shoes said, 'Not a problem anymore.'

Donkey-dung laughed. 'Sorted.'

I pulled the pillow over my head, shutting my eyes so tight I could hear my eyelashes grinding together.

Angry-man said, 'Sorted? Are you brain-dead? You chopped down the money tree.'

'I never chopped a tree...' Donkey-dung began.

Angry-man interrupted, 'What shop did they get you from? Morons-R-Us?'

'He's Baz's cousin's boy,' Clean-shoes said, sounding tired. 'Every family's got one'

'Not every family sends one out on a job that needs half a teaspoon of brains.'

'He only had thirty-two quid in the till,' Donkey-dung said unwisely.

'We wasn't interested in the till,' Clean-shoes said, in the faux-patient voice that could easily explode into more violence. 'You knew that.'

And then someone kicked me in the ribs.

'Knock, knock,' said Angry-man.

'Who's there?' I gasped. It was, I thought, the only right response.

'Sid,' he said.

'Sid who?' I was almost retching.

'Sid up, and fucking tell us what you're doing down there.'

I struggled up, leaning against the jars of instant coffee, hugging my bruised ribs. I couldn't stop words from hopping like frogs out of my mouth. 'I got bored and decided to count cockroaches.'

I stared up. There were three of them now. Angry-man of course. He was about forty-five with a thin, lined face and a bitter mouth. He wore Buddy Holly glasses.

Clean-shoes' shoes were indeed clean. He was the kind of well-fed type you might have bought a house from. But his smooth plump face was puckered by a scar that ran diagonally from brow to chin. He held a vermilion knife.

Donkey-dung was dressed like a rapper half his weight and twice his IQ. He was squirmy and jittery. I guessed his agitation had something to do with the white powder clinging to his nose hair. 'Earth tremor, danger –
      it's the fool who has the gun.
      There's snow on his nose.'

Five, seven, five. Perfect, if only it made sense.

'What's five, seven, five?' asked Angry-man.

'Did I say that out loud?'

'Yes.'

'There were five-hundred-and-seventy-five cockroaches,' I babbled. I couldn't tear my eyes away from the red knife. 'But I may have counted the same ones twice. They live in families and care for their young, like humans.' I had no idea if this was true, and I had even less idea why I was talking or why the three men were still listening. Maybe, like me, they had no idea what to do next.

'Shall I shoot her now?' Donkey-dung asked no one in particular. He pointed his gun at a spot between my eyes. I turned my head away and found myself looking directly at Angry-man. His eyes were pavement grey.

'You look like Buddy Holly,' I said.

'Are you an expert on mid-fifties pop music too?' He asked, without any change of expression.

I began, 'Well, "A long, long time ago, I can still remember how the music used to make me smile".' I watched him casually pick up a can of Campbell's tomato soup. He rolled it between his palms, nodding at me encouragingly.

'That used to be my favourite song,' he told me almost dreamily. Then like a striking snake he uncurled his right arm and belted Donkey-dung a terrible blow on the side of his head.

Donkey-dung dropped like a large bag of custard. He bounced, wobbled and then lay still. Blood seeped out of his ear and the corner of his eye.

As he was falling the gun flew upwards and Angry-man caught it neatly with his left hand.

'Who the hell let that moron out with a weapon?' Clean-shoes said, fiddling with his knife. They both looked at me and burst out laughing so I knew I must look utterly terrified.

Clean-shoes said, 'Does it have to be "Bye-bye Miss American Pie" now?'

'What do you think?'

'I think, unless we come up with a watertight explanation we might as well kebab *ourselves*. This was not supposed to happen. This was business. The rag-head would be tough – we knew that – but they always fold in the end. He was no fool.'

'Unlike Baz's cousin's boy,' Angry-man said. 'Now we have two deaths and no dosh.' He looked down at Donkey-dung's inert body without emotion.

'Death by tomato soup,' I heard myself saying.

'She ain't helping,' Clean-shoes said.

'Say something else,' Angry-man said to me.

I was choked by tears so I said very softly, '"I don't remember if I cried the night I heard about his widowed bride."'

'Oh yes,' Angry-man said gently. 'The death of Buddy Holly. Okay, Miss American Pie, who are you really?'

'The innocent bystander,' I said.

'You're the effing corpse,' Clean-shoes said. 'Is *everyone* bonkers in this shit-hole shop?'

Angry-man put the gun in his pocket and ran a well-kept hand through dark hair where age had begun to scribble messages of mortality.

He was the undercover cop, I decided. He was treading the fine line between bad guy and good cop – trying to be part of the gang without compromising his moral self.

He hadn't managed too well so far: three deaths, one gun, one knife and a tin of tomato soup. But the soup was *his* weapon of choice and he *had* saved my life with it. Hadn't he?

He moved close to me and patted my cheek. His hand was hard, dry and warm. 'It's shock,' he told Clean-shoes and me. 'Snap out of it – there's nothing you can change. You're caught in a shit-storm. Get used to it.'

'I'm a life coach,' I said, only because it rhymed with cockroach. 'A life and death coach, and I always prattle when I'm scared.'

The two men, fat and thin, stared at me. Clean-shoes said, 'You mean you tell other people what to do?'

'No,' I said, 'I advise them about how to do what they want to do.'

'I want to get out of this place,' Angry-man said.

I pointed to the back door.

'Safe,' he said. 'Unseen.'

'Then send him.' I jerked my thumb at Clean-shoes. 'Send him out first and see what happens. You need more information. "Wise men say only fools rush in" or out.'

'You calling me a fool?' Clean-shoes asked angrily.

'It's a song,' Angry-man said sounding tired. 'Elvis. Heard of him? Miss American Pie here seems to have a thing for lyrics.'

'You asked the question,' I said. 'If *he* asked the question the answer would be different.' My voice was wobbling dangerously.

'Aha,' said Angry-man. 'What if I change the question? We *both* want to leave safe.'

'That's where Donkey-dung would have been an asset,' I said.

'How about *you're* the asset?' Clean-shoes said.

'Good thinking,' Angry-man said. 'We let her out the back door and watch her run to the nearest cop.' He considered me, head tilted to one side like a curious raven. 'There's something not right about you. Are you on medication?'

'Only a little,' I told him, trying to keep my voice steady. I desperately wanted to cover my lies with another lyric, haiku or joke.

'On day release from the funny farm?' Clean-shoes was playing with his knife – now rusting with Mr Hanif's nephew's drying blood.

'No.' Then, unable to stop myself, I blurted, 'But I do live only a stone's throw away from a family who all died mysteriously from head injuries.'

'Wha?' Clean-shoes scowled, but Angry-man burst out laughing. He said, 'We should go quickly, before people start to wonder why the shop's closed.'

'Yeah, and figure out what to tell Big Baz later. Is there a bog somewhere?' He was looking at me.

'Must be,' Angry-man said. 'You got that nervous bladder thing again?'

'Fuck off. I was thinking about her.' He jerked his chin at me.

'My bladder's okay,' I said.

'Where's the bleeding bog?' Clean-shoes shouted, making me jump.

'I don't know,' I said, 'I've never been back there before.'

'Go and look!' Clean-shoes screamed into my face. His spittle hit my skin like instant infection. I could feel every disease he'd ever had burning into my eyeballs and boring through my lips and cheeks. The man didn't need a knife: he could kill just by standing too close.

Sputum kills poets, I thought. But I managed to say, 'Are you going to slice my heart out among the Beaujolais bottles?' I tried to step backwards into the shop. Clean-shoes cut off my line of escape.

'He's going to kill me,' I said. 'He wants me to die in the loo of a lousy inconvenience store.'

'Is that the plan? Angry-man sounded incredulous.

'Nah, fuck off,' said Clean-shoes. 'Well, yeah, it makes sense, don't it?'

Angry-man just stared.

Now he's going to take the gun out of his pocket, point it at me until Clean-shoes relaxes. Then he'll shoot Clean-shoes and we'll escape into the night, hand in hand. I'd definitely seen *that* movie.

But Angry-man kept right on staring. My silence was certainly not going to save me.

'Or,' I said, thinking wildly, voice trembling, 'there's the hostage alternative. That way you could make some money and no one has to get hurt.'

'Too complicated,' Clean-shoes said.

And then my phone rang.

A couple of months ago Keisha programmed 'Crazy Little Thing Called Love' into my phone as a ringtone. So we all heard Freddie Mercury singing, 'I gotta be cool, relax, get hip and get off my tracks' from the depth of my pocket.

'Gimme your phone,' Clean-shoes hissed.

Angry-man was laughing grimly. 'Good tune. Better give the man your phone. "And take a long ride on my motorbike",' he sang along with Freddie.

I fumbled in my pocket and took out my phone which I nearly dropped because my hands were sweating.

'Do we *have* to kill her?' Angry-man asked. 'She makes me laugh.'

I handed my phone to *him*. To my dismay he answered it and I clearly heard Keisha say, 'Where are you, Mina? You're on in ten minutes. You don't sign in, you lose your slot.'

Keisha avoids unnecessary words, a talent I wished I shared just then.

'She ain't coming,' Angry-man said, and switched the phone off. He wasn't wasting words either.

'Why did you do that?' Clean-shoes asked. 'Stamp on the fuckin' thing.'

'I'm considering the hostage option,' Angry-man said. 'Let's just sodding walk out of this door right now before anything worse happens.' He put my phone in his pocket and replaced it in his right hand with the gun which he jammed in the middle of my back. 'You lead,' he ordered. 'Open the effing door and walk out. Any funny stuff and I'll pop you. Got it?'

Clean-shoes said, 'Forgetting something, genius? The sodding car? Kyle's Beamer?'

'Get his keys. Meet us round the back.'

I needed a role-model – but who? The Tomb Raider? The Warrior Princess? The Vampire Slayer? Wannabe Poet doesn't cut it as a Twenty-first Century fantasy female.

Would I be better off if I went running in my spare time, built up my muscles at the gym, lost weight, got a new haircut? I was pitted against a bloody knife, a gun and a man who used a can of soup as a lethal weapon. What did I have to compete with those? Silence, lies and compliance? They weren't weapons, they were terrified responses. How many dark paths had silence, lies and compliance led women down?

Words? Tiny verses that didn't have to rhyme – orphaned words that had no music to give them emotional punch. How many lives had they saved?

Clean-shoes appeared holding Kyle's keys. Angry-man prodded me with the gun. I stepped carefully towards the back door, unlocked it and opened it a crack. I sniffed the cold night air.

We stepped out into the service alley that ran behind the shops and felt sharp September wind on our faces.

Clean-shoes turned right and marched away to find Donkey-dung-Kyle's car.

Angry-man put his arm around me and pulled me close – my back to his front, handgun digging in between us.

'How come you like the same music as me? You're too young for Freddie Mercury.' Kidnap was feeling suspiciously like an embrace.

I said, 'How's the evening going for you so far?'

'Fucking bollock-shite,' he breathed into my ear. 'You?'

'Don't laugh – I was feeling lucky so I stopped in for a lottery ticket.'

Of course he laughed. I hoped he would. I said, 'If you won the lottery, what's the first thing you'd do?'

'Buy a seaside house in Thailand. You?'

'Buy a time machine, go back and decide not to buy a lottery ticket.'

He laughed again. Then, 'But if you did that you wouldn't buy the winning ticket so there'd be no time machine.'

'But you wouldn't have a gun in my back.'

'But *I'd* of still been forced to go out on a job with a total piss-pants berk who fucked up the whole bleeding show. My fate was sealed.'

'Fate,' I murmured. 'Or bad decisions. Not my first, obviously.'

'What was your first?'

I paused. My voice started to wobble. 'Not going into my mother's business.'

'What business?'

'She's a jeweller of sorts. She buys broken or unwanted jewellery, melts down gold, resets stones in modern settings. Sells to South-East Asia mostly. It's a really nice earner.'

'Hmmm.' He sounded thoughtful. 'What about your dad?'

'Drunk. Abusive. Haven't seen him for years.'

'Same here.' He sounded surprised. 'So, how much would your mum pay for your safe release?'

'Don't know. How much would you want?'

'Don't know. Never thought about it before.'

'Well, my mum isn't worth millions.' I tried to calm the vocal tremble. 'But she might think about crowdfunding. She's an enterprising woman.'

He shrugged. I felt the gun rise and fall. He said, 'See, I'm knee deep in the shark pool.'

And then a car without headlights crawled up the alley towards us. Angry-man pulled me back into the doorway.

Clean-shoes got out saying, 'I thought you'd scarper.'

'I thought you would,' Angry-man responded.

'I got honour.'

'Yeah, yeah,' Angry-man said, sounding less than convinced.

Then the door behind us jerked open so suddenly we nearly fell backwards. Kyle lurched out to the sound of breaking glass. He had both arms clamped around a carton of wine bottles. The bottom of the box was damaged so he was dropping bottles one at a time like a dull-witted hen laying eggs.

'Look what I found,' he announced proudly. Blood ran sluggishly from his nose. He didn't notice. 'Are we leaving?' he asked. 'Move over, I'll drive.' He managed to save the last bottle and standing, swaying, in the midst of shattered glass and spilled wine, he unscrewed the cap and took a slug.

Angry-man said, 'You asked one of us to drive. You fell and hurt your head, remember?' He opened the rear door of the BMW and half ushered, half shoved Kyle and his bottle onto the back seat.

While he was doing this, Clean-shoes popped the trunk open, and, without warning, threw me inside. I just had time to glimpse a mess of beer cans, dog food, cartons of cigarettes, muzzles, leashes and dry cleaning bags before he slammed the lid shut and left me in the dark.

'I can't breathe!' I screamed. But I couldn't see or hear either. I could smell exhaust fumes and I could feel hard edges digging into my back and legs. My head was crammed at an odd angle against what I supposed was a wheel arch. My right arm was trapped by the weight of my own body.

'Let me out!' I shrieked. 'I can't breathe.' My voice stopped six inches from my mouth and I knew no one wanted to hear me, no one wanted to see me, no one wanted to help me or keep me safe. My throat constricted as surely as if Clean-shoes was throttling me. A sensation like a balloon full of worms filled my chest and began to expand to bursting point. This must be panic, I thought. I will die if the bubble bursts.

Breathe, I thought, while there is still some air: in slowly, out slowly.

I wriggled experimentally and found I could bend my knees a little more. I could relieve the pain in my neck a bit and wriggle slightly to push some of the cruel cans out of the way. But there was no comfort.

Out of the blue came the sensation of being an infant crying in the dark. After a while I gave up because somehow I knew with tragic certainty that no one would come to pick me up, cuddle me and feed me. I was screaming for what I could not have and something inside me died.

My name is Mina and I grew up with secrets. I couldn't have friends over for tea or sleepovers so I didn't have friends. My mother, father and I lived in a series of one-bedroom furnished flats, flitting in the dead of night when we couldn't pay the rent. My father was an alky and my mother was obsessed with him. She didn't seem to mind him hitting her and she only moved out when he started to get interested in me in the wrong way. It was something she never forgave me for. After that she pulled herself together somewhat and found work with a local pawnbroker.

Me? I made stuff up and lived in a land of secrets, lies and dreams. You know, the other world, where you're safe, warm, rich and popular. The world where you win prizes and approval instead of being the kid in the back row who never puts her hand up and who tries to make charity shop clothes look like a personal choice.

Well, listen: don't feel sorry for me. I could do that all by myself. And I didn't wallow in it. I got weekend jobs waitressing and shelf-stacking. I saved every penny and I left home as soon as I knew I had a half scholarship to a university in the West Country.

I sold my virginity for a thousand pounds to the owner of a bar chain called Pigs In Clover, which set me up for the first few week's rent.

Did you believe that? Yes? Don't feel too bad about it – it was a story I told a library friend at college knowing it would circulate and make me look more interesting. It was the sort of story I'd previously only told myself when I was trying to figure out how to survive financially without parental support.

Sometime in that first year my heart began to dream of real skills, and I took a Saturday morning job telling children stories at a city centre library. I started with tailored versions of Kipling and Hans Andersen. But soon, bored with familiarity, I enlisted the children's help: I asked them the age-old question, 'What do *you* think happened next?' These sessions were so successful that I was approached by a publisher to collect and write them down. It was the beginning of my fame as a children's writer.

Did you believe that one? Okay, well it's partially true except, of course, there was no fame and certainly no fortune. But a tiny Bristol press and printer did bring out a slim collection and the books sold out. But no one suggested a second edition. There has been no interest in my work since then.

As for my claims to have a rich mother willing to crowdfund my release from imprisonment? I haven't seen her for years and I don't know whether she's alive or dead. My connection with her was weakened when we moved to a two-bedroom flat in a north London high-rise and she started to refer to my tiny bedroom as the 'spare room'. She also used my wardrobe for her overflow clothes even before my final year at school or my acceptance at uni. I mattered less to her than her frocks and shoes.

Not only am I fighting panic and breathlessness, I must, must, must fight my deep-rooted feeling that confinement in the boot of Kyle's Beamer is my place in life. He is a murderer. He is stupid and probably a coke-head. Yet he owns a saloon with a trunk large enough for a fully grown woman and a load of dog food. What would my therapist say?

Do you believe I can afford one? No. You're right – that's not what I spend my money on.

Keisha would say, 'Stand tall, Mina, get out of your own light.' Which is difficult when you're lying in the dark with your knees crushing your boobs. So I did what I always do when circumstances become the spade I use to dig up the decaying bones of the past: I put up all my Keep Out signs and occupied my own private territory.

At the moment I am in 17th Century Japan following Matsuo Basho into the Deep North. I carry his Knapsack Notebook and he is not at all bothered by the fact that for this journey his disciple is a woman. I stand beside him, contemplating plum blossom 'behind the shrine-maiden's house'. Although I do not know what a shrine-maiden is or what she does.

Basho is about to explain when the car stops with a jolt that I can feel jarring every bone in my spine. Plum blossom falls in a rotting clump at my feet and car doors slam. Three slams: one for Kyle, one for Clean-shoes, and one for Angry-man: the gun, the knife and a can of soup. Mr Hanif and his nephew die all over again.

While I'm here I'm safe, I thought, suffocated but alive. When they come for me they'll kill me. They'll have to. I am the other witness. This is what the hero in the movies is for – to prevent the inevitable from happening. Which is what Angry-man did: he prevented D-Dung-Kyle from shooting me between the eyes. He averted my inevitable death. Does that make him a hero? Or was he actually preventing another gunshot that might be heard and reported? Was he saving *himself* from further involvement in a calamity he never intended and couldn't control?

On the one hand this, on the other hand that. Or maybe, I thought, it's two sides of the same hand:
'The palm of your hand
strokes my cheek, while your hard fist
punches my teeth out.'

Not a useful concept. *Is* poetry useful? Does it feed the hungry, heal the sick or warm your bones on a winter's night? No, no and no. But it's keeping me sane right now – not because I'm reading it and it's bringing comfort to my aching heart – no, again. It's because, however crappy, I'm making it. It's the act of making that stops me shaking. Don't sneer – it doesn't have to be good; it just has to be done.

I don't know how much time passed before I heard voices. By then all my muscles were cramping and I thought I was running a fever.

The car started and the painful journey continued. I didn't want to cry, because I couldn't blow my nose or dry my stinging eyes. But there was nothing except pain left, and when Angry-man at last opened the lid of the boot and hauled me out I couldn't stand up. The arm I had been lying on was numb, purple and puffy and I had a nose bleed which had run into my hair and ear.

He said, 'Bit of a mess, aren't you?'

We seemed to be on a dirt track between pine trees. It was raining. The silence, after the noise of the grinding engine, made me feel I'd been struck deaf. I could only just hear Angry-man's voice. He said, 'Nothing to say? Not so gobby now, are you?'

I couldn't answer. I let the rain wash my face and hair. It dripped into my mouth as I gasped, and diluted the taste of my own blood.

He had an umbrella in one hand and Kyle's gun in the other. A shovel was leaning against the rear of the car.

He said, 'Do you know what you're supposed to do now? Eh?'

I still couldn't speak so he went on, 'You're supposed to dig your own grave, lie down in a convenient position so that I can put a double tap into the back of your bonce, all neat and professional, without having to look at your face. Like it?'

There it was. Out in the open. Dig your own grave. You're food for the worms. Fiction and non-fiction alike: the Nazis, The Godfather, Syria, The Sopranos, Afghanistan, The Wire and beyond – an endless stream of stories celebrating men's violence. And women's need for rescue.

My guts turned to water and my legs to jelly. I croaked, 'I need to pee. Can you wait?'

'You're kidding me,' he said, an expression of disbelief on his quirky not quite handsome face.

'No,' I replied, not knowing where my voice was coming from. My puffy hand and arm were burning. My back was shooting pain down my legs. Is old age like this? I thought. Is this what my hero, the one with the gun, is rescuing me from? I reached in my bag – which was still hanging across my chest – and drew out a bunch of tissues. I waved them at Angry-man as I staggered to my feet and hobbled off behind the nearest tree.

'Dig your own grave,' I threw at him as I squatted as effectively as I could manage.

When I'd finished I limped away from him and his gun.

'Fuck off – I'm running away,' I told him when after only a couple of strides he caught up with me. 'Can't we pretend I distracted you with a clever lie and then took off into the forest like a deer, never to be seen again?'

I stopped. Escaping certain death was just too painful at the moment. He looked me up and down. I knew I was a sorry sight. It's hard for a woman, a film and music buff like me, not to be MTV beautiful in circumstances where beauty always saves the blonde chick in danger.

He grinned and jerked the gun at me. 'Tell you what,' he said, 'show me your tits and maybe I'll let you go.'

I could actually feel my jaw drop. I thought, What's *wrong* with this man? And to my horror my second thought was to remember what underwear I'd put on while dressing for a poetry slam. Was it pretty enough?

'What if you don't like my tits?' I asked shakily.

This time he laughed out loud. 'I'll decide that,' he said. And any hope I had left disappeared.

'No,' I said. 'You take me back to Streatham first.'

'I got the gun.'

'So shoot me. But I won't show you my tits or dig a sodding grave for you.'

'Got a lyric for this?' he jeered.

'"Would it be enough for your cheating heart if I broke down and cried?"' I said, without even thinking.

'*It's Only Rock'n'Roll,*' he said. 'And I do like it.'

The rain bounced off his umbrella, but I was drenched and shivering violently with cold and shock.

He stabbed at the night air with his gun and, obediently I walked back towards the car. And I wondered if it was my subconscious choice of lyrics that was keeping me alive. This man was old enough to wear a watch – was that the signal I was responding to? How would he react to something from the present century? I didn't want to find out. Experience tells me not to change what's working. I needed this man's approval to survive the night.

At the car he taped my hands together and fixed me to the seat beside him. He laughed and called the procedure 'a little light bondage'. And I was so grateful not to be stuffed back into the boot that I said nothing. God help me, I even smiled.

He interrogated me about where I lived, and who I lived with: Streatham and nobody. He looked at his watch and told me it was just after three in the morning. 'Not many nosy buggers around,' he said. And I agreed. I was being agreeable.

We drove for nearly an hour along nearly empty roads and only stopped when we got to the South Circular. Then he tied my scarf around my eyes and placed his own dark glasses over the blindfold. He drove on for a few more minutes before stopping again and switching off the engine.

Blind, aching and immobile, I could only wait for his next move. I comforted myself by thinking he wouldn't shoot me in Kyle's BMW. The constant tension was too much. Unwisely I relaxed a little.

I waited for him in the dark, and he wasn't long. We were switching cars, he told me, as he untied me from the seat and manhandled me into something else just as big. It was still raining. This time the ripping sound told me I was gaffer-taped to the back of the seat. I couldn't move an inch.

'Is this your car?' I asked as we moved off.

'Yes, so don't throw up or pee on the seat.' He sounded almost jolly.

He was even less likely to shoot me in his own car, wasn't he?

'Where are we going?' I asked, rather than, 'Where are you taking me?' I wanted him to think of me as half of 'we' or 'us'. Wouldn't I be safer that way?

'You'll find out soon enough,' he replied.

You're enjoying this I thought, before remembering he was in danger too. I was a danger to him, and that was why he was so dangerous to me. It was a toxic lock.

And yet, I thought, you wear Buddy Holly glasses and look as though you read books. I had made so many mistakes about men you'd think I'd know better than to make a judgement based on a guy's spectacles.

The first time I met Keisha was at a club in Camden. The DJ was hot and everyone was on their feet. Me too. Just stompin' joyfully. Then a big, good-looking guy edged over and danced in a tight circle around me. I gave him the eye, and was moving closer when an equally big woman hipped me out of the way. She said something to me but the music was too loud.

'What?' I shrieked, annoyed.

'Mine!' She screamed.

What a bitch, I thought and danced away.

Later, at the bar, she tapped me on the shoulder.

Oh fuck, trouble, I thought, mainly because her eye shadow was silver and blue. But she paid for my mojito and said, 'That's Grant. We been together three years, but he can't resist a lone dancer. So best I step in before misunderstanding. See, then I get vex. No one has fun when I vex.'

The bitch became my best friend and Grant proved to be an almost reliable boyfriend.

In her club schmutter she looked aggressive and possessive. In fact she was protecting all three of us from drink-fuelled agro. And *she* read books – which I never would have guessed judging by her mascara. She is an activist; I am an observer. This suits both of us.

Angry-man and I were dangerous to each other, which suited neither of us – especially me since I was tied up and he had the gun.

I was very tired and extremely frightened so I asked, 'Is the dumb guy going to be okay?'

'What's it to you?' he replied. Then, 'Is your name really Mina?'

'No,' I said, shocked he'd remembered. 'It's a made-up stage name.'

'Stage? I thought you were a life coach.'

'So? Don't you do stuff in daylight that isn't clobbering stupid blokes with canned goods and tying up women?'

He started to laugh but cut it off sharply. 'Is that what you think of me?'

'That's what I see.' Mistake.

'What *did* you see?' He asked so casually that that my hair tingled. This was the crux.

'Nothing. I heard a shot and went down flat.'

'What else did you hear?'

'I covered my head with both arms,' I said, voice shivering. 'Didn't know anything till someone kicked me. I was hiding, but, you know, "nowhere to run, nowhere to hide".'

There was a long pause, then he said, 'Um, Martha and the Vandellas?'

I nodded. To him this was a quiz and lyrics were his specialist subject.

'I'm not so good with women,' he confessed.

No shit, I thought, but said nothing.

I could hear and feel his body move when he braked or slowed for turns. His thigh, so close to mine, oozed heat. He smelled of sweat, cologne and maybe gravy. There was no hint of spice on his breath. This guy, I guessed, ate straight white English. Picturing him, I remembered he had dressed smart casual when he went out to... Do what? Intimidate, rob, force Mr Hanif into doing something? I nearly asked. I nearly said, 'Are you a gangster?' Blind, I felt disembodied and therefore immune to consequences.

At last I said, 'Mina is a street performer at weekends.

'Are you successful?'

'No.' I was telling the truth for once.

'What would a life coach say about that?'

I put a smile into my tremulous voice. 'If the client is young and has no responsibilities I say, "If you love it, if you want it, have a go – a serious, all-in go". I think the worst thing about getting old must be to realise you wasted your youth and energy by playing safe.' I liked that answer.

There was a pause. Then Angry-man said, 'I want to fucking hit you.'

I could've swallowed my tongue.

He said, 'I ain't young.'

'You aren't old either.' I was running to catch up.

'Too old to try out for Millwall. I was good as a kid – captain of football at my school. I was scouted when I was fourteen. But my effing mum wouldn't hear of it. "You're too young," she said. "Get a proper job," she said. "Your uncle Eddie is doing great in the butchering. He goes to Spain twice a year." I wasn't even playing safe for meself. I was playing safe for her. Some of us never had a youth. We were too fucking busy trying to be our mother's father. Geddit?'

'Yes,' I said chastened. But it didn't give him the right to hold a gun on me, tie me up and blind me.

He braked and jerked the handbrake on. 'Gimme your bag,' he said roughly.

'I can't,' I told him.

'Bugger,' he said. The car wallowed as he got out and opened my door. One minute my bag was safely hanging across my body under the seatbelt and gaffer tape, and the next he'd cut the strap and was ripping it away from me.

He did this without cutting the tape that bound me. I tested the restraints and found that I still couldn't move an inch.

He wanted my bag presumably to get at my keys. If he wanted my keys it must be because we were outside my house. If I could ease just one hand out of the sticky binding I could lean on the horn, make a ruckus, attract attention. But gaffer tape is famous for good reason: my washing machine is held together by gaffer tape. I am part of Angry-man's car.

I have neighbours in the street. Maybe one of them, soothing a fretful child, would hear me scream. Maybe, though, they've all heard about Mr Hanif's murder and will be too scared to respond. Maybe his shop, just round the corner from here, is swathed with police bunting – blue and white ribbons dancing in the wind and rain, announcing his catastrophe. My neighbours might be terrified.

I call, 'Can anyone hear me?' And my voice bounces off the windscreen like a ping-pong ball. I can hear autumn rain suddenly sharpen to ice, irritable hail thrown like pins at the glass. But confined among the man-smells of fuel, leather, cooling metal and gravy, waiting for the worst, I am warm and comfortable.

He has taken my satchel-shaped bag with my keys. In it are two notebooks full of handwritten jottings, observations and a small bunch of polished poems. The poems are already as safe as poems can be in binary code in a computer. But there is no copy of night thoughts and word plays that might or might not prove useful. My notebooks are like seed packets: some seeds will grow; some are duds. The trick is in deciding which is which.

I had picked out three linked verses for tonight – tonight, which is now over and turning too fast or too slowly, into morning – while I hang suspended between yesterday and tomorrow.

I think about the three verses and cannot remember a single line of what I felt so intensely, worked on so slowly and changed so often. Tears burn my eyeballs and are sucked up by the blindfold. I was grieving for the woman who I was before I stopped to buy a lottery ticket.

If I survive the next few hours probably I'll say I was grieving for Mr Hanif and his nephew. But now, because I may have no future, I've no one's good opinion to lose by being honest.

Movie scenario: one, I kneel on the floor and he does what he said he'd do in the woods – he fires through a cushion to muffle the sound – two bullets in the back of my head. I would only hear the first shot. Two, he shoves me into my tiny shower stall and, pulling my head back by my hair, produces the fishing knife I have not yet seen and slits my throat. The camera lingers on the splashed Psycho tiles and the blood swirling clockwise down the drain. It will hurt a lot for a short time. Three, he will fake my suicide by hanging me by my own belt from the hook behind the door. I suffocate slowly. This probably won't work as I am not good with rawlplugs and the hook may not bear my weight. It could turn into a comedy. Four...

This is what my brain does while I wait for Angry-man. It also looks at the scenes where Woman in Danger breaks her captor's hold by throwing her head back and nutting him on the bridge of his nose, causing so much pain and shock that she has time to escape. Feminism says that Woman in Danger should save herself.

This woman in danger is thwarted by gaffer tape. She has no secret weapon. The only thing that might help is that Angry-man, in spite of his apparent strength and certainty, seems confused. He has already saved my life once and, at another time, changed his mind about killing me. But confused men are unpredictable, and unpredictable men are a menace to powerless women.

He seems to like me. I don't get why. I am a witness against him and his colleagues. He has accepted the job of killing me. The odds are against me, but why has he brought me home? If, in fact, that is where I am.

The truth is that, blind and paralysed, I know nothing at all. I might as well be that baby, left to cry in a dark room. Defeatist or realist? You tell me. My fear shimmers, ice cubes under my skin, and tightens like the belt around my throat.

The car door opened just as I gaped to scream. Which made it very easy for Angry-man to stuff a wad of tissues into my mouth and slap more gaffer tape over the top of it. My stomach heaved – the gag reflex is well-named.

Angry-man cut me loose and dragged me out of the warm car. He shuffled me across the wet pavement and through a door into a narrow hall. My hall, which I share with two other tenants, smells of garam masala, toasted cheese, and take-out kebabs. There was the scrunch of mail and flyers under my feet which told me there was no one in the house but me and Angry-man. He hustled me downstairs and through my door.

He'd found my basement flat, my burrow, my home. He shut my door. We stood in the room that was kitchen, sitting room and office. My kitchen: I knew I'd left the pan half full of five-bean curry on the stove. I'd forgotten to put it in the fridge before making sure I'd selected the right three verses and rushing out full of excitement and hope.

Powerless in my own safe home, I thought.

He said, 'Not much of a place. Maybe you should be your own effing life coach and tell yourself how to get on and find somewhere better. Your curry would be all right if it had some meat in it. But I suppose you're one of those vegans, one of those faddy people who are so superior about your diet and the sodding polar bears and all that crap.'

I just shook my head because of course I couldn't answer him with a gob full of toilet paper. Up to a point, though, he was right-ish about me. He seemed to be looking for ways to criticise me, but, oh shit, I still wanted him to like me. His hot, hard hand was clamped around my upper arm and I wanted him to stroke my wet hair and say, 'Be a good girl and I'll let you go. We can put this rubbish behind us.'

I turned towards him and kicked him. My shoe connected with something but all it did was make him laugh.

'No one would ask *you* to try out for Millwall,' he jeered. 'You write poetry, don't you? How much money does that make you, eh? I mean, my TV screen's bigger than your bed.'

He shoved me backwards onto the couch which, like everything else, was disappointingly close to the middle of the room. But it was covered by a glorious, anarchic riot of shapes and colours, a throw that Keisha made.

While I was off balance and before I could kick out again, he pulled my boots off.

'Shit,' he sneered, 'you've even got a hole in your sock.'

But it's a clean sock, I wanted to say. It may not be designer or dainty but everything I wear for a poetry reading is always freshly laundered. It's a mark of respect.

'Now you listen to me,' he went on as if I had any choice. 'I've got your keys. I know where you live. Even better, I got your phone. I got all your contacts, all your music, photos, your Internet history. I got your whole sorry life here in my pocket so don't you ever, *ever*, think you can get away from me if I decide you won't die here and now. Do you hear me? Do you understand?' He pulled my hair. My squeak of pain was swallowed by bog paper. It occurred to me that I could eat and swallow half the bloody gag.

He said, 'Fucking nod if you get the picture, dummy.'

I nodded.

He said, 'You've read all these books but you're the one tied up.'

I nodded again. He had a handful of my hair and a grip like a plumber's clamp around my arm. He was so close I could smell my five-bean curry on his breath where before I'd only smelled gravy. If I could have found anger… But I couldn't. All I could think was, What am I supposed to do now? Sightless, voiceless, handless. What did Captive Heroine do to save herself, to prove her power, when the villain had her phone and his gun in his pocket? Well, for starters, she'd have foreseen the danger and never allowed herself to be made voiceless, sightless and handless. The Vampire Slayer, the Warrior Princess and the Tomb Raider added failure to my helplessness.

Failure, in any case, stalks me like a pack of hyenas in the night, laughing as they circle my wounded body: 'Not strong enough,' they snigger, 'not clever enough, not mentally tough – you'll never be a published poet. You thought Angry-man might be the hero, the undercover cop, didn't you? You thought he liked words and read books. How many mistakes have you made about men? Well, "dummy", this one may be your last.'

Angry-man hauled me to my feet by my hair. He pushed and kneed me through the door to my bedroom.

'You never even made the bed,' he said. 'You're a slut, ain't you? Look at you – I never seen such a slummock.' He gave me one almighty shove.

I crash-landed face down on the bed. I tried to roll over so that I could use my knees and feet, but something cold and hard whacked my temple and his arm fell like a rock on the back of my neck forcing my face into the pillow.

He said, 'Lucky for you I like dirty girls.'

*

After he'd gone I remained, numb, exactly where he'd left me. I heard two doors shut but he had my keys. He could come back whenever he chose.

He didn't choose. I rolled onto my side, raised my bound hands to my face and pulled the blindfold down. The light was on. What had been done had not been done in the merciful dark. Then I made myself scream by tearing off the gag.

315

I tried to scramble off the bed but my jeans were twisted round my ankles and I nearly fell on the floor. One small problem at a time, I thought.

A kitchen knife was too big to handle so in the end it was nail scissors that, millimetre by painful millimetre, snipped my hands free. The blades were curved so I kept scratching and poking my own wrists as I tried to keep purchase on the gaffer tape. But nevertheless I freed myself and when I looked I saw the same marks of self-harm and inept suicide attempts I'd seen years ago.

Only then could I stumble to the door and bolt it.

One tiny step at a time, I thought as I undressed and stuffed all my clothes into a thick black rubbish bag.

I knew I shouldn't shower, but how could I not? I knew for certain he hadn't used a condom and that was the sort of evidence needed by forensic science, but how could I live with myself if I didn't scrub myself down to the very bone? In any case the police weren't an option. His threats were specific. He had my mobile phone and I didn't have a landline. I couldn't ring the cops, a locksmith, or, more urgently, Keisha.

So, knowingly, I made the mistake nearly all women in my situation make: I showered until my skin was red and raw.

When I was dry and dressed in a warm, loose tracksuit I looked around to see what else was missing or damaged.

He'd eaten a lot of my curry straight from the pan and left the lid off. He'd drunk two bottles of Cobra beer from the fridge, leaving the fridge door open. He'd emptied my bag and taken my wallet with my credit and debit cards and all my cash. But he'd left my notebooks – like a rejection.

In the corner where my desk was I found that he'd smashed the screen of my iPad but left my clunky old computer untouched. The man who wore Buddy Holly glasses and looked as if he read books had swept my dictionaries, thesaurus and mythology books off their shelf. They were lying trampled, face down, on the floor. Like me.

I thought, This only happened to my body. My mind is innocent.

This was true and utterly untrue. I opened my computer and wrote to Keisha, heading my email SOS.

There was something yellow and slimy in my mouth, something acid in my throat. I cleaned my teeth a third time, then threw up more acid.

*

It was noon before Keisha showed up. She said, 'Grant's in the car. Can he come in?'

I said, 'No.'

She looked at the raw oblong around my mouth where the gaffer tape had ripped off a layer of skin. She said, 'I thought, y'know, you got lucky and that's why the guy answered your phone.'

She said, 'Shall I send Grant to the pharmacy? What do you need?'

I said, 'The morning-after pill.'

She said, 'No point saying you should report this?'

I said, 'He's got my phone. He knows where *you* live too. He knows where Grant works. I'm so, so sorry.'

'Not password protected? No? Well me neither. That gonna change.'

She said, 'Hanif dead? He did that too?'

I said, 'He didn't pull the trigger, he didn't cut the nephew. But he was there. He let it happen.'

She said, 'Why you alive?'

She looked at my damaged wrists. She said, 'Why you still alive, Mina?'

I said, 'I thought he liked me.'

She looked at me and then burst into tears. She said, 'Always the wrong one feel the shame.' We sat really close and watched Twilight till Grant came back with a morning-after pill.

Grant said, 'I'll kill the bastard.'

'Fuck off, Grant,' said Keisha.

*

Keisha, Grant and I found a large dilapidated ex-shop to rent in a failed high street north of Kensal Rise. We turned the ground floor into a sort of craft gallery and vintage clothes shop. Grant does repairs on sick and dying white goods. We call it Second Chance. We are doing surprisingly well in this weirdly depressed economy.

The week after we moved I wrote a letter on a found-computer which was soon sold on to a student. We printed it on a reconditioned printer – also sold. Wearing surgical gloves, I put it in a self-sealed envelope which I then wiped carefully with a weak bleach solution before dropping it into a post box five miles from Kensal Rise. It was addressed to the detective who was supposed to be looking into the killing of Mr Hanif and his nephew.

I wrote, 'Mr Hanif was shot by a man called Kyle. He is the child of a cousin of someone called Big Baz. He drives a BMW saloon. I think he might be involved with dog fighting or dog racing.

'Two other men were in the shop with Kyle. They both seem to be employed by Big Baz. Both indicated that they were not supposed to have killed anyone. But one of them stabbed Mr Hanif's damaged nephew when he became hysterical.' I described Clean-shoes as best I could.

Keisha, hanging over my shoulder, smelling of fresh paint, said, 'What about the angry man?'

I said, 'He saved me from Kyle.'

'How many times you been out of this house since we got here? And why you stopped writing?'

So I added a description of Angry-man, but I did not say, 'He wears Buddy Holly glasses and looks as if he reads books.' Nor did I say he was a lyric junkie who had warm hard hands and who would find me wherever I tried to hide.

I am grassing him up. Sort of.

Why? Well, Keisha thinks I need revenge and closure. She certainly sounds as if she does. Because of course Keisha has a past too.

And Grant says, 'You gotta make him pay for what he's done.'

They're right. I've told them so many times. And they've persuaded me that my letter is the safest way to point a finger.

They think I'm afraid that, in spite of all our precautions, Angry-man will find me.

But what really worries me is that I am a masochist and I'm afraid he won't.

I'm afraid my letter to the cops is really a letter to him. He said that if I ever grassed on him he'd find me wherever I was. So am I saying 'Come and find me'?

See, if Grant asked me about this I would explain, saying, 'If he finds me here I'll be able to kill him myself.' And it's true, I sleep with a kitchen knife under my pillow and a claw hammer beside my bed. If I knew how to buy a gun I'd probably have one of those too – me, a lifelong pacifist.

I keep Basho's *On Love And Barley* next to the hammer, and paper and pencil beside that. But I don't read or write.

If Keisha asked me to explain I'd tell her that if I hurt him as badly as he hurt me it would redress the balance and I'd be able to start writing again.

But real poets are powerful, and if Angry-man taught me anything it is that I have no power. Therefore I cannot be a poet. All the action heroes, the Slayers, the Warriors, the Raiders, are their own saviours. I wasn't. I failed as a feminist too. Even worse,

I wanted him to like me. Sometimes I hope he's thinking about me.

But sexism doesn't work that way. I know it in the marrow of my bones. And yet... And yet the sick longing for his approval is still there, gnawing like a rat on my heart.

*

My guru said, 'You *did* save yourself.'

'In what parallel universe?' I asked. 'Haven't you been listening?'

'You found the humanity in him,' she said, rocking backwards in her lush office chair. 'You shared lyrics and stories. You say he saved your life when Kyle put a gun to your head. But in fact you saved your own life by reminding him he was a human being.'

'And then he nearly killed Kyle,' I reminded her.

'Nobody's perfect,' she said. And waited patiently until I stopped laughing.

'Obviously he was angry,' she went on. 'Of course he made you suffer for it. He put himself in danger by not killing you.'

'Twice,' I said.

'With horrible consequences to you, so try not to sound smug. We are most definitely not talking about love here.'

And then Zoom time ran out. But she sent me a supplementary text which read: 'You lit a spark of humanity in a killer – that's what poets do.'

Keisha said, 'She right, dumb-arse. Words your strength, not action. Write, damnit.'

But I didn't: I couldn't find strength or beauty. Worse, I couldn't find meaning.

Then, nine days later, when I was sitting at the shop's work table diligently re-stitching and restoring a loved-to-death Jean Muir frock, Keisha and Grant came thundering down stairs. She plonked her iPad on top of my work.

'Look!' she shouted.

I looked and saw a page from the Streatham Signal Online. She keeps in touch with news from South London.

'C'mon!' she ordered, her dark eyes blazing with excitement.

The headline read, 'Convenience Store Killer.'

I read aloud, '"The killer of much-respected local corner shop owner Mr Mo Hanif and his nephew Al was, as reported last week, charged with double murder and later released on bail." Much-respected?' I interrupted myself. 'Double murder? Where did they get this shite from? Mo and Al? Why do they always diminish Muslim names? And why did nobody tell me they'd caught Kyle?'

'You missing important stuff.' Keisha snatched up the iPad from in front of me. 'Listen: "Kyle Carter, who had several previous convictions for Demanding Money With Menaces and, more latterly, an outstanding charge of causing Actual Bodily Harm, was himself gunned down in a gang-related drive-by shooting in Camberwell late last night. 'We do not yet know if Mr Carter was the target of the shooting or the accidental victim of random street violence,' a police spokesman said. 'Our investigations are ongoing and will be exhaustive.' This reporter is sceptical about the accidental nature of the slaying and wonders why, with so much violence in his background, Kyle Carter was ever released on bail." There!'

'Where?'

'You're off the danger list,' Keisha said impatiently.

'It was a protection racket,' Grant said. 'That's why your angry man was so angry. Mr Hanif was supposed to be alive and paying, not dead and a danger. The gang honcho – Big Baz for sure – must have finally got pissed at bailing Kyle out and him nausing up business. He was offed by his own family. Stands to reason.' He was leaning against the door at the bottom of the stairs. 'You can't be a threat to your angry guy anymore. It's all down to Kyle. Case closed.'

'But when I wrote to the cops,' I began, 'I said there were three men.'

'Won't matter,' Grant said. 'The cops have been paid off. Why do you think, with a record like his, Kyle was out of nick, and on bail? Again. That can only happen with cop cooperation. The cops want a perp. They got Kyle. Kyle got dead. End of story. Angry-man's bosses think you're buried somewhere off the M4 because that's what he was ordered to do. So he can't tell them you're still kickin', can he?'

I cut in, saying, 'So who wrote the anonymous letter? It can only have been me.'

'But only the angry man *knows* that,' Grant said impatiently. 'He and the berk with clean shoes would say there must have been someone laying low in the storeroom listening in. And the guy with clean shoes probably believes it.'

'Big assumption,' I said.

'I know I'm right. Besides it doesn't mention an anonymous letter anywhere. Why not? Because no one wants to say in public there was a witness. Why? Cos the only one the bad guys know about for sure is a corpse in the woods.'

He continued, making up the story as he went along: 'The truth is Kyle was always a liability so they got rid, after snitching on him to the cops. Everyone satisfied. And your angry guy can't snitch on you cos he's got more to lose than you have.'

'So you can start coming out with me to street art stuff and slams again,' Keisha said. 'You can stop farting around with old clobber and start doing what you're good at.'

'She's pretty good at finding classic clobber and refurbing it,' Grant reminded her. 'It's money for jam – don't knock it.'

'Not knocking. Just saying.'

*

Ten months later: he hasn't come for me and now I wonder if he ever will. Can I actually be longing for what I dread?

After a muggy, sweaty night of fragmented sleep I rolled over and picked up the book that yesterday I wanted to hide on a high shelf. It fell open to Basho's poem: 'Girl cat, so thin on love and barley.'

I wondered if I was a girl cat.

For the first time in ages I was the only one in the house. Keisha and Grant were in Ireland with Grant's dying dad.

Alone, I was waiting wearily for the knock on the door; waiting for a man to put a 'double tap' in the back of my head. Or waiting for him to give me an armful of white chrysanthemums and apologies for the harm he'd done me.

I made a large mug of tea and went down barefoot to the shop floor. It would be a couple of hours before I'd open up, so I sat at my table and picked up a pair of silk velvet Isaac Mizrahi trousers and continued to mend a ripped seam. I would have to alter the other leg to match – in which case the overall size would be closer to a 10 than a 12. I made a note in the workbook to remind me to put that on the ticket. Tiny soothing stitches, working with my hands, knowing what to do next – all was well.

I was roused from the rhythm of the needlework by loud buzzing. A super-large wasp was trapped against the shop window. There was no peace or rhythm in its frantic efforts. Every now and then it would fly slowly round the room and circle my head before crashing back against the window. Wasps fly slowly and observantly, in sharp contrast to the speed and fury of their head-banging struggles.

Without thinking, I picked up the pencil. I wrote:
'Angry wasp, decide –
come in, go out, decide *now*.
Don't leave me waiting.'

I found a glass and a postcard, and opened the shop door. I trapped the wasp under the glass and slid the postcard between the glass and the window. Then I carried the furious, vibrating trap out to the street. I removed the postcard and shook the glass.

Instead of flying free, the wasp fell out onto my bare foot. Before I had time to register that there must have been water in the glass and the wasp's wings were too wet for flight, it stung me.

I was shocked and outraged: I'd helped it escape, but it stung me and it really hurt.

While I was hopping around, cursing fluently, the postman arrived. He looked at my swelling foot and said, 'You should put something on that – looks nasty.' He saw the wasp crawling away and casually stepped on it, squashing the magnificent black and yellow armour between shoe and paving stone. 'Nasty buggers, wasps,' he said, handing me a few envelopes and striding away.

I looked at the pitiful mess that had once been a fierce creature. I felt the heat and pain of its poison. Tears tickled my cheeks. I thought, is this relief or grief? I went back inside and relocked the shop door.

After I'd treated my foot with ice and antihistamine cream I made another mug of tea and returned to my worktable. My hands were still shaking so, instead of picking up my needle, I looked at the envelopes.

One was addressed to me. There was no note inside. I shook it out onto the table and a flimsy pink square of paper detached itself from its prison and floated down onto the silk velvet.

It was a single lottery ticket. My heart banged furiously against my ribs, like a trapped wasp trying to escape. And I thought, Do I feel lucky or unlucky?

Like the wasp I can see freedom but can't reach it.

Or is that what Angry-man feels? Will either of us ever be free? Even if we never meet again are we shackled together by what happened the last time I was feeling lucky?

HARD HEARTS

Shelly was trying and failing to keep her mascara attached to her eyelashes. 'Last night when I came home, I still had the key in my hand,' she said, 'but I thought I was in the wrong flat. I'd bought salmon steaks for our tea but there was no fridge to put them in or cooker to cook them on. And he took the mattress. But he left me with the wooden bed frame.'

So I was thinking, Okay, he has a van but not a big one.

Shelly was crying now, and even Hard-hearted Hannah, as I'm sometimes called, admitted that she had just cause.

'I made the sandwiches he took to work. Just the way he likes them, and a chocolate cupcake and a ripe pear.'

I pushed my box of tissues across the desk to her. She'd run out of her own although she'd only been in the office for seven minutes.

'He doesn't like apples,' she wept.

In my experience, the broken-hearted often fixate on irrelevant details. Nevertheless I wrote 'Hates apples' on my iPad underneath the heading 'Michelle Cameron: Missing her lying thieving boyfriend.'

I noticed she'd turned white as a gnawed bone and her teeth were starting to chatter.

She's still in shock, I thought. What would a soft-hearted Hannah do?

'Tea or coffee?' I asked.

'The fridge and cooker belong to the landlord,' Shelly said. 'Coffee please. What should I do?'

'Have you reported the theft?'

'He's my *boyfriend*,' she began with the dreaded note of indignation that doesn't bode well for rational conversation.

'If you don't have a crime number your landlord will make you responsible for replacing stolen goods.' I went off to make the coffee. I didn't want to hear the next bit where she'd tell me how she couldn't betray the lying, thieving, probably cheating bastard to the law because she still loved him and wanted him back.

But I was thinking, Okay, he has access to a midsize van and he has friends to help him carry a double mattress and a fridge as well as everything else she owned. If it was a professional moving firm he'd have taken the bed frame too.

I found three customers at the take-out window so I made one cappuccino and two flat whites for them; two Americanos with hot milk for Shelly and me.

Digby was sitting at a table doing a sudoko puzzle, looking bored and ignoring paying customers. He's four foot seven inches tall, built like a brick shit-house – even his muscles have muscles on them – but once a week, usually on a Wednesday, he wears a navy blue A-line mini skirt and refuses to stand on the block that helps him reach the coffee machines. He claims that the perverts we call customers look up his skirt. Once, when I was still on the force, I tried to arrest him for causing an affray outside the Wheatsheaf on the High Street after someone called him a 'pigmy poofter'. Even now I don't know which half of the insult he objected to most. I couldn't arrest him because I was laughing so hard. Of course that was on a Wednesday. Today's a Wednesday too.

We have an arrangement, Digby and I. Among other things, I'm not supposed to see a private client today. For this reason he isn't talking to me now. He'll wait till we're alone; then he'll give me a mouthful, fire me, and I'll try not to laugh.

I took the Americanos, plus sugar, through to the office.

Shelly greeted me with, 'I know you're right but… ' while I reminded myself that Michelle Cameron was not really a pathetic loser. Before the sickness that changed everything she'd taught dance and exercise at a studio called You Can Do It. She'd had a large enthusiastic following – most of whom were still following her online.

Lying, thieving boyfriends can turn even the most intelligent, entrepreneurial women into losers.

I took a few notes while she sipped coffee and got to the inevitable speech that began, 'I just want to know what I did wrong,' when I interrupted her with my inevitable rejoinder: 'Crap question.'

'Excuse me?' she said from behind another handful of tissues.

'The right question,' I said, trying not to yawn, 'is "What did *he* do wrong?" Let's get some details. Photos?'

She dragged her phone out of her bag. I waited while she switched on and searched for her album. She froze suddenly and looked at me with a stricken expression on her face. 'It's gone,' she said, her voice cracking. 'The whole album's been erased.'

'Blimey,' I said, thinking, Wow, this bloke's serious and thorough. I reassessed my chances of finding him quickly.

*

Shelly met Ryan at a pub quiz less than six months ago. She was leading an exuberant team called Plus-size Samba; he wasn't in a team – merely watching from the sidelines. They moved in together only eight weeks later.

'We just clicked,' she said, blushing. 'I *know* – way too quick. But, well, nobody'd been interested for at least three years.' Her impressive chest heaved in a sigh that came from the depth of an abandoned soul. 'Then suddenly, there he was – a dream-come-true: I never thought I'd ever find someone who cared for me like Ryan did. It was as if we were being sung about in the same love song. That's what I don't understand – when I went to work yesterday I left him in bed and as I was opening the front door he called me back for a last kiss. He was so *tender*.'

Having been tenderly shafted myself a time or two, there wasn't much I could say about that. But I let her ramble on because the details of her story would help me decide whether Ryan Wilson had picked her as a soft mark from the beginning or if he was just another coward who couldn't bring himself to say, 'Sorry, this isn't working for me anymore.' The fact that he'd taken everything he could fit in a van was a clue that the first hypothesis would be the correct one, but hey, I like to keep an open mind.

Coincidence had a lot to do with it. They were both flat-hunting when they met; they were both fed up with furnished accommodation; they both loved Sean Baker movies, and they were both lonely. People get together for worse reasons, so I had nothing to say about that either.

They spent their nights at her place because he said he was ashamed of the hole he lived in.

Who paid the deposit on the new flat? 'I did – he was strapped for cash at the time but he paid the rent.'

'Are you sure about that?' I asked.

'What do you mean?' She almost looked frightened.

'Well, if he didn't you'll probably find an eviction notice on your welcome mat sometime soon.'

I changed the subject because she looked so scared and asked what her friends thought of Ryan.

'They loved him,' Shelly said sadly. 'They thought we were perfect together.'

'What about *his* friends?'

'I never met any of his friends.' Her lips tightened. 'You think I'm a total idiot, don't you?'

'No,' I lied. 'But I'm afraid *you're* beginning to. Blaming yourself won't help. Get angry instead.'

But she didn't seem ready for anger. Instead she said, 'He went to College in the States and his previous job was in Portugal somewhere. He said he wanted to settle down.'

Settle down? All I could think of to say was, 'Call the cops and change the effing locks.'

*

A quick internet search told me Ryan Wilson did not appear on any Electoral Register and there was no Cassidy Community College in Minnesota. Social media came up with several Ryan Wilsons – none of whom fitted the profile – and my totally anonymous informant on the force said he had no presence on the PNC.

'He's a bloody ghost,' I muttered.

'What you gonna do now?' Digby asked after demanding a brief outline of the case. This was not normal. Usually he ignored weeping women and the trail of wet tissues they left in their wake. This time he'd watched with interest as Shelly left Digby's Crap Sandwich Shack. Probably it was the impressive chest. I didn't ask. There's a lot about Digby I don't want to know.

*

The sisters, Alice and Bette, met me at the aforementioned Wheatsheaf on the High Street. They were both in the original Plus-size Samba quiz team.

'We didn't notice him on the night,' Bette said. 'We were having a good time.' They both sipped the rum and cokes I'd bought them.

'To tell the truth,' Alice said, 'we didn't meet him properly till after they moved in together. But of course we heard about him.'

'We heard lots,' Bette agreed. 'Sickening, really. You know, flowers, chocolate, love notes, chocolate, fancy meals, chocolate. She was bowled off her feet.'

'She was a regular ten-pin,' Alice said. 'He was so effing perfect we thought she'd made him up.'

Bette nodded. 'It happens. I wouldn't blame her. Being single for years sucks.'

I nodded. I knew about that.

'So we persuaded her to let us meet him,' Bette went on. 'We went to dinner – medallions of lamb and all the trimmings – and there he was. Perfect.'

'Tall and tanned, even in November.'

'Fair brown hair, blue eyes, broad shoulders, lovely suit and manners, slim.'

'And, worst of all… ' The sisters exchanged a significant glance. Alice continued, 'He was at least five years younger than her.'

I said, 'Oh, kill him right now.'

They relaxed. 'That's what we said afterwards.' Bette looked wistfully at her empty glass.

Alice said, 'He was so sodding wonderful we thought she'd hired him from an escort agency.'

'Seriously?' I asked, a fresh idea lodging in my suspicious mind like a stone in my shoe.

'We were jealous,' Bette said.

'Not any more,' Alice said, now sombre.

'Poor Shelly,' they said in unison.

I thought they were kind enough to mean it.

*

Next day, Digby was standing on his block stuffing falafel and salad into a pita sandwich.

I said, 'I don't care how fit this sodding ghost is, he couldn't hump a double mattress down three flights of stairs, load it into a van and not be seen.'

'Neighbours?' He wrapped the sandwich in greaseproof paper and started on a salmon and cream cheese bagel.

I was making four cappuccinos and pouring them into four customer-owned mugs. Our Thursday walking club was outside waiting for its breakfast. I said, 'I canvassed six neighbours and no one heard or saw a thing.'

'Boring,' he said. 'Order up. Take these to the hatch, you lazy cow.'

'Fry your bollocks in batter,' I said and took the food and drinks to the hatch. 'What's it all to you anyway?' I added when I got back.

'I'm bored. The take-out trade just don't tickle my sociable side.'

'You're as sociable as toothache.'

'You wouldn't recognise a lonely man if he spat in your soup,' he said moodily. Which might have explained his interest in Shelly's chest. But I couldn't help feeling he was lying just for the fun of not telling me useful facts; something an ex-cop knows all about.

*

BettaGettaway, Ryan's supposed place of work, was a long way from where he and Shelly had lived. There was a 'Business Closed' sign on the door and someone had been sleeping rough in the doorway. But peering through the grime I was surprised to see movement inside. I tapped on the glass, but there was no response. I tapped harder, then harder still. That must've given the woman inside a clue about my character because she came to the door and opened it an inch.

'If you're from the council,' she said wearily, 'I'm doing my best to clean up, but I'm on my own. And there's no way the Chaneys will ever pay the refurb bill you slapped on them. Also they decamped to Belize before Christmas. I'm the only one left.'

Before Christmas, if I was calculating correctly, was before Ryan met Shelly. But I said, 'I'm trying to trace a guy called Ryan Wilson who used to work here. Can you help me?'

She stared at me and then opened the door wide. She was wearing jeans and a sweatshirt, her hair was covered with a scarf and she held her broom like an offensive weapon.

'Are you joking?' she asked. 'Ryan Wilson died of pancreatic cancer five years ago. I should know. He was my uncle.'

We stared at each other, but she went on, 'Look – this business went bust when the sickness started. A travel agency can't survive a travel ban. The boss and her hubby went AWOL. They left the online side of the business with me and now I'm being hassled for back rent, rates and repairs.'

I almost turned tail but there was something about this woman… In spite of the smudged cleaning clothes, physically she was the image of Shelly. So I said, 'Well, buggeration. Dump the broom and come out for a coffee or something stronger. It's on me.'

Outside a street bar, drinking Irish coffees, Lara said, 'Are you saying there's a guy somewhere who said he worked for BettaGettaway, pretending to be my uncle?'

'How would he know about your business and that your uncle's name is safe to use?' I watched her turn this over in her mind. Then I went on, 'He's nearly six foot tall, fair brown hair, blue eyes, slim but well-muscled, has an all-year tan.'

'Oh,' she said. 'That sounds like Ian.' A tear glistened, swelled and dripped.

I sighed and handed her the tissue I'd already concealed in my left hand.

*

'She bought him a car,' I told Digby. 'She *did* go to the police when it was certain he'd done a bunk, but she just *gave* the damn thing to him so no crime was committed.'

'He's *good*,' Digby said and moved away sharpish before I could kick him.

My phone rang. It was Shelly. 'You were right, Hannah – he didn't pay the rent. I'm going to be evicted.' She was crying so hard I had to wait before repeating my advice about reporting the crime.

'Lara's car?' Digby asked after I'd hung up.

'I'll see if there's any record of the bloody thing being re-registered. But that may take a while.'

'Where do these women keep their brains,' Digby asked gleefully. 'In their D cups?'

When I didn't answer he went on, 'This guy's got a type. Pity you're as flat-chested as you're hard-hearted. Otherwise you could be bait.'

'Pity you're such a warped little bigot,' I replied, emphasising the word 'little.' This usually annoyed the brown stuff out of him. But not today. I was disappointed and got up to leave.

'Oy, where you off to?'

'Tanning salons. Maybe the creep's vanity will trip him up.'

'Not till after the lunch crowd,' Digby crowed. 'I see dozens of pizza slices in your future. And don't look at me like that. Remember what it was like conducting confidential business on a park bench, before I took you in out of the kindness of my heart?'

The thought of kindness and Digby's heart in the same sentence left me speechless.

*

It started to rain heavily after lunch. Rain is a death sentence to take-out catering but it left me free to pursue the elusive Ryan-Ian Wilson.

Before I tried tanning salons I called the man-with-van businesses in Shelly's neighbourhood. The first and fourth numbers clearly indicated a switch to deliveries since the sickness. The second gave me a disconnected tone. The third, a machine, asked me to leave a message. The fifth number was actually answered by a human being who said Georgie would ring me back this evening. The sixth attempt produced a male voice who asked what I wanted. I gave him the story I'd prepared for the other five: that during a house clearance at Shelly's address a couple of items had been mistakenly removed. The man said someone would ring back but he had no record of such a job. A baby was crying in the background and he hung up before I could leave my name.

Telling Digby I would pick up the bread and dairy deliveries that'd failed to arrive in the morning I drove first to the suppliers and then to the smart area where all the beautiful people who hadn't managed to fly south this year went to top up artificial tans.

It was a depressing experience for someone as vitamin D deprived as I was – doubly depressing because I'd compensated with an excess of chocolate and slobbing out in front of Netflix. I was not cheered by the toned and slender models pictured in the posters and brochures. And in case I missed the point the people behind the reception desks were fit enough to make a grown woman weep.

My story was that a guy I'd given a lift to had left a bag containing a pair of expensive Church brogues and an Apposta shirt on the backseat of my car. All I knew was that his name was Ryan or Ian Wilson and he regularly used a tanning salon in this area.

It was a story designed for peacocks of all sexes with short attention spans. Okay, so I'm a liar and somewhat contemptuous of the pretty people who are contemptuous of me. I have a job to do. I'm responsible to my paying client and not to the self-righteous prigs hogging all the moral high ground. I do whatever it takes. It was an attitude that eventually got me fired off the Force.

I hit pay dirt when, wet to the bone and ready to go home, I trudged into FauxSun, the most expensive, luxurious salon at the best address in the area. There I met Valentina, a trans so gorgeous that I gasped and said, 'Bloodyell, you take my breath away.'

Which made her smile a wondrous smile and hand me a pink towel.

'You poor dowdy ol' hen,' she breathed in a bogus American accent.

'You're far too exquisite for a smack in the kisser by a wet hen, but less of the old if you don't mind.' I rubbed the worst of the rain off my hair, and after that we got along fine.

For all the wrong reasons she didn't believe a word of my story even after I'd resorted to a version of the truth. 'Left you at the altar, did he? Lucky escape, if you ask me. That's one weasel on the make.' She sang a line or two from Just a Gigolo, making some rather basic hand and hip gestures to go with her breathy tenor voice.

'How do *you* know?' I asked. 'You're *so* not his type.'

'Don't you just say the *sweetest* things?' She waved a graceful hand at her surroundings. 'Since you ask – okay you didn't, but anyway – I am an online influencer with a fast-growing following.'

'If you aren't already famous,' I said sincerely, 'you ought to be. But tell me how you know Ryan-Ian.'

'I think you mean Sean,' she said, 'your average Brenda-with-low-self-esteem's wet dream. He sees my boss once a month in her upstairs boudoir and receives a free deluxe treatment in return. Fair enough – this place is obscenely expensive – but you're on a freebie and you don't tip your body-stylist even if she's *me*? That's not just cheap, it's insulting.'

'Once a month?' I said. 'When's his next appointment?'

*

'So you found him,' Digby said flatly. 'What's Shelly gonna do – kill him or kiss him?'

'If she's got a brain in her head,' I told him, 'she'll shop him to the cops and get back as much of what she's lost as possible. But it can take a woman years to reclaim her brains after she's been worked over by an expert.'

'If I didn't know you better I'd think you sympathised.' He slapped some cheese, ham and pickle between two slices of rye bread. 'So what did she say?'

I was timing eggs and whipping up a batch of tuna mayo for the lunch crowd. 'I rang her when I got home last night, but she didn't pick up so I left a message. Actually, that's odd.' I looked at my watch. 'I thought she'd come straight back to me.'

'She's probably been out on the pull, got lucky and forgotten all about him.'

'And you call *me* hard-hearted?'

'You *are* hard-hearted,' he said, mean and moody. '*I'm* merely damaged.'

I could've told him about damage, but there were dozens of tuna salad sarnies to make. When I finished I rang Shelly again.

This time the call was picked up but not by Shelly. 'Who's this?' a hesitant voice asked.

'Hannah,' I said. 'Backatcha.'

'Alice,' she said. 'We met on Wednesday.'

'What's up?'

'I'm at St Georges Hospital with Bette and Shelly,' she told me in a hushed bedside voice. 'Shelly was attacked yesterday evening. And the doctors say the only reason she isn't dead is because Bette and I arrived with armfuls of pillows and a duvet before he could finish the job. But the guy knocked Bette over running away and she's broken her ankle.'

'Was it Ryan?' I should've said, My god, are *you* alright et cetera, but I forgot.

'It wasn't Ryan,' she said, sounding angry. 'It was a big bastard in a red sweat shirt with a cricket bat. He was wearing a surgical mask and his head was shaved. It was all too quick. The police were rude to me and Bette for not noticing more, so don't *you* start.'

'Wasn't going to,' I protested. 'What about Shelly – can she talk?'

'She's still confused and they're watching her for brain damage. I'm waiting to pick Bette up.'

'Okay,' I said. 'I'm very sorry. Tell Bette I said so. But I will have to talk to the cops about Ryan and Shelly.'

'I already told them about Ryan,' she said. 'And about you. And they laughed their heads off when I said the only address I had for you was the Crap Sandwich Shack.'

'Oh perfect,' I said, ringing off.

'You know this is all your fault,' Digby said.

'Excuse me?'

'This is all down to you kicking over anthills. You wouldn't know tact and finesse if they walloped your ugly bum.'

'My ugly bum's prettier than your hideous face,' I snarled as I snatched up my bag and coat and slammed out of the Shack.

I was angry because it *was* my fault. Someone I'd talked to knew I was on to Ryan. Or maybe they thought I was Shelly and *she* was on the verge of tracking him down. Who had I talked to? Bette and Alice were off the hook. And Lara was surely another victim. But Valentina thought *I* was the abandoned lovesick loser. And I'd left messages with two van drivers. One of whom might identify Shelly by her address.

Which meant Ryan-Ian-Sean had at least one accomplice who owned a cricket bat. Which in turn meant that what looked like a cruel and ugly break-up was something more. Why else would Ryan or his battering mate risk adding Grievous Bodily Harm to simple thieving? GBH carries a much bigger tariff.

As I was thinking logical thoughts and walking to where I'd parked my car, I met a cop coming in the opposite direction. It was DC Len Mathis. He stopped the regulation six feet away and, with the familiar sneer on his pasty face, said, 'I hear you're looking for a man, Hannah. Well, good luck with that – I, for one, wouldn't touch you with surgical gloves on.'

'Thank the good lord for small mercies,' I said with a dramatic sigh.

Pleasantries over, he said, 'We know you're involved in the attack on Shelly Cameron.'

'Now that I'm not a cop,' I began, 'this is exactly the unnecessary, provocative tone of questions I've come to despise. You know perfectly well that I was hired by Ms Cameron to find her lying, thieving boyfriend. If you want to know what my thinking is just ask politely. I know it's against your religion, but you might find it saves your time.'

I could see my car and I skirted around him.

'Okay, okay,' he said, catching up and walking beside me a few feet apart. If there's one good consequence of the sickness it's that arses like Len can't get up in my face.

'I'm investigating a serious assault,' he began.

'Yes,' I interrupted, 'on *my* client – for whom I'm investigating a missing person.'

'Assault's the more serious crime and should take precedence.'

'So let's co-operate.'

'I seem to remember you got canned for… what was it? Oh yeah, not co-operating and shoving your Sergeant into the Union Canal.'

'Have a nice life,' I said, illustrating my words with a middle finger protruding vertically from a clenched fist. I opened my car door.

'Where's your sense of humour?' Len asked. 'Seriously, Hannah, what do you know about the assault?'

'Nothing. Except that two people who met him are positive the assailant is not the man *I'm* looking for.'

'Yeah, the Who-ate-all-the-pies pair. I dunno about deaf, but they're both blind and dumb. What I'm wondering is if *you've* come across anyone who could be an accomplice.'

I sometimes blush that I ever sniggered at cop humour. I said, 'I have no evidence that anyone I've met in the course of my investigation is associated in any criminal way with Ryan Wilson.'

'Yeah, yeah,' Len said, rightly dismissing my cop-speak as deceptive and faintly insulting. 'How about we play "I'll show you mine if you show me yours"?'

'Okay,' I said, making up my mind in a hurry. 'The individuals I've met so far are women who have been severely let down by the man I'm trying to trace.'

'Not useful,' Len said.

'No,' I agreed. 'But I have made a list of local man-with-van operations.'

'Why?'

'Because Ryan needed help emptying Shelly's flat and the helpful individual would know where the goods were taken. Which would help me find the creep who stole them.'

'How would that help *me*?'

'Well,' I said, imitating patience, 'the case has become more serious, and you asked me about accomplices. So if I should happen to find, for instance, a bloodstained cricket bat behind the driver's seat of a removal van, I might earn enough points to be reinstated on the force.'

He laughed. 'Fat chance,' he said. 'Gimme the list. Don't make me fuck you up worse than you are already. I could send Health inspectors to your place of work. How would that go down with the Mighty Midget?'

So, whining and grumbling, I handed him my list. Triumphant and crowing he grabbed it and turned away.

'I never wanted to see yours anyway,' I mumbled to his retreating back. 'I bet you haven't even got a little one.'

As soon as he was out of sight I adjusted my posture from loser to… okay, trickster. If anyone was going to blunder into a big bastard with a blood-spattered cricket bat I wanted it to be Len, not me. And if he wasn't curious about anything else he could stay ignorant.

I jumped in my car and drove to St Georges.

Shelly was awake but very groggy. Alice was with her, arranging flowers, cards, and chocolates. I'd forgotten to buy so much as a mouldy grape.

'Before you ask,' Shelly said in a slurred voice, 'I can't remember anything. One minute I was waiting for a delivery and the next I was here. It's confusing.'

'Of course it is.' Alice sat and took her hand.

'That's okay,' I said. 'I just wanted to see how my client is. I don't usually lose them this quickly.'

Alice snorted with laughter, but Shelly said, 'Oh yes, you're Hannah. I hired you, didn't I?'

Alice and I exchanged a glance.

Shelly's rainbow-coloured face creased with effort and distress. 'Did you find him?'

'I might have,' I said. 'Do you still want him found?'

Tears meandered between the swellings and abrasions. She said, 'What's his name? I can't seem to remember his name.'

'That's alright,' Alice said. 'You need a little sleep. You'll feel a lot better tomorrow.' She planted a goodbye kiss on Shelly's wrist and whisked me out of the ward before I could say 'Ryan Wilson'.

'There's something a bit cold about you, Hannah,' she said while we waited for the lift.

I said, 'Shelly paid me to do a job for her. So I want to do it. Also I think she was whacked as a warning to call the dogs off – or, since it's me, the bitch.'

We got into the lift and didn't speak again until we were outside the building, sipping cardboard containers of sour, vending-machine coffee. Then Alice said, 'At least the bastard who did this to my friend wasn't Ryan.'

'But when the cops find Shelly's attacker I'm positive we'll make a connection. I've already given them a lead which, if they have any brains at all, they'll follow up.'

Alice's eyes filled with tears. 'It's like she's been beaten up twice in as many days. You didn't know her before, but she was a force of nature. She wasn't just teaching us to dance or whatever – she was teaching us pride and how to live joyfully, accepting who we are.'

'It's good she has friends like you,' I said cautiously. Live joyfully? How do you manage that one? But I added, 'I'm not a friend; I'm a hard-hearted hired hand. I'm not crippled by emotion. I have to think clearly even if my client's in hospital looking like a tower block fell on her. So, here's a question for you: at the dinner party when you met Ryan did you or your sister take any photographs?'

'Yes.' She fumbled her phone from her pocket and found the right sequence in her album. As I'd expected, Ryan was always blurred or turning away or hidden behind Shelly. Even so there was useful information.

She'd just finished forwarding the pictures from her phone to mine when a text from Bette came in and she hurried away. I chucked the rest of the horrible coffee and went back inside the hospital, taking the lift up to Shelly's ward. There, to my astonishment, I found Digby sitting in the chair next to her bed. The toes of his Nike's only just brushed the floor when he swung his legs. Although Shelly was sleeping, his hand covered hers.

Not at my most articulate, I said, 'What the fuck… ?'

'Piss off,' he replied. 'You'll wake her up.'

'If she wakes up and the first thing she sees is your ugly mug it'll probably kill her. What the bloodyell are you doing here?'

'Keep your fat nose out,' he said. But when I reached for the security bell he hopped off the chair, saying, 'Okay, okay. If you must know, I recognised her when she came to the Shack to see you. She was too busy crying her eyes out to notice *me,* but years ago we were in the same West End production of Cats. We even had a little, um, thing.'

Of course I knew that, before the sickness killed off live performances, he'd had an intermittent career as an actor. He was even in a Kinks tribute band. But the thought of him having a 'thing' with my client made my eyelids shrivel.

Even more urgently, the information that he'd been in Cats rang a bell in my head so loudly that I all but dragged him out of the ward and down to the vending machines. This time I tried the hot chocolate, which tasted like tepid mushroom soup, and we went outside with the smokers.

'She was in Cats?' I said.

'She was a good dancer,' he said. 'Really solid chorus line fodder. She could do everything – tap, western, free jazz. Anything with a big cast of dancers.'

'And you? I didn't know you could dance.'

'Never asked, did you,' he said sulkily.

I should've shut up, but I had to open my big gob and say, 'Well, there *had* to be kittens in Cats.' Which was why Digby flung half a cup of coffee at me. I should know better by now. As it was I only just prevented him from storming off by employing some squirmingly abject apologies and promising to open up and work Saturday at the Shack – on my own and unpaid. Digby drives a hard bargain.

Finally I got to ask him the question I would've asked Shelly if she'd been awake and *compos mentis.* I showed him some of the pictures Alice had taken of her bright, colourful living room. On the wall, at the dining end, there was a large, elaborately framed theatre poster for Cats. It was behind Ryan who was caught in the act of turning towards Bette. You couldn't see his features at all.

'Is that the sadist who broke Shelly's face?' Digby stabbed the screen as if his finger was a blunt instrument.

'No,' I said. 'That's the sadist who broke her heart and robbed her blind.' I tapped the screen and enlarged the photo, dragging the image of the poster to the centre. 'Anything special about that?'

'I've got one of those,' he said. 'There was some sort of Cats anniversary.'

'But is anything identifiable about it? See, the furniture et cetera, looks nice but it's all, y'know, flat pack stuff. There's a possible line of enquiry if something unique turns up on eBay. The only possibilities here are the art on the walls.'

'I see what you mean,' Digby said. 'Maybe you do have a think-box up there between your ears. Well, we were all given a whole bunch of posters to sign with white pens – so the signatures would show up on the black cat's face. We each got one. The extras were sold at a charity auction. They're collectors' items now.'

'Worth something?'

'Oh yes,' Digby said proudly. 'I had mine framed and put up in the Shack when I first opened. But some jerk offered me fifty quid for it so I took it home for safety. It was worth twice that even then.'

'That's really useful,' I said.

'I helped you?' he said, his mouth puckering in self-disgust. 'Well I'll sew my lips together with knotted string and a rusty needle before I do that again.' And he stomped away without another word. Who wouldn't love a boss like that?

*

The next day I had a whole list of things more important than opening the Crap Sandwich Shack in time for the dog walkers and the breakfast mob. But a deal is a deal, so for a couple of hours I was up to my elbows in fried egg and bacon rolls, sausages and hash browns, even scrambled eggs and avocados. In my experience vegans don't walk dogs or eat breakfast at take-out cafés with the word Crap in their names. When naming his empire Digby's First Rule of the Sandwich Shack was 'Read the words above the door and stuff your complaints where the sun don't shine'. You might say the clientele is, in that respect, self-selecting.

It being Saturday, breakfast morphed into brunch and then into lunch. I got to the afternoon, dehydrated, but with only a few cuts and burns.

Digby turned up at 3:45 precisely just as I was pulling down the shutter over the serving hatch. I knew he'd been watching for several minutes. If I'd closed the Shack even thirty seconds early there would've been a tantrum. Instead he cashed up while I raided the first aid kit. He did smile rather spitefully at my sliced thumb which was still bleeding, but, just to prove there are a few miracles left in the universe, he made no critical remarks.

Then he said, 'Fancy a beer?' Without waiting for a reply he took two bottles of Tiger beer from his private stash at the back of the fridge and hooked the caps off, inviting me to sit with him. I had to pretend not to be astounded.

He took a long swallow from his bottle and announced, 'I'm doing this for Shelly, not for you. Got that?'

'Loud and clear,' I said, and took a gulp of my beer. 'I'm listening.'

'But you never listen,' he complained. 'You're too busy thinking up zinger come-backs.'

He had me there, but I kept my expression neutral and cocked my head like therapists do in the sitcoms. He was waiting for me to crack. When I didn't, he said, 'Okay. So, this morning, while you were poisoning the perverts, I did a search for sellers of theatrical memorabilia and I found this.' He smart-thumbed his smart phone and pushed it across the table. He was showing me an eBay entry offering a cast-signed, original, full-size Cats poster in mint condition for three hundred pounds, or nearest offer.

'There are several of these on sale,' he told me, 'but this one is Shelly's.'

'How do you know?' I asked, bringing up the photo of the item. 'Where's the frame? Shelly's had a curly, gilded frame.'

'The seller would take the poster out of the frame to photograph it, dummy. Otherwise, one, the glare on the glass would obscure the picture, and, two, you might see the seller's reflection. He's a dirty bastard thief so he wouldn't want that.'

'Makes sense,' I said admiringly, and before he could get suspicious I added in a sceptical tone, 'Even so, how do you know it's Shelly's poster?'

He took the phone back and tapped the photo so that it enlarged full screen. Then he enlarged it further. 'Because,' he said like a magician pulling a dove out of his sleeve. 'Because of *this!*' And he turned the screen to face me.

Now I could see the signatures quite clearly. And, centre frame, there was Michelle Cameron's flowery handwriting, while next to it was Digby's illiterate scrawl.

'So?' I said. 'You said you both both signed hundreds of these.'

'Look closely,' he commanded. 'At the hearts.'

And then I saw them: the i in Michelle and the i in Digby were crowned with little white hearts.

'Why Digby,' I crowed. 'You romantic old fool!'

'That wasn't *me*,' he said. 'Shelly made me do it. You can't think…' But I was trying so hard not to laugh that I didn't hear the rest. Digby in love! Or, more likely, Digby pretending to be in love – priceless either way!

I said, 'So this is the only Cats poster in the world where the i's in Michelle and Digby are dotted with little hearts?'

'The only one on the market,' he snarled furiously. So there had been two, and he owned the other one.

He chugged down the rest of his beer, burped loudly and offensively, and marched to the fridge – another for him, none for me. He had a face on him like a slammed door so I started to forward the eBay entry to myself. I wasn't quick enough. He snatched his phone back as soon as he saw what I was doing.

'Too late,' he said. 'I already offered two-twenty cash for a quick sale.'

'Are you *mad?*' I was outraged – this was going to be tricky enough without Digby blundering around like a wild elephant in a petunia patch. 'This is *my* case; you've no business sticking your buggering beak in.'

'Shelly isn't a case,' he said snottily. 'She's my *friend.*'

'And when did you last see your *friend?*'

'Yesterday,' he said, all smug and righteous.

'And before that? When she was, as you say, "crying her eyes out". I was *so* impressed by the way you put your arms around her to comfort her.'

'Don't you start that game with me Ms Stony Heart, when all you got to offer is an Americano and a fistful of paper towels.'

We glared at each other, fight-faces forward.

I don't know what I might've said next if a knock hadn't sounded at the door, and a loud voice yelled, 'Police! Open up.'

Instantly, Digby picked up the cash bag and threw it into the back of the supply cupboard; we've had unwelcome visitors just after cashing-up time before. He hurried to the place behind the counter where he keeps two ball-peen hammers. 'Answer that, Hannah,' he said, chucking a hammer to me. I caught it one-handed and went to the door. I moved the blind aside and peered out from behind the Closed sign.

'Sod it,' I said. 'It *is* the police.'

I opened the door and Len Mathis strutted in saying, 'Got a cup of coffee for a hard-working cop?'

Digby shot me a warning glance just as I was shooting him one.

'Something frothy,' Len suggested. 'Oh and a nice thick ham sandwich would go down a treat.'

I could see Digby making a visible effort not to slay Len with a joke about thick ham and a thick pig.

While this was happening I slid Digby's phone into the pocket of my nauseatingly stained apron. I took the apron off and put it in the dirty laundry bag.

'Make the officer a sandwich, Hannah,' Digby said in a strangled voice.

'Make it yourself,' I replied in case Len might suspect I'd had a personality transplant or there was something to hide. But in the end, grumbling about overtime, I put on a fresh apron, new surgical gloves and mask and made Len a sandwich. I used the ham that had passed its use-by date, smothered it with English mustard, cut it in half and slammed it down in front of the pig who was sitting like an effing king, waiting to be served.

'I've been here since six this morning, on my tod,' I growled at both men. 'So whatever you want, make it snappy.'

'That list you made me,' he said with his mouth full. 'Van drivers.'

'What about it?'

'I gave it to a probationer to follow up and the silly cow lost it.'

'Make your own effing list. I'm supposed to work without pay for two lazy-arsed men and feed you as well?'

'Aren't you interested in finding the bastard who beat up your client?'

'More interested than you are, for sure,' I said, but I fished my iPad out of my bag and copied the names, addresses and phone numbers onto a sheet of paper. Before handing it to Len I sent another warning glance to Digby before saying casually, 'Actually I might have a line on some of the stolen household goods.'

He snatched the paper from my hand and stuffed the last of the sandwich into his already bulging cake-hole. 'I told you,' he spluttered through half-chewed bread and ham. 'Assault is a proper crime. Your client didn't report the theft of household goods – so, as far as I'm concerned, there was no crime. Pots and pans are your bailiwick, not mine.' With that, he swigged down the cappuccino Digby'd made for him and swaggered out of the Shack still chewing.

'What game are you playing?' Digby asked. 'You practically told him about the Cats poster.'

'Why don't you use your nut for something other than cracking eggs?' I was tired and clatty. Even my hair smelled of bacon. 'Didn't you notice my wily use of the phrase "household goods" to arouse his contempt for womanly things? I wanted him to say, in front of a witness – *you* – that the theft of Shelly's stuff was not a crime and was of no interest to him. Now he can't accuse us of interfering with police business.'

'Oh, right.' Absent-mindedly he popped the cap off another bottle of Tiger and handed it to me. '*Us?*' he asked. 'Have you decided not to disembowel me for "interfering with gumshoe business"?'

'And did you see that I hid your phone in case Mr Plod took an interest in your research?'

He hadn't noticed. I retrieved it from the laundry bag, wiped it and, instead of handing it back to him, I started where I'd left off and forwarded the information to my own phone. This time he made no objection.

I said, 'So you offered two hundred and twenty quid for something the seller wants three hundred for?' My skin was sticking unpleasantly to my underwear. I took another swallow from the bottle. Beer does make me feel mellower, but it makes me think worse.

'Yes, but,' Digby said, 'dicking around's quite normal. I said I'd pay more if he had a frame to fit and that it'd be a quick cash sale and I'd collect it. No postage, packing or insurance. Sellers like that these days.'

'What did he say?'

'Nothing yet. He'll wait to see if there's a better offer so that he can screw more out of me. Then I'll try to find out more about him – like a pick-up address. All I know at the moment is that he's "in the London area".'

'Okay,' I said. 'Do whatever you have to do to secure the sale. But you've got to swear on your effing life that you won't do anything without telling me. These are *not* people you want to screw with alone.'

'You think I can't handle myself?'

It was the beer talking. And unfortunately it said, 'Of course you can. If you couldn't you'd never get any sex.'

We parted on our usual terms and I went home to look for another job.

*

Of course there aren't any other jobs that'd provide me with almost enough to live on, flexible hours and the use of a tidyish office behind a kitchen. But that's alright because Digby never found anyone else masochistic enough to work for him for more than two days.

After half an hour in a steaming hot bath I lay down for five minutes. I didn't wake till nine on Sunday morning.

The Shack is closed on Sundays. I rolled over and would've gone back to sleep except that my phone was winking at me like a dirty old man.

There were two messages from Digby. The first had come in at about eleven last night. It said, 'I think I've nailed the bastard. Call you tomorrow. I'll need two-hundred and seventy-five quid in used notes.'

'What?' I howled as I leaped out of bed and stood barefoot on my hairbrush.

The second message had arrived twenty minutes ago. 'I'll pick you up in half an hour. Bring the money.'

'Are you insane?' I spluttered, spitting toothpaste at the bathroom mirror while hopping on my uninjured foot.

Nevertheless I was standing on the kerb outside my building, wearing nearly clean jeans and the sort of jacket I'd never wear to work, when Digby rolled up in his modified VW Golf.

As I slid into the passenger seat he said, 'Got the money?'

I just looked at him. He waited. So I said, 'You owe me two weeks' wages. You can't have banked yesterday's take yet.'

He said, 'This is *your* case, remember? I'm not laying out nearly three-hundred pounds on your behalf.'

'*You* insisted on doing the deal for *your friend*. It was your idea.'

'It should've been your idea. If you were a proper gumshoe you wouldn't need me to think for you.'

'If you were any sort of friend to Shelly you wouldn't have made me waste my time working non-stop for nine hours yesterday while you swanked around tickling your phone.'

'I'll stop and you can bugger off right now,' he said, stamping on his modified brake pedal. 'Or you can fasten your sodding seat belt. I don't want to replace my bleedin' windscreen just because you went through it.'

I fastened my seat belt, and yelled, '*Stop tailgating that bus!* What's more, we aren't going to *buy* Shelly's poster. Are you stupid? We're going to threaten to turn him in for fencing stolen goods. Who is he anyway?'

'His seller name is Bizarre Bazaar7.'

'Eh?'

'Bizarrebazaar7 – all one word. He doesn't need a real name. That's why I offered to collect. And we'll still need to show him the money, dummy.'

'Then stop at a cash point and get the money out. All *I* have is fifty-two quid. You owe me two weeks and Shelly's cheque was stopped. I think the lying, thieving bastard cleaned out her bank account. So who're *you* calling dummy?'

We bickered all the way to a cash point and then we bickered all the way to a rundown row of shops at the weirder end of Clapham. But by then we also had a plan that was smarter than his first suggestion which was that I sit on the seller while Digby kicked his head in.

Number 159 London Road looked like a pop-up shop. It drooped beside a failed nail bar as if failure was a contagious disease. There was some second hand furniture in the window posing as antique.

Digby drove past slowly while I took a few pictures on my phone. The street was Sunday-quiet. We U-turned and came back. Digby parked in front of the shop and used his phone. He said, 'I'm outside now.' And, 'Yes, I've got it. Where are you?'

'He says he's coming down,' he told me, climbing out of his seat onto the narrow pavement. I crawled from my side and crouched behind the front wheel, camera pointing at the shop door. Digby stood to one side giving me a clear shot at whoever opened up. From a quick glance, I thought that someone was examining Digby through the glass. Since he was the height of an eleven-year-old child he didn't look at all threatening. After a short pause the door opened and I pressed the button that started my video.

'Hi,' Digby said as if he was just a friendly buyer. 'Good to meet you at last.' He was wearing a surgical mask which helped his pretence no end.

'Yeah, yeah,' the other man said. He was solidly built, about six feet tall, his head was shaved and, for a few seconds at least, he wasn't wearing a mask. Then he hauled something grey and nasty from his pocket to cover his mouth. He said, 'Dunno why you bother, I'm not asking you in for coffee and cake. Where's the money?'

Digby pulled a wad of notes out of his pocket and held it up for inspection, saying politely, 'I'd like to see the poster now, please.'

'Those ain't the nuggets we agreed,' the big bloke said.

'The rest's in the car. I'll get it as soon as I see the poster.' Digby was being so patient and polite I could hardly believe it was Digby.

The bloke stepped back into the shop and re-appeared with a poster. It was framed in black plastic – not Shelly's gilded piece of fancywork. But Digby knelt down and examined the picture minutely. I waited, keeping Digby, the poster and the big bloke on my screen as best I could.

Finally Digby got to his feet and gave the thumbs-up sign. He said, 'Okay, this is what you're selling for two hundred and seventy-five pounds, framed, right?'

'Right,' the big bloke said impatiently. 'Now where's the rest of my dosh?'

'*Where?*' Digby asked.

It'd all gone so well. But now Digby had to open his big mouth. I was already chucking my phone into the backseat of the car, getting ready to pound across the pavement when he said, 'Where's your dosh? Up a syphilitic camel's backside, you thieving son of… ' And then Digby sailed through the air and landed with a huge thump on the roof of the VW.

I left him there.

I am *not* a short person but to avoid a fist the size of a ham hock, I tackled the big bloke low. My left shoulder caught him below the knees and he went down, hitting the pavement with a thud and a crack.

While he was down the *real* short person landed on his chest and started kicking his chin with stacked-heel Cuban boots. An excellent if foolhardy response to being hurled onto the roof of a car.

It gave me a split second of Big Bloke's stunned immobility to twist up and stamp on the bastard's ankles while fumbling in a pocket for my cable ties.

Cable ties are little miracles when it comes to putting a perp out of action. But even with his ankles tied Big Bloke managed to sit up and grab Digby by the throat.

It was his second, or was it his third, mistake. I'd lost count because by strangling Digby he'd moved his hands and wrists close enough together for me to cuff him with another cable tie.

This did not help Digby because Big Bloke wouldn't let go. So I gripped his earlobe, digging my fingernails in hard enough to draw blood, and bellowed, 'Police. Release your victim. Do you want to add murder to trafficking in stolen goods?'

'Aaargh-urch,' went Digby. 'Who the fuck you calling a victim?' His face was turning an interesting shade of lilac. But when Big Bloke relaxed his grip Digby fell back and rolled away gasping like a weary walrus.

Big Bloke was trying to break the cable ties and swearing like a stand-up comedian. He was ballyhooing loud enough to raise the dead and I didn't need an audience. I grabbed him by one elbow and dragged him off the street into his shop. Digby followed bringing the Cats poster with him, placing it out of harm's way.

I flicked Big Bloke's bleeding earlobe, just to remind him I meant business, and said, 'Do you want me to shut your filthy mouth with parcel tape or are you going to do yourself a favour and help me with my enquiries?'

*

As well as informing the police that Big Bloke was tied up in his shop, I left a message on Len's private line. 'I've found the man who probably assaulted Michelle Cameron – Billy Allsop. He's certainly in possession of some of her stolen "pots and pans" and he fits the description.' I did this while still in the car outside Allsop's premises. I hoped the cops would hurry because while questioning the twat I heard a baby crying upstairs. And I was sure some woman with really low expectations in life would come down and cut the cable ties as soon as the ruckus was over. 'You poor darling,' she'd say, and instead of thanking her he'd recover from his humiliation by slapping her around.

Of course you could say Billy Big Bloke had himself been assaulted by Digby and me. But as Digby sophisticatedly said, 'He started it.'

As a precaution I took Digby to the casualty department at St Georges to have his injuries checked. While there I took photos of his back and throat.

'I wish you'd taken photos of Bastard Billy's face too,' Digby lamented. 'I did damage. I loosened a few of the animal's teeth.' He was still pumped.

I waited till he was cleared for take-off because he wanted to see Shelly and bring her the Cats poster himself. That day he was his own hero.

Shelly was awake. Although her eyes were shut she had her ear buds in and was crooning along to something. In a nice bluesy voice she sang, 'That man's got a heart like a rock cast in the sea...' She was swollen-faced and bedraggled.

Digby unexpectedly hung back, holding the poster in front of him like a shield.

Bloodyell, I thought, Digby's shy!

'What you listening to,' I asked by way of an opener.

'Bessie Smith.' She removed the ear buds. 'Saint Louis Blues. I'm wallowing.'

'Oh crap!' I said disgustedly.

She ignored me. 'Oh my god!' she said. '*Digby?* What on earth are you doing here?'

So I had to witness their sappy re-union and hear Digby's explanation of how brilliantly he'd found her poster and his epic battle with Big Billy Bastard Bloke.

I thought I'd puke if I had to listen to another one of her, 'Oh Digby, you're so brave,' interjections, so I said, 'Okay, Digby, enough with the war medals.'

And he said grudgingly, 'Hannah helped.'

If there'd been a VW Golf handy he'd have made another dent in its roof.

He'd definitely outstayed his welcome as far as I was concerned so I said to Shelly, 'I think, with Digby's help, I've found the man trying to fence your stolen goods. The cops will likely prove he was the van driver who helped Ryan clear your flat *and* that he was the guy who beat you up… '

'That was your fault,' Digby interrupted.

'Take a hike, Digby,' I said. 'I need to talk to my client in private.'

'Oh, do let him stay,' Shelly said. I saw, with a spasm of nausea, that she and he were holding hands. Nausea turned to annoyance: how broken-hearted do you have to be to find consolation in Digby?

'I'll stay as long as you want,' he said in a peaches and cream tone I didn't recognise.

'Oh *gak!*' I said, forgetting to be professional. 'Shelly, we need to talk about money. Your cheque bounced. For the last four days I've been working for free. If you still want me to find Ryan Wilson you'll need to finance the search.'

Shelly looked totally stricken.

Digby said, 'They call her Hard-hearted Hannah.'

I gave him my evilest grin and said, 'You know what my per diem rate is – are you going to guarantee payment for your friend?'

'No, no, no,' Shelly said to him. 'I'd *never* let you do that.' She withdrew her hand from his and turned her blackened, bloodshot eyes on me. A better woman would've felt guilty. But as well as hard-hearted I was hard-up Hannah.

Digby left before Shelly could find out how ungenerous he could be.

When we were alone, she said, 'I have a savings account. I wasn't trying to cheat you.'

'It's okay. When you wrote the cheque you didn't know he'd cleaned out your account.'

'Alice insisted I talk to the police,' she said humbly. 'You were right. I really did need a crime number. I've stopped my credit cards, done all the sensible things. It's just… '

'I know,' I said, almost bored. 'You can't believe someone you loved could act so cruel and ugly to you.'

'Yes!' she said. 'I don't know if I'll ever get over it.'

'Try,' I said. 'You'll cripple yourself if you don't.'

'You've found him, haven't you?'

'Well, I know where he'll be at three-thirty tomorrow afternoon.'

'I want to see him,' she said without pausing for thought. 'I've got questions. I need answers.'

'But what will the liar's answers be worth? And will the doctors let you out of hospital?'

*

Next morning, early, Digby and I were forced to serve Len the sort of breakfast that ought to clog his arteries and make him drop dead at our feet. Free sausages, bacon, eggs, beans, hash browns, fried bread as well as toast and marmalade poured down his gullet while he informed us of the iniquities we'd committed the day before.

For once Digby and I backed each other up successfully. Digby reminded Len he'd said he wasn't interested in the stolen goods even though I'd told him I'd found some of them. And my video proved that Billy Big Bloke was offering stolen goods for sale *and* that he'd perpetrated the first aggressive act on poor little Digby. We swore blind neither of us had claimed to be police officers and that the violent man had to be restrained to prevent further injury. Digby's bruises and abrasions were examined. As were the disastrous nests of cables and wires I was going to sort out for him with my pocketful of cable ties. Cable ties were not offensive weapons. I forwarded the video to Len's phone along with Alice's photos of Shelly's dinner party. These might help Len identify more of her property.

Did he return the favour by telling us what Billy had said under caution? He did not. So I didn't tell him about Digby hawking into his coffee cup. We parted on our usual terms. He did not leave a tip.

*

I hired a van with a backdoor lift because Shelly and Bette were both in wheelchairs. Alice would push Bette; Lara had made herself responsible for Shelly. Shelly and Lara were getting along like sisters – warm and intimate, as well as watching each other like hawks.

I turned the radio to an easy listening station. Patsy Kline was singing Crazy. I would've changed stations but the other four women began to sing along. How come all women but me know the words to Crazy? I was already jumpy about the afternoon and Crazy made it worse.

We parked around the corner from FauxSun – two minutes away even by wheel chair. It was three-twenty. I was waiting for Valentina to call.

I had questions about Valentina. Why was she helping me? Was it because Ryan was a tightwad? She certainly showed no fellow feeling for his victims, and there was no reward involved. All I could offer her, it seemed, was drama. Would drama be enough?

Five women in a van – two of them among the rolling wrecked. There were too many of us, and too few. How was I supposed to make Ryan listen to Shelly? I still had a pocketful of cable ties, but if cable ties were all it took to make a mean man listen, I'd cash in my savings and buy shares in the company that made them.

Patsy Kline sang, 'And I'm crazy for loving you.' I thought, Why the effing hell do we let ourselves get our knickers in such a twist about *men?* And the phone rang.

Valentina said, 'He's crossing the pavement right now. He's opening the door. He's… ' Her voice dropped to a breathy drawl, 'Well, hiya, Sean. How're you today? Take a seat. I'll rustle up an espresso and see if the boss is ready for you.' She rang off.

I said, 'He's here. Let's roll.' I hopped out of the van and ran round to the back. I'd kept my voice level but I was jittery with impatience. I should've got the wheelchairs out of the van earlier. But how could I when I didn't know which way Ryan would come? I couldn't afford to let him see women he'd recognise. Now I felt as if I was regimenting goldfish – the backdoor lift took for ever, and then the women, even Shelly whose face still looked like a war zone, straightened their clothes and patted their hair.

'Let's *go*,' I said for the third time. My brain was pinballing – might Ryan sense something was up? Would he pick up signals from Valentina? Would she give the game away, and by the time we got there would he have scarpered?

But we trudged around the corner and at last came to a stop outside FauxSun. At which point I noticed that there was no wheelchair access. Bloody typical, I thought – only the young and fit would be catered for; the halt and lame had no need of professional tanning.

'I'll have to bring him out,' I said.

'Wait a minute,' Lara said shaky-voiced. 'What's to stop him running off?'

'*You'll* have to,' I said. 'Zone defence.' And, without explaining, I opened the salon door and marched in.

Lounging on a leatherette seat, casually elegant and thumbing through a copy of Esquire, was the object of desire who'd caused heartbreak, physical injury, loss of confidence, and loss of money and property. Ryan-Ian-Sean Whatever – another damn dude with a talent for mendacity, meanness and megalomania.

He really *was* attractive. Even Hannah the hard-hearted could see that.

He looked up when I opened the door and instantly gave me the sweet, quirky smile of a man whose mission in life is to be adored. Then he turned back to his magazine.

Valentina appeared in the inner doorway.

I said, 'Ryan Wilson?' My fingers curled round the cable ties in my pocket.

'You've made a mistake,' he said in a pleasant tone. 'That's not my name.'

'It was till five days ago,' I told him, matching his soft speech. 'There's someone outside who wants to talk to you.'

'I'm sorry.' His voice only froze slightly. 'You're mistaken. I have an appointment here.'

'Not hardly,' Valentina said cheerfully. 'The boss had an urgent call. She sends her apologies. I have to close the salon for an hour.' She swayed gracefully towards him, rhinestones glittering, making shooing gestures with her exquisitely manicured hands, coming so close that he had to stand up and take a step backwards.

'Get off me, freak,' he said.

'Ooh,' I said to Valentina. 'True colours?'

'I guess that's why he was such a goddamn ungrateful customer,' she said sadly. 'Who knew?' She moved closer, and I opened the street door.

He jinked round me, slippery as an eel. I grabbed for his arm and missed. But after only one pace onto the pavement he came to such an abrupt halt I barrelled into him.

I gaped in amazement. I'd left four trepidatious women outside, two in wheelchairs. Now there were twenty or thirty women spilling onto the road.

'Is that him?' someone at the back of the crowd yelled. 'I can't see.'

'That's him,' Shelly and Lara called back in unison.

'Tasty,' someone else said.

'Tasty but treacherous,' came from the middle of the throng.

'A moment on the lips,' Valentina crooned. 'A lifetime in therapy.' Her musical tenor voice carried, and laughter broke out.

Without speaking Ryan tried to escape back into the salon. But Valentina and I were blocking the door. More women joined us and he was surrounded.

It was extraordinary – there were big women, little women, skinny, plump, young, old, black, white, brown, yellow. Alice whispered beside me, 'I got in touch with all Shelly's classes and I suppose some of them brought friends. Aren't they wonderful?'

I was still too gob-smacked to answer. But Shelly spoke up from her wheelchair. She raised her poor tie-dyed face and spoke. 'Ryan,' she said, 'what did I do to you? What did I do so wrong that you left me without a word, stole from me and had your cousin beat me up?'

Ryan ignored the question and instead said in a loud voice, 'I haven't got a cousin.'

'Billy Allsop,' I said, just as loudly. 'He's in police custody right now and he's spilled. His shop and your lockup are under the microscope. We know he called you, telling you that the owner of the flat you and he'd just cleaned out was asking questions. He told us that you ordered him to put the frighteners on her. But he made a mistake; it wasn't Shelly who rang him. It was me.'

It was my turn to be ignored. Ryan moved closer to Shelly. 'Sweetie, you *know* I'm not violent,' he said gently. He reached out and cupped her poor bruised chin in one shapely hand. 'I'd never do that to you.'

Lara knocked his hand away, and said, 'Answer the question.' She'd dressed for the occasion, wearing tailored slacks, a slim-fitting sweater and high-heeled boots. Her hair was silky and fell to her shoulders. But Ryan's eyes passed over her without interest.

'You don't even recognise me, do you?' she said, outraged. 'You took months of free board and lodging from me. I gave you a car, fuck it, and you stole my dead uncle's identity. And now I don't even *exist* for you.'

Shelly repeated, 'What did I ever do to you?'

Someone in the crowd yelled furiously, 'What did *he* do to *you?* That's the question.'

Someone else piped up, 'You're always late with the child support.'

Then, 'You forgot my birthday.'

'You never unload the dishwasher.'

Some of the women were laughing now. Ryan managed to look beleaguered and contemptuous at the same time. A lot of us recognised that expression.

Then one woman at the back yelled, 'You raped my daughter.'

An ominous murmur followed. This had stopped being a game. I said, 'Hey! This is one man, not all men. He may be a liar and a thief but I'm sure he isn't… ' I was out-shouted by a babble of voices.

I rounded on Ryan and said, 'Listen arsewipe – answer Shelly properly. Your only chance is if they think you're really sorry.'

He nodded, so I raised my arms and yelled, 'Let him speak to Shelly.' Gradually the women fell silent.

Ryan turned to Shelly and began, 'I'm sure you're a perfectly lovely lady, but this was never about you… '

Mayhem broke out again: 'Why is it *always* about *you?*' came from several directions.

'Why do you always flirt with my sister?'

'You gave me an ironing board for my anniversary present.'

'Give it up, Hannah,' Valentina called. 'The guy's too stupid to save.' She raised her voice again, singing out over the babble, 'Hey, sisters, let's see what he's made of, eh?' In one practiced motion she stripped Ryan's coat off his back. She looked at the label and called, 'Armani. I wonder who bought this for him.' She flung the jacket into the crowd. Laughter welled up – the mood had shifted again. Somehow the jostling pushed Ryan over, and while he was down Alice pulled one of his shoes off and chucked it into the wonderful rabble, screaming, 'Mahabis! Any takers?' Soon, women were giggling and squabbling over their prizes. And Ryan was stark naked.

To complete his misery, it started to rain. But the weather might have saved him from physical injury.

Umbrellas went up and the mob began to drift away, shouting, 'Get well soon, Shelly,' and 'we'll be thinking of you.'

'Aren't they lovely?' Shelly asked.

I was neither surprised nor overjoyed to see she was crying again.

We left Ryan cable-tied to the nearest lamppost with the words, 'Liar and thief' written in scarlet lipstick on his back.

'Well, that was fun,' Valentina said, as ten of us crammed into the van. We made our way to the Wheatsheaf for a few glasses of sparkling wine.

It would be the Law's turn to give the lying, thieving boyfriend a hard time.

My client was satisfied so that ended my involvement. Tying a nude man to a lamppost was not the professional way I wanted to close the case, but if it worked for Shelly I'd live with it.

NOTES FROM AN UNTIDY DESK

I want, here, to say something about the stories, and to pay tribute to some of the people who have kept the short story alive in a sometimes unfriendly or indifferent market.

One of the Heroes is Doug Greene, founder of Crippen and Landru, who published my first collection of short stories, *Lucky Dip and other stories*. He commissioned 'Mr Bo', a Christmas story, and didn't complain about my less than enthusiastic attitude to the season.

Doug was also responsible for the wonderful *The Verdict of Us All*, edited by the equally wonderful Peter Lovesey. It was conceived as a celebration of the great H.R.F. Keating's 80th birthday. 'Kali In Kensington Gardens' was my homage to Harry's Indian Inspector Ghote series.

Later, when it was Peter's turn for a birthday party, Doug asked Martin Edwards to edit *Motives for Murder* in his honour. This was perfect for me because Peter sets his Diamond series in my home town so I could write 'Ghost Station' without any location research.

Martin has become a Hero in his own right, editing *Deadly Pleasures*, the Crime Writers' Association's Anthology, for which I wrote 'Day or Night.'

But, from my point of view, the biggest Hero and Star of the short story world is Janet Hutchings who, to push a metaphor further than it should go, runs an orphanage for those of my stories no one has requested. She is the editor of *Ellery Queen Mystery Magazine*. Without her a lot of us might have a full-to-bursting bottom drawer.

Nearly all my stories are written because they have to be and not because someone has asked for them. But sometimes there is a purpose. For instance 'Art, Marriage and Death' was a birthday present for my friend Gail. The most important character is Gail herself. Her rather dim sidekick is Liza. Apart from that the demands of fiction triumphed over truth or reality at least nine times out of ten. It's a good example of how facts metamorphose into something unrecognisable. After all, I'm nobody's dim sidekick, am I? Or am I?

'The Old Story' was written for a panel Michael Z Lewin, Peter Lovesey and I put on for the CrimeFest convention in Bristol. The title of the panel was *The Ideas Experiment* and it was intended to demonstrate that, given identical source material, three writers would produce three utterly dissimilar stories. We picked, as a starter, a three-line News In Brief article about pensioners turning to crime, and the result was three wildly different stories. So different, in fact, that Janet Hutchings placed all three in the same edition of her magazine.

'A Hand' began with a trip to Whitby. Initially I was attracted by the weird and wonderful palaeontology of the place but I ended up fascinated as much by the weird and wonderful history and folklore – the Hand of Glory being an example. Even the name itself is totally misleading.

It isn't necessarily the crime, criminal or victim that interest me. Sometimes it's those closely associated and how they cope or fail to cope with the aftermath. Often, because it's a convenient trope, the media and popular perception put the blame on the mother. As a mother myself, and knowing what it's like to accept responsibility for my own failings, I sometimes identify with the women who feel the guilt but who had no power to anticipate or prevent something dreadful from happening. This is what 'Whole Life' is about. Superficially though, the story started when I saw a single trainer, laces flapping in the wind, on top of a bus shelter. I was on a treadmill at the YMCA gym at the time and, as everyone knows how boring life on a treadmill can be, I was staring out of the window waiting for something interesting to happen on the street below. Even a single shoe can snag a empty mind.

'Ghost Station' and 'Day Or Night', along with 'A Hand', 'My People' and the last part of 'Health and Safety' feature a young police officer, Shareen Manasseh, who comes from an immigrant family of Mizrahi Jews. She seems never to belong anywhere and is shifted from one job to another without ever finding a permanent home in the police force. I suppose I was, for once, exploring my own background and the sense of impermanence that follows a second-generation immigrant around like a faithful dog.

'Life And Death In T-shirts' began when I was helping a friend rationalise his wardrobe. No matter how holed or stained, every t-shirt I attempted to sneak into a bin bag had an important memory attached. This simple beginning became the vehicle for a story about the sometimes fatal mistakes lonely women can make.

'My People', a study in divided loyalty, had its beginning in an Action taken by Extinction Rebellion. The police overreacted, and the excitement, fun and good intentions of taking part in a protest about climate change turned ambiguous and nasty. It was exactly the right time and place for a second generation immigrant, Shareen Manasseh on an undercover assignment, to face the dilemma of not being accepted by an establishment organisation.

Often short stories arrive after I've finished a novel. I work very slowly so a full-length novel can take several years and be quite exhausting. At a time like that I think I may never have another fresh idea again – the well has run dry. So, however slight an idea is I tend to pounce on it with relief. It was like that with 'I Am Not Fluffy' which was inspired by an action a friend and I took when we were disgusted by a certain part of our city being used by pubbers and clubbers as a urinal. We began to write messages in chalk to the offenders. The messages could be not only critical but downright rude so, in a spirit of writerly irony, we signed them 'Fluffy' which was about as inoffensive a name as we could think of. Unusually, I became my own inspiration.

Just because a story is short doesn't mean that the subject has to be either single-issue or superficial – although, sometimes I wish *mine* were shorter and lighter. But sadly the older I get the more complicated life seems and the more consequences matter.

I wrote 'When I'm Feeling Lucky' after I'd finished my modern Gothic Horror Novel, *Gift or Theft*. It was just as the first wave of Covid-19 began to strangle social life in England, so the consequences of toxic interaction were most definitely on my mind. In the wake of my fears about climate change and the geo-political mess we were making of our planet it appeared that the all-powerful human race was at the mercy of a speck that couldn't be seen and couldn't even be properly called an organism. It derailed our lives, our jobs, our economies. We'd been warned for sure, but actually we hadn't seen it coming.

I was feeling disturbed, distracted and dystopian so I began to write about a young woman going out to meet her friends one evening. She's feeling lucky so she stops to buy a lottery ticket and then someone else's aims and ambitions overpower hers and her life changes for ever.

However grim the story was, I was happy to be able to write it because I was so unsure about what sort of world we would find ourselves in when we emerged – if we ever did – from a weird sort of quarantine. I felt then, and to some extent, now as if I'm suspended between yesterday and tomorrow without being able accurately to assess today.

This is not a bad place to inhabit if you're a science or future fiction writer, but it isn't a good place for me. I need to observe, understand and find meaning in what I see around me. I know I write fiction but in a very deep way I do not feel as if I'm making anything up.

Liza Cody Bath 2021

ABOUT THE AUTHOR

Liza Cody is the award-winning author of many novels and short stories. Her Anna Lee series introduced the professional female private detective to British mystery fiction. It was adapted for television and broadcast in the UK and US. Cody's ground-breaking Bucket Nut Trilogy featured professional wrestler, Eva Wylie. Other novels include Rift, Gimme More, Ballad of a Dead Nobody, Miss Terry, Lady Bag, Crocodiles and Good Intentions, and Gift Or Theft. Her novels have been widely translated. In 2019 she won the Radio Bremen Krimipreis.

Cody's short stories have been published in many magazines and anthologies. The collection of her first seventeen appeared in the widely praised Lucky Dip and other stories.

Liza Cody was born in London and most of her work is set there. Her career before she began writing was mostly in the visual arts. Currently she lives in Bath.

Her informative website can be found at www.LizaCody.com which includes her occasional blog. You can also follow LizaCody on Twitter.

Printed in Great Britain
by Amazon